For Dermot and Alice

## Note on the Author

Sharon Owens was born in Omagh in 1968. She studied illustration at the University of Ulster at Belfast from 1988 to 1992. She has been married to husband Dermot since 1992, and they have one daughter, Alice.

Her bestselling novels *The Tea House on Mulberry Street*, *The Ballroom on Magnolia Street*, *The Tavern on Maple Street*, *The Trouble with Weddings* and *It Must Be Love* are also published by Poolbeg Press.

To read more about Sharon, visit her web site www.sharonowens.co.uk.

# Also by Sharon Owens

# Acknowledgements

Thanks to everyone at Poolbeg, especially Paula Campbell and Gaye Shortland.

Thanks to all at Penguin, especially Clare Ledingham, Mari Evans, Lydia Newhouse and Samantha Mackintosh; and to all my other publishers around the world.

Thanks to everyone in the media for their continued support.

Thanks to my family for believing in me.

Thanks to my late Great-uncle Benedict Kiely for being my inspiration.

Thanks to my friends for emails, phone calls, lunches and laughter.

Thanks to my husband Dermot for loving me all these years.

Thanks to our daughter Alice for being the light of our lives.

And finally, thanks to the readers who make it all possible.

I really hope you enjoy this story.

With very warmest wishes.

# 1

## The Gift

"Oh, go on, Ruby! Why don't you? They're absolutely gorgeous," Jasmine said encouragingly. The two women were standing looking in the window of a fancy shop in Victoria Square shopping complex in Belfast. It was five o'clock on Christmas Eve but the shops were still thronged with people enjoying the Salvation Army carol service and the general festive spirit.

"I'd love to, but they're so expensive," Ruby said.

"Yes, they are. But didn't you say that Jonathan needed a new pair of brogues?" Jasmine replied.

"Yes, I did. His favourite shoes have got a bit worn and these ones are so lovely," Ruby sighed. "Just look at the stitching. It's perfect."

"Well then?"

"But £400 for a pair of shoes?" Ruby said doubtfully. "I always get Jonathan a coffee-table book about NASA or photography. You know, something small like that."

"A book about NASA! Ruby O'Neill, you can't give your husband a book for Christmas," Jasmine said, shaking her head in pity. "I mean really, a book? Would you ever get real? Books are only stocking fillers."

"He likes books."

"Oh Ruby!"

"He does. He really likes those big, heavy, coffee-table books."

"Just buy the shoes."

"Our monthly mortgage isn't much more than £400."

"That's it. I give up."

The two women had been firm friends for the best part of a year. Ever since Jasmine had come to work alongside Ruby in a small but successful clothes shop on the elegant Ravenhill Road, close to the heart of Belfast city centre. Theodora Kelly owned the shop. She was a sprightly spinster of eighty-two and wore her hair in silvery white waves like the Queen's.

Jasmine was twenty-seven years old. She was tall and super-slim with dark blue eyes and waist-length, honey-blonde hair. Ruby was thirty-one and had hazel eyes and a sleek, black bob. But sometimes she might as well have been fifty-one as far as Jasmine was concerned. Ruby was simply too sensible for her own good.

"Lighten up, Ruby O'Neill! Scrooge himself wouldn't have a look-in with you," Jasmine muttered under her breath.

But Ruby heard her. "You single girls don't have to be as careful with your money as the rest of us," she began, trying her best to be tactful.

"Yes, we do, excuse me. We have rent to pay," Jasmine protested at once.

"Well yes. Rent, of course."

"Extortionate rent, I might add. I probably pay more to rent my one-bed apartment than it costs some couples to buy a big detached house. If they bought before the boom, that is. And I have nobody to split the utilities with."

"True," Ruby admitted, biting her lip with indecision.

2

"Maybe I should start buying Lotto tickets again?" Jasmine said in a dejected voice.

"No, don't do that! You said they were becoming addictive," Ruby reminded her.

"Oh, so I did! Right! Let's wrap this up. Can you afford the shoes?" Jasmine asked matter-of-factly.

"Yes, I suppose I can," Ruby replied.

"Okay. Listen to me, Ruby. Why don't you go mad for once in your life? I've only been in your house a few times but Jonathan has more than enough books already from what I can see. So nip in there immediately and buy your husband a decent present for Christmas," Jasmine commanded, elbowing Ruby through the crowds and straight up to the black marble counter.

"I'd like to see that pair in a size eleven, please?" Ruby stuttered, pointing at the shiny leather brogues.

The young assistant duly placed the heavy black shoes in front of Ruby and took a deep breath. The sales pitch was long and complicated and she was very tired.

But Jasmine was in a hurry. "They're perfect. We'll take them. And can you gift-wrap them as well? Thanks," she said firmly.

Ruby meekly handed over her credit card, keyed in her PIN and exchanged the usual pleasantries with the assistant.

"Well done, Ruby – he'll be so pleased he'll be chasing you round the house all week," Jasmine said casually, tossing her long hair over one shoulder and checking out her glittery eye make-up in a huge Rococo mirror on the wall.

"I hope so," Ruby whispered to Jasmine as she felt her face begin to redden with excitement.

"He will. He'll totally love those shoes," Jasmine smiled. "Well, if that's us done shopping we can treat ourselves to a quick steak sandwich and a glass of wine in the bar next door. There's live music on all day. And the lead singer's quite sexy," she added with a laugh.

"Yes, okay," Ruby agreed. "You go ahead and order for both

of us and I'll be across in a minute." The assistant had taken the shoes off somewhere for gift-wrapping. "Just a fizzy apple juice for me, mind. I'm driving."

"Right," Jasmine said, clutching the giant carrier bag containing her fabulous new white mohair coat from River Island. She'd just got 50% off in a pre-Christmas sale. "I love shopping but I have to say I'll be wearing flat pumps next time."

"Off you go then," Ruby told her. "I'll be along in a minute. And try not to get into any trouble. Find out if that singer has a jealous girlfriend with a bad temper before you go batting your eyelashes at him."

"Hey, you watch it! I hardly ever get myself into trouble, Ruby. Nine times out of ten the trouble comes to me," Jasmine said resignedly. "Is it my fault so many guys seem to find me attractive?"

But Ruby knew she was only joking. Or maybe half-joking . . .

"Okay, I'm sorry," she sighed. Jasmine was a great friend, really.

"Right then. Don't hang about in here chatting to the staff and keeping them back," Jasmine said, laughing. "I've a party to go to at eight thirty this evening."

And off she went marching across the street in her spike-heel boots, skin-tight jeans and short leather jacket. Her long legs were attracting discreet, appreciative glances from most of the men in the vicinity, Ruby noticed. Ruby didn't get admiring looks nearly as often, though she was rather attractive herself. But when men glanced at her full-length black overcoat and her sleek black bob and biker-style boots they knew she wasn't the type of girl to be chatted up on a windblown city pavement. Ruby wasn't exactly intimidating, but there was something about her that was somehow, simply, unapproachable. She was aware of it but she didn't mind. Jonathan was the only man she ever wanted to notice her or fancy her or love her.

And so Ruby was glowing with happiness as she sat down at her kitchen table later to admire the fancy, flock-style wrapping on

Jonathan's gift. There was also a big, black reflective ribbon on the box that caught the light from her little glass lantern and dazzled like a thousand stars. The gift looked very expensive indeed wrapped up like that.

How exciting, she thought, gradually getting used to the idea of splashing the cash. Even if it was only very occasionally.

Jonathan would be home from work soon. They'd be having a few drinks in the office, no doubt. And giving each other silly or naughty gifts in the traditional Secret Santa. But Ruby knew her husband would never drink and drive. Or risk hurting anyone's feelings by giving them condoms (for any man with more than two children) or a saucy peephole bra (for the office flirt) for Christmas. He'd be having only soft drinks. And he'd bought gift vouchers in M&S for the Secret Santa, knowing that the person he was supposed to be buying a gift for was a bit short of money that year. Jonathan O'Neill was the sexiest man Ruby had ever met but he had impeccable manners and the kindest heart as well, it had to be said. And that was precisely why Ruby had fallen for him in the first place. Yes, her Jonathan was the perfect package.

She touched the gift-wrapped box again lovingly and her heart gave a little wobble of excitement. Maybe Jonathan *would* chase her round the house all over the holidays? Maybe next year they *would* have their first child? Then she poured herself a small glass of Merlot and just sat there happily for a minute admiring the glossy black and silver packaging. Outside the kitchen window the sky was an inky-violet colour with just a smattering of stars visible between the ghostly clouds. Soon Jonathan would be home and they would have a cosy supper and then decorate the tree together – it should be delivered any moment now – and take a walk down the road to view the decorations in other houses. Then they would curl up together on the sofa to watch telly.

Filled with a renewed sense of hope about maybe falling pregnant that month, Ruby jumped up from the table and began to get things ready. She switched on the central heating and the various table lamps. She opened some last-minute Christmas cards and slotted them into her trendy wire cardholder in the hall. She set a beef casserole into the oven to heat through. She stacked the dishwasher and filled the washing-machine and snapped them both on happily, thinking where would she be without her mod cons? She did a quick vacuum of the hall rugs and tidied up the coats on the coat-stand.

There, she said to herself. The house looks perfect now. What else was I supposed to do? There was definitely something else? Oh yes, I've got to phone home.

Ruby took the phone into the kitchen and speed-dialled her parents' large house in the countryside. It lay at the end of a very long, very dark driveway in County Fermanagh in the west of the country and Ruby had never liked it much when she was growing up. Her parents had made a lot of money selling off Ruby's father's family land in the 1980s so the council could build more social housing, and they'd been living off the proceeds ever since.

"Hello?" Ruby's mother said hesitantly.

"Hi, Mum! It's me," Ruby said brightly.

"Hello, dear," came the usual subdued reply.

"Merry Christmas, Mum!"

"Yes indeed, and the same to you."

"Have you got everything ready for tomorrow then?" Ruby was hoping she could entice her mother into a cosy chat. It was a faint hope but it was always there. "Everything ready? What are you talking about? There's only the two of us here," her mother said in a flat voice.

"Yes but there's still an awful lot to do, isn't there? Pudding to set in the steamer, cream to whisk, tablecloth and napkins to press, and the turkey to stuff?"

"We'll manage well enough, Ruby. I'm only cooking a breast

6

of turkey from the supermarket this year. Last year we couldn't eat the half of it. It went in the bin on Boxing Day."

"But it wouldn't be Christmas without a turkey!" Ruby persisted.

"Whatever you say."

"You sound a bit tired," Ruby said in her most sympathetic voice.

"You phone me up and then tell me I sound tired? That's not very nice of you. I'm fine."

"Okay, okay. I'm sorry I spoke."

"No really, I'm fine," Ruby's mother sighed.

"What's wrong, Mum?"

"Nothing's wrong. Nothing at all."

"You can tell me if there is?"

"I'm fine. Jesus!"

"You could both come to me for Christmas Day? I have the whole house decorated," Ruby said hopefully. "You're still welcome to join us tomorrow."

"You know I like to stay at home, Ruby. Burglars never take a day off."

"But you have the alarm now?"

"I don't like to use the alarm."

"Oh Mum!"

"It's so noisy when it goes off."

"It's meant to be noisy," Ruby said gently.

"Anyway what use is it? Nobody would hear it blaring and beeping: not all the way out here. The whole place would be ransacked and wrecked and nobody would be a bit the wiser."

This was familiar territory: Ruby's mother's lack of faith in her state-of-the-art burglar alarm.

"And you're sure you don't want us to come and visit you instead?" Ruby asked.

"No, not at all," said her mother sharply. "Are you out of your mind? I hear we might have snow coming, for heaven's sake. I won't have you both breaking down on the road and freezing to death. Not on my account! And if you did make it this length, you might be stranded here for days and then your own home would be broken into."

They both sighed heavily.

"Okay, Mum. Well, I'll see you sometime then?"

"Yes, sometime."

"And I hope you have a lovely day tomorrow."

"Yes. You too."

"Say hello to Dad for me, won't you?"

"I will surely. He's out in the garage, smoking a cigarette."

"Right then. Merry Christmas again."

"Yes, yes. Bye, dear."

"Bye, Mum. Love you."

"Yes, same here."

Ruby hung up feeling slightly disappointed as she always did after speaking to either one of her parents. They didn't like a lot of fuss and hugging and kissing and "silly nonsense" as they put it. They liked to stay at home for Christmas and they didn't like the stress of having to entertain visitors. Even Jonathan was still classed as a visitor after seven years of marriage and ten years altogether as Ruby's partner. Oh well.

Next she rang Jonathan.

"Hello, love, how's the party going?"

"Hi, babe – oh God, it's been totally hilarious. My sides are sore laughing. Somebody bought Robert a pair of super-strength odour-eaters and he went buck-mental and pushed the Christmas tree over and broke the lights. Then he fell on top of it and got all caught up in the tinsel. He is so plastered."

"Poor Robert. Are his feet really smelly?"

"Just a bit."

"Oh, God love him! What did Susan get?"

Susan was the office chatterbox.

"Wait for it. A dog's muzzle."

8

"Oh Jesus! No way! Was she raging?"

"No, she was delighted with it. She's wearing it now. It's a white muzzle with pink stones on it. She said she's going to wear it in bed tonight and drive her boyfriend wild with lust."

"She's not shy then?"

"No, she's not shy. She's a proper nutcase. No, she's a good laugh really."

"She sounds it. Will you be leaving soon?" Ruby asked eagerly.

"Yes, I will. It's all winding up here now anyway. I just have to drop some papers off to a client in Ballynahinch and then I'll be straight home. Took ages to sort out the accounts. They were in such a muddle."

"Ballynahinch? But love, that's miles away. Can't it wait till after Christmas?"

"Not really. It's a bankruptcy case. It's urgent. There's going to be an auction on the 26th. I *am* the boss, after all, so it's only fair I drop off the papers. And this lot are wasted anyway."

"Oh well then. Poor guy going bankrupt on Christmas Eve."

"Yes, he's a farmer. He tried going organic but it didn't work out for him. I'll just be an hour or so, I promise."

"The traffic's pretty crazy," Ruby reminded him.

"I know, I know. But then I'll be off work for two whole weeks," he said brightly.

"Me too. Won't it be heaven?" she sighed. "All those lovely lie-ins?"

"Oh yeah! Wonder what we'll do with so much free time! I can think of one thing, at least!" He laughed and added, "I love you."

"I love you too," she replied automatically.

"That's my girl. I won't be too long."

"Okay. I made a casserole last night, by the way. It's heating in the oven as we speak."

"Brilliant. I can't wait. The party nibbles were great but not the same as one of your casseroles."

"Ha! Thanks," she laughed.

"Oh, has the tree arrived?"

"No, not yet."

"They're leaving it a bit late, aren't they?" he said, a little anxiously.

"You didn't forget to order it?" she joked.

"No, I didn't!"

Jonathan always liked to decorate the tree late on Christmas Eve. It was a sort of tradition of his, as was the walk along the Ravenhill Road to look at the other trees sparkling in bay windows and hallways. They'd hold hands like teenagers and finally kiss by the garden gate on the way home.

"Oh wait a minute, there goes another round of party-poppers," said Jonathan. "Hey, watch it, you lot! You'll burn the bloody building down! That carpet cost a fortune too!"

There was a riotous cheer in the background as a handful of poppers exploded. Jonathan collapsed into a fit of laughing. "Did you hear that, Ruby? Fuck's sake! They're a mental bunch in here. Robert's lying asleep in the corner and even that almighty bang didn't wake him up."

"Jonathan, listen, I bought you a lovely present today," Ruby said tentatively. She just couldn't help mentioning it, could she? Silently, she chided herself but the words were out now.

"Did you really? How exciting!"

"Yes. Jasmine talked me into it."

"Jasmine, huh? Sounds pretty expensive then. Actually I bought you something special too."

"Did you, honestly? Shall we swap gifts at midnight tonight?"

"Okay. If you like?"

"Be careful coming home, won't you? The traffic is bumper to bumper."

"I'm always careful," Jonathan said tenderly.

"Yes, I know. See you soon then?"

"Very soon. Bye, love."

"Bye."

Ruby hung up and sipped her wine thoughtfully. Jonathan hadn't sounded cross at all about her lovely present. In fact he'd sounded strangely pleased. She smiled at her reflection in the darkened window.

"He'll love the shoes," she told herself. "I just know it."

# 2

# The Tree

Ruby was just starting to doze off in her favourite armchair when suddenly there was a loud knock at the front door.

Startled, she spilt some red wine down the front of her black crewneck sweater.

"You silly eejit!" she said to herself, setting her glass down on the table. What am I like, she thought. Just because I've gone a bit mad with the credit card I'm all on edge.

She quickly dabbed the wine off with a tea towel and went rushing to answer the door, expecting to find the carol singers from her local church outside. Yawning widely, she opened the door.

"Tree for Ruby O'Neill?" said a tall man with longish brown hair tucked behind his ears. He had earnest-looking, dark brown eyes with the beginnings of some serious crow's feet around them.

Ruby was relieved when she realised it wasn't the carol singers. They were a lovely gang but they usually sang and sang until every drop of heat had been drained from the house. And she always had to stand there smiling at them like an idiot while Jonathan hid in the kitchen, giggling at her embarrassment. They must have come earlier when she was still out with Jasmine. And then she felt guilty that she hadn't been in the house to give them a few pounds for their collecting tin.

"This *is* the right address?"

Ruby realised she was just standing there, gazing at the tree man. "Yes, yes, it is. Excuse me – I just thought you might be the carol singers."

"Sorry, I'm not," the man said shyly.

"No, you're not."

"Hope I've not come at a bad time?" the man said, glancing into the hallway behind her.

"Not at all," Ruby said and then she smiled warmly at him. Not the usual young guy from the garden centre, but he seemed nice enough. Lovely brown eyes actually, she thought. Handsome almost, even though he must be about forty-five, forty-six? Lovely deep voice. It was very calming.

"The tree? You still want it?" the man asked, reaching down to pick it up from where it lay on the tiled path.

"Yes, indeed I still want it."

He straightened up again. "Eight foot spruce? No stand required. Yes?"

"That's right. I've still got my stand from last year."

"Okay. That'll be thirty-five quid, please."

"Surely. Just a minute." Ruby darted back to the kitchen to get her purse.

"Cheers," the man smiled as she paid him. "And a Merry Christmas to you."

"Merry Christmas yourself," Ruby said at once, pulling the heavy, netted tree further into the hall. "Are you new at the garden centre?"

"No, I'm from Camberwell. I'm the head gardener there. I'm the only gardener there to tell you the truth. But head gardener sounds better."

"Camberwell? The stately home?"

"That's right. We're selling trees now. Been growing them commercially for ten years and the first lot were just ready to sell this Christmas."

"I see. How lovely!"

"Yes. The garden centre sold a fair few of them for us. I was just there actually, to take away any unsold ones. You were the last address on their list. And I said I would drop this one off to you on my way home. Save them the bother of coming out in this traffic. Tom's the name. Tom Lavery."

"And I'm Ruby. Ruby O'Neill."

"Yes, I know. You were on the list."

"Oh, of course I was . . ."

Tom reached out his hand and Ruby quickly checked her own for telltale drips of red wine. But it seemed clean enough. They shook hands firmly. Ruby noticed that although the air outside was freezing cold Tom Lavery's handshake was warm and friendly. They exchanged a brief glance and then pulled their hands apart again.

"Right, thanks very much, Tom. So I've got myself a posh tree this year then?" Ruby said, eager to get the netting snipped off and the fat, fragrant tree fully decorated. She had 120 red berry lights and a box of papier-mâché Santa figures and angels by Gisela Graham to hang on it.

"Oh there's my buzzer," she said, hearing her oven-timer pinging. "I'd better turn the oven off."

"Yes, okay, I won't keep you," Tom said, turning to leave. "Bye now."

"Thanks, Tom, safe home," Ruby said brightly, waving him down the path and then softly closing the front door behind him.

Sitting in his Land Rover, Tom Lavery turned the heating up and rubbed his arms to try and get his circulation going again. For some reason he'd suddenly gone all weird and shivery. He knew he would have to take a minute to catch his breath before he could drive away anyway. His heart was pounding in his chest like a sledgehammer. Thumping so hard he was sure he'd have a heart attack.

What am I like? he scolded himself. God help me, I'm like a teenager with a hopeless crush. Where the hell did that come from?

It'd been years since he'd felt like this, long years since he'd felt anything apart from impotent anger and endless grief. And regret for all the things they'd never got around to doing before Kate died. And the soul-destroying loneliness that had haunted him since losing her.

"Stop it," he said aloud. "Get a grip! Pull yourself together, man."

He turned his head towards Ruby O'Neill's three-storey Georgian house. The lights in the front room were suddenly snapped on and the rose-patterned walls were brightly illuminated by a beautiful vintage-looking chandelier with glass droplets. The room was full of white-painted furniture and two huge white sofas that were piled high with pink and white cushions.

Nice room, he said to himself. If you like pink!

He shouldn't have stayed there looking at this beautiful woman he had just met but he couldn't help it. Because, even though his pulse was racing along at what must have been a dangerous level, he was still filled with curiosity.

"Curiosity killed the cat," he murmured softly.

As Tom watched, Ruby dragged the huge tree into the bay window and fitted the stand onto the base of the trunk. Then she stood the whole thing upright, quickly tore off the net, fluffed out the branches and looked at the tree from several angles to find the best one.

"Clever move," Tom said softly. Not so easy to put up a tree that size all by yourself.

Kneeling down, Ruby inched the Christmas tree into the perfect position and then left the room, coming back two minutes later with a glass of red wine and a large box from which she began to pull decorations. Tom noted how her glossy bob was as sleek and shiny as a raven's wing. She was quite tall with an hourglass figure but it was her stillness and grace that he was fascinated by. She seemed to possess an inner peace that Tom would have given anything for.

"Ruby O'Neill, who are you?" he whispered.

As Ruby stood there gazing at the tree and holding up various large and spindly decorations against its luxurious blue-green branches, Tom finally shook himself out of his daydream, started up the Land Rover and pulled slowly out into the rush-hour traffic.

Ah, would you wise up! What's the use in looking? he sighed. She's married. She must be married. She had a wedding ring on. And even if she weren't spoken for, a beautiful woman like that would never be interested in a man like me in a million years. And anyway I can't be over Kate. Not yet. I'll never be over Kate. God, what am I going to do? How am I going to get through another blasted Christmas on my own?

And then he sighed and forced himself to stop being so defeatist. He wasn't really on his own. Not really. For he had Noah his faithful black Labrador to talk to and to bring out for walks. Noah had been Kate's dog. She'd bought him as a puppy and named him Noir. But over the years the name had somehow morphed into Noah and the new name seemed to suit the dog much better. So Noah it became. Now if it weren't for Noah and the gardens at Camberwell to look after he really would be close to the edge tonight.

He inched his way towards the Saintfield Road and, as he drove, he made a mental list of all the things he had to do that night. He had to pick up dog food from the supermarket. Then call Kate's parents in Hillsborough and wish them a Merry

Christmas. Then drop off the three unsold trees at a YMCA near Camberwell. They'd said they'd be grateful for any donations this year, no matter how late, for they were having a big party on New Year's Eve. Then he had to water the eight Christmas trees in Camberwell House and check the greenhouses for frost. And he mustn't forget to put the garden centre money in the safe. And then if he was feeling up to it he might go for a pint or two in his local pub. But only if he felt in the mood for a chat. It was hard to be alone on Christmas Eve sometimes. But then again sometimes it was even harder to be with people who didn't understand what he was going through.

They mean well, he reminded himself. I mustn't get irritable with them when they tell me that time is a great healer. I know I just have to bite my tongue and nod and say thanks for the advice.

But sometimes Tom Lavery just wanted to stand in the middle of nowhere and roar his head off.

When Tom got back to Camberwell, Noah ran out of the gates to greet him. And Tom slowed right down so the dog wouldn't get giddy and run under the wheels.

"Steady, boy, steady," he warned, through the driver's open window.

He parked the Land Rover at the back of the house and went hurrying into the kitchen to see if there was any supper going spare. Occasionally the cook at Camberwell House, Mrs Kenny, would leave a dish of lamb stew or a bowl of chicken salad for him in the staff fridge. Luckily tonight there was a tasty selection: a big bowl of chicken soup, three buttery rolls filled with Cheddar cheese and cold ham, and six mince pies wrapped in tin foil.

"You're a gem, Mrs Kenny," Tom said happily to the empty kitchen, cheering up for the first time that day.

Back on the Ravenhill Road Ruby was also eating a solitary

supper. She helped herself to a second bowl of beef casserole and shook her head as she sprinkled salt and pepper on it.

I hope the traffic isn't too bad, she said to herself. I bet it'll take ages to get to Ballynahinch and back in this freezing cold weather. Jonathan should have used a courier to deliver those papers instead of going himself. He's far too conscientious sometimes. Just because it's his firm, and there's a recession on, and he doesn't want to lose business or to have to let any of the other accountants or office staff go. There might be ice on the roads by now! Black ice maybe! Or a stupid lorry broken down and it's blocking the whole road? The police will be out directing traffic if it gets any worse. And then people will be stuck for ages and getting hypothermia.

And then she scurried over to switch on the small portable telly and lose herself in *EastEnders*. At least on the soaps people were usually guaranteed to be having a worse time than you are, she thought sagely. As the programme began, the familiar figure of soap matriarch Pat Butcher went racing across the street, her face set into a grim mask of anger, obviously on an urgent mission of some kind.

No point in moping about like this and worrying myself sick, Ruby told herself sternly. That soft-hearted husband of mine is just chatting to that poor guy who's gone bankrupt or something. Trying to cheer him up for Christmas. Or maybe he's stopped off to buy some more wine or chocolates or maybe the new *Radio Times*? But then again, that would only add ten minutes to the journey . . . For heaven's sake, Ruby O'Neill, would you listen to yourself! You'll turn into your own mother one of these days if you're not careful. Always expecting disaster round every corner. Too afraid to enjoy yourself in case life leaps up and bites you on the bum!

Ruby poured out another small glass of wine. Then she sat down to watch the portable TV. Somehow she thought Jonathan would make it home sooner if she waited for him in the kitchen. It was silly of her but she felt it would feel lonely to go and curl up on the sofa in the good room. Anyway the kitchen was nice and warm because the oven had been on.

"Right, come on then, what are you up to, Pat Butcher?" Ruby said, determined not to fret any longer. Jonathan would surely be coming in the door any second and hopefully he would be so hungry he wouldn't even notice that she'd been getting a bit fed up waiting for him. And if he didn't hurry up she'd go ahead and decorate the tree on her own, so she would! And if he said anything whatsoever to her about their precious tradition she'd give him a good stern lecture on how he was becoming a complete workaholic these days. Top accountant or not! Christmas Eve or no Christmas Eve! Men could be so damn stubborn sometimes!

"May God be good to you and your big earrings, Pat Butcher!" Ruby said then. Poor old Pat had had more than her fair share of heartaches over the years, she thought. I bet it won't be two minutes before it all kicks off *again* in the Queen Vic . . .

# 3

# The Accident

However, by nine o'clock, Ruby was getting seriously worried. She was standing by the bay window at the front of the house, peering up and down the street for any sign of her husband's car. In seven years of marriage Jonathan had never been home this late on Christmas Eve. She'd sent him three text messages and called him twice but there'd been no reply. Surely he hadn't given in to peer-pressure from the lads at the office and gone back into Belfast City centre with them after his trip to Ballynahinch? Surely he hadn't gone to the pub for a proper booze-up? After all the drink they'd had already? How could he have forgotten to give her a call and let her know he was okay? He knew she had no one else coming round to visit this evening. He knew she'd be alone in the house on Christmas Eve. Was she being a total shrew, she wondered then? Wasn't her husband allowed to have a bit of fun after working so hard all year?

"Okay, calm down and just get the tree finished," she told herself sternly.

With her heart fluttering she unwound the two long strings of crimson berry lights, draped them expertly on the branches and switched them on. Then she hung all twenty of the elegant Christmas figurines on the tree, spacing them out carefully.

"He's missed the decorating now, but never mind," she said to a papier-mâché reindeer. "Out on the rip! And me stuck here fretting about him! Do you know I'm tempted to go and have a lovely soak in the bath . . ."

But of course she didn't.

Eventually Ruby decided to play the fussy wife and start ringing round the pubs that Jonathan might be drinking in. The Merchant or The Errigle or the Europa, maybe? But as she was walking toward the telephone in the hall it began to make its high-pitched electronic chime. She snatched up the receiver.

"Jonathan? Is that you? Where are you, love?"

"Hello? Am I speaking to a Mrs Ruby O'Neill?" a man's voice asked.

He sounded very solemn. Ruby's heart seemed to lurch to one side.

"Yes, you are," she said shakily.

"Is your husband called Jonathan O'Neill?" the man asked. "He has a silver BMW?"

"Who is this?" Ruby said, her face and hands turning cold with nerves. Was this a wind-up by Jonathan's mates in the office? She'd stop speaking to the lot of them, so she would.

"This is Mr Doonan. I'm a consultant at the Royal Victoria Hospital."

"Oh my God, what's happened?" Ruby gasped and she sat down on the little chair beside the telephone and began to tremble.

"I'm very sorry, Mrs O'Neill, but your husband has been involved in a serious traffic accident. Can you please come to the hospital straight away? Have you anyone who might come with you?"

"Yes, yes. I have someone. I'll be right there. A&E, is it?"

"Yes, take care now. Goodbye."

Ruby clattered the handset into its cradle and then immediately lifted it again and called Jasmine. But Jasmine wouldn't be at her apartment in the Bell Towers, Ruby remembered suddenly. Jasmine had said she was going to a party tonight.

"Please God, let Jasmine have her mobile switched on," Ruby wept.

She hung up and dialled Jasmine's mobile number instead.

"Jasmine, please answer, please answer," Ruby sobbed as the phone rang and rang.

"Hey, Ruby, what about ye! Merry Christmas!" Jasmine yelled eventually, seeing Ruby's name on the caller-ID display. "God, I'm as drunk as a skunk already here."

"Please Jasmine, you've got to help me," Ruby begged.

"What is it?" Jasmine asked, sobering up instantly.

"It's Jonathan. He's in hospital."

"What happened? An accident?"

"Yes, a road accident."

"How is he?"

"I don't know. They didn't say. Or wouldn't say . . ."

"Right," Jasmine whispered.

They both knew this was not a good sign.

"Will you come with me to see him?" Ruby pleaded. "Please? I'm in a right state here."

"I will surely. Can you pick me up? The party's just a few doors down the street from my place but I'll have to run home and change. I'm in a mini-skirt. Can you pick me up at the main entrance?" Jasmine couldn't afford to run a car of her own since moving to the Bell Towers.

"Fine, fine," Ruby said through her tears. "I've had two small glasses of wine myself but I'm sure it'll be okay. Anyway I'll never get a taxi so late on Christmas Eve. I'll be there in two minutes."

"Okay."

"Thanks, Jasmine," Ruby said gratefully, slamming the phone down hard and running to the kitchen for her coat and car keys.

Minutes later she was pulling up at Jasmine's apartment building, sounding the horn and crying simultaneously. She'd forgotten to switch off the lights on the Christmas tree back home but none of that mattered now. After a few more agonising minutes, Jasmine came racing out of the main door and Ruby stepped from her car and called to her friend across the road.

"Hey Jasmine, I'm over here! There was nowhere to park on your side."

"I'm coming," Jasmine shouted as she sprinted across four lanes of traffic and leapt into Ruby's ancient Audi. "Are you all right, love?"

"No, I'm not all right."

"Jesus, Ruby, I'm really sorry . . . But he'll be okay . . ."

"What if he isn't? I've to find this Mr Doonan . . . and I've been drinking," Ruby wept. "What'll he think?"

"It's Christmas Eve, you doughnut! Who hasn't been drinking? Come on, woman, you can do this," Jasmine urged.

"Okay."

Ruby pulled out into the traffic and turned right towards the Ormeau Road.

"Please God, let him be all right," she said over and over as they nudged slowly through the Holy Lands district, down Great Victoria Street and across to the Falls Road.

"This damn bloody traffic! Does it never stop?" Ruby wept again as the lights turned defiantly red. She jammed on the brakes and thumped the dashboard with frustration. "Have all of these stupid, bloody people got no homes to go to?"

"Ruby, maybe you'd better try and calm down a bit or we'll be in an accident ourselves," Jasmine soothed.

"Okay, you're right. Sorry. I'm sorry for losing my temper. Thank God you're with me, Jasmine. Thanks for coming with me tonight . . ."

At last the hospital gates loomed up eerily before them in the car headlights.

"Now listen to me, Ruby. You must be positive when you see Jonathan," Jasmine began carefully. "You mustn't let him see you this upset. You'll make it harder for him, say he is quite hurt."

"Yes, I know, I know. Oh God, Jasmine! Something terrible has happened. I just know it," Ruby said as she parked the car sideways across three disability spaces in the nearest car park. "Never mind the ticket-machine. Nobody will be checking it this late on Christmas Eve. Come on. Hurry!"

"It'll be fine, Ruby," Jasmine said hopefully as the two women linked arms and went scurrying towards A&E. "Everything will be just fine, you'll see."

"Excuse me, Nurse, we're here about Jonathan O'Neill. He's been in some sort of accident," Ruby began.

"A road accident," Jasmine added helpfully. "This is Ruby O'Neill, his wife."

"Please tell us what's happened to him?" Ruby asked as Jasmine put one arm round her friend and prayed for good news.

Ruby was trembling from head to foot. She hadn't been inside a hospital for years. She was feeling surreal already. As if she'd accidentally wandered onto the set of *Casualty*, or something.

"Just take a seat and I'll let the doctor know you're here," the nurse said calmly.

"But is my husband badly hurt?" Ruby pleaded.

"The doctor will explain, Mrs O'Neill."

"Please tell me something? Anything?" Ruby begged.

"Ruby, will you let the nurse do her job?" Jasmine whispered quietly, giving Ruby's arm a gentle squeeze.

"Just tell me he's okay?" Ruby persisted.

"Mrs O'Neill, would you please take a seat? Thank you." The

nurse turned away from Ruby and Jasmine then and began tapping hard on some buttons on her computer.

"It could be something routine," Jasmine said brightly as she led Ruby away from the counter. "A broken arm or leg? A cracked rib or a spot of concussion, perhaps? That's likely it, you know: it's concussion and they're taking him for a scan, just to be on the safe side."

"If that's all it is then why won't they tell me?" Ruby sobbed as the other people in the waiting area stared at the posters on the walls in an embarrassed silence.

After ten minutes, the consultant came hurrying into the Accident & Emergency department: a tall man in his late fifties with a shock of pure-white hair and a healthy pink glow on his face. He ushered Ruby and Jasmine down the corridor and into a small private room furnished with two plain armchairs, a small matching sofa and a low, wooden coffee table. Ruby saw a big box of tissues sitting pointedly on the table's highly polished surface.

"Oh sweet Jesus Christ, I knew it, I knew it!" she wept, collapsing onto the beige sofa in a crumpled heap. "He's dead, isn't he? Isn't he?"

The doctor was slightly taken aback. Usually the relatives went into denial at this stage. They normally needed some convincing before they would accept that a loved one had died.

"Has Ruby's husband actually . . . *died*?" Jasmine whispered incredulously at that point.

"Well now, I'm afraid the news is not good. He's on life support at the moment. But I'm sorry to say . . . there's no hope." The doctor shook his head sadly.

"Oh Jesus!" Jasmine said eventually. "Oh, sorry! Sorry, I didn't mean to say that, Doctor."

The doctor just nodded and sighed.

"No, he can't be going to die! No way, I can't believe it," Ruby gasped then, her eyes wide with shock. "Jasmine, I think I'm going to be sick . . . There must be some mistake? Doctor? Have you done everything you can to save him?"

"Yes, we have."

"There must be something?"

The doctor shook his head.

A small silence descended and then Ruby began to cry noisily.

"What happened, do you know?" Jasmine asked, sitting down beside Ruby and hugging her tightly.

"A lorry clipped Mr O'Neill's car on the Carryduff roundabout. He swerved into a stone wall. His neck . . . was broken."

"Oh Jonathan! It can't be true," Ruby cried. "Not my Jonathan, he's an excellent driver. The traffic wasn't moving quickly enough for an accident like that to happen."

"Apparently it was."

"Jesus Christ," Jasmine said. "Sorry."

"He wouldn't have suffered, Mrs O'Neill," the doctor said. "I can assure you of that. There was a witness. A man who attended the scene within seconds. The lorry driver was going too fast apparently. Didn't slow down as he entered the roundabout. He couldn't stop in the icy conditions, or so he said. He's been arrested."

Ruby didn't answer the doctor. Her mind was floating somewhere high above the hospital building. Thinking to herself, well, Jonathan wouldn't have to worry about her spending all that money on a pair of shoes after all. Jonathan wouldn't need new shoes now, or anything else, ever again. She closed her eyes and began to moan in a very low-pitched voice.

"Mrs O'Neill, are you all right?" the doctor asked gently.

Ruby nodded vigorously. She was all right, yes. She just couldn't form any coherent sentences at that precise moment. That was all.

"Do you want to ask me anything?" the doctor said. "About what happens next? Before you see your husband?"

Ruby turned away from him, just as the nurse downstairs had recently turned away from her. She couldn't bear to speak to anyone.

Outside the bare windows a soft dusting of the purest white snow was beginning to fall. Ruby watched the twirling flakes with a surreal sense of detachment. She felt numb and frozen.

"Ruby?" Jasmine asked.

"No, thank you," Ruby said eventually. "I can't think of anything."

"Then we'll go upstairs?" the doctor ventured.

"Thank you, Doctor," Ruby said politely.

"Yes, thank you," Jasmine said in a whispery, shell-shocked voice.

"Would you like a little something to calm you down?" the doctor asked discreetly.

"No, best not," said Ruby quietly. "Not yet anyway. Not yet . . ."

"Yes, good," the doctor agreed. There were far too many people taking tablets for their nerves, in his opinion.

"Could Ruby have a quick cup of tea?" Jasmine asked suddenly. "She's gone all cold and shivery on me."

"That would be nice," Ruby whispered. "I do feel slightly faint as it happens. Must be the heat in here or something. Hospitals are always far too warm, aren't they?"

"They are," Jasmine said soothingly.

"I'll see to it," the doctor said, going out of the room.

Minutes later a nurse brought in some tea things on a tray. Ruby's heart was fluttering wildly in her chest. She thought she might have heart failure with the stress of it all but she honestly didn't care if she did. Was it only an hour or so ago that she'd been decorating her Christmas tree and sipping red wine? Dreaming of expensive shoes and long lie-ins and new-born babies with silky-soft cheeks?

"He was so young," she whispered to Jasmine. "Only thirty-eight."

"You've got to be strong now," Jasmine told her, handing her some tea with two sugars in it.

"Yes, I know, I know."

Pull yourself together, Ruby hissed internally at her startled reflection in the darkened windows. Oh, pull yourself together right this minute, Ruby O'Neill. What sort of a woman are you anyway? People die all the time.

But it wasn't just anyone who had died, was it? No, it was her gorgeous lover, her best and closest friend in the entire world, her fabulous husband Jonathan. A great gulp of panic rose up in Ruby's chest and she half-coughed, half-gasped for air.

Jonathan was dying.

"But I don't want him to be dead!" she wept. "It's not fair! I don't want him to leave me like this. We had so many plans for the future. He was my best friend! I have nobody else, not really . . . Just you, Jasmine . . . My parents are hopeless, just hopeless. I can't go on living without Jonathan. He can't be dead, he can't be! We were going to try for a baby; we were going to be a proper family. I bought him expensive shoes for Christmas . . ."

"Ruby love, poor love, poor love," Jasmine said gently, pulling Ruby closer to her.

"No!" Ruby wept.

"Take slower breaths," the nurse urged.

"I think I might try a pill actually, please?" Ruby said in a faltering voice.

The nurse produced a small bottle of white pills from her pocket and gave her one.

"We'll go upstairs soon," the doctor decided. Things were only going to get worse, the longer they sat here in this emotional vacuum.

"Are you okay now, Ruby?" Jasmine asked her.

"I think so," Ruby said in a small voice, gulping down hot, sweet tea to take away the bitter taste of the tablet. "Let's go."

The doctor and the nurse exchanged concerned glances as the four of them made their way towards the elevator and got in. Ruby seemed marginally calmer now.

But when the lift came to a juddering halt Ruby's heart went into a tailspin all over again. Somehow she managed to speak briefly to another doctor about Jonathan's organs being donated. Jonathan's neck had been broken but otherwise he was in perfect health. They'd been keeping him on life support until Ruby could see him, the second doctor explained. And if it was okay with Ruby they'd like to take some of her husband's organs. Ruby just nodded, asking nothing more. Then she was allowed to see her husband. Jasmine braced herself as they went into the room.

"He was always so good-looking," Ruby said in a faraway voice, tenderly kissing Jonathan's forehead and placing her slender hands over his larger ones. "Gorgeous man. Wasn't he always absolutely gorgeous, Jasmine? I mean, isn't he gorgeous?"

"Jesus, Ruby, yes indeed. I'm so very sorry," Jasmine said, tears slipping down her shocked and pale face.

"He had lovely, big, blue eyes," Ruby continued softly. Holding her breath in at the end of the sentence to keep hysteria at bay. "Ice blue. The first time I looked into those beautiful blue eyes of his I knew I'd love him forever. He paid my bus fare home from college one night. I'd lost my purse; do you see? That's how we met. We were so happy together. I only wish I'd realised just how happy we were before it was too late." She had to hold onto Jasmine for a moment then to stop herself from grabbing something heavy and wrecking the room with it.

"We're very sorry we couldn't do more for your husband, Mrs O'Neill," the second doctor said respectfully.

Glancing at her husband's bare shoulders Ruby had a sudden image of Jonathan lying in bed with her, their arms wrapped around each other after making love. He looked as if he were only asleep. Such a warm-hearted and sexy man! Shy to begin with but great fun when you got to know him. He was still warm, still breathing. He couldn't be lost to her forever, could he? Ruby's heart seemed to fold up on itself like an Origami swan.

"Are you really sure there's no hope?" she said.

"There isn't. I'm sorry," Mr Doonan replied sadly.

"Really? Are you really sure?"

"Yes."

"I'll pay for more treatment? Even if he has to go abroad? I'll sell the house. I'm sure it's worth half a million . . ."

"It wouldn't do any good, I'm sorry."

"Ruby, don't torture yourself," Jasmine whispered.

"But I love him so much."

"I know you do," Jasmine sighed.

Ruby kissed Jonathan softly on the lips.

"Okay then, I'm ready," she said finally.

Quietly and efficiently, the machine was switched off. Eventually they all left the room and went to stand in the corridor.

Ruby wept until she couldn't breathe and her eyes were raw and sore. Jasmine wept too. Even the nurse was visibly upset.

"I want to go home now," Ruby said then, suddenly feeling completely numb. "I don't want to be here when they . . . when they . . ."

"Okay, I'll drive," Jasmine told her.

"Are you still drunk?" Ruby asked as they got into the car.

"Just a bit," Jasmine admitted.

"Are you able to drive? Only I don't think I can manage it. I'm shaking all over."

"No problem."

"What time is it?"

"Eleven thirty."

"It's still Christmas Eve," Ruby said dully.

"Yes."

Jasmine automatically switched on the radio. Ruby switched it off again.

"No radio, sorry. If they play a sad song I'll kill myself," she said.

"Okay. Sorry."

The traffic had thinned out considerably by now. Ruby barely spoke as Jasmine drove home at a snail's pace.

The red berry lights were glowing brightly in the bay window as Jasmine carefully parked the car outside the house.

"Thank God there were no cops about," she said. Her hands were white with gripping the steering wheel so tightly. "I've never done that before, I swear to you."

"I know you haven't. Thank you, Jasmine," Ruby said, beginning to cry again.

"Come on, Ruby love. Let's get you inside and warmed up a bit. Yeah?"

Ruby's key in the lock sounded horrifically loud and the house rang with silence when they stepped into the hall. Jasmine closed the front door softly behind them. They went through to the kitchen at the back of the house in a kind of daze. Ruby switched on the radio to a talk station and then turned it down very low so she could still hear the presenter's voice but not very much of what he was saying. Anything to drown the silence.

"Shall I make us some tea?" Jasmine asked.

"Yes, please. Actually I think a brandy would be better. Make mine a double, would you?"

"Right. Where do you keep the glasses, again?"

"On the dresser," Ruby said, pointing.

As the two women sat down at the kitchen table, cradling their drinks, they saw Jonathan's Christmas present sitting on a chair. The glossy wrapping now felt like a reproach.

"I'm so sorry, Ruby," Jasmine sighed.

"What for?"

"Making you buy that gift," Jasmine said, nodding towards the prettily wrapped box.

"Don't be silly," said Ruby. "It was a lovely idea. They are beautiful shoes."

A few minutes passed in silence.

"Can I phone anyone for you?" Jasmine asked then. "Family? Friends?"

"No," Ruby sighed. "Jonathan had no family to speak of. His parents died a few years ago. He had no siblings. Isn't it funny? I have none either. And I don't want all his colleagues to land round here on top of us tonight. Not on Christmas Eve! I'm not ready for all that yet. I'm not ready for people."

"No, of course you're not ready for *people*. But what about your own parents? Surely I should ring them?"

"Oh, it's all right, I'll speak to them tomorrow morning," Ruby said flatly. "They'll be off to Midnight Mass by now anyway. They wouldn't miss Midnight Mass if the world were coming to an end. They'll be sitting up as straight as pokers in the front row, clutching their best missals and their best Rosary beads and muttering their good intentions to Saint Anthony or Saint Jude or something. Praying for other people when they should just go round and *talk* to them . . ."

"Okay," Jasmine said carefully. She had no idea what Ruby was muttering about. Jasmine was Church of Ireland. Not that she ever darkened the door of her local church unless it was a special occasion. Religion was for the oldies in God's Waiting Room, Jasmine reckoned; for those who had nowhere else to go on a Sunday morning.

"I won't be holding a big wake if that's what you're wondering," Ruby continued.

"No?"

"No. I'm Catholic but Jonathan was Presbyterian. And anyway, he wasn't overly religious. He wouldn't have wanted anything too fussy. He once said that a quiet cremation was the most civilised thing to do when someone died. Lots of white flowers but no words spelt out in the hearse. Nothing too . . ."

"Common?"

"Over the top."

"Right. You must do what you think he would've wanted ..."

"I just want to sit here for a little while, Jasmine. By myself, if you don't mind? And you don't have to come here tomorrow, you know? Or even tonight – I'm sure you have plans for Christmas Day?"

"Would you listen to yourself! Don't be daft, Ruby. Of course I'm staying here tonight. And as long as you need me. All over the Christmas holidays. That's not a problem. Sure I'd only be partying and talking pure rubbish otherwise."

"But you said you had a big family get-together to go to," Ruby reminded her. "Your mum will be cooking a goose and everything, you said."

"Hush, woman, I'm going nowhere. I'll just give my parents a ring to let them know where I am, now you mention it. And then I'll fix us some supper."

"Yes, go ahead, the phone's in the hall. But I don't want anything to eat."

"You must have something? A little drop of soup?"

"No, really. You go on up to bed, okay? The guest room is on the first floor. It's the pale blue room with the red curtains and bedspread. You'll find some towels and pyjamas in the airing cupboard next to the bathroom."

"Okay. But just shout if you need a hug. Right then. Goodnight, I suppose . . ."

When Jasmine had left the room, Ruby drained her glass and poured herself another large brandy. Combined with the pill she'd taken earlier the effect was pleasantly insulating. Her head felt as heavy as lead. And her heart felt as fragile and light as an empty birdcage.

Better watch it, she told herself quietly. Mustn't take to the drink! Don't want to end up a raving alcoholic, now do I? Muttering to myself at bus stops. The neighbours avoiding me. Wearing two odd shoes to the shops.

Then she lifted Jonathan's gift and went to the sitting room to place it reverently beneath the Christmas tree. She sat down gently beside the tree, sipping brandy and sobbing until the cold morning light stole across the rooftops and it was Christmas Day.

When Jasmine came tiptoeing down the stairs at nine o'clock the following morning she discovered two things. One: Ruby fast asleep on the sofa, fully dressed and reeking of brandy. And two: outside, it was snowing heavily.

# 4

# The Aftermath

"Ruby? Wake up, sweetheart," Jasmine said softly, rubbing her friend's arm gently.

"What is it?" Ruby mumbled, still deep in a brandy fog.

"You'll do your back in sleeping there like that."

"Leave me alone please, Jasmine. I'm fine."

"No, you're not fine. You'll be crippled, woman. Come on now, up you get."

"No, please just let me sleep."

"Ruby O'Neill, you're still legless and you need to go to bed. Wake up this minute or I'll phone one of my brothers to come round and carry you up the stairs." Jasmine heaved Ruby into a sitting position and carefully tried to pull her off the sofa. Several of the pink and white scatter cushions toppled onto the floor. Jasmine cleared them out of the way with her foot.

"I'm really tired," Ruby groaned.

"I know you are," Jasmine soothed her.

"I want to sleep."

"Yes, I know. Can you walk upstairs? You'll be much cosier in bed."

"Okay, I'll try."

"Good girl. How much have you had to drink anyway?"

"Not that much."

"Oh yeah? Looks like it!"

Ruby staggered to her feet and Jasmine supported her slowly up the wide stairway, gripping onto the banisters for extra security at every step. Ruby was asleep again before her head had even touched the pillow. Jasmine slipped off Ruby's chunky boots and folded the plump duvet across her body. Poor Ruby was in a right old state, Jasmine thought to herself. She wondered briefly if there was any point in falling in love herself. If this was what happened to a girl when the fairytale came crashing to an abrupt end? Maybe she was better off playing the field and not getting too attached, too soon?

"You have a good sleep now and I'll check in on you later," Jasmine whispered softly. She closed the curtains and stole out of the room as quietly as she could – even though Ruby was sleeping so soundly that a Lambeg drum falling down the stairs wouldn't have woken her up at that point.

As Ruby's neighbours on the Ravenhill Road celebrated Christmas by tearing open their selection boxes and unwrapping their various presents, Ruby lay curled in a tight ball, lost in a long and meandering dream about herself and Jonathan. Sometimes they were young again and larking about as students, drinking cheap lager in the Union bar. And sometimes they were getting married, laughing and giggling about how crazy they were to be running away. Eloping like film stars, Jonathan had said. Like film stars . . .

"I bought you something nice too," Ruby heard a man's voice say. And suddenly she was sitting bolt upright and wide-awake in the bed, wondering if Jonathan's ghost had come back to visit her.

"Jonathan, are you there?" she whispered, not wanting to scare him away. Or indeed make Jasmine think she was going mad.

But the room was deathly quiet and still.

"Jonathan, it's okay, you can talk to me. I won't tell anyone," she added tearfully. But there was no sound except the soft drift of snowflakes being blown up and down the street outside.

It's what he said to me on the phone last night, that's all it is, she thought after a few more silent minutes. He said he'd bought me something nice. I wonder what it was.

And then remembering it was now Christmas Day, Ruby slipped out of bed and began to search for her lovely present. She carefully opened the wardrobe and had a rummage in the back but there was nothing there except for several neatly boxed pairs of her own boots and shoes. She looked in Jonathan's bedside cabinet and in his chest of drawers but again she could find nothing except perfectly pressed T-shirts and expertly folded socks.

I had so much time with him, she thought. I had all that time. *We* had all that time. And yet I wasted it ironing T-shirts and folding socks and putting shoes into boxes. And he wasted his time driving papers all over the place for his clients to sign. Why didn't we spend more time *together*? Why didn't we spend our time together doing nice things?

But that question, like so many others, had no satisfactory answer. Ruby sat down on the bed and racked her brains. It must have been jewellery, she decided. Jonathan must have bought her some jewellery. Wasn't that what some men bought for their wives for Christmas? Usually Jonathan bought Ruby a knick-knack for Christmas because she preferred glass candlesticks and pretty cushions to real jewellery. But this year he must have changed his mind.

"So I'm looking for a small box," she decided.

She looked around the room for a clue.

"Where would he have hidden a small box?"

And then her eyes came to rest on his favourite acoustic guitar propped up in the corner of the room on a black metal guitar-stand. He didn't play very often any more but he just liked the look of the guitar sitting there, he'd once said. Ruby tiptoed across the carpet and gently reached in behind it. Her fingers touched something feathery and light, and when she lifted it out she saw it was a tiny box.

"Oh Jonathan," she sighed. She stared at the box for a few moments and then she carefully opened it up. To her amazement it contained a diamond engagement ring. And when she examined it under her bedside lamp she saw that he'd had it engraved with the words, *I love you, Ruby. From J.* Ruby tried the ring on her finger. It fitted perfectly.

Damn you, she thought. You always said you'd buy me a nicer ring someday. Damn you for being so perfect. I wish I'd never met you now. I wish you'd been some awful husband who was getting on my nerves all the time. I wish you'd been a loudmouth drunk or a hateful womaniser or a lazy bloody lump of a man and then I could be glad to be rid of you.

She got back into bed and pulled the covers over her face to muffle her sobs. And she cried and cried until her head was about to split in two and her eyes were raw and sore all over again.

When Jasmine came into the room at lunchtime to check on Ruby she was fast asleep once more, the new ring now warm and snug on her finger. Jasmine saw the empty box and the old ring inside it on Ruby's bedside cabinet and guessed what had happened.

Wow, he must have been a really special guy, she thought.

A gentle knock at the front door distracted her then and she fled downstairs to answer it before the noise woke Ruby up. It was too dark a day to make out the two figures on the other side of the glass. She prayed to God that it wasn't a couple of priests or reverends as she quietly eased the door open. She usually felt quite nervous in the company of the clergy.

"Mum! Dad! Thank God it's only you. What are you doing here?" she said happily, ushering her parents into the hall and closing the door again as a flurry of snowflakes blew onto the pristine hall carpet.

"We're visiting you, Miss! It's bloody freezing out there," Jasmine's father complained. "My back has nearly seized up, it's that cold."

"And the roads round our way are like a bottle," her mother added helpfully. "Wee rascals have been pouring water on the roads so they can slide on them."

"You shouldn't have come across town in this weather," Jasmine scolded them.

"I had to see my only daughter on Christmas Day," Mrs Mulholland said firmly.

"Yes, we were bored with only our five sons and their girlfriends, wives and children to talk to," her father said, kissing her cheek gently with his ice-cold lips.

"Oh my God, you're frozen solid," Jasmine said, horrified. "Come through to the kitchen before you collapse on me. It's much warmer in there. "What's in the bags, Mum?"

"Well, I brought over your funeral outfit from the flat, just in case you didn't like to leave Ruby on her own, to go and fetch it yourself. Wasn't it great I had the spare key? And there's some hot food as well," her mother smiled.

"Hot food? I was hoping you'd say that," Jasmine said happily. "And thanks for getting my funeral outfit for me. Even though it's not a funeral outfit! It's a black hat and coat I bought to wear to a fancy dinner in the Europa Hotel last year."

"Oh aye, sorry. How's Ruby?"

"Fast asleep. Shocked to the core. Devastated for all time. Drunk as anything. Gutted. Take your pick," Jasmine sighed.

"The poor creature. Are there any family here so far?" her father asked.

"No, they both come from small families. Friends have been phoning but I've been telling them Ruby's asleep. I don't think she's really taken it all in yet anyway. She had a bit of an episode in the hospital when they told her, poor love. I thought she was going to go loopy on me."

"Aye, it'll be about a year before she accepts that he's gone," Mr Mulholland said wisely.

"I'm sure Ruby can't face eating much at the moment but you should have some dinner," her mother said then, setting her bag of food on a chair and looking around for the cutlery drawer. "This is some fancy kitchen, I'll say that much," she added, gazing round at the green-painted units and the grey granite worktops.

"Ruby and her husband did most of the work themselves," Jasmine said. "Ruby told me it took them two years to source all this stuff cheaply and get it organised. She loves her wee trinkets, doesn't she?" she added, as Mrs Mulholland admired various pretty jugs, bowls and baskets on the dresser.

"Yes, she does. Right, can I stick your dinner in the microwave to revive it? Where is it?"

Jasmine pointed. "It's behind that door."

"Right. And maybe you could make us a coffee to take the chill off our bones?"

"Surely I will, Mum. And thanks for coming over here today. I really missed you this morning," Jasmine said. "I really, *really* missed you both this morning but of course Ruby needs me now. She has nobody else to come and sit with her. Not really. Not anyone that she wants to see, in her current state."

"That's all right, love," said her father. "We're here now and we'll be only a phone call away if you need us."

Then they all sat round the table to a strange Christmas dinner where Jasmine wolfed down two helpings of roast goose and roast potatoes while her parents drank coffee and looked on lovingly.

Ruby opened her eyes and blinked hard a few times, vaguely confused by the eerie whiteness of the master bedroom. She glanced at the clock on her bedside table. It was seven o'clock. Seven o'clock in the *evening* on Christmas Day! Yes, it must be evening by now, she decided. But the light coming in at the edges of the curtains was strangely soft and flickering. The entire room was glowing like an angel's halo. And then Ruby realised what was happening: it must be snowing heavily. Perhaps it had been snowing all day? The flickering patterns across her bedroom walls were the shadows cast by the snowflakes as they fell around the streetlight directly outside her window.

"Jasmine?" she called out in a worried voice. "Are you still here? Is it snowing?"

"Yes, it's snowing and don't worry, love, I'm still here," Jasmine said immediately from the bottom of the stairs. "You're awake then? I'll be right up with some food for you."

A few moments later Jasmine knocked on Ruby's bedroom door and came in with a high-sided tray. On it was a plate of dinner covered with tin foil, as well as two strong painkillers and a pot of tea.

"I found the empty brandy bottle lying under the coffee table," Jasmine said grimly, setting the tray on the edge of Ruby's bed. "Thank God it was only a small bottle or you might not have lived to tell the tale . . . Sorry . . . Your head must be opening."

"Yes, well, I do feel as if I've been hit with a hammer but that brandy did the trick," Ruby grimaced. "I'd never have slept otherwise."

"Fair enough. Eat up now. You had no supper last night. Or anything else all day today. I don't want you keeling over on me. Come on, sit up."

"Where did this lovely food come from?" Ruby stuttered as Jasmine whipped off the tin foil to expose a magnificent roast dinner that Nigella Lawson would have been proud of.

"Mum and Dad were here earlier," Jasmine said shyly. "I hope you don't mind?"

"Of course not."

"They brought us over some goose and a few mince pies and so on. I've just heated your dinner up in the oven. I was going to wake you now anyway."

"Thanks, Jasmine."

"And Mum and Dad said to say how sorry they were to hear the sad news. They left some boxes of teabags and biscuits and a couple of trays of sandwiches as well, bless them. They just assumed there'd be a wake."

"Me being a Catholic and all?" Ruby smiled weakly.

"Yes. They were almost afraid to come into the house in case they interrupted the Rosary or tripped over a priest or something."

"Or got fatally splashed by Holy Water?" Ruby smiled. "I hope you made them a cup of tea?"

"I did, of course. Coffee, to be precise. Mum couldn't say no to a peek at your kitchen, once she knew there was nobody else here. She said to say your house is just lovely."

"Did she? The wee dote! I must phone her later to thank her for this lovely food. Remind me, won't you?" Ruby reached for the knife and fork. She was almost frightened by the throbbing hangover she could feel gathering behind the bones in her forehead. "Is the snow very deep?"

"Yes, a record for Belfast, they said on the news. Eight or nine inches in some areas! It's supposed to snow all night tonight as well. I don't imagine it will have cleared for Saturday. Good job the funeral parlour is only two minutes up the road, I suppose."

"Yes, I suppose. Did they get in touch?"

"Yes, they rang this morning. And this afternoon too. They said they would call back tomorrow morning though. Just to confirm flowers and music and so on. I reminded them to have only white flowers on the casket."

"Thanks, Jasmine. And there was no problem with the date?"

42

"No. A church service and a burial would have been much more difficult to arrange at Christmas time, they said. But a simple cremation service is fine."

"Okay. Thanks. I'm so glad Jonathan mentioned cremation to me that time, Jasmine. I couldn't bear to stand in a cemetery in the snow. With the wind cutting through us all like a knife. There's nothing sadder than a funeral in the snow."

Ruby closed her eyes and, dropping the knife and fork, pressed her hands over her mouth. She must not cry like a Banshee now. Not with the hangover from hell pressing at her skull! Her exhausted brain would simply implode with the added pressure.

"I found this engagement ring," she said, showing her hand to Jasmine.

"I noticed it earlier. It's beautiful."

"It's my Christmas gift from Jonathan."

"Yes, I guessed that much. Here, will you please try and eat a bite of this dinner before it gets cold? I daren't risk keeping it warm for much longer. You might get food poisoning or something. Roast goose isn't exactly what I'd usually recommend after a night on the drink. But you do need to keep your strength up so have a little bit, yeah?"

"Your mum's a terrific cook," Ruby said, trying a small forkful. "This is delicious." She didn't like to tell Jasmine that the very thought of rich food made her feel ill.

"Good girl. Now, a few of Jonathan's friends have been on the phone. They saw his car on the news and put two and two together. I said I would let them know about the funeral arrangements later on today. And Theodora was here earlier leaving flowers for you. Bless her soul. She walked all the way up the Ravenhill Road in her little furry boots. She wants to come to the funeral, of course."

"Yes, the funeral. Oh Jasmine, is this really happening? For a split second when I woke up there I thought it'd all been a bad dream."

"It'll be all right," Jasmine said gently. "I'll not leave your side for a single second, I promise. And don't worry about inviting anyone to a hotel for dinner afterwards. There won't be anywhere available at such short notice, I'd say, in any case."

"Well, I might ask a few people back here for tea and cakes maybe. I'll see how I feel. Did my parents phone?"

"They did, yes, at ten o'clock this morning. And just a few minutes ago too. They didn't seem to know what had happened when they called the first time. They said they'd been out gathering firewood and so on. And they hadn't heard the news."

"Gathering firewood? That's a new one. I thought they had a gas fire in their kitchen. Anyway they never listen to the news much or bother with any newspapers really."

"Oh, okay. So I told them. Was that all right?"

"Yes, thank you, Jasmine. Thanks for everything. When will they get here? It'll be a three-hour drive in this weather, I fear."

"Ruby, the thing is . . . they're not coming. They said they'd been snowed in."

"What? They're not coming at all?"

"No. I'm sorry. That's why they rang back. The village is completely cut off, they said. The heaviest snow in living memory. The roads are much worse in the west of the country. No one can get in or out of Blackskull village even with a tractor."

"What about the funeral though?"

"Well, they said they would try to make it . . . but that it was very doubtful."

"Should I ask for it to be delayed?" Ruby fretted. Oh God, this damn bloody snow! I don't want to delay it all now, Jasmine, in case I go crazy or something."

"I don't know, love. Maybe the snow will be cleared off the main roads by tomorrow afternoon and they can make the trip?"

"Maybe. But I doubt it." Ruby's eyes filled up with fresh tears. "I might have known something like this would happen. They always manage to find some excuse not to visit me, Jasmine. It must be two years since they've been in this house. I can't believe it."

"Shush, now. They can't help being snowed in, Ruby. Will you take another tablet, please? Just the one, yeah? I think you should."

"I haven't got any tablets."

"The nurse dropped some off this morning. So just pop one in, okay? And then we'll not mention them again?"

"Okay," Ruby agreed. "Just the one. Thanks for staying the night, by the way. I really appreciate it."

"Don't mention it." Jasmine slipped the tablets out of her pocket and placed one into Ruby's hand. "There you go, get that down you."

"God help me, I'm a walking disaster area."

"You're doing fine."

"I'm hopeless."

"You're not."

Ruby ate a few more mouthfuls of lunch and then she laid the fork down and made an apologetic face at her friend.

"I'm sorry for crying all the time, Jasmine. My head's just clean away with all this. It's mental. We were going to start trying for a baby, you know? This very Christmas!" Ruby closed her eyes again and tried to pretend she was somewhere else or someone else.

Jasmine just patted her hand uselessly. There was nothing left to say. Instead she poured some tea for Ruby and sat silently beside her while she drank it.

"Come on, then, love," Jasmine said eventually. "Up you get, if you're finished eating?"

"Get up? What for?"

"To freshen up. I'll run you a nice hot bath, yeah? For I'm sure you haven't enough energy to stand up in the shower."

"Do you know, I probably haven't. You're an angel, Jasmine Mulholland. An absolute angel! Thank you from the bottom of my heart."

"You're welcome, Ruby. Sure I know you'd do the same for me."

# 5

## The Funeral

On Saturday morning, the two friends put on their sombre funeral coats and hats and ventured out into the sparkling white snow-scene that the Ravenhill Road had become. A fresh blanket of snow had covered everything in sight. The terraced Victorian and Edwardian houses had been transformed into giant, iced cakes. The cars parked along the edges of the street were huge snowballs on wheels. The garden railings had become delicate cobwebs that sparkled in the weak morning sunshine and even the bare branches of the trees were heavy with great clumps of blue-white snow. Most of all it was exceptionally quiet.

"I think most people have decided to take the day off work," Ruby said in a half-whisper, threading her arm through Jasmine's for moral support.

"It's Saturday, Ruby," Jasmine said gravely. "You've lost track of the days."

"Yes, I think I have," Ruby replied, feeling slightly embarrassed. "That's what happens to people when they start swallowing happy pills, I daresay. Next thing, I won't know the name of the current Prime Minister."

"Shush now, you're doing fine," Jasmine soothed. "It's an easy mistake to make. There's always less traffic on the Ravenhill than on the Ormeau Road anyway. And you've only had two pills so far. It's not like you'll be on them forever."

"No, not forever," Ruby sighed, squeezing Jasmine's hand softly.

They crunched up the street together, leaving two meandering trails of footprints behind them. Surprisingly there were lots of cars in the car park of the funeral home.

"Looks like a big enough crowd," Ruby murmured nervously.

"It'd take more than a bit of snow to keep the locals at home. Jonathan was very well liked," Jasmine chipped in at once. "I'll be stuck to your side like glue all day, don't you worry."

"You're a good and dear friend," Ruby told her.

In the glass entrance porch there were two magnificent displays of white hothouse roses with trailing fronds of ivy, ferns and other greenery. Even in the chilly morning air, the heady scent of the roses filled Ruby's heart with love and she could almost hear Jonathan's voice calling to her: *I love you*.

"I carried a posy of white roses on my wedding day," Ruby said flatly. "I thought we would be together for a hundred years."

"Oh Ruby, I know, and it's all so unfair."

"Jasmine, God help me, I don't think I can go in there," Ruby said, glancing through a glass panel in the inner doors, at the packed benches and the forest of white flowers within, and sensing the air of finality that these things meant. "I'm afraid I might make a complete fool of myself. Jesus, no, I can't do it. I'm going home. God! Where did you put the rest of those tablets? I need one quick."

"Come on now, sweetheart, you'll be fine."

"I won't!"

"You will. It's time to do this one last thing for Jonathan," Jasmine urged her. "You know how you said he liked funerals to be relatively dignified."

"Yes, he did say that, didn't he? Okay then. But stay beside me, promise!"

"I will. I promise."

Clutching one another tightly they pulled open the heavy wooden doors to the main room and despite the heat emanating from within they continued to shiver as they took their seats in the front row.

Ruby almost collapsed when the brief ceremony began but she managed to make her mind switch off somehow. And she gazed instead at the beautiful wreaths sent by herself, by her boss at the clothes shop (Miss Theodora Kelly herself), by Jonathan's many friends in the accounting business and of course, by dear Jasmine and her family. Ruby couldn't spot a wreath from her own parents amid the sea of blooms but she was sure there was one up there somewhere. The music began and Ruby squeezed Jasmine's hand tightly for moral support and then simply closed her eyes and tried to breathe normally . . .

And then she just let her thoughts wander back to the days when she and Jonathan had met as students at a bus stop outside Queen's Union. She remembered the draughty bed-sits they had shared, the candles dripping wax down the sides of cheap wine bottles, the chips-and-lager suppers. She thought about the day he'd proposed to her, buying the small engagement ring with his first decent pay packet. Their perfect wedding day in the Scottish highlands: they'd decided to elope to Scotland rather than force Ruby's devout parents to witness a "mixed" marriage. Then their idyllic honeymoon in the cosiest cottage in the world, the luxury of a bath that was big enough for two. Then buying their large but rather dilapidated house on the Ravenhill Road and fixing it up together, planning for the future, kissing by the garden gate . . .

Ruby sobbed quietly at the end and shook hands with the other mourners. She thanked the undertakers and she admired the flowers and she did discover a small wreath containing long white trumpet lilies that had been sent by her parents. Ruby read the message on the card "*With Deepest Sympathy, From Mr and Mrs Nightingale*", and was grateful for that much, at least.

And then she and Jasmine were outside again in the snow and it was over. As they set out for Ruby's house with the other mourners they didn't notice a reporter from the local paper taking their picture.

On the night of her husband's funeral service Ruby could not sleep. Lots of people had come back to the house for tea, drinks and sandwiches, and Jasmine's mother had arranged it all and served the food beautifully. Ruby marvelled again at the kindness of this woman she had never met before. And tried not to be angry with her own parents for being snowed in at Blackskull village. It wasn't their fault that the country was seeing the heaviest snowfalls for decades. But they were an anti-social pair of old relics when all was said and done and they could have made the effort for their son-in-law's funeral. No doubt Jasmine's parents would have made it; perhaps some families were just more *determined* than others to keep in touch, Ruby fretted. She should have phoned them back, she supposed, but she was too cross with them today. She'd do it tomorrow.

Ruby tried hard to sleep but sleep would not come. She didn't want to take yet another tablet and she was afraid to open another bottle of brandy. She lay stiffly on her own side of the bed until she thought she would scream with frustration and grief. In the end she decided to get up and do something useful to pass the time until morning. So she quietly tidied and dusted and cleaned the kitchen until it shone, and sorted out the recycling into plastic crates in the small laundry room at the back of the house. At two o'clock in the morning she sat beside the Christmas tree in the sitting room, leafing through old photo albums, crying softly and pressing her cheek to Jonathan's wedding photo. At three o'clock she made herself a mug of hot chocolate and curled up on the sofa with a soft throw over her legs, sipping her drink slowly to make it last longer. Meanwhile Jasmine was fast asleep in the main guest room, having insisted on staying with Ruby for another couple of nights.

Ruby brought her friend a piping hot cup of tea at half past four, hoping to find her awake so they could have a good long chat. But Jasmine was sleeping soundly, the duvet pulled right up to her eyelids. Ruby smiled and left the room again as quietly as she could. It was so lovely of Jasmine to give up all her parties and the chance to bump into someone special under the mistletoe. Ruby didn't know how she would have managed without her over the last couple of days.

She didn't think of the years ahead, though. The years ahead were simply too frightening even to contemplate.

A couple of days later at Camberwell House, Tom Lavery sat for a long time in his potting shed staring numbly at Ruby's picture in *The Belfast Telegraph*. The photographer had taken her picture as she came walking out of the funeral home arm-in-arm with her friend Jasmine Mulholland. Ruby's face looked frozen as if all the life had been drained out of her.

There was a picture of Jonathan too, taken on his wedding day seven years before. He was a very handsome man. Tom had to admit that. Clean cut and intelligent-looking with a nice suit on him and a kind yet mischievous smile on his face. The article said that the lorry driver had been banned from driving until the case went to court but that it was unlikely he would be found guilty of causing death by dangerous driving. A lack of evidence apparently. A single eyewitness was not usually enough to secure a conviction.

The *Telegraph* had quoted one mourner as saying that the service was "very thoughtful and beautiful". No doubt the reporter would have been disappointed with that, hoping for some ranting against the other driver.

"Poor, poor woman," Tom said sadly and beside him Noah pricked up his ears and looked sympathetic. "Ruby O'Neill's a widow, Noah boy. She's on her own now too. I wouldn't wish on anyone what she's about to go through. Not on my worst enemy."

Slowly he folded up the newspaper and slipped it into a drawer in his ancient old filing cabinet. Then, worried that somebody would find it there and think he was stalking Ruby O'Neill, he took it out again and laid it gently on top of the recycling pile by the door.

"Come on, you," he said to the dog then, pulling himself out of his comfy armchair near the small gas stove. "Not much to do today. Let's go out for a walk, yeah?" Noah leapt up and went to the door eagerly and Tom slipped a warm coat on and they went outside together. "Just a quick stroll," Tom added, more to convince himself that he wasn't being cruel to Noah, to take him out walking in eight inches of snow. But he needn't have worried. Noah took one look at the depth of the snow and immediately trotted back inside. He lay down in his warm and blanket-lined basket near the heater and refused to get up again.

"Have it your own way," Tom said, leaving the door ever so slightly ajar and going out by himself. That dog of his was spoilt rotten.

As he crunched laboriously around the grounds, Tom's mind couldn't help wandering back to that solemn picture of Ruby and wondering how on earth she was going to cope. He'd been a widower for several years and he didn't seem to be getting any better. In fact he thought he was getting worse. The more he cut himself off from people, the harder it was to get back into the swing of things. But then again, the day had never come when he actually felt ready to start behaving "normally" again.

Let's face it, he said to himself. I am practically a social recluse.

And it was true. He hardly ever left the estate unless it was to run an errand for work.

At least Camberwell House and the gardens were looking as beautiful as ever. They were always at their best on a snowy day like today when the silently accumulating snow highlighted the formal topiary and the many architectural details of the house. Tom checked that all of the outbuildings were secure and then he collected Noah from the shed and drove home to his lonely cottage on the very edge of the estate.

His little home was surrounded on all sides by a dense planting of Christmas trees but since losing Kate he'd not bothered having one inside the house. Tom lit the fire, fed Noah, ate a microwave dinner and switched on the TV for company. But he barely watched what was on the screen. Noah lay on the sofa beside him, his wise eyes half-closed with contentment.

"What are we like, boy?" Tom said softly, patting the dog's head and then pulling a warm throw across his own chest. "A real barrel of laughs, the pair of us. Well, it'll be a New Year soon, Noah. I don't want to tempt fate but maybe next year I'll stop being such a miserable sod. Maybe next year I'll stop wishing it was me who'd died instead of Kate."

It wouldn't be a fresh start for Ruby though, he thought sadly. And he closed his eyes with the pain of remembering Kate's funeral and the madness he'd felt in the months following it. Months when he thought he would go out of his mind with grief. Yes, Ruby's agony was only just beginning.

# 6

# The House

But yet, life continued, as it always does. Even though life seemed to be moving in slow motion for Ruby O'Neill. And even for Jasmine Mulholland, who had missed out on all the festive fun and riotous New Year parties. In a few days Jasmine went back to her spotless apartment and Ruby spent countless hours curled up beside her Christmas tree, bathed in the warm red glow of the berry lights. Sometimes she would sit holding Jonathan's new shoes in her hands. Sobbing loudly and having hot flushes of panic and then cold sweats of misery and then sleeping for hours and hours and hours.

The police came to see her twice but nothing more could be done until the court case went ahead, they told her. They suggested Ruby join a bereavement group but she said she wasn't anywhere near ready to talk about what had happened. And furthermore she had no desire to be held up as the poster-girl for forgiveness and maturity. She wasn't ready to forgive anybody for Jonathan's death. Definitely not the lorry driver! And not even Jonathan himself! She'd asked him to take Christmas Eve off work so they could go and do some last-minute shopping together. Theodora had given herself and Jasmine a half-day off, after all, and so they'd closed the dress shop at lunchtime. But no, Jonathan had said he had a difficult case to tie up and then there was the office party to go to. He couldn't miss that or they'd all be teasing him and calling him an old woman. And then he had to make a quick dash to Ballynahinch . . .

No, Ruby wasn't ready to start talking to the professionals just yet. She was still trying to come to terms with the reality of losing her husband in the first place. She had made no plans for the future, she told the police. No plans at all.

And that was why Ruby simply continued to get up in the mornings and get dressed and go walking quietly into work. She served the customers and she cleaned the shop and she chatted to Jasmine about trivial things. She placed Jonathan's ashes on his bedside table and set a framed photograph of him in front of them. She wasn't ready to do anything further with the little bronze urn. Every evening she wandered round the house, tidying rooms that were already tidy. And every night she cried herself to sleep or paced up and down the stairs like a restless ghost. She flushed the rest of her little white tablets down the loo and banned herself from buying any more alcohol. Another week relying on brandy to get to sleep and she knew she'd be past the point of no return.

"I'm not about to become a burden to anyone," she said bravely to her reflection in the bathroom mirror. "Least of all to poor Jasmine. I have nothing left now but my dignity and I'm sure as hell not going to throw that away along with everything else."

Occasionally she rang her parents. And tried not to notice how little they rang her back. Her parents found any amount of excuses not to visit her in Belfast and she said she was too exhausted to go and see them in Blackskull. On a subconscious level both Ruby and her parents knew that their relationship wasn't strong enough to cope with a death in the family.

The insurance people organised lots of legal papers for Ruby to sign. Jasmine's mother sent regular food parcels. All the neighbours were very kind: sending flowers and asking if Ruby needed any errands running. Ruby thanked them all over and over and prayed for the day when she would wake up and start to feel normal again. Privately she didn't think she would ever feel normal again.

Seven months later, however, the cogs and wheels of life were turned again by the mysterious hand of fate. And the clothes shop where Ruby and Jasmine worked was put up for sale. The two women were given only three months to find other jobs. Surprisingly Jasmine was terribly upset. Normally the resilient type, Jasmine was almost in tears when Theodora told them she was finally selling the shop and retiring to Essex to live with her widowed sister Amelia. Ruby's recent troubles had reminded her that time was very precious, she told them.

"I see," Jasmine said sadly. "Well, I'll definitely miss the old place. I've been very happy here. But obviously you must do what you think is for the best, Miss Kelly," she added, nodding her head as if she thought it were a terrific plan.

But the fact remained that Jasmine absolutely adored working in the classy shop and would rather have died than don a regulation supermarket body-warmer. If nothing better came along, that is. She had to work somewhere after all because she had rent to pay. Ruby on the other hand wasn't too devastated. Yes, the shop had been her salvation since Jonathan's death. It had given her a reason to get out of bed in the mornings and get dressed and eat breakfast. But a job was simply a job to Ruby and she knew she would find something else eventually. With the house paid for, thanks to Jonathan's recent life insurance cheque, and a fair amount of her own savings in the bank, Ruby knew she wouldn't starve. Unlike Jasmine, who was determined to stand on her own two feet financially, and not go running home to her parents' tiny terraced house on Sandy Row at the first sign of trouble!

"Ah well! What a bummer! I'll really miss working with you, Ruby," Jasmine said glumly when Theodora had given the shop a quick inspection and then gone to visit a friend for the day. "What are the chances we find new jobs in the same place? Or even close enough to meet for lunch every now and then?"

"We might be lucky," Ruby said, polishing one of the display cabinets until it gleamed and then rearranging the costume jewellery within. "The new owner might keep us on here. And if not, then we'll surely be snapped up by somewhere else. With all of our experience in retail! Come on, love, cheer up."

But Jasmine wasn't so sure. Perhaps the other nice clothing shops would be finding it harder and harder to make a profit in the new economic downturn? She fretted about it all morning.

"We could finish up in the Odyssey cinema, the pair of us. In red overalls or something! Shovelling popcorn into those giant paper buckets," she sighed heavily. "Mopping vomit out of the bogs at midnight . . ."

"Don't even joke about it, Jasmine. Do you know, I wish Theodora hadn't bought these huge great amber pendants. They're absolutely lovely and everything but not very practical. I mean I might wear one but a normal person would laugh their head off if they got this whacking great lump of a thing as a gift."

"Yes, that'd be a nice pendant if it was a bit smaller. But anyway, Ruby, I'm fed up. This shop was so handy to my flat as well."

Jasmine loved her trendy, one-bed apartment in the Bell Towers, a fabulous new housing development that was built on the site of the old Ormeau Convent. She was so proud of her airy home and its clean, modern lines and the generous built-in storage in the bedroom. She was always talking about her chocolate-brown kitchen counter-tops and her recessed bathroom spotlights. The rent was considerably higher than what she'd been paying in her last place. About one hundred and fifty pounds higher, to be precise. But Jasmine had solved that particular problem by giving up cigarettes and Lotto tickets. Not to mention Sky TV, drinking wine during the week and eating fish suppers that cost nearly five pounds a time.

"Still enjoying the high life then?" Ruby teased. Jasmine's apartment was on the fifth floor of the complex. She had her own little wrought-iron balcony with potted plants on it and a metal chair for people-watching on Sunday afternoons.

"Yes, I am, thanks for asking – I do love living on my own," Jasmine said happily, all delighted with herself despite the bad news about the shop being sold. And then she was quiet again, fearing she might have reminded Ruby of Jonathan's death. "I mean it was very strange at first, yes, living by myself. Worrying about burglars and possible weirdos in the other apartments and so on. And having nobody to talk to in the evenings was a bit lonely. But now it's great! No mess and clutter belonging to other people! No need to listen to a lot of nonsense and gossip and boring trivia all the time. Though it *would* be nice to meet a decent man for a change and maybe have a little bit of old-fashioned romance. Though I *don't* want to get lumbered with a live-in lover just yet obviously. And all that music crap that most guys seem to accumulate! Huge bloody speakers or amps or whatever they're called. And crates of vinyl and at least two guitars gathering dust . . . oh! I'm sorry. Jonathan had guitars, didn't he? Oh, I'm so sorry, Ruby. I'm making everything worse with my stupid rambling . . . I'll make us a sneaky brew, shall I?"

(If Theodora knew they were drinking tea outside of their official lunch-break, and in the actual shop itself instead of the kitchenette, she would give them both a stern lecture on Health and Safety.)

"Yes, please," Ruby smiled. "I'm sure Theodora won't be so quick to enforce the rules, now she's selling up and moving on."

Then, as they were thoughtfully sipping their mugs of Punjana, Ruby had an idea.

"Jasmine Mulholland, brace yourself! This is going to sound mad but I'm going to put in an offer for the shop," she announced in a breathless whisper.

"You're going to do what? An offer for the shop! For this place?" Jasmine was completely surprised. "Can you really afford it?" she asked, her heart fluttering with hope and excitement. Was it only a few months ago that Ruby had been dithering over buying a mere pair of shoes?

"Yes, I think so. You see, I'm going to sell the house," Ruby said firmly.

"But the cost of it, Ruby! I mean, Jesus Christ, the cost of it! I mean, do you think that's wise? You have the house so nice."

"Yes, I know it's lovely. But it's time I downsized, don't you think? I haven't even cleared Jonathan's things out of it yet. The whole place is like a shrine to him and I'm just pottering about in it since he died. Kissing his photograph in the middle of the night like some mad Victorian hermit." Ruby looked as if she was going to burst into tears but then she took a deep breath and continued. "Jasmine, it's now or never."

"But still, moving house is a really big change to make at any time, in anyone's life," Jasmine remarked carefully, worried that Ruby would sell her lovely home on a whim and then miss it dreadfully. "A bit too much for you to take on, maybe? He's only been gone for seven months. Why not wait a bit longer?"

"The shop will be sold to someone else if I wait a bit longer. And I will be able to cope with a big change. I'm thirty-two now, not seventy. Didn't you swap your rickety old bed-sit for a fabulous new place? No troublesome garden to maintain and a cute balcony to sip your morning coffee on! Didn't you say your whole life was transformed by having decent storage in the bedroom, and lots of light flooding in through those big windows during the summer evenings?"

"Well, yes, I know all that. But I had nothing to lose. I was only renting an old dump anyway. And I don't remotely like gardening. And besides, where will you live if you sell the house? Renting is only money down the drain. I only rent because I've no hope of getting a mortgage, not on my pay packet. I mean, I've only got one bedroom . . . oh, but you're welcome to my sofa-bed for a few weeks!"

"Jasmine, love, don't panic! There's no need for you to worry about unwelcome lodgers cluttering the place up! I know what you're thinking! Yes, I do. Jasmine, you sweetheart . . . Look, I know you love having your own space. But I won't be crashing at your place! Isn't there a perfectly good flat up there?" Ruby nodded towards the stairs.

"Oh yes . . . But it's full of stock and spiders," Jasmine said in a gloomy voice. "And I don't know if it's a proper flat. There's a loo but no shower or bath. Wouldn't you need to have a separate front door put in at street level? And that would mean a whole palaver with the rates office and the insurance people?"

"I suppose there would be a lot of forms to fill in, yes. But sure what else have I got to do with my spare time? I always wanted to have my own business but Jonathan was so sensible where money was concerned. He didn't want us to take any major financial risks."

"Nothing wrong with being sensible," Jasmine said kindly, wiping a telltale cup-ring from the counter with a piece of kitchen paper.

"Yes, I know. But Jonathan isn't here any more to worry about taking financial risks, is he? It's only a small shop I'll be running, not a major factory. And, besides, when I'm in charge we can have a cup of tea whenever we like and we can leave the shop at lunchtime to run a few errands. And what's more I'll even allow you to go to the loo without asking my permission first."

"Wow, really? Why didn't you say so? Now that's a different matter altogether," said Jasmine, pretending to swoon with happiness behind the counter. "Though I promise not to leave the cash register unattended. But don't say I didn't warn you if you have any regrets down the line. Some people can get very emotionally attached to their houses."

"I think I'll manage," Ruby smiled. "The house is far too big for me now. And as for the business, haven't I worked here for years? I think I know how to run a small business. And besides I did go to Art College in my younger days, you know? I do know a good design from a bad one."

"True. At least you wouldn't have bought those great big pendants."

"I definitely wouldn't, you're right there. Okay, I'm going to have my house valued as soon as I can get it staged for the buyers. I need to do this, Jasmine. I need to move out of my comfort zone and do something new before this little burst of courage deserts me forever."

"Okay, Ruby. Good luck, love."

"Thank you."

And so it was decided.

Theodora Kelly was delighted when Ruby told her she'd like to buy the shop. She agreed to give Ruby six weeks to get her finances in order before she accepted any other offer on the property. There was a steady stream of potential buyers to look at the premises but no firm bid on the table as the weeks went by. The looming recession was putting people off or so it seemed. And Ruby began to think that her dream of owning her own business might be coming true at last.

In the meantime she had a lot to do. Every evening after work she forced herself to choose at least five items belonging to her late husband and then she sorted them into poignant little bundles in the drawing room. One pile for the charity shop, one for the bin and one for keeping. On her day off she would take a stroll to the Action Cancer shop on the Ormeau Road and hand over a couple of fat carrier bags full of clothes. Or she'd go sadly outside to the wheeled bin in the yard and have a private little cry before closing the lid on a pile of Jonathan's old socks or rusty razors. Or she'd lovingly wrap some treasured personal item belonging to him in tissue paper and parcel it up for the move. She wouldn't have room for much in her new home so she kept only a limited amount of things like his wedding ring, his new shoes, his reading glasses and his good leather wallet. She donated his four acoustic guitars, his cameras and his massive collection of photography books to the local church community centre. As well as most of the dishes in the kitchen and a small dining set.

Eventually there was nothing left in the house except for the larger pieces of furniture and the carpets and curtains. And Ruby knew the moment had arrived when she finally had to let go of the marital home. Her hands shaking, she telephoned a local firm of decorators and arranged for the entire house to be re-painted inside and out. A nice fresh ivory, she said; that would show off the house's architectural details and high ceilings to perfection. When the paint was dry she had all the hardwearing beige carpets replaced with an expensive ivory wool blend. The old curtains were gently folded into bin bags and dropped off at the Castlereagh dump. She ordered some smart Roman blinds in a neutral fabric and marvelled at how pretty they looked and how much bigger the rooms appeared to be when they were drawn up. The tiny front and back gardens were neat and tidy already so there was nothing else to be done there except invest in a couple of tall, steel pots for the front doorstep and plant them up with fragrant lavenders.

The estate agents agreed to conduct the viewings while Ruby was out at work. She was simply feeling too emotional to do it herself, she explained. There was nothing valuable that anybody could pocket when the agents weren't looking, she told them. Ruby had already put all her most precious keepsakes into three sturdy wicker hampers and Jasmine was currently storing them at her apartment in the Bell Towers. The only items left in the house were a few tasteful props. Some pale church candles sitting in the various grates and a set of pretty white china on the kitchen dresser. The agent was convinced Ruby's house would sell quickly despite the increasingly difficult market conditions.

"It's perfect," he said, shaking Ruby's hand as she handed over a spare set of house keys. "The nicest house we've had on our books in several years."

As expected, the house was sold to a couple of well-heeled first-time buyers within a week and Ruby discovered that she had made enough money to buy the shop outright. The paperwork went through without a hitch so that was an added bonus. There weren't too many sales going ahead in the city that year and all parties concerned wanted to seal the deal as soon as was humanly possible. So Ruby packed up her everyday clothes, stored them in four cardboard boxes in the kitchenette at the shop and that was that.

On the day that Ruby handed over the keys to the new owners she had to have a little glass of red wine in a nearby pub first to steady her nerves. She could have let the agent arrange the hand-over for her but she felt it would be good for her rather fragile self-esteem to do it herself.

"I can't imagine why you'd ever want to sell this absolutely amazing house," the young woman said when Ruby showed her and her husband into the hall that afternoon, delight beaming like sunshine from their faces. "We loved it from the minute we walked in the door."

Ruby studied their happy expressions and didn't want to spoil this great day for them by telling them that her husband had died nine months previously. And that she had to get out of the house now or else she would spend the rest of her life in it, sobbing over what might have been and the unpredictability of life in general.

The young couple were university graduates just starting out on life's journey and it wouldn't have been fair on them. He was a handsome dentist in navy chinos, with athletic arms and perfect teeth. And she was a pretty, blonde primary-school teacher in a pastel sheath dress and matching cardigan. They had worked hard at college for several years to be able to afford such a big mortgage (though a handy legacy had provided half of the asking price, the estate agent had told Ruby) and they deserved a cheery word from Ruby now. The estate agent had obviously also decided not to tell them Ruby O'Neill had recently been widowed. Ruby wondered whether they had seen her photograph in the local newspapers. If they had, they clearly didn't make the connection now. Perhaps they'd been away on holiday at the time, Ruby thought to herself.

"Let me just assure you I was very happy here," Ruby said breezily. "It's a great house in every way, isn't it? But now I'm starting my own business and I need to downsize a little. And I simply won't have the time to enjoy these lovely big rooms any more. Still I hope you'll look after the house for me? It's a dear old place and it deserves to be treated well."

"Rest assured we'll take very good care of it," the young man said. "We aren't going to change anything structural or even re-decorate. It's all so fabulous and clean and nicely done. We love the blinds and the carpets. And thanks for giving us the wardrobes and the other bits and pieces," he added politely. "We really do appreciate it."

"You're very welcome," Ruby smiled, swallowing back her tears. "The furniture won't fit into my new place so you might as well have it. It was hard enough getting those bigger pieces moved from room to room when the new carpets were being fitted. I daren't even think about how hard it'd be to get them down the stairs. Now, the wardrobes haven't got woodworm or anything. So please remember to check for woodworm if you buy any antiques, won't you?"

"We will indeed."

They all smiled warmly at each other. A sudden burst of strong September sunlight lit up the fireplace in the sitting room. Ruby could tell they were anxious for her to leave now. They wanted to go running from room to room, kissing and hugging and deciding which room to make into a study or a nursery or a dressing room. She looked at her watch to let them know she would soon be departing.

"Could I just go round the house for one last time, please?" she asked them shyly in the hallway. "Just to say goodbye to it?"

"Yes, of course," they said right away. "We'll go out to the little garden at the back and enjoy the spot of sunshine. Just let us know when you're ready to go?"

"I will, thank you."

And so Ruby went up to the top of the house and made her way slowly down again. Stopping for one short moment in every room, just remembering . . . something Jonathan had done or said . . . some little memory of him that she would treasure forever. That time he'd kissed her ankles tenderly when she was halfway up a ladder dusting the picture rails in the master bedroom. The other time he'd brought her breakfast in bed and hidden weekend tickets to Prague under the butter dish.

As she was glancing out of the bedroom window for the last time she was surprised to see a little robin redbreast perched on the windowsill. It was looking right up at her with its head to one side.

"Hello there," Ruby said, smiling down at him. "What are you doing there? I've got no crumbs for you today, I'm very sorry to say." The bird continued staring up at Ruby for another few moments and then suddenly it took off and flew towards the park on the other side of the road.

"Oh, Ruby O'Neill, you're getting fanciful in your old age, talking to birds!" she said to herself.

And then it was time to go down to the kitchen again via the other reception rooms and wave out the window at the new owners and let them take over the running of the house from her.

"I'll be off now," she said brightly, laying the keys formally on the kitchen dresser.

The young couple just nodded and came inside and waited respectfully in the kitchen as Ruby let herself out the front door.

"Cheerio, and the best of luck to you both," she called back over her shoulder.

"Bye, Mrs O'Neill. And thank you."

As Ruby pulled the front door closed a wave of grief threatened to overwhelm her. But she thought of her little shop and of Jasmine's constant friendship and of all the great changes she was going to make to the business. And so she turned her face towards the sunshine and went strolling briskly up the Ravenhill Road as if it were a perfectly normal autumn day like any other.

# 7

# The Shop

Ruby was almost glad the renovations at the shop had taken so long and caused so much noise and dust. And that the meetings with the planning people and the insurance people seemed to have gone on forever. Because she was so bone tired each night her head barely touched the pillow before she was out for the count. Some evenings she thought she would fall asleep while she was still standing at the bathroom sink brushing her teeth.

She'd moved into the rooms above the shop and was spending her nights sleeping on a mattress on the floor while the new layout was completed and the entire building re-wired. Jasmine had offered Ruby the use of her fancy suede-effect sofa-bed umpteen times, of course. But Ruby knew she was only being polite. Anyway, she thought it was actually kind of cosy lying there each evening beside her portable telly, with a kettle perched nearby on a biscuit tin. And living on fish and chips from the takeaway on the nearby Ormeau Road had put a few much-needed pounds back onto her frame. It felt a bit like a camping holiday, in some ways. There was hardly any housework to do. And besides, she had grown used to her own company in the evenings. It was lovely chatting to Jasmine constantly about anything and everything, of course. But they had all day to do that. Then at night Ruby would gratefully embrace the solitude and the silence.

Jonathan would have been very proud of her. She knew that. He wouldn't have wanted her to go on living in that big five-bedroom house all by herself for another forty years. This way she would always have something to do. Seasons and special occasions to plan for in the shop, endless customers to chat to and of course Jasmine for company. For as long as Jasmine decided to go on working with her at any rate. To this end, she was still paying Jasmine's wages even though the shop had been closed for a few weeks. Yes, this way there was just a small chance she might not actually go crazy with loneliness. The doctor had offered her anti-depressants, naturally, especially during the empty days just after the funeral. Everybody was on them nowadays according to Jasmine, who seemed to know half the city. But Ruby had said no, thank you very much. She preferred to deal with being a widow the old-fashioned way. By keeping herself busy during the day and then crying herself to sleep at night.

And whenever she felt out of her depth or remotely tearful Ruby would sit down with the cute little sewing machine that she'd bought in her student days and just zone out for a few hours. Forcing her mind to concentrate on her stitching and on creating neat seams instead of thinking of other, sadder things. Her sewing became quite a valuable distraction for Ruby, in fact. She had completed seven soft velvet evening bags in the months since Jonathan had died. Nothing she might ever have any use for really. Just pretty things in their own right, because Ruby loved pretty things. The bags were all neatly packed away in the wicker hampers in Jasmine's apartment, to save them from the omnipresent dust in the flat.

Keep busy, she kept telling herself. I must remember to keep busy.

However, when all the building work was finally finished after six long weeks and the plaster and paint had dried, the little place did look rather splendid. Especially the flat upstairs with the recessed spotlights that Jasmine had recommended in every room. Or rather that Jasmine had insisted upon.

"I'm telling you, Ruby, those miserable old dust-catcher pendants are so last century," she'd said firmly.

And some soft, cream carpets completed the look.

Ruby totted up the final cost of the new décor and wrote out some basic calculations on the back of an old envelope. Just to remind herself exactly how much money she needed to make in the shop each month to keep ticking over. With no mortgage to pay and only one member of staff on the books it didn't seem an insurmountable figure. She was glad she'd chosen a pale pink shade of paint for both the inside of the shop and the flat above it, because the newly revamped premises looked positively glowing with light and freshness. The old display cabinets in the shop had been spruced up with a few coats of duck-egg blue and then rubbed back at the corners to look antique. She'd had the shop floor-tiles professionally cleaned and a fancy new awning fitted over the front window. With her very own name printed on it: *Ruby O'Neill*, on a classic background of elegantly narrow pink and white candy stripes.

She didn't have much furniture in the flat yet but she decided to keep that little project on the back burner for the time being. Someday when she was really ready to face the world as a confident single woman she would go hunting for some nice cabinets and curios for her new home. A fat floral sofa or two, and some pretty cushions and rugs. But for now it was neat and tidy and strangely pretty in a monastic sort of way. With only a café table and two chairs in the small kitchen, a modern white sofa in the sitting room and a bed piled high with plain white pillows in the bedroom. She had a nice tasselled standard lamp by the bed to read by. And she had her clothes hanging on a chrome rail she'd rescued from the old stockroom. Yes, it would do for now. The main thing was the shop and it did look heavenly. Even Ruby with her modest and self-effacing nature had to admit that her shop was easily the prettiest one in the city. And Jasmine agreed with her.

"Ruby O'Neill, I have to tell you in all honesty I've never seen anything half as beautiful. In all my life, really!" Jasmine cried when she turned up for her first full day back at work after the renovations. "I mean, I knew you could do it, certainly I did. But this is even better than I thought it would be. Isn't it great to see the back of all that dreary beige? Dear Theodora, she was a great one for beige, wasn't she? And all those wobbly old rails have been replaced by pretty wardrobes, oh my God! And I love the new awning. So shiny and swish! It looks like something you'd see in Paris. It's really dinky! I could see it from half a mile up the road."

"Thanks, Jasmine," Ruby laughed. "That's the general idea. I thought it would be a bit of free advertising for us. And it'll be even nicer when the flowers start to bloom in the window-boxes next summer."

"Yes, yes . . . Now, Ruby, please don't take this the wrong way or anything, but do you think it'll look *so* nice and maybe *so* expensive that people will be afraid to come in?" Jasmine asked thoughtfully. "I don't want to sound like a wet blanket or anything. And I did promise not to be negative. Because all of this is absolutely to-die-for! But you know what Belfast folk are like? They tend to shy away from anything too OTT in case they can't afford to buy the stuff once they're in the door. Because then they'd be mortified."

"Possibly, yes. It *will* look a tiny bit intimidating at first. But when people see some of the things I'm going to put in the window they'll be reassured that we aren't the sort of shop where only millionaires are welcome. I'll have little coin purses in there and nice fluffy bedroom slippers and padded hangers. You know? Little luxury trinkets to tempt the impulse shopper."

"Right."

"And then they'll come in and see that our prices are actually quite reasonable and that the clothes and shoes are really high quality . . . They'll last a lifetime."

Jasmine nodded in agreement. She decided not to ask Ruby if the shiny awning was insured against vandalism. Now really wasn't the time to sound like a doom-and-gloom merchant. Hopefully the shop would look so lovely and serene that the young hooligans of the city would be afraid to come near it.

"It's all so terribly exciting, really it is. You know what? I just adore the smell of fresh paint in the morning," Jasmine sighed, taking it all in. "My apartment felt like this for about six weeks, as I recall. There's just something about the smell of fresh paint that makes me think of new beginnings."

"Let's drink a toast to new beginnings then? I've got a bottle of bubbly on standby," Ruby said happily, thinking of the small bottle of champagne she had in the fridge in the doll-sized kitchenette at the back of the shop. "I mean, let's drink a toast after we've got the shop ready for opening?"

"But aren't we going to have a big glossy re-launch?" Jasmine asked, slightly puzzled.

"No, Jasmine. I'm sorry but we aren't. I don't want to tempt fate by getting ideas above my station. Do you understand? I know it sounds daft but I'm going to try and sneak this little adventure under the wire. I don't want to set myself up for any more bad luck. No, I thought we would simply re-open and just let the new shop grow on people. You know? Let the legend spread by word of mouth? Like the Harry Potter books."

"I suppose you're right."

"We'll still have a little celebration though, just you and me on

SHARON OWENS

our own," Ruby said brightly. "We'll go out to dinner tonight, the pair of us. Yeah?"

"But Ruby, you haven't been out for dinner since Jonathan died," Jasmine said quietly. "You said it would feel like you were betraying his memory if you went out for a nice meal in a restaurant without him."

"I know, I know. But we'll go somewhere that's nice and friendly and not too brightly lit or stuffy, yes? What about that big Italian place on the Malone Road? They were always lovely and easy-going in there. I'm sure they wouldn't throw me out on the street if I started sobbing into my garlic chicken."

"Okay," Jasmine agreed and gave her friend a little hug. She understood how hard it would be for Ruby to overcome the reclusive pattern she had fallen into since losing her husband.

"We'll choose a table near the door and then if I do start welling up we can simply ask for the bill and make a quick getaway," Ruby announced. "I'll bring cash so it'll be even quicker to pay. My treat, by the way! And we'll have a couple of cocktails, too."

"Sounds perfect."

"Brilliant! Now let's get these boxes open and the new stock out on display," Ruby said with a determined burst of enthusiasm in her voice. "And let's group the outfits together by theme and by colour and not by size like we used to?"

"Shall we put all the old stuff down the back on the sale rail?" Jasmine asked. "Or should I say, the sale *wardrobe*?"

"Yes, but let's also hang it nicely, by colour. So it doesn't look too haphazard? And we'll not put the big sign saying SALE back up either. We'll just attach new price tags and keep it all very discreet."

"Right. We can just tell customers about the bargains if they ask?"

"Yes. And I got these nice new bags made. No more beige plastic carriers for us, Jasmine."

Ruby carefully opened a large cardboard box and lifted out a batch of pink and white striped paper carrier-bags with black cord handles. All bearing Ruby's name in black curly writing, on a pretty, white, oval-shaped label. Two sizes: one little, one much larger.

"Wow, what fabulous bags! Were they terribly expensive?" Jasmine couldn't help asking.

"Not really. Okay, they were a little bit expensive. But I think they'll be worth it in the end. So every customer gets a bag even if they're only buying a purse or a bangle, okay?"

"Okay. Just one last thing?"

"Yes?"

"Is anyone allowed to sit on that amazing armchair?" Jasmine pointed to a huge, overstuffed, pink floral, handmade designer armchair that had come all the way from London by recorded delivery.

"I suppose so," said Ruby reluctantly. "But definitely not if they're drinking tea or coffee. In tribute to dear Theodora and her obsession with Health and Safety! And may the sun shine on her in her retirement years."

"Hear, hear!" Jasmine said eagerly. "Won't it be weird to have a cup of tea where we don't have to go running for the kitchenette every time Theodora arrives at the door? Honestly, I think I've developed a phobia of little old ladies."

"Yes, I know what you mean," Ruby replied, laughing. "Isn't it great not to have anybody standing over us at long last?"

"It is."

Filled with hope and a creeping sense of excitement the two women quickly hung up their new stock in the freshly painted shop. Ruby arranged some of the nicest outfits and accessories in the window along with a few of her crisp new carrier bags. Jasmine vacuumed up the dust created by the packing boxes and then folded all the leftover cardboard into bags for the recycling lorry. By lunchtime they were ready to turn the lovely vintage door-sign to OPEN.

"Here goes," Ruby trilled, cracking open the champagne and pouring some into two tall pink glasses.

"Here's to new beginnings!" Jasmine said, clapping her hands and admiring the luxury armchair again. "Here's to the most stylish boutique that Belfast has ever seen!"

# 8

# The Ravenhill Road

As December approached, Tom Lavery thought again of Ruby O'Neill. Or rather he allowed himself to think of her without feeling guilty about it. Not that she'd ever been very far away from his thoughts during the eleven months that had passed since he'd first spoken to her. And shaken her hand on the doorstep of her lovely home on the Ravenhill Road. But as the Christmas decorations went up again now around the city he couldn't help wondering how Ruby would get through her first Christmas on her own. He knew from bitter experience that from now on everything wonderful that had once reminded Ruby of something happy would probably only remind her of how much she had lost.

Despite all that, Tom half-hoped that Ruby would order a fresh tree again, so he could at least call by and wish her a Merry Christmas. Or just say hello, even. *Merry Christmas* might be stretching it a bit, given the circumstances. But no order appeared on the list at the garden centre. And when he drove past her elegant house on the Ravenhill Road one day on his way to deliver some topiary tubs to a nearby restaurant he was dismayed to see a young couple coming out of the house instead. They pulled the front door shut behind them and walked happily down the short, tiled path to the street. The woman had a small pregnancy bump and the man was very protective and careful of her. They were holding hands. Tom slowed down and glanced in through the bay window. The pink rose-patterned wallpaper was gone from the sitting room. In its place were some large modern prints and a couple of tall chrome lamps. In that instant Tom knew that Ruby had sold her house and moved away. And his heart was pierced by yet another painfully sharp arrow of loneliness.

Christ, would you pull yourself together! He sighed loudly. She wasn't even your friend or anything. You meant nothing to her. Five minutes after you walked away from the house that night she probably forgot you ever existed. Come on now, get real.

Still it'd been comforting somehow to think of Ruby pottering around in her pretty pink house. Tom sorely missed a feminine presence in his life. And even one as remote as Ruby O'Neill's had been something to think about during the long lonely nights in his isolated cottage on the Camberwell estate. Cheery Mrs Kenny and her tasty leftovers from the kitchen were the nearest things he had to a family life these days. But he didn't like to hang around the café at Camberwell too much in case he might get drawn into a harmless conversation about gardening with some of the visitors. God, he was such an oddball nowadays, he thought to himself. Breaking out in a cold sweat if anyone cornered him and started asking about plants.

"Well, I never claimed to be the life and soul," he said aloud. Is it my fault if the majority of the people in this fucking country could talk the leg off a table, he thought. Is it my fault if I don't want to go spilling my guts and telling everyone about my personal life? Maybe I'm the normal one and they're all too nosy and pushy."

However, just as he was sinking deeper into his dark mood he spied the pink and white awning outside the clothes shop a little further up the road. He drove alongside and read Ruby's name on it and he understood at once what had happened. Ruby hadn't moved away from the Ravenhill Road altogether. She had only moved on a little bit. She must have bought over that dress shop? It must be the same Ruby O'Neill. Well, good for her!

Tom duly delivered his consignment of topiary (six squirrel-shaped ivy plants in mock-pewter containers) and then decided on the spur of the moment to park the Land Rover and go for a gentle stroll along the street. Just to stretch his legs, he told himself. Not to be an old nosy or anything like that! No, just to prove to himself that he wasn't turning into a nutty, anti-social recluse. Even though he knew in his heart that he *had* turned into a nutty, anti-social recluse years earlier.

"I'm fine," he said to himself. "I'm *fine*." And then he decided to shut up in case anyone saw him talking to himself on the street.

However, Tom's heart leapt as he passed the window of Ruby's shop and shyly glanced in. Without noticing he was doing it, he stopped walking and just stood there, his hands clenched tightly in his pockets with sheer nerves.

"Oh my God," he whispered to himself.

There she was. Casually sipping a cup of tea or coffee, and smiling at something the other girl was saying to her. That must be Ruby's friend Jasmine, by the looks of it. Tom remembered her from *The Belfast Telegraph*. The shop was a pastel cave of femininity with lots of delicate mohair sweaters and embroidered coats on padded hangers. And fluffy slippers and dainty hats and beaded scarves in the window! (Not the type of thing that his late wife Kate had worn at all. Kate had lived in jeans.) But it was very pretty and sparkly all the same. Ruby reminded Tom of a magpie with her sleek black hair and her elegant white face and her obvious attraction to glittery things.

Suddenly Ruby turned her head and glanced in Tom's direction and a flicker of recognition crossed her face. Jasmine turned also and peered right out at him. Ruby set her cup down on the counter and smiled at Tom. She even raised her hand and managed a friendly little wave. Jasmine's eyes were wide open with curiosity. Tom waved back as best he could with his heart beating wildly.

Then he began to blush furiously. His face, his hands and even his toes were flushing and uncomfortably warm. He felt as if he were flirting with another woman behind Kate's back. What an eejit he was for even coming here today! Ruby would think he was following her. Or maybe coming in to buy something, in his tatty old gardening clothes! He absent-mindedly reached out and touched one of the window-boxes as if he'd been admiring the delicate winter plants in it and not Ruby herself. But it was no use pretending anything now for Ruby was walking towards him. Dear God, she wasn't going to invite him into the shop to meet her friend, was she? The state of him in his oldest clothes!

Tom's courage deserted him like a flock of startled starlings. He turned on his heel and fled back down the street and around the corner to his waiting Land Rover. By the time Ruby had come out of the shop door and down the street to look for him, Tom was speeding back towards Camberwell with his heart in his mouth.

You damn fool, he chided himself as he left the city limits and took the turning for Camberwell. That was a clever move, I must say. Well done, mate! Now she'll think you're a stalker and a hopeless one at that. Leering in the window at her and then running away like a kid knocking on doors. Get back home for God's sake before you do any more damage. You're not safe to be let out, so you're not.

"Who was that?" Jasmine asked Ruby when she came back into the shop.

"Oh, it was nobody," Ruby muttered uselessly, knowing full well she was about to be interrogated.

"It was *somebody*," Jasmine said quietly. "I saw him looking at you. He knew you, Ruby. And you knew him. And he was quite the rough diamond, as my mother would call it. Come on and tell me. I want a name at the very least."

"Honestly, Jasmine, he was nobody special. Just this guy who brought my Christmas tree last year, that's all. I don't know him at all."

"Oh, I see," Jasmine smiled. "Just the handsome gardener, huh? Lady Chatterley's Lover, and all that jazz? Now I see."

"No, Miss, you don't *see* anything," Ruby said firmly.

"Why did you go outside then?" Jasmine asked.

"To be sociable. To say hello."

"Okay, to be sociable," Jasmine said meaningfully. "Whatever you say."

"I don't think he remembered me anyway," Ruby added. "Or if he did, he only wanted to nod hello. He didn't want a big long chat. Sure he legged it when he saw me coming. Probably thought I was going to try and sell him something. Or ask him to move along and stop cluttering up the footpath."

"Probably," Jasmine agreed, her eyes twinkling with mischief. "Yeah, that was it. He was afraid you were going to ask him to move along. Because everybody knows that shopkeepers do actually own the pavement outside their shops!"

"Cheeky cow!"

"Are you getting a Christmas tree this year, Ruby, I wonder? Perhaps that's what he was going to ask you before he bottled it?"

"Oh no, I don't think so," Ruby said quickly. "It's far too soon to be getting back to all of that, I should think. Besides, there's not room for a real tree in my flat. Not a decent size of a tree anyway."

"I might get a real tree this year," Jasmine said then. "There's more than enough room in my flat. Thirty foot long, my sitting room is! Where did you buy yours last year?"

"The garden centre at Saintfield," Ruby said casually before disappearing into the kitchenette to fetch a duster.

"Is that right? I might just pop up there after work," Jasmine said, as if to herself.

"He doesn't work there in case you're getting any bright ideas," Ruby called out from the kitchenette. "He's only their supplier."

"Right. Where does he work then, this mystery man of yours?" Jasmine wanted to know.

"I'm not telling you, sweetheart! Even I'm not that stupid." Ruby smiled to herself as she delayed meeting Jasmine's eye by tidying up the cleaning cupboard for a few minutes.

"Ruby dear, I can find out where he works easily enough," Jasmine said stubbornly.

"I'm sure you can," said Ruby. "You're very resourceful."

"We should keep him in mind. He looked pretty handsome to me. A pretty handsome, if slightly older man, admittedly," Jasmine said casually. "Just older enough to be sexy, mind. Not *too much* older . . ."

"He's nice enough," Ruby agreed, momentarily forgetting to be discreet. "I like his long nose. Even though it is a tiny bit crooked in the middle. He has nice eyes too. Kind eyes. He looks as if he might be a nice sort of person, don't you think?"

Jasmine's matchmaking tendencies suddenly went into overdrive.

"Maybe he's got a tiny wee crush on you?" she ventured.

"Oh no, I doubt it," Ruby said, snapping back into defence mode.

"Why wouldn't he have a crush on you? You look just like Juliette Binoche since you got your bob cut. And he's got that arty, dishevelled look down to perfection. You'd be perfect together when you think about it," Jasmine said, getting slightly carried away.

"Oh Jasmine, you're a hopeless romantic," Ruby sighed. "Arty and dishevelled, indeed! He's a gardener, you poor eejit."

"Somebody has to be romantic," Jasmine countered. "Somebody has to go on believing in happy endings. Right! He was a bit scruffy, this mystery man of yours, we can't deny that, but I bet he scrubs up well. And you're pretty tall too so you'd look fine together."

"It's all very lovely, your little scheme, but it's not going to happen," Ruby said firmly, coming back into the room and standing on a chair to dust the chandelier. Even though it didn't really need dusting but she was feeling too fidgety to sit down.

"I know, I know I'm running away with myself here, and it's far too soon for you to think of falling in love again," Jasmine said gently.

"It'll always be too soon for me to fall in love again," Ruby replied calmly. "Anyway, I'd be hopeless at dating again and all that stuff. I was so used to Jonathan, you know? I never even looked at other men in that way. I think my romantic radar or something that's necessary in my brain, for fancying a new man, has shut down."

"Maybe that's true," Jasmine sighed. "But you never know."

"Jasmine, I think we have a customer," Ruby said as a well-dressed woman rang the doorbell.

"Okay, I get the message," Jasmine muttered, buzzing her in. But all the rest of that day Jasmine couldn't help wondering who Ruby's admirer might be and if there was any chance at all that Ruby might actually consider the possibility of falling in love again one day.

# 9

## The Velvet Handbags

Ruby and Jasmine were laboriously carrying the wicker hampers upstairs to Ruby's flat. Ruby felt it was time they took up residence in the corner of her new bedroom. And also Jasmine needed to clear some space in her apartment so she could put up a few Christmas decorations. She didn't say anything to Ruby but she had a lot of socialising and partying to catch up on this year, since devoting the previous Christmas to nursing Ruby through her bereavement. And Ruby didn't say anything to Jasmine either but it was a huge step for her to be moving Jonathan's things into her new home for the first time. It was almost like admitting to herself that he wouldn't be coming back, that these things of his were only keepsakes now. And not Jonathan's own private possessions, waiting for him to come home again and claim them.

Unwrapping everything carefully, Ruby examined them once more and then placed them lovingly in the bottom drawer of her brand new armoire. They fitted perfectly.

"What's this?" Jasmine asked, as one parcel split open revealing a dark-red evening bag with a fat velvet ribbon for a handle.

"Oh, it's just something I made to pass the time. You know, on the nights I couldn't sleep after the funeral?" Ruby replied, emotion welling up in her chest at the sight of it. "It's a little handbag."

"But this is so pretty," Jasmine said. "I love the satin lining."

"I made seven of them," Ruby admitted shyly.

"All the same colour?"

"All the same design but different colours. One dark red, one midnight blue, one jet black, one baby pink –"

"One pale gold, one apple green and one deep purple," finished Jasmine, discovering the rest of the treasure beneath several layers of soft tissue paper.

"Silly of me to make seven evening bags that I'm never going to use," smiled Ruby.

"You might use them someday," Jasmine said kindly.

"I don't think so."

"It'd be a shame to just leave them in a drawer though," Jasmine said, tidying up the bows on the front of the bags and placing them in a neat line on Ruby's bed.

"What else would I do with them?" Ruby asked, reaching to put them away again.

"Sell them in the shop?" Jasmine suggested suddenly.

"Oh, I couldn't do that," Ruby protested.

"Why not? It's exactly the type of thing we sell."

"But we don't sell hand-made things."

"Well, we do, sort of. Everything is made by somebody, somewhere."

"But I don't think these are good enough," Ruby said firmly.

"Are you kidding? They're fine. They're lovely and I think they should go straight into that big glass case by the window, with your lovely new labels attached to them."

"No, really –"

"Shush!"

And with that Jasmine swiftly collected up the seven bags and went hurrying down the stairs before Ruby could stop her. Within five minutes she had all seven bags nicely stuffed with balls of the softest tissue paper, neatly labelled with the price and on display in the glass case. The velvet bags looked sumptuous and rather decadent resting there under the tiny, rainbow-effect spotlights.

"One hundred pounds each?" Ruby said doubtfully when she came downstairs a short while later. "Fifty quid would have been plenty."

"Nonsense, Ruby O'Neill, would you ever stop being so bloody humble, please? This is an exclusive fashion boutique, not a bargain basement. That's a very reasonable price considering all the effort you must have put into them."

"Okay! Don't have a fit! They look quite pretty, I suppose," Ruby agreed slowly, "when you see them nicely displayed like that."

"Yes, indeed they do. Now let's have a cup of tea to celebrate," Jasmine said, nipping into the kitchenette to brew up. Yet again.

"The power to drink tea at a whim is going to your head," Ruby laughed. "No wonder you're never out of the loo."

"Yeah, well, we won't have a minute to spare once the Christmas rush kicks off," Jasmine said sheepishly. "So we might as well get all the tea we can into us now. Build up a good store of caffeine."

"I hope we're rushed off our feet," Ruby said then. "I hope we won't have time to eat or sleep or talk or even think, we'll be that busy."

And she wasn't only thinking of the money.

"It'll get better, Ruby," Jasmine promised.

"Will it?"

"Sure. The world is full of Merry Widows, and widows who just make do, or so my dad says. And he knows everything about everything."

"Maybe. But I'm not your average Merry Widow. I loved my husband so much it took my breath away sometimes. I still can't believe he's gone. Some days I forget he's dead and I think he's just away on business or that he's left me for another woman or something. It's stupid, I know, but I can't quite accept it, still."

"I know. Maybe it would help to just remember the good times? That you loved him and that he loved you? So many people seem to live for years and years and never really love anybody. Never even really *care* about anything that's important."

"I know," Ruby said thoughtfully.

"Will we change the subject now?" Jasmine asked.

"Yes, please," Ruby smiled.

"And just one more thing? Can I please put a few baubles and things up around the shop? Not too much, don't worry. Just a few Christmas bits and trinkets? Just to set the tone for all the party frocks and so on?"

"Yes, okay," Ruby said. "I think I'll go upstairs and look over the books for a little while," she added sadly, swallowing back her tears. Christmas decorations were a bit of a reminder for her . . .

"Okay," Jasmine said quietly, pretending not to notice. "I'll give you a shout when I'm finished, yes?"

"Yes, yes," Ruby agreed, making a beeline for the door.

She dreaded Christmas Eve coming. But it would come eventually and there was nothing she could do about it.

I'll go to bed early and I'll sleep right through it, she told herself as she went up the stairs and into her little flat. I'll sleep right through it and I'll be okay. I hope.

# 10

# The First Secret

It was a cold, bright day in mid-December. Ruby's shop had been open for little over a month but business had been thankfully brisk. As expected they were mostly selling coin purses and other glittery trinkets but they were also building up a respectable clientele of regular customers. And they'd sold a small number of designer dresses and jackets too. Everyone said how lovely the larger fitting room was with its little gilt chair and huge matching mirror propped up against the wall. Not to mention the bowl of fresh white roses on the counter and the fancy carrier bags with their distinctive pink and white stripes, especially the smaller-sized ones that were hopelessly cute. Ruby suspected that some of her regular customers were actually collecting the carrier bags because she noticed they only ever bought one item at a time.

And then something strange happened. Ruby and Jasmine were unpacking a crate of embroidered bedroom slippers from Italy one day when Jasmine noticed a short, dowdy woman dressed in shabby black jeans and a washed-out black sweater. The woman was loitering in a suspicious manner outside on the footpath by the bay window. She kept looking nervously up and down the street as if she thought someone was following her. Jasmine thought the female in question might be forty or slightly older. She had long, mousy brown hair tied back in a loose ponytail and she wasn't wearing any make-up. She seemed to be staring intently at the exquisite velvet handbags that Ruby had made.

"Trouble at mill?" Jasmine joked to Ruby, nodding her head in the stranger's direction. "I think we have a nervous shoplifter casing the joint!"

"Well spotted, Jasmine Mulholland," Ruby said. "She might be just window-shopping but if she rings the bell we'll be ready for her." Ruby had spent a little bit extra on having a new doorbell-entry system installed in the shop at the time of the renovations and she was very glad she had. "Mind you, let's give her the benefit of the doubt, yeah? She's hardly going to do an armed robbery on us."

"Oh look out, here she comes," Jasmine hissed and the familiar tinkling chime rang out from a concealed loudspeaker beneath the counter.

Ruby pressed the button, the door opened and the woman stepped gingerly into the shop.

The three of them stood smiling at one another for what seemed an age.

"Can I help you?" Jasmine offered at last, coming out from behind the counter and approaching the customer in a friendly way that disguised her suspicions.

"Thanks, I, um, I was interested in those handbags you've got in the case," the woman said in a gentle, whispery voice. "The black velvet one with the pink lining in particular."

"That one's so adorable, isn't it?" Jasmine said enthusiastically. "A lovely piece, hand-made by the owner here." She indicated Ruby with a little flourish of her cocktail-ring-bejewelled hand. "Shall I fetch it from the display so you can have a closer look?"

"Would you mind? Only I spied it yesterday and I can't seem to get it out of my mind. It reminds me of a party dress my grandmother once had. Actually it reminds me of old perfume bottles, and even of my childhood, if that makes any sense?"

"Does it really? All those memories from one little handbag?" Jasmine said kindly, suddenly feeling quite sorry for the woman.

"Yes, thank you. I thought I might treat myself for my birthday. My fortieth birthday. I daresay my darling husband will only remember to get me the usual bunch of droopy carnations from the petrol station," the woman said sadly. "You know the ones? Going brown at the edges? That's if he remembers to get me anything at all."

"Well, it's the thought that counts, isn't it?" Ruby said brightly. "A lot of men are just too shy or too busy to go to a proper florist, aren't they?"

"Yeah, and there's not always enough parking outside the nicest florists," Jasmine added helpfully.

"Not my husband, he's just not bothered. In fact he goes out of his way to buy me a bunch of rubbish flowers just so I can't say he got me nothing. He's a very clever man, is my husband."

Jasmine and Ruby exchanged worried glances. Perhaps the poor woman was going to break down and sob in front of them?

"So, back to the bag," Jasmine began. "You'd like to see it?"

"Yes, please," the woman said.

Jasmine silently unlocked the display case and reverently carried the black handbag over to the counter. Meanwhile, the woman approached and waited patiently to examine it. Jasmine duly opened the ribbon handles to fully reveal the pink satin lining within. This particular handbag didn't require any hard sell. This particular handbag spoke for itself.

"It's so beautiful," the woman said in a surprisingly soft voice. She traced one finger along the shimmering satin lining and looked wistfully at it. "So beautiful. Hand-made, you said? By the owner?" She glanced at Ruby.

"Yes, indeed," Jasmine said brightly. She knew Ruby would blush and Ruby duly obliged her. "The price is one hundred pounds," she added carefully. Hadn't their would-be customer noticed the price?

"So I see," the woman said calmly.

"It's a bargain really. It's from a limited edition collection," Jasmine told her. "Ruby O'Neill here is a new designer, based right here in Belfast, and she only makes a small number of each design."

"I see."

"There are only seven of these particular bags with the velvet outer fabric and the satin lining inside. And the other ones in the range are all made in different colours as you can see. So each bag is unique and will never be repeated. The price is a sheer bargain, as I said before."

"Well, well. That all sound's pretty special. Okay then, I'll take it."

"Really?" Jasmine said.

"You will?" Ruby was amazed.

"Yes, it *is* my birthday," the woman said firmly. "And I don't treat myself very often. In fact I never do. So I might as well make up for lost time today." She slipped a credit card out of her jeans pocket and placed it carefully on the counter.

Ruby and Jasmine tried to conceal their surprise. They glanced at the name on the card. It said, *Mrs M Stone*.

"Yes. That's me. Mrs Mary Stone."

Jasmine duly wrapped the precious handbag in several layers of soft white tissue paper before popping it into one of Ruby's bespoke candy-stripe carriers.

"Thank you very much indeed," Ruby said, smiling widely. She didn't feel even a slight twinge of regret that the beautiful bag she had made with her own hands was about to leave the shop. It felt okay to see it go to a good home. To someone who might actually appreciate the craftsmanship that had gone into it. Mary Stone might not be the most glamorous woman in the world but there was something gentle about her. And Ruby sensed that there was some inner turmoil going on, that she could easily relate to.

"Yes, thanks very much," Jasmine added. Thinking to herself: you should never judge a book by its cover.

Mary Stone picked up her credit card and her new purchase, turned on her heel and swiftly left the shop.

"Well, that one didn't look as if she could afford a new pair of socks, never mind one of the prettiest things we had in the entire shop," Jasmine said when their unlikely customer had been gone for a few moments. It took both of them that long to get over the emotion of selling the first bag in Ruby's collection.

"I know. But she could be an eccentric millionaire?" Ruby suggested hopefully.

"Or a writer or a poet or an artist," Jasmine agreed.

"True. Lots of arty types make a point of dressing down. But, Jasmine," she added thoughtfully, "it's funny but I've a feeling we'll be seeing Mary Stone again . . . She'll be back."

And in the event Ruby was half-right.

For just before closing time the following day a broadly built man with an upturned nose and a disdainful expression on his big red face pressed the doorbell and came barging into Ruby's shop. Brandishing the one-hundred-pound evening bag and demanding his money back.

"My wife is suffering from clinical depression!" he shouted rudely, right into Jasmine's shocked face. "She's a total bloody basket-case! Her nerves are in fucking bits! How dare you take money from someone who is mentally ill!"

"What? Now, hold on a wee minute, Mister! I'm sorry but your wife had a valid credit card," Jasmine replied, glaring right back at him, her hackles clearly raised. "If she's too ill to shop, then she shouldn't have a credit card in her possession. And I don't think it's very nice of you to describe your own wife in such an awful way. No wonder she's depressed if that's the way you speak about her behind her back. I suggest you leave the premises before we call the police."

"Who the hell do you think you are?" he growled.

"Who the hell do you think *you* are?" Jasmine said angrily "Shouting your head off like that? And telling us your wife is a basket case? You big gulpin!"

"Shut up, you cheeky bitch!" he shouted, his free hand making a fist.

Jasmine immediately reached for a pair of scissors from underneath the counter.

"*You* shut up or I'll cut the tongue out of your head, you big ugly lump!" she roared back.

The man looked momentarily shocked into submission.

"Go on, get out!" Jasmine yelled.

Ruby feared Jasmine was going to snip off the man's expensive-looking tie. Or maybe even his tongue like she'd already suggested.

"Jasmine, I'll handle this, thank you very much," she interjected quickly. "Is there a problem with the handbag, sir?"

"Too right there is, you pair of idiots! You bloody crooks! My stupid wife was robbed in this shop and I want that money back or I'm going to a solicitor."

"Show me the bag," Ruby said quietly and she took it from his clenched-up hands. "Now I'm sorry to tell you this, but the handle has been damaged since it was sold. Look here." She showed him the spot where the stitching had been torn loose.

"Claim it back on your insurance," he barked.

"No, I don't think so," Ruby said firmly.

"It was already damaged when that useless bitch brought it home yesterday," the man accused.

"Mr Stone, I presume? You really must calm down," Ruby began but Jasmine beat her to it.

"No deal, Mr Stone. This bag was not damaged in any way. I wrapped it up myself," she said loudly, her hand hovering above the telephone. "And we have proof *actually*. Because we took photographs of the displays, that very same morning! Now I think you'd better leave. You can't just walk in here and threaten us. I'm not married to you and neither is this woman here. Thank Christ!"

"You'll be sorry you spoke to me like that," he said in a low voice.

"I am very sorry, Mr Stone," Ruby said gently, "but this handbag was definitely not sold to your wife in that condition. And I'm not going to commit insurance fraud just because you've had some sort of disagreement. I suggest you go home to your wife and apologise for embarrassing her like this. Good day to you."

By this time the man's face had turned a livid purple with pure rage but Ruby wasn't afraid of him any more. She had faced worse things in life than a pompous bully who was all riled up because his poor doormat of a wife had bought herself a beautiful velvet evening bag. Mary Stone wasn't mentally ill. Ruby was absolutely convinced of that. She might have been depressed though. And who wouldn't be? Married to a great ugly oaf like that? But no way was Ruby having her finest work thrust back so rudely into her face.

"You haven't heard the last of this," he thundered as he went storming out the door, slamming it hard and leaving the beautiful handbag behind in Ruby's trembling hands.

"What a rotten piece of shit," Jasmine spluttered. "Trying to involve the pair of us in his crazy marital problems! The money was nothing to do with it. That suit of his was by Armani. He's just a control freak. Fat ugly pig! Some people are just unbelievable twisters. Who the hell does he think he is?"

"Jesus Christ," Ruby gasped, waving one hand in front of her mouth. "That was pretty brutal. We're lucky he didn't punch the two of us."

"Aye. Mind you, I'd have stabbed him with the scissors if he'd laid a finger on either one of us!"

Ruby went very pale.

"Are you okay, Ruby?" Jasmine asked.

"Yes, just promise me you won't stab a customer?" Ruby murmured. "Not unless it's absolutely in self-defence?"

"Aye, all right. You were great, by the way. It was all I could do not to go for him. What an absolute git!"

"Yeah, he was. And that's another thing, Jasmine, could you please try *not* to shout and roar in the shop when we have a customer? Even when it's an awful customer like him?"

"Oh, yeah, right. I will."

"Thanks. And thanks for sticking up for me." Ruby took several deep breaths. "I'll make us some tea, shall I? I think we've earned it. And let's keep this bag close by for when Mary Stone comes back to claim it. I'll put a few stitches in the handle and it'll be as good as new. Poor woman! No wonder she looked so browbeaten yesterday! Married to that great slug. Wouldn't the very thought of him touching you make your skin crawl? Yuck! By the way, if he comes back here don't let him in."

"Too right."

Three days later, Mary Stone came back to the shop. Still wearing her scruffy jeans and shapeless sweater. But this time sporting the faded remains of a world-class bruise on her left eyelid. And her bottom lip was slightly swollen and cut.

"I'd like my handbag back, please?" Mary said, smiling and then wincing as the skin above her left eye crinkled up in pain. "And before you ask, yes, my husband did hit me for spending a hundred pounds on a handbag. And no, I'm not sorry I did it because he spends fifteen thousand pounds a year on football tickets. And yes, I have left him."

"Oh my God," Jasmine said, open-mouthed with shock.

"Good for you," Ruby said, producing the black handbag with the pink lining from beneath the counter. "I knew you'd be back and I've repaired the damage for you. I'm sorry about that – unpleasant – episode with your husband. But we couldn't refund the money after we saw the bag was damaged."

"Yes, that's fine. He tried to pull it to pieces but it was too well made. The worst he could do was damage the handle. Thank you very much for keeping it for me. I've been trying to find the courage to leave that bully for over nine years now. It was this handbag that finally gave me the motivation to do it," she said happily, clutching it to her chest. "It was so beautiful sitting there in the glass case. And it made me remember that I was beautiful once and that I believed in myself once. And that my life doesn't have to go on being so miserable any more."

"Well done, love," Jasmine said, choking back her tears. "If you can't buy yourself a lovely wee handbag after nine years of marriage it's a poor enough show."

"We've been married for twenty years," Mary grimaced. "But it's only been really bad for the last nine. I don't think he ever forgave me for losing my figure or my salary after the children were born. We have five kids."

Jasmine and Ruby were speechless with righteous anger. They simply couldn't fathom the logic behind such cruelty. Ruby had always believed that married couples should love each other unconditionally. And once again she pondered the sheer unfairness of losing Jonathan when they'd loved each other so much. They'd not even had one serious argument in all their time together. They'd bickered a bit over little things, surely. But they'd never gone to bed without making up again.

"Do you think he'll leave you alone now though?" Ruby asked tactfully. "And us, for that matter? Should we be contacting the police with a request for increased patrols along the Ravenhill, or whatever?"

"I shouldn't think there's any need for police protection," Mary said, trying hard to smile despite her bruise. "I don't think he'll be bothering any of us for some time."

"Why not?" Jasmine asked quickly. "You haven't gone and poisoned the vile creep, have you?"

"Jasmine!" Ruby scolded. "Don't be outrageous."

"It's okay," Mary laughed. "Ouch, that hurt! No, I haven't poisoned him. Though I've often felt like it, to tell you the truth. But no, I finally went to the police to tell them about his so-called *unreasonable behaviour* towards me."

"Wow," said Jasmine. "Well done yourself!"

"Yeah. When he hit me that day I just knew it was going to be the last time he would ever hit me. And I also knew I wasn't going to let him get away with it. He's been arrested. And held overnight as it happens."

"Oh, wow again," said Jasmine.

"Not for years of bullying me though. Isn't it hilarious? They got him for resisting arrest and assaulting a police officer. Still, all's well that ends well. I've taken the children and we're staying in a refuge for battered wives. We'll be moving to England as soon as I can get things organised. I have some old school pals there who'll help me to find part-time work and a new place to live. I might even end up working with horses in the countryside or something. I was always great with horses when I was younger. The children would love to live in the countryside, they said."

"Well, that's quite something," Jasmine sighed, almost weak with relief. "Our very first experience of arrest in the retail trade."

"So I just wanted to say thank you for standing up to him," Mary said quietly to Ruby and Jasmine. "I don't think anyone else ever has. And you two really rattled his cage, I can tell you! Especially since you were only 'a couple of stupid women in a stupid handbag shop', as he put it. I just wanted to say thanks for showing me that I didn't have to be a drudge cowering in the corner any longer. Whatever happens, I'm free of that awful man. I'm divorcing him immediately."

Ruby simply nodded, while Jasmine reached for a crisp carrier bag and parcelled up the contentious handbag for a second time. Then Mary took her precious purchase and went breezing towards the door.

"Thanks again," she called back over her shoulder as the door to Ruby's shop swung open. "I'd like to say I'll be seeing you but I don't expect I'll be back here for years and years, if ever. Cheerio!"

And the door pinged shut again.

For a few moments both Ruby and Jasmine were too shocked and saddened to comment.

"That poor woman! Did you see the state of her eye? Of course you did. There, but for the grace of God, go I . . . Well, it's my turn to brew up."

Jasmine made tea while they digested what had happened.

"I think she's been bottling her feelings up for far too long, Jasmine. It was good for her to say it out loud, I daresay. Anyway, what else could she have said with a shiner like that? It would have been mortifying for all of us if she'd pretended she'd walked into a door. Do you suppose she'll be all right now? And the children?"

"Yes, she'll be fine," Jasmine said confidently. "Once a bully understands that it'll be more effort for him to go on tormenting his current partner than it'll be to find a new victim, the innocent party is pretty much home and dry."

"Unless he's a total psycho?" Ruby pointed out. "Then he might track her down and kill her?"

"Obviously there's always a chance of that, yes."

"Oh Jasmine . . . Why has the human race lasted so long?" Ruby pondered with a sad shake of her head. "It's so fucked up."

"Because all we single women live in the hope of finding a little gem like your Jonathan, that's why," Jasmine told her kindly. "Chocolate biscuit?"

"Go on, then. Just bring the bloody tin in here, in fact. We're allowed extra biscuits when we've just rescued a customer from an abusive relationship."

The two friends munched their way through half a packet of milk chocolate biscuits in near-silence. Jasmine reflecting on how close she had just come to stabbing someone in a fit of bad temper. And Ruby realising that perhaps it was time she stopped defining herself by her marriage to her late husband. Or at least it was time she stopped dwelling on her loss for every hour of every day. Now that she had seen what clinging to a man for twenty solid years had done to Mary Stone. Even clinging to a good man like Jonathan hadn't been an altogether good idea, as it had left her so broken when he'd died. No, emotional dependency of any kind was clearly not the road to happiness.

"Jasmine," Ruby said eventually, "I don't know if there's a secret, or maybe a list of secrets, to being happy . . . but I'll tell you this much. The first secret of happiness is to be emotionally independent. You know what I mean? You can't expect another person to *make* you happy or to *give* you happiness. Or even just *allow* you to be happy, as if you've got to ask their permission or something? You've somehow got to create happiness within yourself and let nobody else touch it or take it away."

"Well done, Ruby," Jasmine agreed at once. "Ten out of ten for observation. It's obvious really, isn't it?"

"I suppose," Ruby mumbled, through a sip of tea. It might have been obvious to Jasmine all along but it was something Ruby herself was only beginning to understand.

# 11

# The Maze at Camberwell

Tom loved it when the weather took a downturn. It wasn't something he was proud of, especially as he worked as a professional gardener in one of the wettest climates in Europe. But in recent years he'd come to associate bouts of damp and windy weather with a kind of inner peace and outer tranquillity. For when the grey foreboding clouds rolled in and the sky was suddenly dark with the promise of torrential rain, the bruising pressure on his heart always seemed to lift a little bit. Heavy summer downpours were his favourite. The huge, fat raindrops bouncing off the dried-up flowerbeds and the pebbly pathways and eventually pooling in the centre of the formal lawn. For one thing it saved him many hours of watering and tedious soil maintenance. And for another it gave him a bit of much-needed privacy as the chattering visitors went dashing towards the warmth of the café and the well-stocked souvenir shop.

He'd worked as the head gardener at Camberwell House for most of his adult life. He'd been the only gardener on the payroll most of the time. But it looked better on his staff ID badge if they pretended there were a few other green-fingered minions toiling away in the background. The truth was that Tom had been the sole person employed to look after the grounds of the estate for a few years now. The house and gardens cost an awful lot of money to maintain. And most of the estate's annual income went to support the current owners' second home and very comfortable lifestyle in the Bahamas. So Tom and Mrs Kenny the cook did their best to keep the place ship-shape and the cream teas up to standard. And they silently hoped that the current owners of Camberwell House would someday sell it on to someone else who actually cared about heritage and about precious and ancient things.

In the meantime, whenever the rain came on, Tom would take refuge in his official headquarters: the large wooden potting-shed, painted dark green, and tucked away behind the kitchen garden at the back of the house. There he could relax in his comfy old armchair while Noah curled up in his basket and slept in the blue glow cast by the gently flickering gas heater.

The shed was where Tom stored his packets of seeds and most valuable gardening tools. He also kept a tin of biscuits, a bottle of whisky and a framed photograph of his late wife Kate. Not that he was a heavy drinker. He definitely wasn't. He'd seen other people's lives ruined by drink, entire decades written off, and he didn't want that to happen to him. But on particularly rainy afternoons he would put his feet up on a small bench, pour a large whisky for himself, and just reminisce.

It had been five years now since Tom had lost his beloved wife to breast cancer. And some days he still woke up thinking he'd dreamt it all and that she'd be lying in the bed beside him. He was almost grateful he had so much work to do at Camberwell because it kept him busy for more than twelve hours each day. He had endless hedges to clip and feed, the kitchen garden to cultivate, the raised flowerbeds to protect from frosts and pests, and the Christmas tree plantation to keep an eye on. That last project had been his own idea: a way of gaining valuable income from some watery fields with a rather dull view onto an electricity sub-station. The trees surrounded the Camberwell estate on three sides now and acted as a kind of physical barrier between it and the outside world. And even better, Tom had also discouraged the bored teenagers of the city from popping over to vandalise the estate by starting a rumour that the plantation was haunted.

Tom laughed now as he recalled starting the rumour on impulse a few years earlier. Weary of collecting empty drinks cans, smashed cider bottles and crumpled cigarette packets from the plantation, he'd told the young girls working in the café that he'd seen a ghost there one night. The ghost of an old man wearing Edwardian clothes and with only one arm, limping towards the statue of an angel in the centre of the plantation. Nobody could say why the pretty statue of a weeping angel had been erected in such an unlikely spot but the general assumption was that it marked the resting-place of a favoured dog or horse. In any event the excitable waitresses had lost no time in spreading the story. Soon the rumour was all over the city, and the empty cans and bottles and the smouldering cigarette butts were no more.

People were so afraid of the dead, Tom thought now, as the rain thundered down onto the wooden roof of his cosy little hideaway. People didn't realise that the dead could do them no harm. It was the living they had to be wary of. For if ghosts really did exist then he would have seen Kate again by now. He'd hoped and prayed for a nightly visitation for five long years but his lonely bedroom had remained resolutely ghost-free. And if Kate had been able to come back and let him know she was all right then she surely would have done. No, his bedroom had been sadly, tragically empty for half a decade.

He had to catch his breath suddenly as an image of Ruby O'Neill came completely unbidden into his mind. And the way she'd behaved with such dignity at her husband's funeral. No ugly rants against the other driver. No embarrassing pictures of her shouting insults, her face all twisted with rage – which he was sure the photographer had been staking his bets on.

Ruby O'Neill was beguiling and wise-looking, as well as beautiful. There was something otherworldly about her that he could not easily define or hope to forget. That routine delivery of a Christmas tree had stayed with him over the last year and he didn't know why. He'd only been collecting the unsold trees from the garden centre to pass them on to the YMCA. Otherwise he would never have met Ruby in the first place. If he'd been five minutes later arriving at the garden centre that day, someone else would have delivered Ruby's tree to that lovely house on the Ravenhill Road. And their paths would never have crossed. Strange the way these things happened sometimes.

Yes, Ruby O'Neill was very attractive in a serene and sophisticated way. Not like Kate's freckle-faced and bubbly beauty. Not like Kate with her bright red mane of curly hair and her all-natural, dressed-down style. Ruby O'Neill had perfect cheekbones and arching eyebrows that were as sharply defined as blades of grass. But it was definitely about more than that. Something in her expression told Tom that she too was enduring extreme grief. That day at the funeral, in that picture of her in the newspaper, she'd looked so different already from the happily flustered woman he had shaken hands with. And that other time at the shop, even though she'd smiled at him, he could tell right away that she was struggling to contain her sadness. Was there something he needed from Ruby, he wondered? Would it help him to talk to someone whose heart had been truly broken also? Would Ruby understand how he felt? Only half-alive himself, most of the time. Would she be able to save him from his loneliness? Would they be able to save each other?

How could he find out more about her? He couldn't ask

anyone he knew if they'd ever heard of her. They would only assume he was getting over Kate. And start treating him normally again, and he wasn't ready for that. Oh, it was all madness anyway, he thought grumpily. He wasn't ready to let another person into his heart. And he wasn't ready to put up with being teased about having a new girlfriend.

"Forget it," he said to nobody in particular. Though Noah pricked up his ears and growled softly. "What does it matter? I'll never see her again or speak to her again. And anyway I'll never stop loving Kate, and no doubt a fine woman like Ruby O'Neill isn't looking for a relationship with a scruffy old curmudgeon like myself."

He was only forty-five but Tom knew that his weather-beaten face was lined and worn already, and usually he made no effort whatsoever to tidy himself up. In fact, he went out of his way to live up to his reputation as the hard working but anti-social head gardener of Camberwell. It meant that nobody ever bothered inviting him to awkward social gatherings that he had no interest in attending.

But as the rain continued to hammer down on Camberwell House and its surrounding gardens and outhouses Tom's thoughts were interrupted again by Ruby's smiling face thanking him for the delivery of the Christmas tree and casually wishing him a Merry Christmas. Something nobody who knew him well had dared to do since Kate's death. Strangers had said it, of course. But with them it had meant only politeness; Ruby seemed to actually mean it.

"I felt normal that day," he told Noah. "Only for about half a minute, of course. It was a good feeling. It scared me too. I mean I haven't felt normal for a very long time. I didn't know what to do with myself." Noah yawned and went back to sleep.

Tom checked the calendar on the wall. The winter programme was winding down now and the New Year parties would soon give way to the coach-loads of summer visitors who would come from far and wide to walk through the newly restored box hedge maze and marvel at its mystery and complexity.

"Better check the maze again, I suppose," he sighed. "If it's going to be the star attraction next summer."

Yes, when the rain stopped he would get his bale of string and go and make sure the tightly packed green walls of the huge maze were perfectly straight and uniform, and also do a bit of light clipping. Sweep up any leaves that had blown in and collected in dark or damp corners. Check that none of the large blue and white pebbles on the pathways had cracked or come loose with the cold.

"As if we haven't enough excitable day-trippers to feed and water in this place already," he said to Noah's sleeping face. "But hey, all that grand living in the Bahamas has to be paid for somehow. Yes, I know! Why don't I leave here and get another job somewhere else, one that pays better? Because I can't be bothered to, that's why."

So he would check the maze when the rain stopped. Okay. Then he would get on with a bit of light weeding in the kitchen garden. It was always easier to loosen the weeds after a rainstorm when the soil was wet and broken. He had to fork over the compost heap too and plant seven mature birch trees on the driveway to replace some that had died off. Hopefully by the time he lay down in his bed that night in his small cottage on the edge of the estate he would be much too tired to think about Ruby O'Neill and that telltale faraway look in her eyes. He could go straight to sleep and dream of Kate instead. He felt he was being unfaithful to Kate by even thinking of another woman. But still he couldn't help wondering if Ruby had had a reasonable Christmas. And if he'd made a terrible first impression on her the Christmas before, in his old clothes and shabby boots. And his Land Rover that was falling to bits and loaded up with unsold Christmas trees. Ruby's shop was perfection itself, he'd noticed. No, probably she had forgotten him already. *Forgotten, forgotten, forgotten*, the rain seemed to say.

Well, that was the end of the story now, he thought sadly. For how could a man like himself with so much sadness in his heart ever get to be even casual friends with a woman who was carrying so much sadness of her own? The rain began to ease off and Tom felt fidgety all of a sudden.

"Got to get out of here, Noah," he sighed. "Got to keep busy."

Patting Noah softly on the head, he put on his wax hat and jacket, slipped out of the shed and went across to the maze, taking a bale of twine, a yard brush and his sharpest clippers with him. His own heart might still be smothered in thorns of loneliness and self-imposed solitude but at least when the maze was unveiled to the public in the summer it would be nothing short of perfect. As the rain slowed down and became just a mist, Tom clipped and tidied and swept and cleaned. Burning off pounds of nervous energy, using up all those lonely hours. Thinking of Kate laughing at something funny he had said, and then thinking of Ruby smiling out at him from her little sparkly shop, and then trying not to think about anything at all.

# 12

# The Second Secret

It was lunchtime on New Year's Eve. Ruby had decided to open the shop for a few hours just to capitalise on any last-minute trade. And also because she had made no other plans and didn't want to rattle round the flat all day on her own. She'd told Jasmine she could have the day off if she wanted to go somewhere special but Jasmine said she had made no real plans either. She'd actually turned down quite a few party invites for New Year's Eve itself just in case Ruby might have a breakdown or something. But she'd told Ruby she thought she was coming down with a cold, just so they wouldn't spend the day arguing about it.

Anyway she'd been to a few parties in recent weeks and there hadn't been much male talent in evidence. Jasmine had an awful suspicion that all the nicest guys were either gay, married or had emigrated to Australia or New Zealand. All those irritating TV shows showing pasty-faced families from the British Isles living it up on Bondi beach were to blame, Jasmine reckoned. She might consider going to Australia herself if she had better qualifications but no doubt they had enough shop girls to be getting on with. Oh well, she just supposed she'd have to make the best of things here in dear old Belfast. Both jobs-wise and men-wise!

Speaking of Belfast men, Jasmine wondered if she dared ask Ruby about that shy-looking man again. The one who grew the Christmas trees for the garden centre.

"You liked that guy a wee bit though, Ruby, didn't you?" Jasmine asked gently now, as Ruby knelt down to retrieve a stray Christmas bauble from underneath one of the painted wardrobes.

"What on earth are you talking about, Jasmine Mulholland? Who am I supposed to like?" Ruby asked as she put the bauble back on the counter display.

"That handsome older man? Well, old-ish. It was hard to tell what age he was really, under all that tatty clobber of his. You know the one who was peeping in at you a few days ago? Who was he, really? Do you know him a bit more than you're letting on, seriously?"

"No, I don't know him at all, Jasmine. Truly! He delivered my Christmas tree last year, that's all. I told you that's all it was. And I do not like him in that way. Are you completely mad?" Ruby said crossly. How could Jasmine even joke about such a thing? With Jonathan only gone a year?

"Come on now? Don't be so defensive with me, Ruby. I'm only asking! It's just that I saw a funny look in your eye this morning when you were tidying the Christmas decorations on the counter. You looked happy for the first time in a long time. Weren't you?"

"For your information I was recalling the time Jonathan took me to an Art Deco hotel in London for Christmas. They had big glass baubles exactly like this one here, hanging on a huge Nordman tree in the foyer. Now listen, we must've let the vacuuming slip in recent days? I mean to say, this bauble must have been lying under there for a while without either of us spying it."

"Sorry, Ruby," Jasmine said at once. "I didn't mean to sound insensitive. I was just being a romantic fool again. Pay me no heed. I'm always on the lookout for romance where clearly none exists."

"That's okay. And I'm sorry for snapping at you. It's just that I could never fall in love with another man, Jasmine. Not ever! I feel like Jonathan only left me yesterday."

"But you're so young, Ruby. Just thirty-two! It's far too soon for you to say it's all over for you in the love department?"

"Jasmine, it might not be too soon for a lot of other people. But it's as much as I can do to keep the shop going and keep myself neat and tidy and remember to eat three meals a day. I'm telling you there'll be no romance in my life for a very long time to come. If ever."

"But you did look at that guy in a strange way that day."

"That's because he was looking at me in a strange way. He must have mistaken me for someone else, that's all. I'm sure he doesn't remember me. Perhaps he was going to come in and buy a gift for his wife or his girlfriend but then he chickened out? You know how some men are terrified of girly shops?"

"Okay, I'm sorry I spoke. I'm just being silly – it must be due to my current man-free status. Hang on, Ruby. Look, there's somebody outside, staring at the evening bags. A nice-looking man as it happens. Could we be about to make our second sale?"

Ruby's heart lurched with hope and anticipation. She'd begun to look on the sale of her beautiful handbags as a sort of omen. Hopefully if this customer was interested in one of them she could take it as a good sign for the New Year. Could she dare to believe that her shop was really going to be a long-term success?

"That guy is still looking," Jasmine whispered.

"Well, don't stare at him then, in case you put him off," said Ruby, getting out her duster and giving the glass counter a nervous polish. As if on cue the doorbell rang and the man came in, obviously ill at ease in this cosy nest of feminine frivolities. He was tall and slim and very handsome.

Jasmine checked at once to see if he was wearing a wedding ring. He was. She rolled her eyes and turned away.

"How much is that dark blue purse-thing, please?" he said fake-brightly to Ruby.

Jasmine looked at Ruby carefully. Would Ruby dare to ask for the full amount? She decided she would let the boss handle this sale on her own. Jasmine smiled at both Ruby and the customer and then she began to price some pink umbrellas with barley-twist handles that had just been unpacked.

"Um, those particular bags are one hundred pounds each," Ruby said in a shy voice. She could hardly bring herself to say the words out loud.

"Oh. That's quite a lot . . ."

"They're all unique, do you see? I made them myself. Here, I'll show you," Ruby told him, reaching the bag out of its case and setting it reverently on the counter. "See the lemon lining there? A real labour of love."

"Unique, did you say? Oh well, in that case I'll take it," the man said, beginning to perspire slightly. He was a person who felt extremely out of place beside fluffy white slippers and padded lilac hangers. But the blue velvet bag had caught his eye for some reason and he just knew he had to have it. He placed his debit card on the counter as Ruby swiftly wrapped the bag and then expertly swiped his card.

"It's for my wife," the man said suddenly in case they thought he was buying it for himself. "I'm not a cross-dresser or anything mental like that. Though now I've said it I suppose you'll be convinced it is for me."

Ruby and Jasmine exchanged mischievous glances.

"It takes all sorts, mate," Jasmine said, winking.

"Jasmine, stop it," Ruby commanded.

"Sorry," Jasmine sighed.

"No, really, it's for my wife," the man said again.

"I'm sure she'll love it," Jasmine nodded, grinning.

"Jasmine, I said stop it. Now then, I hope your wife just loves this bag. It can be used as an everyday bag or to store jewellery in or to keep for special occasions. It's very strong really but don't let it get wet please or the velvet will darken slightly."

"Okay, I'll tell her," the man said, knowing he'd never remember what Ruby had just told him. "She's not been very well, do you see? That's the worrying thing. Not too well, overall, no."

"Oh dear," Ruby murmured. "I'm sorry to hear that." Ruby smiled warmly at her latest customer. It was quite hard for the average Belfast man to be so revealing about his personal life. She knew that for a fact. She smiled at him. He seemed to relax a little bit.

"Yes. She's been very down-in-the-dumps for the last couple of years actually. Very down, if you know what I mean?"

"You mean she suffers a bit from the 'auld *depression*'?" Jasmine asked bravely.

"Jasmine, thank you!" Ruby said. "Look, I'm so sorry," she said to the slightly flustered man.

But Jasmine wasn't sorry. Maybe Ruby's beautiful handbags were about to lead to another bout of soul-searching, she thought to herself.

"It's okay really," the man said after a moment. "She is depressed. I mean, I told her that all I want is for her to get well. It's what we all want, all the family circle. But I'm worried she's giving up. She can't be bothered talking to any of us any more. Even small talk seems to wear her out."

Ruby and Jasmine made sympathetic faces.

"Bless her," Jasmine nodded.

"Yes, it's very frustrating. She won't take her pills or eat properly or even take the vitamins that her doctor recommended. She's lost interest in Christmas altogether this year. Even though she always used to love baking the cake and so on. She won't give up smoking cigarettes either. Just sits smoking cigarettes all day on the sofa, getting more and more unfit."

"Oh dear," Ruby said again. "That sounds like a bad case of depression all right."

"She won't talk to me about anything, either serious subjects or silly ones. I don't know what to do with her, basically."

"Oh dear," Ruby soothed.

"Ah well . . . Sometimes I feel like shouting at her . . . but naturally I wouldn't do that. It might make me feel better but it definitely wouldn't do my wife any good. Sorry, I'm rambling away here, I don't know why I'm telling you all of this," he finished lamely.

"Listen, we both wish you and your wife the very best possible outcome," said Ruby at once, slipping some complimentary scented room-sachets and a box of embroidered handkerchiefs into the crisp carrier alongside the blue velvet handbag. "We can't understand precisely what you must be going through, of course. But it must be awful for you not being able to do anything to help your wife. Mind you, I'm sure that just being there for her means a lot. More than you think, probably."

"Thank you," the man said, brightening up a little. "I know it's true that depression is a very common ailment. It's just that sometimes you feel like you're the only person whose world has fallen apart, don't you? And you don't want to be a bother to anybody so you keep your worries to yourself."

"Indeed you do," Ruby smiled. "I really hope your wife will be fine though. And you'd do well to look after your own health too, you know? And not just your physical health? Have you tried calling MIND for advice? Often it's the carers who come off worse in the end, so they say. Oh Lord, I'm making it worse now . . ."

"It's okay, thanks. Yes, I should call them, shouldn't I?"

"Well, yes. Yes, maybe you should? And you might take some of those vitamins yourself and try to eat properly, even if your wife

110

can't face too much food right now? And keep the house nice and tidy for her too maybe? I always find that a cosy house is a tonic for me when I'm feeling under the weather. Buy her some flowers occasionally?"

"I will indeed. Thanks very much for all the advice."

"You've probably heard it all before, but sure it's got to be worth a try? And I'm sure this lovely gift will cheer her up immensely," Ruby said finally, setting the candy striped carrier on the counter. "And I wish you both a very happy New Year."

"Happy New Year!" The man lifted his precious purchase gently and nodded farewell to Ruby and Jasmine. He backed out of the shop and went walking down the Ravenhill Road with a new spring in his step.

"Poor guy," Jasmine sighed, watching him from the bay window. "His wife doesn't know how lucky she is to have him. This shop is turning into a drop-in centre for the terminally miserable. I hope he hasn't just gone and spent money they really can't afford."

"I've a feeling his wife needs a little surprise right now," Ruby said quietly. "To remind her that the sun will come out again one day. Hopefully that little gesture of his will turn out to be worth every penny."

"Here's hoping," Jasmine agreed.

"You know what, Jasmine? While we're all opening our hearts today, you were right about there being a weird kind of spark between myself and that guy the other day. But I have no idea why. We have met before, like I said. But it was just the one time, and even then it was for, like, two minutes. He's the head gardener at Camberwell House. And truly, I was only happy today because I didn't think I'd be able to cope during my first Christmas without Jonathan. And in the end it was okay. Well, not okay exactly, but not a total nightmare either, like I was expecting. So I was just happy that I made it through the holidays, you know? That bauble reminded me of Jonathan and our trip to London."

"Okay."

"And that guy? Okay, his name is Tom Lavery . . . But he had nothing to do with me being happy today. Yes, he's quite handsome in a rugged and ragged and repressed sort of way. And yes, I did feel a tiny bit attracted to him when we first met, for some bizarre reason. I mean, I thought he was nice when we met last year, before I knew about Jonathan's accident. But I would never consider even flirting with him now. Nothing like that! It's far too soon. And anyway he's obviously married because he was wearing a wedding ring."

"You looked at his hands then?"

"No, I didn't look on purpose."

"Are you sure about that?" Jasmine smiled.

"Yes, I couldn't help noticing a ring, that's all. When I paid him for the tree last year I saw it glinting against his skin. He had very tanned skin and very dark brown eyes. And I wondered if he had Spanish or Italian roots maybe?"

"*Interesting*," Jasmine said, biting her lip so she wouldn't say something out of place and cause Ruby to shut down any tentative feelings she might be having for this new man.

"So there you have it," Ruby concluded. "He was quite nice to talk to but he obviously wasn't available, and I'm certainly not looking for a boyfriend right now."

"Right you be," Jasmine said carefully. "That's the end of it, so. My lips are sealed."

"Okay."

But it wasn't quite the end of it.

"Is that why you didn't have a tree this year, Ruby? Because you didn't want to meet him again? Tom Lavery? Because there was some sort of chemistry there?"

"No, silly. I just didn't want a tree, that's all. Sure I could have got a tree anywhere, not just from Tom Lavery or that particular garden centre."

"True."

"Right. That's two evening bags sold anyway so we've only five to go."

"Do you know, Ruby, I hope we don't sell another one for a few days yet. I don't think I can take any more earth-shattering revelations just at the moment," Jasmine sighed.

"Yes, that poor guy, I hope his wife gets better soon," Ruby said glumly. "At least she still has her husband to look after her. And he did seem a very caring sort of husband."

"Are you serious? Ruby, the woman sounded like a lost cause to me. Did you not hear what he said about her?"

"I heard him."

"She just sits about, he said. Doing nothing, saying nothing. No interest in Christmas any more. Can't be bothered baking a cake. Can't even be bothered to talk to her own family."

"Oh my God," Ruby said quietly, her eyes wide with shock.

"What is it? Have you left the cooker on upstairs?" Jasmine asked, glancing toward the ceiling.

"My mother, Jasmine! My mother."

"What about her?"

"I think *she's* depressed," Ruby said in a frightened voice.

"Depressed? How come?"

"She's been like that for years. Like that man's wife. No real interest in anything. Can't be bothered to talk to me on the phone . . ."

"But someone would have noticed if she was really bad," Jasmine said, shaking her head in disbelief.

"Who would have noticed? I'm never there any more. She's never here."

"Your father then?" Jasmine suggested.

"No, he's too used to her. He probably wouldn't notice if she'd got any worse in recent times. My God, is it really over a year since I visited my own parents? Where has all the time gone?"

"It was their duty to come here and visit you, Ruby. You were the one who was suffering. Anyway, the neighbours would have told you if your mum wasn't well."

"I don't think so. They never see the neighbours. They live in the middle of nowhere, Jasmine. And they don't like visitors. I mean, they say hello to everybody after Mass and so on, but it's not the same as having proper friends, is it? It's not the same as having friends you can confide in. Oh my God, I bet my mum's been depressed for years and I'm only just realising it. That's why they didn't come to Jonathan's funeral, don't you see?"

"But they couldn't come because of the snow, remember?" said Jasmine.

"That's true. But why didn't they come to see me afterwards? In the New Year? No, the truth is they didn't think Mum could face it. Or face me." Ruby's eyes filled with tears.

"Now Ruby, don't cry. It's not your fault."

"It is my fault. I should have done something."

"Like what?"

"Gone down there more often? Insisted on spending Christmas with them? I don't know what exactly. But I should have done something."

"Well, go and visit them now," Jasmine said, beginning to add up the takings. "You just get in the car and land on them without phoning ahead, and see what happens. Stay the night and see in the New Year with the pair of them. Then you'll see if your Mum's truly depressed or if they're just a pair of anti-social old culchies. No offence! We can shut the shop for a couple of days, can't we?"

"Okay, yes, I'll do that."

"Good girl. I'll keep an eye on the place while you're away."

"Will you be okay on your own tonight?" Ruby asked Jasmine.

"Surely I will. Somebody at the Bell Towers will be having a few drinks and I'll get myself invited along, don't you worry. And if not, there's always a party at my parents' house in Sandy Row. Only the oldies dancing to Abba, but it's usually a laugh."

"Thanks, Jasmine," Ruby said, drying her tears on a leftover Christmas napkin. "I'll set off as soon as we close the shop today. I'll just throw a few things in a bag and drive straight down there. I've just got to make sure they're okay."

"Yes, you do that."

"That's the second secret, isn't it?"

"Come again?"

"The second secret of happiness? Good health! Of both the body and the mind. That's the second secret of happiness."

"Secrets of happiness? You need to get out more, Ruby O'Neill," Jasmine said primly, shaking her head in mock-pity.

"Yes, I know I do," Ruby smiled back at her. "I need to do lots of things, Jasmine love. And getting out more is only one of them. But first of all I need to check on my crazy parents."

"Drive carefully please, won't you?" Jasmine said, looking away shyly.

"Don't worry, I will," Ruby promised.

"And go easy on them when you get there? Yeah?"

"I will."

"They can't help being a bit weird, I'm sure."

"Okay."

"They *are* from the country, remember?"

"Yes . . ."

"How much? A hundred pounds? Are you kidding me! Are you stone mad?"

Ruby and Jasmine didn't know it then but at that exact moment the recipient of the second handbag was clambering up off her saggy sofa and heading for the power-shower. For if her long-suffering husband had been reduced to wasting their precious savings on overpriced velvet handbags that she'd never realistically be able to use, then it was high time she was up and about again. And back in charge of the family finances.

"A hundred quid indeed!"

They must have seen the fool coming.

"You could have got some home heating oil instead! Or new vinyl for the bathroom floor! Or a bloody gate for the front garden that doesn't squeak like a scalded cat every time somebody walks through it! Are you nuts or what?"

"I'm going out for a drink," her husband said to her quietly. "You may do whatever the hell you like."

And out he went, closing the door softly behind him. She watched him walk down the street, away from her, and something that felt like tension in her heart seemed to unwind a little bit.

Maybe she could get a refund, she thought to herself.

And after a good long shower she finally started taking her anti-depressant medication and booked a much-needed appointment at the hairdresser's. She'd get her roots done and about six inches chopped off the length.

"I look a complete fright," she told the stylist. "Honestly, you'll die when you see the state of me. No, you will! Okay, see you then, cheerio!"

She lifted the midnight blue handbag and then threw it across the room in disgust.

"Idiot man!"

Then again maybe she *would* keep the handbag forever as a reminder of how out-of-touch she had become in recent years?

"And this house could do with a bloody good clean," she wheezed, tossing her ciggies and matches into the kitchen bin.

Eventually she decided to keep her packets of anti-depressants in the midnight-blue evening bag with the bright lemon lining. At least that way she wouldn't forget to take the damn things.

# 13

## The Village

Driving all the way down the wide grey motorway and then along the much more winding roads of Fermanagh, Ruby racked her brains with the effort of remembering. Her mother had always been a very private and refined sort of person. Never the type to giggle and gossip or go out boozing with the girls. Or use "bad language". Or do silly things like flinging a burnt saucepan into the garden pond like Jasmine's mother once had. According to Jasmine all the fish had died the following day after eating the bits of charred curry. But no, Ruby's mother was never the type to go making a show of herself in public. And that was why she'd stayed hidden away behind those dry-stone walls and those big heavy gates. Not because she was a depressive, reclusive, anti-social or snobby oddball. But because she was a supremely private person . . .

"But she must be depressed?" Ruby said aloud after a few more minutes spent deep in thought. Arguing with herself as a soft blanket of silent rain enveloped her car. She must be depressed on some scale? That's why she didn't come to Jonathan's funeral last year? Okay, there was snow. But she could have come after. But she knew that I'd notice she was acting differently and that I'd say something to her . . . that I'd persevere until she admitted she was depressed. Oh Dad, why the hell didn't you tell me?

But she knew very well why. Her father hadn't mentioned anything to her because he knew she was still grieving for Jonathan. Ruby's father was absolutely Old School: where boys did not cry and spouses did not go telling tales on one another. Ruby turned up the heat in the car and swallowed down a giddy urge to swing the vehicle round and go straight back to Belfast and her cosy apartment above the shop. She longed to dive under the quilted covers and drift into a blissful sleep and just ignore it all.

Ignore them like they've ignored me this last year, she thought, feeling a headache beginning to take shape behind her eyes. Driving in the dark always gave her a headache. At least the snow they'd had this winter had cleared away. Oh, Mum. Poor Mum.

For an entire year she'd been secretly furious with her mother for not being more supportive after Jonathan's death. And all the time the poor woman was probably struggling with her own demons. Ruby had always felt that her father was a bit too accepting of his wife's moods. A passive foil to her mother's more overbearing nature . . . When all the time he must have been terrified that something like this would happen someday: that his wife would tip over into full-blown depression.

God, it never ends, Ruby thought. Why can't I just have normal parents? To make up for not having a husband any more, or a child.

Then the rain got heavier and Ruby was forced to concentrate on her driving. After three hours' driving in total, and with her heart in her mouth for most of the way, Ruby carefully guided her old Audi in through the large iron gates and along the narrow lane to the house. The grass track up the centre of the narrow road was overgrown and untidy. The trees also seemed not to have been clipped for many months.

"Oh Mum, this is a bit weird," Ruby said aloud. "What the hell's going on?"

And suddenly there it was, not so much a mansion as an oversized Irish farmhouse. The familiar grey walls with their moss and lichen spots sent a shiver down Ruby's spine now, as the house was lit up by the car headlights. She'd never liked this forbidding building. It had always felt rather sinister to her as a child, as if the house had a resentful personality of its own. And it hadn't wanted Ruby and her parents living in it.

But tonight something was different. Even before she had parked the car and had a good look at the house Ruby knew it had changed. It had lost something of its austere nature and had somehow become slightly defeated instead. Mature weeds dotted the messy gravel, and the laurel hedges hadn't been trimmed in ages. The curtains were not tied back in their usual symmetrical perfection. The doormat was sitting crookedly on the step and there was an empty cigarette packet lying by the boot-scraper. Ruby parked her car neatly to one side of the house, rang the doorbell, held her breath and waited.

"Daddy?" she said slowly when her father answered the door wearing an old cardigan and smoking a cigar. A cigar!

"Ruby!"

"Are you smoking cigars now?" she asked him anxiously. "Or is it just for New Year's Eve? Why are there no lights on? Have you had a power cut?"

"Ah, Ruby love," he sighed gently. "What in the name of God are you doing here?"

"Thanks a lot, Dad. It's good to see you too."

"I didn't mean it like that."

"How did you mean it, exactly?"

"You shouldn't have come all this way without telling me first."

"Why not? It's not a bloody Embassy, is it?" Ruby said,

beginning to bristle. "Do I need an appointment now to see my own parents? Where's Mum? It's freezing cold out here. Aren't you going to ask me in?"

"Your mum? Well now, that's the big question. Who knows what she's up to?" he sighed again. "Not me, that's for sure. I'm only her husband."

"Right, that's enough of this big, stoic act," Ruby said boldly, elbowing past her father and marching into the double-height hallway. "I want to know what's been going on here. I want to know why you've not come to see me in a year? I want to know where my mother is. You and me are going to have a little chat, Dad. I think I know what's wrong with Mum."

"Oh, I'm too tired for his, Ruby – I was awake all night last night," he protested. But it was no use. He shuffled backwards from the front door and swung it shut with one foot. Ruby was already halfway down the hall.

"Daddy, what's all this about?" Ruby gasped when she got to the kitchen and witnessed the scene of devastation within. Empty pizza boxes were stacked in a teetering pile by the bin, empty cigarette and cigar packets lined the windowsill, and several cheap lighters lay in the fruit bowl. Dirty plates were scattered everywhere, the curtains were closed and crumpled, the sink was smelly and ringed with old cups and sticky spoons.

"Dad, this kitchen is a pigsty. And it reeks of smoke."

"Well, what did you expect? I didn't know you were coming," he said hopelessly. "If I'd known you were coming I'd have tidied up."

"Dad, until this moment I would've said it was an urban myth that men can't tidy up after themselves. But this is ridiculous! Could you not have walked ten feet outside to the bin? Could you not have opened a window to let in some fresh air? Has Mum left you or what?"

"Yes, Ruby. She has left me. If you must know."

"What? Are you kidding me?"

"She left me three weeks ago."

"What are you talking about, Dad?"

"You did ask," he said, tapping his cigar ash into an empty pizza box.

"Dad, don't do that. You'll set the house on fire. Now, I was only joking about Mum leaving you. Do you mean to tell me she really has walked out?"

"I'm afraid so, yes."

"But you're sixty-eight years old, for God's sake! She's sixty-five. You can't just split up at your age. You've made it all this way. You can't just give up now?"

"All the same, apparently we have. She's not here at any rate. Two minus one equals one, Ruby. As the man says, do the maths."

"It's, do the *math*, Dad. It's an American saying. Oh my God, this is just too weird." Ruby sat down gently on a kitchen chair and closed her eyes. "Okay, I'll be calm, I promise. Just tell me what happened."

"There's not much to tell," he said quietly, waving his cigar in a hopeless sort of gesture. "One morning she was cleaning the house as usual. Sweeping out the ashes in the good room. And I asked her, was she not a few days late putting up the Christmas decorations? And she just stood up, threw down the brush and dustpan and told me she was bored to death."

"Bored to death? Those were her exact words?"

"That's what she said, yes. Bored to death. So I said to her, well, let's go out for a drive or something. And have lunch in town. And she said no. I'm not just bored with the housework, she said. I'm bored with everything."

"Everything?"

"Yes, everything. That's what I said as well. Bored with *everything*? And she said yes. She was bored with Christmas, bored with me, our marriage, the house, the village . . . her entire life to date. And, well, everything."

"Christ and all the angels. What did she do then?"

"She went upstairs, packed a small suitcase, phoned a taxi and left me."

"I don't believe it. Where did the taxi take her?"

"To the airport."

"And you didn't try to stop her?" Ruby spluttered.

"Not after she said she'd have me arrested if I did."

"You're winding me up?"

"No, I'm not. I rang the taxi firm after she'd gone. They said she'd asked to go to the International airport. You know, up near Belfast?"

"I know where the airport is, Daddy."

"Aye. No real rush on her, they said. They said she hadn't decided yet where she was going so there was no big rush."

"Oh my God. And you haven't heard anything since?"

"Nothing. Not a squeak from her! Look, I'm not too worried. I mean we both have close relatives in London. I've a hunch she's gone to stay with one of them maybe? Have a wee holiday on her own, like?"

"Why didn't you tell me?"

"Ah, Ruby. Because I thought she'd just go to London for a couple of days and do some Christmas shopping and then come home again. I didn't think she was really going away for good. I still don't know if she *has* gone away for good. She could be back any minute. She's always been a bit moody, as you well know."

"So you were on your own all over Christmas? The whole time?"

"Yes, I was indeed. And I was fine."

"But when I rang on Christmas Day you said Mum was cooking the dinner. You said to me that she said hello."

"Ruby, I lied to you, pet."

"Oh Dad. What are you like?"

"I didn't want to worry you. It wasn't too bad in the end. I had a few drinks and watched a film on the telly. Went for a long walk by the lakes. She'll come back when she's got the restlessness out of her system."

"How do you know that?"

"She does this from time to time. Though usually she only goes to the seaside. A guesthouse in Galway or Donegal, or maybe Dublin for a bit of shopping. Five days was the longest she stayed away before this. And she never took her passport before. I didn't even know she had a passport actually. We've never been abroad."

"How long has this sort of behaviour been going on, Dad?"

"Oh, I don't know. A few years."

"How long exactly?"

"What are you now? A policewoman?"

"Tell me, Dad."

"Forty-odd years?"

"Fucking hell."

"Now, don't be swearing, Ruby love."

"Did it never occur to you that Mum might be depressed?"

"Of course it occurred to me. I'm not completely dense, Ruby. But what could I do? She wouldn't go to the doctor. She said they would only fill her so full of tablets that she'd rattle. Or else they'd stick her in the asylum and throw away the key. We always managed with her moods, Ruby. It wasn't perfect but we always managed."

"They don't lock people away any more, Dad," Ruby said gently.

"They used to, in our day. Hundreds of them were shut away in that big, ugly asylum in Tyrone. Especially any women who were bad with their nerves, the poor souls."

"Yes, but that was fifty years ago."

"Well, your mother had an aunt who was committed once. After she had a baby, it was. Probably it was only post-natal depression or whatever? But you don't forget something like that in a hurry. Last we saw or heard of Cissy, she was roaring her head off in the doctor's car. She died in that place. Of heart failure or so they say. My guess is they gave her too many tablets."

"Oh my God! Listen to me, Dad. Things are different these days. They don't commit people any more just for being depressed. Look, I'm going to stay and help you now, okay? We'll phone everybody we know and try to find out where Mum is. Right? We'll open the windows in the morning and light the fires to freshen up the house. And then we'll dust and vacuum so it all looks lovely for when Mum gets home again. We'll buy some flowers for the hall and maybe an artificial Christmas tree? You'll never get a fresh one at this late stage. And then we'll persuade Mum to get some proper help for her depression."

But Ruby's father was barely listening.

"No, Ruby. No action whatsoever will be taken. She may not be truly depressed. She may just be restless. Nobody is happy all the time unless they're simple, Ruby. And to hell with the tree! Christmas is over now anyway."

"Fair enough on the decorations. But *no action will be taken*? What on earth do you mean?"

"We'll do nothing at all, Ruby. I don't want you to do anything or touch anything or say anything to anyone."

"But why not?"

"Because when your mother comes back I don't want her to know that you've been here. I just want her to come back and tidy up the house by herself and then we'll carry on as normal. That's why I'm leaving all this mess. So she'll have something to do when she returns. She'll be all guns blazing with the duster when she comes back. And she'll need some housework to do. That's usually how it goes."

"But this isn't normal at all, Dad. This is completely weird behaviour," Ruby said, her eyes filling up with tears.

"No, it isn't. It's the way your mother and I like to do things around here, that's all."

"Dad, please let me ask her doctor for some advice? Or maybe I should ring the police?"

"Not a bit of it, I absolutely forbid ringing the police. She's a *restless* woman, Ruby, that's all. She's far too intelligent to be stuck out here in the countryside with nothing to do but dust and polish all day long."

"But she never wanted a career, did she?"

"Oh, she did surely but she never got the chance to go to college," Ruby's father said flatly, as if that would explain everything. "When we were young it was only the children of the gentry that could afford an education. By the time I came into the money it was too late for your mother to go to college."

And then Ruby began to lose her temper. "Dad, to use one of your own phrases, would you ever 'change the record'? Don't even start on me with that old chestnut about the gentry getting all the chances. It wasn't the Famine era, you know? It was only the late 1970s. Mum could have gone back into education any time she wanted. You had plenty of money and only one child to bring up. You could have hired a nanny for me, and a housekeeper for the rest of it. That's a lot of nonsense to say Mum never had any chances. She's just punishing you for being so passive and nice and understanding."

"Stop it, Ruby."

"I won't stop it. She's out of control."

"I was lucky that she married me. I was lucky that she agreed to settle out in the sticks."

"Oh please, it's so pretty here in Fermanagh. This gorgeous, big house! Well, it could be perfect if you'd paint the outside of it and put in a few lights along the drive. I don't know why you didn't do it years ago but never mind that now. You could have moved closer to the village or even into Enniskillen town. Or you could have moved to Belfast to be near to me. Your only child, remember? Mum could have trained as a nurse or a doctor or anything."

"Ah no, you have to do these things when you're young. Not when you're thirty-five and all the other students think you're only an old eejit trying to join in their fun. And she would have been thirty-five by the time she'd got all the school exams she needed to get into university."

"Oh, what's the point of even trying to talk to you, Dad? You're just as bad as she is. You're both daft if you ask me. All of this diva stuff is just the result of the two of you being idle rich and bored stiff and plain silly. The grounds haven't been touched in months so obviously this situation has been going on for some time."

"What would you know about it?" he asked suddenly. "Away up in Belfast with your own fancy business and all your swanky friends?"

"What? I don't have any swanky friends . . . Dad, are you mad altogether? Just my old neighbours and a few friends from school that I see for coffee about once a year. Do you even know your own daughter at all? Have you forgotten that I lost my husband last year? You didn't even ask me how I coped with the funeral."

"I didn't like to bring it up."

"You what?"

"I didn't want to upset you, Ruby."

"Dad, Jonathan is dead. He died in a car accident. Dad, are you listening to me? On Christmas Eve, it was. I'm never going to forget that as long as I live," Ruby said angrily. "Ah, what's the use? You'd rather die in agony than have a straight conversation with your only child. I really don't know why I bother. I should phone the Samaritans whenever I feel like a chat. I really should!"

"Don't be cheeky to me! I'm sorry if I'm not the father you wanted me to be," he said huffily.

"I just want you to be like most other fathers, Dad. And for Mum to be like most other mothers. You know? To take an interest in the little things in life? To ask me how I am, to hug me when we meet?"

"You could have moved back here after the funeral?" he accused her. "If you wanted to be so close to us."

"What? So I could see the two of you fighting and carrying on in a bit more detail?"

"We can't help being the way we are, Ruby. We were brought up to be private people. It's all gone too far in the other direction if you ask me," he said, staring up at the ceiling. "All kissing and pawing at complete strangers!"

Ruby sighed heavily. Obviously there was going to be no hug from her dad tonight.

"Well, for your information, I'm a grieving widow, Dad, with a small dress shop on the Ravenhill Road. And my best friend is also my employee. And not a day goes by that I don't long for Jonathan to come walking in the door and tell me the whole thing has been a bad dream. We loved each other so much. But what would you know about my life? You and Mum sitting here, playing your silly games, with all your money in the bank and all this spare time on your hands! Wasn't it lucky for the pair of you that I didn't have a whole bunch of kids before my husband went and got himself killed? Then you'd have to act your age and behave like proper grandparents and maybe help me out for a change. Every street in Belfast is crawling with Granny-nannies! The economy would collapse without them. Yes, lucky for you, I've got no children. Then we'd see how self-obsessed you really are. The pair of you!"

"Well, now you're just being hurtful – I think you'd better go home and calm down, Miss," Ruby's father said quietly, lighting up another cigar.

"I'm thirty-two years old, Dad. You can't talk to me like that any more. I won't be told to calm down."

"I'm still your father. And I do think you'd better go now."

"Don't you worry, I'm going," Ruby told him, walking stiffly to the door. And utterly outraged that her father was going to let her drive for another three hours! She turned to face him again. "But it's time you grew up a little bit yourself, and stopped this permanent teenager routine of yours. Nobody cares, Dad. The neighbours don't care about you. They don't know enough about you to care. Fermanagh doesn't care what the hell you do out here in the middle of nowhere. You're keeping up a big show that nobody *cares* about. You need help, don't you see?"

"You don't understand, Ruby. Your mother will be back soon. And when we next meet up, I don't want you to mention this, do you hear me? There's no need for doctors sticking their noses in, and all that nonsense. She's just the flighty type. You're making a mountain out of a molehill."

"Yes, whatever you say. Happy New Year! See you, Dad," Ruby replied, closing the front door behind her and getting back into her car with as much dignity as she could muster. "You can phone me, and you can come to Belfast to visit though," she said to nobody in particular. "I'm not coming back to this house again until my parents start acting like proper adults."

Ruby's father didn't come to the window to wave her away. And Ruby didn't look back as she went driving softly down the weed-strewn gravel drive. If her father wanted to sit there alone with his cigars and his crazy notions about keeping up appearances then so be it. Ruby didn't have the energy to convince him to speak to a doctor or a counsellor. If he thought it was a normal thing for his wife to go missing occasionally as some sort of compensation for a lost career, a fantasy lost career, then who was she to argue? Personally, Ruby had had enough drama for one day.

She drove home to Belfast in silence. Savouring the dark, empty roads and the feeling of being alone yet still connected to the world around her. She would have a hot bath and then get tucked into bed with a hot chocolate, she decided. She would spend all of New Year's Day in her warmest dressing gown. She'd watch the repeat of Jools Holland's music show on the telly, and make cheese on toast when she got hungry. She'd think of Jonathan and have a little cry to herself. And she'd text Happy New Year to Jasmine and to her other non-swanky friends in the city. She'd fall asleep tonight and tomorrow night knowing she was doing her best to be normal in a world that was sometimes very far from normal. Yes, if her parents got some thrill out of sulking and huffing and hurting each other in their twilight years then that was their business.

"I won't ring him," Ruby told the steering wheel as the lights of Belfast came into view three long hours later. Her head was splitting with the effort of driving for so long in the dark. It was five minutes to midnight. "I swear to God I won't interfere again. No matter how long it takes! I'll keep my trap well and truly shut. I won't say another word."

And she meant it.

Even though her head was telling her to go straight inside and call the police and have her own mother registered as a missing person. But no, if that's the way her parents wanted to play the game, then so be it.

Two days later, Ruby's father called her on the shop phone to say that her mother had been in touch, thank God.

"Where is she?" Ruby asked wearily, thinking that she'd have to go and fetch her silly mother home again now.

"She's in America," he sighed. "In New York . . . I guess Donegal wasn't far enough away for her this time . . ."

# 14

# The Third Secret

It was April now. Ruby and her father were still not speaking to one another very often. And there was still no sign of Ruby's mother coming back from New York. She'd called home a few times, told them she was okay and that she wanted to be alone for a while. Ruby was mystified: there was nowhere more peaceful than Fermanagh and nowhere more crowded than New York City, surely? But she didn't want to get any more deeply involved in her parents' marriage. She didn't have the emotional strength for it yet. So the three of them were firmly in their trenches and there was no sign of a white flag being waved any time soon.

"Don't ask," Ruby would sigh, if Jasmine ever brought the subject up.

It had been a quiet morning in the shop but all that was about to change. The doorbell pinged sharply several times and Ruby glanced up from tidying the cash register to see a dark-haired, orange-skinned young woman peering eagerly in the window. She came barging noisily into the shop the second Ruby pressed the release button. Nearly getting stuck in the doorway, in fact, she had so many bulky shopping bags draped over her muscular arms.

"Oh my sweet Lord, it's only official wild child Rebecca McCann! We were at school together," Jasmine said to Ruby at once, turning a worrying shade of pink. Ruby could see immediately that Jasmine wasn't exactly Rebecca McCann's biggest fan.

"Jazzy babes, me auld mucker, what about ye?" Rebecca screeched. "And just call me Becky. I'm not fuckin' royalty, you know!"

"Um, Becky, how're you keeping?" Jasmine faltered, her wide-open eyes clocking Rebecca's expensive clothes and shoes. Tarty enough admittedly, but still very expensive-looking . . . And a huge great diamond ring that was flashing on her engagement finger. Jasmine couldn't help assuming that the bold Becky had netted herself a rich boyfriend. A bit galling when Jasmine considered herself much better-looking and classier than poor old Becky and her Page Three wannabe persona. Becky had crow's feet already, she noticed, not to mention a few nose-to-mouth lines. Probably all those single ciggies puffed in various bus shelters in her formative years, Jasmine thought bitchily.

"Hey, I'm keeping the very best, ta very much for asking. Did you not hear the good news, Jazzy babes? I only went and won the freakin' Lotto last month," Rebecca laughed loudly, throwing her head back and her mouth open to reveal two perfect rows of neon-white American veneers.

"You did not? Jesus! Did you really?" Ruby exclaimed, as Jasmine swayed a little on her feet and seemed to have to gasp for air.

"I did indeed. I won seven million freakin' quid," Rebecca trilled, her heavy eye make-up giving her the look of a startled Panda. "I'm being interviewed about it on UTV tonight. Fancy me being on the telly! Fame at last! And it'll be in the national papers as well. Mind you, I'm bricking it – I never take a decent photograph when I'm nervous."

"Seven million pounds? Should you not be keeping that sort of news to yourself for fear of being kidnapped or something?" Jasmine managed to splutter. "You'll be shoved into the back of a van one of these days by some out-of-work terrorists and never seen again."

*Hopefully* never seen again, Jasmine's expression seemed to add.

"Jasmine, please don't upset your friend," Ruby warned. "I'm sure the Lotto people have warned Becky here about such things already."

But Rebecca wasn't too worried about her personal security.

"Stuff the terrorists! They'll have their work cut out to kidnap me, Jazzy babes. I've got two bodyguards on the payroll," she explained with a casual wave of her manicured hand. Both women stared at Becky's inch-long nail extensions, painted white and red, and studded with blue stars.

"Bodyguards?" Jasmine gasped. "You've got bodyguards?"

"Aye, I have surely. Two lovely lads that I got from an agency in London! Ex-military: they're well fit. Biceps like grapefruits! I'm moving away from Belfast soon anyway. Going to live in a villa in the sun. Swimming pool and all the rest of it! I can't say exactly where, just yet, I haven't made my mind up. But I'll be out of this freezin' dump before long, don't you worry. Who'd have thought it, huh? I've been buying ten tickets every week for years."

Jasmine opened her mouth to speak but no words were forthcoming.

"Well, congratulations to you," Ruby said brightly, trying not to notice Jasmine's neck drawing in on itself in a pitiful retching movement. "Isn't it lovely for someone from Belfast to have won the Lotto? Fair play to you and I hope your good fortune makes you very happy." Ruby was only being polite but Becky didn't seem to notice, or care.

"Cheers, love," Becky said, flicking her tapered fringe out of her eyes.

"What can we do for you today?" Ruby asked then, anxious to get Becky out of the shop before Jasmine tried to strangle her with one of their glittery scarves.

"I want to buy that wee green bag in the window," Becky said, trying hard to point with the weight of six shopping bags on her right arm alone.

"Surely you'd be wanting to buy a Chanel bag?" Jasmine asked sweetly.

"Well, yes, but I wanted this bag for my ma, you see? She said she was looking in your window the other day and she spied this cute wee apple-green bag with a dark green bow on it. She's the one who wants it, not me as such. Mind you it's kinda nice in its own way. Is there no handle on it or what?"

"You put your wrist through one loop of the bow," said Ruby. "I'll wrap it up for you, shall I? And please tell your mum I was delighted she liked my handbag." Then she added proudly, "I made these ones myself."

"Aw, aren't you the clever one? I'll tell her surely, so I will," Becky said, peeling some banknotes off a fat roll in her pocket and dropping them onto the counter as casually as if they were old sweet wrappers.

"Thank you very much," Ruby told her, slipping the money into the register. Yes, she could have given Becky the bag for free, seeing as she was Jasmine's old school "chum" but she didn't want to upset Jasmine any further. The poor girl had veins throbbing on her forehead where previously there'd been creamy smooth skin. Ruby wrapped the apple-green bag in tissue paper, popped it into a striped carrier and handed it over politely.

"Where's your bodyguards today?" Jasmine asked mock-innocently.

"In the car, having a wee smoke," Becky had to admit, and in the process revealing that she'd only brought all her shopping into Ruby's shop in order to show off to Jasmine. Obviously Becky had known already that Jasmine worked there.

"If I don't see you again, good luck to you," Jasmine said through gritted teeth. "Mind you don't get too sunburnt in your new villa, now. Won't you? Remember, Becky, we're so pale here in Northern Ireland that we tend to get skin cancer after, like, about five minutes in a really sunny country. So keep a good look out for any auld moles that are changing shape or bleeding. Won't you, now? They're bastards to cure, once they get established, those auld melanomas . . ."

Finally, Becky looked slightly crestfallen.

"Moles?" she said, trying and failing to frown through her Botox.

"Aye, they're desperate!" Jasmine sighed.

"And congratulations again," Ruby added, nipping out from behind the counter and opening the door wide for Miss Rebecca McCann, now one of Belfast's wealthiest citizens. "Fancy that! A Lotto winner standing in this very shop!"

"Cheers," Becky said and then she was laughing again. "Oh, and I'm engaged too. Did you notice the ring at all?"

"Oh yes, isn't it bloody huge?" Jasmine agreed spitefully. "I wasn't sure if it was only glass?"

"No, it's the real deal. I left my other fella last year. He was a bit of a loser," Becky explained, rolling her eyes. "A wandering eye on him. And that's not all that was wandering, if you know what I mean? Dickhead."

"Oh dear. Well, who's the lucky man?" Jasmine couldn't help asking.

"Jimmy White."

"Jimmy White from our old school?" Jasmine asked in a wobbly voice. Only the best-looking boy in the district! A dead ringer for Matt and Luke (the Bros pop star twins) with his blond crew cut, sharp cheekbones and his bright blue eyes.

"The very same. Met up with him again on Facebook a while back."

"After you won the Lotto or before?" Jasmine said.

"Jasmine, don't be cheeky," Ruby trilled.

"Afterwards as it happens. We got engaged after spending just six days together. But he's not after me for my money if that's what you're worried about," Becky laughed lightly. "He was in love with me from Day One, he said. I mean I bought the engagement ring myself naturally. But he would've bought it if he'd had the money. If he'd had £100K going spare! I mean he does have a couple of kids to support and their mothers are two real hard bitches. Bitches to the bone!"

"God love him . . . I'm sure the CSA has his heart broken . . . Childhood sweethearts, you say? How romantic," Jasmine said, smiling brightly though her eyes were as hard and dark as two chips of flint.

"Aye, love's young dream! Well . . . see ya, Jazzy babes!" Becky finally said and she breezed out the door.

Ruby waved her off and then stood chuckling at the window as Becky piled her shopping into a black stretch limousine with tinted windows, and then half-fell into the car herself. A plume of cigarette smoke drifted out of the sunroof as the car drove away.

"What a laugh!" Ruby said, shaking her head in disbelief. "What a real character she was!"

But Jasmine only went over to the luxury armchair at the back of the shop and threw herself down on it in despair.

"Character, you say? Complete cow, more like," she said bitterly. "Imagine that dozy cow winning seven million quid . . ."

"Banish envy, Jasmine," Ruby said at once.

"What?"

"Banish envy. That's the third secret of happiness."

"Ruby, what are you talking about? You're not making any sense."

"I'm thinking of making a list, you know? I've been thinking a lot about this in recent days. And that's the third secret of happiness, I reckon."

"What tablets are you on this week?" Jasmine asked, closing her eyes with the sheer strain of hating Rebecca McCann.

"Don't you remember my first two secrets? Well, firstly you have to become emotionally independent and then you have to address any ongoing health problems. And then you have to get rid of negative emotions like envy."

"Ruby, that dizzy bimbo just won seven million pounds on the Lotto!"

"So what? You should be happy for her."

"You don't know her like I do, Ruby. She's a gloating, smug little cow. She's rubbing my nose in this – she's loving every second of it. She's the last person on earth who should win seven million pounds."

"Of course she's loving it! She bought her tickets like everybody else, didn't she? Ten of them a week, she said."

"Ah, balls! When I think of all the lovely things I could have done with that money. A nice house for my parents . . . early retirement for them both . . . an adapted bungalow for my cousin in Bangor who's disabled . . ."

"Well, sure, we could all do lots of lovely things with a Lotto win," Ruby said, smiling calmly. "Come on now, pull yourself together, girl. It's only money."

"Easy for you to say. You've got money," Jasmine said curtly.

"The Merry Widow, huh? Sitting pretty on the handy old life insurance?"

"No, I didn't mean it like that and you know I didn't," Jasmine said.

"Yes, you did mean it. And yes, it's nice for me to own the shop and the flat outright but I'd give it all away tomorrow to have Jonathan back."

"I'm so sorry, Ruby. I know you would."

"Apology accepted. But why do you hate this girl so much?"

"Oh, I don't know. She was always a useless trollop. Pinching other girls' boyfriends when we were teenagers. And she was an only child who was spoilt rotten and never had to do any chores. She got to go to all the good pop gigs too. And she used to bully this wee girl in our class who had ginger hair. Called her Fanta Pants for years and years. It just isn't fair."

"Life isn't fair. I should know."

"I know, Ruby, really I do. I know it's not really important. But it's just not fair."

"Just try not to think about her."

"But she's not even grateful, Ruby. She thinks it's all just one big laugh."

"Yes, I don't expect she's aware of what a gift she just got. She seems the simple type, you know? She just goes with the flow. She won the Lotto and now she's shopping up a storm. If I won the Lotto I'd be scared stiff of gangsters following me home and so on. But she's like a child in a toyshop, isn't she? I'd like to be more like that myself in a way. Easy come, easy go."

"Huh. People like her shouldn't be allowed to buy Lotto tickets," Jasmine said bitterly. "There ought to be a screening system."

"Oh, Jasmine, that's a bit extreme!" Ruby smiled.

"I bet she goes to live in some lovely place," Jasmine said then. "A millionaires' paradise. With an outdoor seating area and a massive swimming pool. And staff to clean up after her. And she'll have nothing to do all day but shop and gad about in a chauffeur-driven car. Like a proper WAG."

"Some WAGs never look all that happy to me. It must be hard living with the pressure of being in the public eye. And a thick husband."

"True."

"Anyway, by the looks of all that shopping Becky was doing

she'll be broke in two years' time," Ruby said wisely. "A stretch limo and two bodyguards just to go shopping? And maybe that Jimmy of hers is a lying, cheating gold-digger? He has two kids, she said. Well, that's not a good sign, is it? If he's going to leave his children behind and move abroad with Rebecca? A decent man would never move that far away from his kids."

"Oh Ruby, you can always cheer me up, thank you. Jimmy was a bit of a boozer too as I recall. By the time he was thirteen he could neck two litres of strong cider and still drive a car in a straight line. And he used to spit a lot. I never could stand boys that gobbed up on the street. I still can't. The dirty gits."

"There you go then. He'll buy flash cars and party his way through Becky's money like there's no tomorrow probably. I mean it's normal to be a bit jealous of Lotto winners but I think you're overreacting, that's all. You've got a good life, Jasmine."

"Yeah, I work in a clothes shop in Belfast and spend all my wages on the rent for a tiny flat," Jasmine murmured.

"Or another way to look at it is, you have a nice easy job near your home and your boss is lovely to you. And your family all adore you and you live in a luxury flat with a balcony and tons of built-in storage," Ruby said solemnly. "And you're lovely looking too. Becky's all hair and teeth really, she's not a patch on you."

"Sorry, Ruby. You're so kind."

"You're welcome."

"Just one more thing," Jasmine sighed.

"Name it," Ruby smiled at her.

"Please don't ever call me Jazzy," Jasmine said softly.

"Okay."

"Or even worse, Jazzy *babes*."

"I wouldn't dare," Ruby said, smiling.

Three weeks later Ruby heard on the local news that Lotto winner Rebecca McCann's fiancé Jimmy White had stolen two million pounds from their joint account and fled the country with it. The police had then foiled a kidnap bid on Rebecca's parents when three masked men approached them in the Homebase car park at Galwally. Guns had been brandished and Mrs McCann had fainted and cut her head on a heavy-duty trolley. The three of them were now in hiding at an undisclosed address in England. Jimmy's abandoned kids were pictured in the papers under headlines such as "*Come Home Daddy. We Love You A Lotto.*"

"Poor old Becky," Jasmine said when Ruby showed her the latest edition of one paper. "I do actually feel a bit sorry for her now. Stupid bitch and all that she is."

And she did seem genuinely sympathetic, Ruby thought to herself. There was barely a twinkle in Jasmine's blue eyes when she said again how very sorry she was to hear about Becky's terrible run of bad luck.

# 15

# The Flower Show

June arrived at last and the sun was beaming down from a perfectly blue sky. After weeks of depressing drizzle and damp weather, it seemed that the sunshine had decided to bless the city with a surprise visit.

"I can't believe I let you talk me into wearing this ludicrous dress," Ruby muttered under her breath, as she stood beside Jasmine in the very long queue. They'd been waiting impatiently outside the first annual Belfast Flower Show for about an hour.

"Shut up, you look lovely," Jasmine soothed. "It's just because you haven't been out-and-about in so long you're a bit nervy. Come on now and settle your old head, there's a good girl."

"Not possible, Jasmine. Not when I look like Nora Batty on HRT or something, God rest her soul, as the saying goes. Are you sure these dresses are only A-line? My skirt feels as flappy as a circus tent. Jasmine, tell me the truth. Have you hired these frocks from a fancy-dress place?"

"Would you stop talking utter nonsense, woman," Jasmine whispered back, trying hard not to laugh out loud and spoil their sophisticated image. "You look good enough to eat. We both do. Full-circle skirts are so in this year. And these floral tea dresses are the absolute height of summer fashion."

"So is caramel cashmere," Ruby hissed, smoothing down the creases on the front of her red and orange dress. At least the pattern was relatively small, she told herself, trying desperately to calm down. Jasmine's frock had giant black and blue daisies on it, with a large black bow on the front of her waistband. And she'd decided to wear electric-blue shoes as well. "As if nobody was going to notice you in the dress alone," Ruby fretted, staring down at Jasmine's size nine feet encased in bright blue sling-backs.

"Ruby, will you try and relax a little bit, please? We'll be in through the gates soon and then nobody will even notice us when they see all the lovely flowers and . . . stuff." Jasmine was craning her neck to check for any celebrities going in by the side gate.

At this last remark Ruby began to giggle nervously. Jasmine knew nothing whatsoever about gardening and she didn't even have a garden to go with her luxury fifth-floor apartment at the Bell Towers. Just a balcony with a couple of pots and a tiny chair on it. But Jasmine Mulholland was obviously determined not to sit at home growing old and boring like Ruby, not when there were so many new events being added to the Belfast social calendar every year. And Ruby couldn't blame her for that. In fact she totally admired Jasmine's spirited personality. She just wished they could have worn something more low-key, that was all. What if there were TV-cameras roaming about! Actually there were bound to be TV-cameras roaming about. Ruby began to perspire heavily under her flawless make-up.

"You *do* look very nice to tell you the truth," Jasmine said suddenly. "That luminous face powder seems to be working well at any rate. You're positively glowing right now."

She could have said she was so nervous she was actually sweating but Ruby just sighed. She had made her point about the dresses. The queue moved forward slightly. It seemed as if their tickets were finally about to be checked and stamped.

"Thank God for some sign of movement in this bloody queue," Ruby whispered gratefully. "I'm dying to stretch my legs. Oh, I hope it doesn't rain. At least the weather looks promising. Seeing as we've only got these so-called shrugs of yours to keep us warm."

"You're welcome," Jasmine said brightly, determined not to let Ruby's fussing spoil the day for them. She threaded one arm through the crook of Ruby's elbow and propelled her friend forward. "Look. There's Jimmy Nesbitt! Oh my God, is that his wife? Isn't she pretty? Her coat is fabulous! Honestly, Ruby, I think the two of us are under-dressed if anything. We should have worn the fascinators like I suggested."

At that Ruby began to giggle again, even though she was feeling very anxious about the sheer volume of people gathering to get into the flower show. But perhaps when they were all in through the gates and beginning to disperse a bit she would feel better? The show was laid out over a generous site. It couldn't be too claustrophobic, could it? And she could always walk home if there were no taxis available afterwards. It wasn't all that far to the Ravenhill, not really. She'd sneaked a comfortable pair of pumps into her handbag just in case her red shoes started to cut into her heels.

"Hooray and we're in," said Jasmine as the queue surged forward again.

But as the two friends finally squeezed through the narrow entrance gates and tried to take in the general layout, Ruby spied her mysterious Christmas tree supplier, Tom Lavery himself. Sitting in the driver's seat of his very old, very battered-looking Land Rover. He was sipping from the plastic cup of a tall, tartan flask. His large hands were black with dirt and even his long brown hair was streaked with patches of dust. He looked almost as fed up as Ruby felt. Attached to the back of his vehicle was a huge trailer full of empty flowerpots and the remnants of dozens of compost bags. He must have been here for ages already setting up an exhibition of some kind, she thought to herself. Ruby began to forget how nervous she was and instead wondered where Tom's exhibition was located and what it might contain. But she said nothing to Jasmine who was already spotting more celebrities sipping champagne in the VIP tent. And wishing aloud that she'd remembered to bring an autograph book.

The two women set off along the designated path and soon they were happily taking in all the different sights and sounds of the flower show. There were endless beautiful summerhouses on display. There were also some very pretty patios, modern-style water-features, classic statuary, whimsical topiary and lavish flowers of every description. And there was lots of room to meander about, Ruby noted gratefully. She'd feared she'd be crushed up against the side of a lorry or something. For ever since moving into her dainty flat above the shop, and not having to even walk up the road to work any more, she'd become slightly phobic of large crowds.

"It's just like Chelsea only far better," Jasmine declared happily. "Lots more room. Hey, anything they can do, we can do better! I told you this would be a good day out. Now there's the peasants' refreshments marquee. What say we have a little snack to revive us?"

"We've only been here for forty-five minutes," Ruby protested.

"But if we hang about any longer they'll run out of the nicest buns. I see they have triple-layer, puff-pastry lemon things on the poster. Come on, quick, or there'll only be plain scones left," Jasmine said wisely. And so in they went through the rather grand doorway which was decorated with pink and lilac bunting. A brass band started up on the other side of the site and a polite smattering of applause rippled round the grounds. Ruby found a quiet table near the entrance to the marquee and Jasmine grabbed a tray and began loading it up with forks, paper napkins and plates. Soon they were sipping pink champagne and attempting to eat two very large, fresh-cream pastries with as much dignity as possible. Jasmine spilled some lemon curd on her dress but Ruby convinced her nobody would notice it amidst the giant daisies. Ruby cheered up and they even managed a little girly gossip about a friend of Jasmine's who was gradually selling off all her good jewellery and hiding the money in a foreign bank account because she feared her husband was planning to divorce her.

"So when she finally gets the solicitor's letter she'll be good and ready for him," said Jasmine approvingly. "She'll have her nest-egg safely tucked away. And she's just going to say she must have accidentally thrown her jewellery wrap in the bin when she was de-cluttering. The two-timing weasel! What is it about some men? Why isn't one woman enough for them? Or are they all creeps, I wonder?"

"I have no idea," Ruby said absentmindedly, tidying up the table and leaving a tip for the waitresses.

"Oh, I'm sorry, Ruby. I know your Jonathan wasn't like that," Jasmine said quietly.

"Shush, that's okay. But don't talk about him please or I'll only cry. He'd have enjoyed all this. He once said he'd like to do the back garden up a bit. Even though it was only small. Even though he wasn't much of a gardener."

"Are you all right, Ruby? You do look a wee bit wobbly."

"I'm fine. It's just I haven't been sleeping very well these last few months for worrying about Mum and Dad."

"I'm not surprised, really. And they haven't kissed and made up yet, isn't it unbelievable?"

"We don't even have an address for her in New York."

"God, I know, that's just awful."

"I know. Just a mobile number."

"Oh Ruby, you should ring them again, both of them," Jasmine said carefully.

"I know I should. But every time I lift the phone I feel so angry with them . . . and yet I know they can't help being the way they are. Stubborn! And I can't help being a very practical person. So I'd only suggest counselling again and that would go down like a lead balloon, do you see? And I don't trust myself to be tactful with them any more. And then I can't ring them after all, because I don't know what to *say* to them any more. My father might have a heart attack if I start pushing things again. He's a very heavy smoker these days, I think. Judging by the way he was getting stuck in to the cigars the last time I saw him. Smoking like a chimney, he was. And if Mum thinks we're on her case, she might take off again and go even further afield this time? Maybe to some bizarre place we've never even heard of . . ."

"Okay, I understand," Jasmine agreed. "Let sleeping dogs lie, huh?"

"Yeah," Ruby sighed. "There's a lot to be said for letting sleeping dogs lie."

"Fair enough," said Jasmine.

"Shall we get on with the rest of it then? The sooner we complete the circuit of exhibitions the sooner we can get out of here," Ruby smiled.

"Okay," Jasmine said again, collecting her handbag and shrug and dusting some icing sugar off her daisy-covered knees. "Come on then."

And so they went strolling along the temporary pathways, stopping to admire each new display and occasionally having a short chat with some of the exhibitors. Jasmine bought a round, fat cactus covered with long, deadly spines and decorated with glittery glass beads, that she said reminded her rather spookily of Rebecca McCann. The two women laughed heartily at that and Ruby was almost glad she had agreed to come to the flower show after all.

Then Ruby's heart gave a tiny wobble as she noticed Tom

Lavery again, standing beside the very last display area before the exit: a miniature box-maze with perfectly flat sides and tops, and dotted with moss-covered statues of angels and fawns. It seemed to have been put together in short sections, which looked as though they had been grown in long flat troughs. People were flocking to go for a walk round it. But because the maze was only about thirty-foot square they had to go exploring in small groups of three or four. Tom seemed quite ill at ease, Ruby thought to herself, as she observed him pushing a stray strand of hair out of his eyes. He'd washed his hands and changed into a smarter jacket by this time but still he seemed very reluctant to be there. He was handing out leaflets and trying to organise the people going into the maze, and also selling box-clippings by the dozen.

Ruby looked around for an alternative exit in order to avoid having to speak to him but there was no other way out available. They had to pass Tom's exhibit directly to leave the show via the main exit or else go all the way back to the entrance gates. And so all she could hope was that he wouldn't remember her. But somehow she knew that he certainly would remember her. And suddenly she felt very excited . . .

But with Jasmine walking here beside her, she couldn't possibly talk to him.

In a flash of inspiration Ruby remembered she had a pair of sunglasses in her bag and she quickly fished them out and slipped them on. Jasmine had bought them for her especially for the occasion. They were ridiculously large and round. With white plastic frames! She would look absolutely daft in them, like a poor man's version of Paris Hilton, but never mind. She would be able to slip past this strangely compelling man and not add to his embarrassment by forcing him to make polite conversation with her. With poor Jasmine salivating with curiosity on the sidelines.

But eagle-eyed Jasmine had already spotted Tom anyway.

"Oh Ruby! Ruby, don't look now but there's your Christmas

tree guy," Jasmine squeaked excitedly. "What's that sign say? *The Box-maze at Camberwell House.* Do you want to stop and say hello to him? Oh, go on!"

"Jasmine, don't you dare say hello to that man. And we're not going into the maze either. We're just going to nod briefly and keep on walking, right? We're nearly finished here."

"Right, Ruby, you're the boss."

But as Ruby was slinking discreetly past Tom's information table Jasmine suddenly realised she had a stone in her shoe.

"Stop walking," she said abruptly, grabbing Ruby's elbow and hopping around on one leg. "Pebble in my shoe! Pebble in my shoe!"

"Wait till we're out the gates at least," Ruby murmured.

"I can't wait. I'm in agony," Jasmine replied.

"You conniving wee witch," Ruby muttered.

"What do you mean?"

"There's no pebble, is there?"

"Yes, there is," Jasmine grinned back at her.

And so Jasmine had to stop, wriggle off her shoe and shake the imaginary stone out of it. And as she held onto the table for support while Ruby stood seething silently beside her, Jasmine said hello to the ruggedly handsome Tom Lavery and began to show a bit of interest in his exhibit.

"That's a fine old maze you have there," she said boldly.

Ruby could have reached for her friend and slapped her but there was nothing she could do, short of storming off in a sulk like a hormonal teenager.

"Well, isn't this all very nice? Love the statues there! Cute! Now you don't know me but I'm Jasmine Mulholland and this here is my friend Ruby O'Neill," Jasmine was saying.

"Yes, I remember," Tom said, looking shyly at Ruby.

"That's right. You two have met already, haven't you?" Jasmine said with a wide grin.

Ruby kept her sunglasses on and prepared to say cheerio but Jasmine wasn't quite finished.

"And your name is Tom, I believe?" she said, smiling up at him. He was very tall. He must have been six foot four to her five foot nine. Jasmine thought that Tom Lavery looked just fine, close up. Not nearly as weird as he'd looked that day rushing away down the road from Ruby's shop.

"Um, yeah, Tom Lavery. Have you ever been to Camberwell House, I wonder? Lovely place for a day out." Tom was blushing like mad. He hadn't meant to mention the house to Ruby and her friend Jasmine but he'd been telling thousands of people all day and somehow it had just slipped out.

"You know what, I don't think we ever have," Jasmine said, all big eyes and fluttering eyelashes.

"We haven't been there yet, no," Ruby muttered darkly.

"Hey, Ruby, we must go to this Camberwell place and check it out some day," Jasmine said, giving Ruby a gentle nudge in the ribs with her elbow.

"Oh yes, definitely," Ruby smiled back, giving Jasmine a daggers-glare from behind her white sunnies. "I can't think why we haven't been already, Jasmine. For you simply love old houses, don't you?"

"I do surely," laughed Jasmine. "The older the better. All those ceiling roses and secret passages hidden behind the bookcases? We'll see you there so, Tom Lavery, it's a date. Thank you very much."

Jasmine reached across the table and shook Tom's hand warmly. He seemed rather surprised but he rallied well and handed over some leaflets.

"These will get you in, half-price," he explained.

And then, without quite understanding why he did it, Tom offered his hand for Ruby to shake also. Ruby gazed at his outstretched fingers for one stunned moment before politely placing her pure-white hand in his darker-skinned one. Tom's large, strong fingers closed around Ruby's trembling palm and immediately a surge of electricity shot up her arm and made her jump. So much so, her sunglasses fell off and clattered to the ground.

"Oh, sorry. Let me," he said, bending down to retrieve them and the magic spell was broken.

As he handed Ruby her glasses Jasmine winked and made a face behind his back. Ruby blushed furiously.

"Camberwell is open six days a week during the summer months," Tom said, automatically falling back into salesman mode. "Monday is our closing day. Hot food served at all times and there are guided tours every hour, on the hour."

"Thank you very much for the leaflets," Ruby said quietly.

"Now let's have a peep at this maze of yours," Jasmine announced brightly.

"Sorry but we've run out of time," Ruby said sweetly. "Must dash. Bye!"

Ruby grabbed Jasmine's elbow and hurried her towards the exit. Tom watched them go with a flicker of disappointment in his dark brown eyes.

"Love is . . . an invitation to view ancient chamber pots," Jasmine said as she tumbled, laughing, out onto the pavement again. Swinging her cactus merrily in its heavily punctured carrier bag.

"I'm warning you, Jasmine Mulholland. If you ever pull a stunt like that again I'll fire you without a second's thought," Ruby said bossily.

"I'm sorry, Ruby," Jasmine said quietly. "But I couldn't help it. Wasn't he rather special? Very intense, you know? I think he has a bit of a crush on you, to be honest. He was blushing like a sixth-former on prom night."

"You're stone mad," Ruby sighed. "You're obsessed with romance. In fact, I think you should speak to somebody about it. It's like an illness with you, it really is."

"Probably. I've been living alone for too long, that's my trouble. I'm looking at love through rose-tinted specs. I'm sorry if I showed you up or anything."

"That's okay."

But Jasmine wasn't a bit sorry. Wedding ring or no wedding ring, she wanted to find out a little more about Tom Lavery. After all, Ruby was still wearing her wedding ring. But she wasn't married. Not any more . . . And there was definitely something there, Jasmine told herself stubbornly. There was definitely some chemistry between the pair of them. She could feel it. For heaven's sake, she could *see* it. They were attracted to one another, she was convinced of that. Now the only problem was, how was she possibly going to get Ruby O'Neill all dolled up, bundled into the car and off to visit Camberwell House without having to slip a sedative into her food first? It wasn't going to be easy. But she was going to have a try. *Nothing ventured, nothing gained*: that was Jasmine's motto.

Ruby was very quiet as they abandoned the hopelessly long taxi-queue and caught a bus home. She didn't even notice when a bunch of chattering schoolgirls in short skirts got on the bus and giggled furiously at their vintage-style dresses. She almost missed their stop, in fact, she was in such a daydream. Jasmine had to snap her fingers in her face to wake her up.

"Penny for them," Jasmine said as they limped up the Ravenhill Road a few minutes later, their new shoes beginning to bite at last.

"Oh, nothing important," Ruby replied. "I was just thinking that maybe we should have gone round the maze for a quick look after all? It wouldn't have killed us to show some interest in it. And it did look very nice. I hope Tom didn't think we were bored by his exhibit, that's all. After all the hard work he must have put into it? He looked so tired. Didn't you notice how tired he looked?"

Jasmine said nothing but instead turned her face away so that Ruby didn't see her smiling from ear to ear.

# 16

## The Fourth Secret

When Ruby got the invite to her old school reunion a few days after the flower show she was tempted to drop it straight into the wastepaper basket and pretend she'd never seen it. For one thing she wasn't keen to go anywhere near Blackskull village. Even though the reunion was being held in the nearby town of Enniskillen. But it was still a trip down Memory Lane and Ruby wasn't feeling very keen on the distant past. Not these days since she still hadn't made it up with her parents. The guilt was smothering her like an old musty blanket. It kept her awake at night and in a permanent state of worry.

She hadn't phoned her father much in the six months and he had hardly phoned her. He hadn't even sent her a birthday card! Though Ruby forgave him for that as he had so much on his mind. Then again, she thought, the old rascal could be playing for sympathy . . . But she wasn't going to give in and start begging his forgiveness for their little spat. Or offering to act as a go-between. No, this time she was holding out until her parents underwent an epiphany of sorts and started acting their age. Even so, the situation had become so strained in Ruby's mind that every time she looked at the phone in her flat she felt an awful fluttering sensation in her stomach. And sometimes she even had a nervous, nauseous flush spreading across her face and neck.

"Am I supposed to report the two of them to Social Services or what?" she asked Jasmine later that morning as the two of them sat chatting over lunch in a café near the shop.

"Search me," Jasmine said, tucking into her food. "All oldies are a bit contrary, aren't they? Manipulative, some of them. Or else going a bit dotty? I mean, not senile exactly but wandering a bit? Confused, I think they call it?"

Ruby decided to ignore that particular comment. The thought of being the only child of two estranged and senile parents was just too difficult to contemplate. But would they be able to divorce if they began to wander in their minds, she fretted.

"Do you really think they're going senile?"

"Ah well, Ruby, I suppose they're far too young for all of that just yet," Jasmine said doubtfully.

"God, I hope so. I mean, what could I say to Social Services anyway?" Ruby continued. "Hello there. Have you got a minute? Now what's happened is, my mum's gone AWOL because she never got to be a big fancy career woman with her very own briefcase and all. And my dad's sulking up a storm and he's let the housework go to the dogs. He's smoking cigars all day long and he's living on pepperoni pizza. And I want you lads to do something about it."

"It's a tough call all right."

"I mean, I can't exactly ask them to give me a mother and a father from a children's picture-book, now can I?" Ruby sighed. "A lovely gentle Daddy with a pretty greenhouse in the garden? And a contented Mummy who's always smiling, and baking big jam cakes, with a gingham apron on her?"

"No, you can't," Jasmine agreed. "They'd think you'd gone mad entirely."

"I mean, if Social Services landed out to the house to do a spot-check and Mum was home again, then she'd know that I know that she'd been away. And then she'd be furious with Dad for telling me and maybe she'd go away again. And then he'd be raging at me, instead of her."

"I know, I know."

"It's an impossible situation."

"It is. Could you not just go and visit them again?" Jasmine suggested then. "Just turn up with a Battenberg cake and a bunch of tulips? And let on nothing's happened? Like your father said he wanted you to? She's likely come home again by now and there's no harm done."

"But that'd be playing along with their little game, do you see? That's pretending that they're both fine and dandy and in good mental health. I don't want to go along with that."

"True. But if it's what *they* both want then why beat yourself up?"

"Yes, I know it'd be easier that way. But still, I think it's better to address these issues, don't you?"

"Who knows what other people's marriages are like?" Jasmine mused thoughtfully, pouring old-fashioned lemonade from a stylish glass bottle. "Maybe they get turned on by the drama of it all? Maybe the make-up sex is mind-blowing?"

"Jasmine, will you please stop it? They're both in their sixties," Ruby said, rolling her eyes. "I think they only had sex once and that was to have me. No, seriously, I just can't see them roaring and shouting, and then stripping off and *doing it* halfway up the stairs. He's too emotionally repressed and she'd be worrying about scuffing the skirting boards."

"Whatever. More lemonade?"

"Cheers. Anyway is there any news on the romantic front for you this week? Any nice men discovered holding up the bar?" Ruby smiled, anxious suddenly to change the subject. "I don't want to think about my parents for a while. I keep imagining Mum's been murdered somewhere and her body dumped down a storm drain. Or that Dad's fallen on the stairs and broken his hip and he can't reach the phone. Why can't they be normal bloody parents and just phone me twice a week like other *normal* people phone their kids? Talk about the shit weather and the price of gas?"

"Um, are we still talking about your parents then?" Jasmine yawned.

"No, sorry. Go ahead," Ruby urged.

"Well, there's been no serious romance lately, no. I met a nice-looking guy on my travels around club-land last week. But when I asked him home for a snog he went straight into the old lusty lunge. Reaching for me on the sofa like an octopus on speed."

"Did he really?" Ruby said, all interested.

"Yeah, he did. Two seconds in the door and he was in porno mode."

"Not even time for coffee and a chat first?"

"No, sadly. He wanted me to do pervy things to him. Asked me to take off all my clothes and prance about in the shower. Feel myself up or whatever . . . He wanted to film me on his mobile phone. Like, yeah! He'd have it all online and pay-per-view before the sun came up. Weirdo."

"Oh my God. You never told me this. Is that the norm nowadays?" Ruby said, giggling.

"Well, maybe it's just me? Maybe I attract the fantasists?" Jasmine liked a bit of raw passion but she wanted friendship and sincerity as well.

"Men have changed so much, or some of them have," Ruby said sadly. "Jonathan and I must have been together for six months before things moved beyond a kiss. Well, maybe it was four months. Well, it was three months definitely."

"It's all quite different now," Jasmine said casually. "All these topless models giving raunchy interviews with one finger stuck in their mouths. They give the impression we girls are all mad for bondage and being spanked over the tumble-dryer. The poor guys are tormented. Like, I always knew they were sex-mad. But now it has to be kinky as well. Me, I just want some good old-fashioned, no frills, honest-to-goodness sex. Preferably with a nice dinner beforehand and a civilised breakfast the morning after. No drugs and nothing *too* pervy!"

"Indeed. And what's wrong with that? I'm so glad I'm not dating, myself. So how did you get that guy out of your flat after his lusty lunge was rejected? Did he go quietly or did you have to Kung Fu him?" Ruby asked. "I'm worried about you now, Jasmine. Maybe you shouldn't let guys into your home any more? Not on the first night anyway? Just to be on the safe side?"

"Ah, bless you, he just called me a flake and a tease and then stormed out. It's funny how quickly you can go off a good-looking guy when he comes leering towards you with his mouth wide open and his breath still smelling of curry sauce and chips."

"Oh my God. What's happened to romance?"

"Once or twice I've had to set off my rape-alarm. That fairly puts a stop to their kinky nonsense. Plus, I let a good, deep roar out of me! Half the building comes running!"

"Christ, Jasmine, that's hilarious," Ruby said, half-shocked and half-amused. "I can just picture you doing that actually."

And then despite themselves the two women collapsed into hopeless giggles.

"One guy fell down the stairs, he was that spooked," Jasmine spluttered. "Calling me all sorts. I said, at least I'm not as desperate as you are, mate. At least I'm still living in the real world, I told him."

"Jane Austen would be turning in her grave," Ruby wheezed. "Can you imagine what she'd have thought of pole-dancing and PVC hot pants?"

"Yeah well, in Jane's day nobody ever really had sex. Only alcoholic prostitutes, God love them. And rich creeps who ended up dead of syphilis before they were thirty. C'mere, we'd better get back to the shop. Lunchtime was over ten minutes ago."

"Okay."

When they got back, however, Ruby couldn't avoid at least a small glance down Memory Lane. For there was a woman standing on the doorstep, looking pointedly at her watch, and also looking slightly disappointed. The warm summer sunshine made her red hair glow softly like an angel's halo.

"Teresa?" Ruby asked gently, touching her on the arm. "It's never Teresa Dunne?"

"The very same. Except I'm Teresa Morris now. Ruby Nightingale, you haven't changed at all. I was just in Belfast doing a bit of shopping and I thought I'd look you up," she said, nodding towards the shop window. "I heard you had your own business now on the Ravenhill Road. Looks amazing!"

"Thanks very much, Teresa, I'm glad you waited for us. We're just a bit late getting back from lunch, that's all," Ruby explained, handing the keys to Jasmine. "Open up, Jasmine, would you?"

"Sure," Jasmine said and she unlocked the door and left the two women to have their little chat outside in the sunshine.

"So Teresa, how've you been all these years?" Ruby began. "You don't look any different from when we were in school together." And she didn't. The same flame-red hair and pink cheeks full of freckles.

"Ah now, you're too kind. Sure it was only fourteen years ago, woman. You look the same yourself. Except you've had your hair cut."

They smiled at each other then, wondering how much they could say without sounding over-familiar.

"I also heard you lost your husband?" Teresa began.

"Yes, it was eighteen months ago," Ruby said, colouring slightly.

"God bless you," Teresa said gently.

"Thanks," Ruby said simply.

"I lost my own husband four years ago, in a farming accident. Did your parents not say anything to you about it? We live not far from Blackskull village. I thought you might have sent a card? Maybe you did send a card, Ruby, maybe you did? But anyway I never got it."

"Oh my God, no. I never knew that," Ruby gasped. Raging again at her parents for not telling her this huge news. "They must have assumed I knew already."

"Well, it's no matter. The tractor overturned in soft ground and it fell on him. It was very sudden."

"Oh Teresa, I'm so sorry."

"Thank you Ruby. You have to struggle on, don't you? And I still have the five children to rear."

"Five children?" Ruby was amazed.

"Yes, two of his, two of mine and the one we had together. We were both divorced when we met but his two children wanted to stay on the farm and their mother's an actress away working in London so I just got on with it. They've all bonded now so when Mick died we decided to leave things as they were. She sends money and visits when she can. She's not really the maternal type."

Ruby suddenly felt slightly giddy. There she was, pottering about in her hobby-shop on the Ravenhill Road, while out in the real world other people were struggling hard on a daily basis. Teresa Dunne, well, Teresa Morris was nothing short of magnificent.

"I'm so sorry," Ruby said again.

"That's grand, thank you. But anyway I didn't come here to bring you down, Ruby. What I wanted to ask you was, do you think that you and me could rock up to the school reunion together? Us being young widows and all? Or have you met someone?"

"No. No, I haven't. Not at all," Ruby said guiltily. But she couldn't help thinking about Tom Lavery. And then she was raging with herself for betraying Jonathan's memory. And then she was raging at herself again for even thinking of her own problems instead of poor Teresa's.

"Oh right, that's okay then. So what do you say? Shall we have a coffee some time and a catch-up? And if we're feeling brave enough on the night, we'll go to the reunion together, yes?"

"The thing is, Teresa, I'm not really sure," Ruby faltered. "I might not go."

"But you got on all right with everyone, didn't you? And it'd be nice for you to see Sister Anne again, wouldn't it? She was always so nice to us, bringing us out to see a play for the last day and everything? We never got her a leaving gift, which I always think was awfully bad of us . . . I'd like to give her something small now: a book or a little ornament. What do you think, Ruby?"

"Yes, she was always very kind to everyone," Ruby agreed.

"Well then, will you keep an open mind about the reunion? We could go along for a while maybe? It's only a buffet and some background music, not a formal sit-down dinner, thank God. I hate those things – they go on and on, don't they? Will you think about it?"

"Surely I will," Ruby said finally.

"Right. Will we swap numbers and then I'll be on my way? Oh, I saw your father at Mass the other day and he was looking very well. Your mother wasn't with him, though. He said she'd gone to look after a sick cousin in England for a couple of months. They couldn't get any home help on the NHS, he said."

"Yes. She's such a pet, isn't she?" Ruby said quickly, amazed at her father and his determination to keep up the pretence of a normal marriage. "Look, Teresa, come here into the shop and let me give you something to remember your visit to Belfast by."

"Are you sure? I hope I didn't seem nosy or anything, by coming here today? I just wanted to keep in touch, that's all," Teresa said softly. "We always used to sit beside each other in English, do you remember? And correct each other's spelling tests?"

"Yes, I remember," Ruby said, almost able to smell the varnish again on the old lidded desks. But hardly able to remember what life was like in the years before she had met Jonathan. Had she really been a person in her own right once? Before she became a wife and then a widow?

She ushered Teresa in the door and told her to have a good look round and to pick anything that she wanted.

"Anything at all," Ruby commanded.

After a minute of thanking Ruby and then several cries of "Oh now, I couldn't take a thing, really," Teresa finally pointed to one of Ruby's velvet handbags in the glass case.

"Are those bags very exclusive?" she said, indicating the gold one. "I just love that beautiful gold bag there. But if it's really exclusive now I definitely won't accept it."

"It's yours," Ruby said, lifting it out and wrapping it up. "I made it myself, so yes, it is very exclusive indeed, and it would mean a lot to me if you'd accept it as a token of our friendship now, and the days we walked to school together all those years ago."

"Oh Ruby, thank you," Teresa said with a quiver in her voice. "That'd be lovely to keep my bits of jewellery in. The little bangles and things Mick gave me before he . . ."

"Not another word," Ruby said, hugging her old friend tightly.

And then they swapped numbers and Teresa was on her way home to Fermanagh with a load of cheap clothes for the children in the back of her car that she'd bought in Primark. And one of Ruby's precious handbags sitting on the passenger seat beside her.

"That was very kind of you," Jasmine said quietly, as Teresa's car went up the Ravenhill Road and out of sight.

"She was always such a lovely girl," Ruby sighed. "What rotten luck, to divorce one husband and then bury the second one."

"Five kids, huh? Fuck me."

"I know, and yet she still bothered to come and visit me," Ruby said.

"Yes, that was nice of her."

"The fourth secret of happiness, Jasmine: hold onto your friends," Ruby sighed. "At least now I know my stubborn old father is still in the land of the living. Even if we still have no idea when Mum is coming home from America.

Then she hung up her coat and got back to work.

# 17

# The Shy Guys

"**R**uby, I've had a genius idea," Jasmine said the following morning.

"Hit me," Ruby said carefully.

"Wait for this . . . ready-wrapped gifts!"

"Um, come again?"

"Right. We pick a small selection of gifts to keep *unwrapped* on display, like? And we wrap up lots of identical ones . . . so that the men don't have to hang about when they come into the shop," Jasmine trilled. "It'll be a godsend for shy guys everywhere."

"Okay, I'll think about it." Ruby said. She wasn't ruling it out or anything.

"But this is a dead cert, Ruby. You see, one of my brothers told me that he hates shopping for presents for his wife, because they always make him wait so long in the shop. You know with the debit-card verification and then printing the receipt? And then the gift-wrapping and the ribbon curling and everything! Twenty minutes, he said he was in a jeweller's last week. Twenty minutes to buy a pair of pearl earrings!"

"But couldn't he have used cash and then bought a small gift bag in Clinton's card shop?" Ruby wanted to know.

"Ruby, he's a *man*. He's not that organised. That's the first thing I asked him, you silly moo. There was a long queue at the cash machine in any case, he said. And another long queue in Clinton's, as far as he recalls. Anyway, I think we should go with this idea and maybe put a little advert in the window? Business has been slacking off these last few days."

"Business always slacks of at the end of the summer," Ruby told her. "Anyone who can find a caravan to rent or a B&B with vacancies is away to Portstewart or Donegal.

"Yes, but you know it *has* been a little quiet lately," Jasmine persisted.

"Maybe it has," Ruby conceded.

"Come on then, what harm can it do? Just a small notice in the window, huh? I'll do all the wrapping? Please?" Jasmine begged. "We'll even round the prices off to save time at the register."

"Up or down?" Ruby laughed.

"Down?" Jasmine tried. "I'm sure it'll be a great hit."

"Okay then," Ruby agreed. "But don't go completely mad."

"All right," Jasmine said happily, getting out their price list to pick a small selection of suitable gifts. "I'll pick cute things that'll be easy for the shy guys to slip into their pockets. I'll buy some lovely paper and ribbons tomorrow too. No more than twenty pounds' worth, don't worry," she added. "And I'll do a beautiful display in the window, yes?"

"Okay," Ruby said, surprising herself with her readiness to relinquish control over her beloved bay window. "Okay then. Why not?"

"Oh, this is going to be so exciting," Jasmine twittered, excitedly jotting down ideas in a tiny notepad.

Ruby left her to it and stood looking out of the window, thinking of Teresa Morris née Dunne. And her sheer bravery in raising five children all by herself on a small farm in rural Fermanagh . . . Never mind climbing Mount Everest for charity, Ruby thought to herself. Never mind all that *Boy's Own* stuff, though of course it was all well and good in its own way. But when it came right down to it women were the superior sex after all. They had more stamina than men, because it was up to them to look after the children. And there were no days off when you were a mother. Unless of course, you were Ruby's own mother!

And then she thought of Tom Lavery again. And she wondered if she'd seriously fancy him if she'd never met Jonathan.

# 18

# The Phone Call

Another few months flew by. And suddenly it was very late on Christmas Eve. Ruby was curled up in bed, wrapped in her warmest dressing gown and trying to pretend that Christmas wasn't happening. Even though they'd been snowed under with extra holiday business in the shop in recent weeks. In fact, Jasmine's idea for ready-wrapped gifts had been going strong for the last six months. Word had spread round the city like wildfire and now hardly a day went past when they didn't have at least three "shy guys" select a gift from the window display, come in and pay for it and then flee the shop again. Five seconds was the current record, Jasmine was always telling people. Five seconds to hand over thirty quid and take possession of a ready-wrapped trinket-box, glittery scarf or pair of stylish earrings. And of course, all the gifts had been specially selected to be romantic and flattering in nature, and none of them were even remotely dull!

"I am a genius!" Jasmine kept saying. And Ruby kept telling her that she needed to get out more. But Jasmine only said she was going to source some pink striped gift-wrap online so the gifts would match the carrier bags.

However, today was the second anniversary of Jonathan's death and Ruby was all alone in her flat. The heating was turned on full blast and the entire flat was immaculate as usual but there were no glittery decorations in evidence. Just a small basket of white winter flowers that Jasmine had bought Ruby for Christmas. Ruby had set the pretty basket on her dressing table so she could see it from the bed when she woke up on Christmas Day.

Jasmine herself was out on a date that evening with one of the "shy guys" from the shop. He'd come in to buy something nice for his mum's birthday and then taken quite a shine to Jasmine herself. Three times he'd come into the shop and bought a gift before he'd found the courage to ask Jasmine out on a date. Ruby hoped Jasmine's evening was going well. She deserved a nice time after such a disappointing year, romance-wise.

Suddenly the phone rang and Ruby almost dropped her mug of hot chocolate onto the pristine padded counterpane.

"My God," she said aloud. "Living alone is turning me into a nervous wreck. Every time there's the slightest noise I leap six feet into the air." She picked up the phone. "Hello?"

"Ruby dear? It's your mother here."

"Sweet Jesus Christ, Mum? Is that really you? Oh, thank God. Thank God you phoned! Now, just don't say you're fine and then hang up again, right! Where the hell are you staying in New York? Tell me before you hang up this time! And will you keep your phone switched on from now on, please?" Ruby got out of bed and began to pace back and forth across her lovely cream carpet. There was a lump in her throat and she was sure she'd be sobbing in half a minute.

"We'll get to that eventually," came the simple reply.

"You're still in America?"

"Yes, that's right."

"I can't believe you did this to Daddy and me."

"Why can't you believe it?"

"Mum! Look, are you cracking up on us?"

"No, Ruby, I'm not."

"Listen, have you had a breakdown or something?"

"No, I have not indeed! Will you stop being such a dramatist? I told your father why I left Blackskull, Ruby. I was bored stiff. Bored stiff dusting the knick-knacks all day long, and then going for a walk down the drive, and then back up it again. And then making the bloody dinner. Same three or four meals, in rotation, for the last forty years . . . I couldn't go on like that forever, could I?" she said huffily.

"Mum, you've been away for a whole year."

"So what?"

"We've been worried sick, for God's sake! When you first left, I asked Jasmine if I should call the police. And she asked her dad for his advice because he knows a couple of policemen. But they said they couldn't do anything whatsoever because you were an adult. And Dad wouldn't hear of us doing anything official, like asking your doctor for advice. And he refused to let me ask the bank if your account had been used –"

"Quite so. It's a free country, Miss. I'm allowed to go travelling without a chaperone."

"But Mum, you never go anywhere on your own!" Ruby was truly exasperated. "Dad drives you everywhere, you know he does! You know the two of you were always like a pair of bookends. Always together."

"Oh, stop your nonsense, Ruby Nightingale. I mean, Ruby O'Neill. I'm still an individual, my dear. I still have a brain of my own. I remembered I had a second cousin out here as it happens. So I got her address and I wrote to her. And then I got myself a passport. I'd been planning it for years. It was really quite simple, in the end."

"But Dad said that the taxi-driver told him that you'd said you didn't know where you were going!"

"Of course he did. That's what I told him, Ruby. I didn't want the whole country knowing where I was going, did I?"

"Oh Mum!"

"And so this cousin put me up at her place and helped me to find a job."

"A job? So you've got a job now in New York, have you? Are you an illegal immigrant by any chance?"

"Yes, indeed I am. Sure the country is full of them. I'm only selling bread in a bakery in Manhattan but it pays the rent."

"I don't believe this. The rent?"

"Yes, Miss, the rent. I couldn't go on imposing on my cousin. I have a one-room apartment just three blocks away from the bakery. A tiny place, it is. The shower is practically in the kitchen and there's no bath but I've made some great pals in the building.

"I really have –"

"Oh Mum, what are you trying to do to us, at all?" Ruby began to cry silently. Tears trickled down her face and fell heavily onto the carpet.

"Ruby, I always wanted a job of my own. I told your father. But he wouldn't let me work in the village or even in the town. He said the people would all be talking about me behind my back, saying I was only looking for attention. So I moved away for a while, that's all. I needed some space. I needed my space."

"Don't you think you've left it a bit late to have a mid-life crisis?" Ruby wept.

"No crisis about me, dear. I just wanted to do something on my own for a change. I'm not a simpleton, you know."

"But, Mum, you know you could've made some changes to your life without going to another country? And by the way, you had no right to leave Dad on his own all this time. All over Christmas! Not just one Christmas either. But two of them now."

"You see? *I had no right*. That's why I had to get away, Ruby. Because nobody ever listens to me! I *have* got rights. I *have*. I can do whatever I want."

"Okay then, fair enough, I'm sorry for being cross with you.

But you've made your point now, Mum. You've worked as an illegal immigrant in Manhattan, congratulations! I hope you're very proud of yourself."

"Don't be cheeky to your own mother."

"Are you coming home now? Or are you afraid you'll be arrested at the airport for overstaying your holiday visa? I could take legal advice?"

"No, I'm not coming home yet. I'm taking painting lessons and there's still six months of them to go," Ruby's mother said breezily. "We meet up in this big empty warehouse every Sunday morning at eight o'clock, and have breakfast together, and then we paint until the afternoon. The teacher is so good at getting us all involved and chatting away about art and everything. It's really amazing."

Ruby's throat had almost closed over with worry. God love her mother, she thought to herself. God love her and her bizarre little attempt to do something different before it was too late and she ended up tottering around the nursing home on a Zimmer frame.

"Okay, listen to me. I'm not angry with you, Mum. Truly I'm not. But still, there are painting courses in Fermanagh. And there are bakeries in Fermanagh too. You could open your own bakery if you wanted to? And Dad is at home waiting for you. And we both miss you very much."

"Ah, but in Fermanagh I'm only that stuck-up Mrs Nightingale from the big house in Blackskull village. And everybody knows my business there. Everybody knows we got the bit of money from selling your father's land. And they're jealous of me. Here in New York I'm just another face in the crowd. And at the bakery and at the painting classes, I'm just Emily from Ireland."

"Mum, they aren't jealous. They're lovely people in Fermanagh."

"They are jealous. I can see it in their faces when they say hello to me at Mass."

"So is that it, then? You're never coming home to Ireland again because of the way people look at you in Mass?"

"I really don't know," Ruby's mother sighed heavily. "I haven't decided yet. Me and a couple of pals are going to paint my digs this weekend and then we're going to see a show on Broadway. We've been looking forward to it for ages."

*Digs*, Ruby thought to herself. Digs?

"Okay then. You carry on, Mum. But will you let me know your address, please? So I can write to you? Just so I know where you are? Please?"

"I will. I'll send you a postcard as soon as I get the chance," Ruby's mother promised.

"Well, if you're that busy, tell it to me now and I'll write it down," Ruby said, reaching for a pencil and paper from her handbag.

"Oh listen, tell you what, I'll write to you. My credit's nearly up here," Ruby's mother said.

"You're not going to tell me where you're living, are you?" Ruby said bluntly.

There was a small silence.

"No, pet, I'm not. I'm sorry but I don't want your father or yourself landing over here and making a show of me in front of my new pals, that's all. I can do what I like now. I'm an adult, like I said."

Ruby suddenly felt very angry. A burning hot flush came soaring up from her chest and spread right around her neck like an itchy woollen scarf.

"You know what, Mum? You're right! You just go ahead and do whatever the hell you like. It's obvious to me now that you never loved either Dad or me all that much."

"How dare you say a thing like that, Ruby Nightingale . . . I mean, O'Neill . . ."

"It's true, Mum. It must be true. You only married him for his money, didn't you? Because he had land! You never loved him at all?"

"No, I did not marry for money. May God forgive you!"

"Yes, you did marry for money. And then you got Dad to sell the land and buy that big house. And then you made him give up his job in the Council to become your companion and your chauffeur. And then you got bored being a lady of leisure so you dumped your husband and sneaked off to America on this third-rate adventure of yours."

"How dare you speak to your own mother like that! Stop it right now, Ruby Nightingale. I mean –"

"Oh, give over, will you? It's your daughter you're talking to, Mum. Not Dorothy and the rest of them at the art class. Spare me the armchair psychology about finding yourself. You always were a detached sort of person. Always obsessed with your own feelings and emotions. Even when Jonathan died, you didn't come to the funeral. And don't blame the snow either! You could have come when the snow melted."

"I'm very sorry about that, Ruby. I wanted to come but I knew I'd be no use to you with my prayers and my beads and my silly old sayings. I knew you'd see me as more of a hindrance than a help."

"I wouldn't have, Mum. I'd have loved you to come to Belfast. You could have come to see me when the weather eased, a few days later. You could have stayed with me for a few weeks and helped me to get back on my feet. I was in pieces, Mum. Jasmine's mother was here. She was here for the funeral – she was making sandwiches for a whole day. She was here on Christmas Day itself, bringing me something to eat. Where were you, Mum? I missed you so much."

"I told you I was sorry," Ruby's mother said sadly. "I'm no good with people, even with my own family. Everything I do and say is wrong. It was always wrong. I was suffocating in that house. You've no idea what it was like."

"Okay, Mum. This is silly – it's just going round in circles. You say you love me but then you run away when the going gets tough. Families should stick together when things go wrong; that's what makes them a family. Don't you get it?"

"I'd better go now, Ruby. I'm tired."

"Okay. But just before you go let me say this: I'm going to advise Dad to sell up and move to Belfast. He's very lonely all by himself in that big house and honestly sometimes, I think you intend to stay in America forever."

"He'll never leave that house, Ruby. He's a Fermanagh man through and through."

"We'll see about that. I think he's coming to a crossroads in his life. He's not as passive as he once was. It's time he got out-and-about again. He's been a bit depressed too, you know? I think the two of you have been a bit depressed for years? Do you think I'm right, Mum?"

"I don't know."

"Will you please have a think about it, then? Dad needs to know where he stands. You can see that, surely? He needs to make plans."

"Okay. I'll be in touch again soon."

"And we both love you very much, Mum," Ruby said gently. "I hope you know that? No matter what happens in the future. We both love you and we want you to come home. It's not too late for us to be a proper family."

"Okay, pet. Thanks."

"Mum, you will take care of yourself, won't you?" Ruby whispered.

"I will, Ruby. I will. Dorothy's been keeping me out of trouble. She knows New York like the back of her hand."

"Okay. Love you, Mum."

"Love you too."

And then the line went dead. Ruby looked at the phone for a few moments. As if she might somehow be able to understand what'd happened to her mother. To make her run away like that, like a teenager high on angst and rebellion? But all she felt was an empty longing in her heart for the sort of cosy relationship with her mother that Jasmine said she had with *her* mother. Was that why she had clung to Jonathan so much, she wondered, because his love had always been more than enough for her? Because he had always made her feel so utterly loved and so wanted?

Well, it was time to stop this silly hankering after things she couldn't have. Wasn't it? Ruby knew then that her mother was a distant and restless personality and that she always had been. And that her father had become used to it, but also quite depressed over the years. And that Jonathan was really dead and that he was never coming back.

"Time to grow up," she told her basket of white flowers.

Then Ruby called her father to see if he had heard from his runaway wife yet. If he hadn't, she'd at least be able to reassure him that Emily was at least willing to have a good long think about her next move. And she was also going to tell her father that she'd be home for Christmas dinner. She'd be home first thing in the morning. So he'd better tidy himself up and also tidy the house. And the two of them were spending the day together; every blessed minute of it and that was final.

# 19

# Camberwell House

It was getting on towards the end of January. Ruby and her father had spent a lovely Christmas together. Tidying and cleaning the house from top to bottom and then going out to a fancy hotel for lunch and drinks by the fire. And Ruby had gently but firmly forced her dad to admit that *he'd* been the one driven to depression by his wife's restless nature over the years. He'd been depressed for so long he hadn't even noticed himself becoming a virtual recluse, in fact. They'd talked it all out over the holidays. He wouldn't go to the doctor, he said. What would be the point? The doctor wouldn't be able to give him back the last forty years. And anyway he didn't regret getting married because his marriage had given him Ruby.

But he'd promised he would make more of an effort to socialise in future. Join the local church choir for one thing. Take up sailing or fishing maybe? And he'd hire a cleaning lady and a gardener to make sure the chores got done properly. He'd drawn the line at moving to Belfast, however. Saying he was a Fermanagh man *through and through* and that he couldn't live without seeing the loughs every day.

Overall Ruby felt he had turned a corner. He still hadn't heard any detailed plans from Ruby's mother. He still didn't know if his wife was ever coming home to him or not. But somehow he was okay about this.

"I'm used to the silence now," he'd said thoughtfully. "It's a different kind of silence when the house is truly peaceful. And it's not the same as when your mother and myself were not on speaking terms, if you know what I mean? It's a restful silence now. Just me pottering about on my own. And the sun coming in through the windows, and the shadows flickering on the walls. And a nice bit of a roast in the oven for my dinner."

"Yes, Dad," Ruby had said, nodding her head sadly. It didn't sound like much of a life to her but what could she do about it? He sounded happy enough and that was better than nothing. And at least they were chatting at least once a week now on the phone . . . and that was the main thing.

So now Ruby was back to her normal routine in Belfast. Though today the shop was closed and Jasmine was dragging her to Camberwell House in a dubious bid to beat the January blues. They were travelling by taxi as Ruby's car was in the garage for a service.

"And by the way, I'm only going with you on this crazy, so-called Girls' Day Out to prove to you that Tom Lavery is a happily married man who doesn't know I'm alive. And also to prove to you that I am not on the prowl for another husband," Ruby muttered quietly, her hands knotted nervously together. "I must be mad, really, to be doing this."

"Oh, shush, you'll enjoy it, you will surely. And you never know, I might meet a nice guy myself. A lovely, country chap!"

"Jasmine love, it's an old house full of oversized antiques and cracked chamber pots and sagging four-poster beds. How on earth are you going to find a handsome and available man amidst that lot?"

"Well, I haven't managed to find one in the bars and cafés and gyms of Belfast in recent years."

"What about your man? Gary?"

"He was okay but a bit soppy for my liking. Still living with his mother? And him thirty-three years of age! I reckon he's just lining up a substitute cleaner for when his old lady kicks the bucket."

"Oops!"

"Yeah. So I'm casting my net a little wider, that's all. Maybe there's a bit more eye-candy on offer in the countryside? Some undiscovered treasure, hopefully?"

"Maybe."

"And maybe the country boys will be a bit more grateful for a stylish catch like myself? And they might even be a bit fitter in bed? You know, what with all that potato digging and such? Your Tom looks pretty good on it."

"God love you, Jasmine Mulholland. I don't know why you bother sometimes."

"Sure why not? Where there's life there's hope I always say. The shop is closed today and we both have nothing else to do. It'll be a laugh."

"We'll see."

"Anyway it's good that you agreed to come with me at long last. I must say you've changed your tune."

"I haven't changed any sort of tune," Ruby said, feeling puzzled.

"Yes, you have. Has your mother's phone call frightened the wits out of you?"

"What are you talking about?"

"Yes, it has, admit it. You're scared stiff that you might turn into a moaning old banshee like her one of these days, aren't you? Mentalist! Slagging off everything under the sun and driving everybody around her up the walls with misery. And then going off the deep end with her bakery nonsense."

"Jasmine, I know my mother isn't exactly full of the joys of spring. But could you please stop putting her down so much? She can't help it. She was brought up in a different era."

"What do you mean?"

"It was all poverty, and religion, and people being hanged for stealing an apple and flogged for having impure thoughts . . . newspapers for tablecloths . . . She probably can't help being a bit unstable. Her own youth must have been a nightmare."

"Ruby, would you listen to yourself! My parents are ancient as well but they're still pretty cheerful. You said to me about a hundred times last week that you were fed up with your mother and her antics of late."

Ruby closed her eyes. "I know I did," she admitted sadly.

"Look, I'm sorry if I sounded bitchy about your mum. It's just that you can't see it yourself, but your mum depresses the hell out of you."

"She does not."

"She does. Look at your father. Poor bugger is that confused he doesn't know whether he's coming or going."

"Maybe he was depressed but he was with her all the time. Years and years of it! I'm not married to her, am I?"

"She *does* depress you, Ruby. Even from a distance."

"How does she?"

"You're always weird for days after you talk about her, or even think about her. And I know when you're thinking about her because you always bite your top lip. Face it, Ruby, the woman was never really cut out for motherhood. I mean, hardcore, full-time, devoted mothering. Quite a lot of women aren't, you know? It's the last great social taboo: reluctant mothers."

"Well, now you mention it, she never did seem overly delighted to be stuck at home all the time."

"No, she didn't. I gathered that much already. And could you blame her? That's why men have always tried to keep women under their thumbs, I reckon. Ever since humans started walking upright and what have you, because men *know* that we women got the raw end of the deal. And they also know what would happen if women gave up trying to keep the world turning. And just behaved as they do. Well, like most of them do. Boozing and fighting and sleeping around. It would all go to hell in a fucking handcart."

"True. What about wars, though?" Ruby countered absent-mindedly. "Men suffer terribly during wars."

"All wars are voluntary acts of aggression," Jasmine said firmly. "Men have a choice in whether or not they start a war."

"What about conscripts?" Ruby asked.

"Don't spoil a good argument, Ruby. Come on, most of them can't seem to get enough of war, whereas childbirth and housework and PMS are just facts of life. And it all sucks! And your mum has just taken herself off for a while to make a point. I'm not saying she's right! I'm not saying I agree with what she's doing. Actually I don't agree with it . . . But this is her teenage phase obviously, even if it is fifty years too late."

"Oh, whatever," Ruby sighed. "I'm far too tired to think about it any more today."

"Yeah, me too. Let's not overthink the situation, okay? She'll come back when she's good and ready, and by the sounds of it there's no point in trying to give her any advice."

"Yes. I mean, no, there's probably no point."

The two women sat back silently in the black taxi and contemplated Jasmine's wise words. And Ruby had to admit, if only to herself, that Jasmine had made some very valid points. Mrs Emily Nightingale was a bona-fide wet blanket. There was no denying that. She'd never had any time for anything that was remotely modern or fun. Yet she complained all the time about life being dull. She always seemed to spend her days waiting for the angels to come and take her home, as she put it. She'd even told her husband not to let the doctors revive her if she got ill and fell into a coma. Not that they'd notice much of a difference in her personality, Ruby thought sadly. Emily Nightingale had wasted her whole life being torn between wanting attention and also running away from it. Ruby only hoped she was happy there among the marble ryes and the giant pretzels and the pastel cupcakes.

The taxi slowed down and indicated that it was about to turn off the main road. A short, meandering drive through mature trees and shrubbery led them out into a small clearing. They could see the magnificent house just a few yards away.

"We're here!" Jasmine said excitedly. "That was pretty quick. It's only about ten minutes away from the city really, say there isn't any traffic. Fancy that! And we're just in time for the last guided tour of the afternoon."

"Come on then," said Ruby quickly, clambering out of the taxi and adjusting her long woollen jacket. This time she was wearing her comfort-zone outfit of high-waist flares, a round-neck T-shirt and a long, embroidered jacket made of the softest wool. All in regulation caramel! And flat suede pumps to match. And a large handbag containing a telescope umbrella, a notebook and pen, a packet of headache tablets, a packet of tissues, two mobile phones just in case one broke down, a pair of gloves, fruit-flavoured sweets for any possible sugar-dips and a small framed photograph of Jonathan.

"You know, I'm actually looking forward to this," Jasmine said brightly.

"Are you really?" Ruby asked, mystified. "I find that hard to believe."

"Sure I am. Think about it! Because after this tour of dreary old spiders' webs, mothballs and dead flies I'll be even *more* in love with my gorgeous apartment. The minute I get home I'll switch on my coffee machine and the central heating and I'll take a power-shower under the recessed spotlights. Ah, bliss . . ."

Ruby rolled her eyes and smiled and the despondent mood was broken. Then the two friends went traipsing carefully across the neatly raked gravel and up to the main door to join the other "gawpers".

As it transpired, the tour was fascinating. All sorts of important historical figures had graced the four-posters and indeed the chamber pots of Camberwell. There were locks of hair from long-dead kings, carefully labelled in a large glass case in the main hall. And not a speck of dust or a dangling cobweb to be seen anywhere. Ruby and Jasmine had a lovely meal of beef stew followed by cream cakes in the pretty café behind the house and after that it was off to the gardens for a wander about. It was a bit cold but there was still plenty to see. The huge box-hedge maze, of course, was the main attraction. There was no sign of Tom Lavery, unfortunately. Jasmine looked for him everywhere but Tom didn't oblige them! When they got to the maze, however, Ruby wasn't quite sure she wanted to venture into the massive, dark-green structure.

"What if we get lost?" she asked dubiously. "There's only an hour or so until closing time."

"It says here we just take a free whistle from this dish and then use it to summon help if we get lost," Jasmine said brightly. "How exciting! To be rescued from a real-life maze by a hunky gardener-type. It's like something from a Jane Austen novel!"

"Oh God, Jasmine, do you ever relax?"

"No. Hey, let's take a whistle each in case we split up. And it says there's a love seat in the centre. We'll take a photo of each other on the love seat, shall we? Come on, look lively."

"I'll give you love-seats," Ruby muttered grumpily.

"Let's go!"

And with that, Jasmine went tearing into the tall and perfectly clipped though rather dark and mysterious maze, with Ruby tripping after her. And clutching a shiny, shrink-wrapped tin whistle she prayed she'd never have to use.

Forty wondrous minutes later, Ruby and Jasmine sat posing awkwardly on the willow bench as a German tourist kindly took a snap of them with Jasmine's tiny camera.

"Isn't it gorgeous?" Jasmine sighed after the tourist had said goodbye and left them alone there. "Don't you wish we could go back in time to an age where nobody used swear words? And where people didn't treat other people like dirt?"

"I think a large percentage of people have always treated others like dirt," Ruby pointed out. "It's just that most people didn't live long enough to get upset about it. They were too busy dying in childbirth or some ridiculously stupid battle instead. Anyway, you enjoy swearing."

"Well, at least they had nicer clothes back then," Jasmine persisted. "No baggy leggings and sweaty tracksuits. Women could hide their big bums under those lovely, billowing ballgowns."

"They did have leggings, Jasmine. Or at least the men did. And I'm sure they were pretty baggy as well. Not many tracksuits though. Definitely not, I'll give you that. Come on, Jasmine, let's go home. I think I remember the way out. It's two left turns and then three right turns and then a left again. And then five right turns . . . If we're really quick we might just get a look round the souvenir shop before closing time. I saw some very stylish white mugs in the window."

"Right. I'm just going to make a wish first. Shush!" Jasmine said.

"You can't make a wish here. There's no wishing well."

"I'm making one anyway."

"It won't work if there's no wishing well," Ruby muttered.

"Nothing ventured, nothing gained. Now will you please shush?"

Ruby checked her watch again as Jasmine made a wish.

"Little amuses the innocent," Ruby added.

"Would that be the sort of thing your mother used to say?" Jasmine asked, winking crookedly.

It was indeed. Ruby instantly changed the subject.

"Come on, you, let's go home," she sighed.

However, when they were trying to find their way out again the two friends got hopelessly lost. They tried to establish their bearings and aim for the general direction of the main house but it was no use. Back and forth they went until they ended up at the willow bench for a fourth time. It began to rain gently and then the clouds rolled in and the raindrops got fatter and heavier. The maze seemed to have been miraculously emptied of people for they met no other living soul as they went rushing this way and that. Desperately trying to remember if they'd passed a particular statue or stone bench. Then the heavens opened and Ruby's light umbrella was useless against the torrential deluge. Soon they were both drenched and Ruby's lovely suede shoes were ruined. After a full hour of frantic walking and two ominous cracks of thunder overhead, Jasmine decided it was time to summon help.

"I reckon these statues are designed to confuse us," Jasmine said wearily. "I bet there's two or three of each one. Okay, here goes."

"I feel really silly now," Ruby complained as Jasmine took a deep breath and blew into her whistle with all her might.

"It's exhilarating making this much noise," Jasmine laughed giddily, having another go. "If we don't get out of here soon we'll catch our deaths. Come on, blow!"

"I'll give it a miss," Ruby said firmly. "You're making enough commotion for the two of us."

Five minutes later they heard a man's footsteps just around the corner and suddenly Tom Lavery was standing before them. His hair was very wet and he was very annoyed-looking. There was an angry red flush creeping up from under his shirt collar.

"Oh, it's you," Tom said, recognising Ruby and Jasmine

despite the fact that their hair was hanging in soaking wet tendrils around their faces.

"Yes, we're so sorry about this," Ruby replied apologetically, almost dying of embarrassment. She was sure her very underwear must be visible beneath her drenched clothing.

"Never mind. You'd better come with me. I've a shed nearby," Tom said, beckoning to them to follow him. "It isn't much to look at but it's warm and dry. The house and shops are closed now and everyone's gone home. The car park's empty. I had no idea there was anyone still around."

"We came by taxi," Jasmine explained. "Ruby's car is having a service."

"Oh, right. Well, I'm sorry you got stuck in here. Someone was supposed to have checked the maze was empty before they closed the gate. But lucky for you I often stay late to finish up any odd jobs that need doing."

"Lucky for us indeed," Jasmine said, her teeth chattering loudly.

"Come on. Like I said, it's warm and dry in the shed and you can have a cup of tea. I, um, I'll drive you back to the city. To make up for the soaking you've had."

He turned on his heel to lead the way.

"Wow, Ruby, who said wishes don't come true?" Jasmine murmured under her breath as Ruby blushed all the way down to her squelching suede pumps.

"Don't you dare start matchmaking, that's all," Ruby whispered as they set off with Tom a couple of strides ahead of them in his olive-green Wellington boots. "I'm not in the mood for any of your Cupid-stuff right now. Plus, I'm soaked to the skin. We'll probably get pneumonia out of this."

"Let's hope your man there has a bit of fire in his grate then," Jasmine giggled furiously, delighted at the thought of a lift home with Ruby's sexy admirer.

The thunder crackled again and the rain stopped coming down in fat drops and started coming down in great grey sheets instead. In no time the three of them were sprinting through the kitchen garden to Tom's dark-green hideaway. Great rivulets of water were coursing along the brick-edged pathways and slapping over the women's ankles. But when Tom flung the shed door open, Ruby and Jasmine were both relieved to find it all very nice and cosy with a gas-heater glowing in one corner. A table and an armchair took up one side and gardening tools were everywhere, hanging from nails in the walls or stacked neatly in willow hampers. A sleepy black dog was curled up in a basket.

"That's Noah. He won't touch you, don't worry," Tom said quietly as the animal opened its eyes. "Steady, Noah."

"Fantastic little spot you've got here," Jasmine shivered, tip-toeing gently across to the heater and warming her hands before its flickering blue and orange flames. "What a lovely dog . . . Thanks very much . . . Jesus, I thought I was going to die of exposure out there."

"Thank you very much, Mr Lavery," Ruby added politely. "I'm so glad you were nearby. We just couldn't remember the way out. No sense of direction . . ."

"It's okay. There's a handy way of telling the way out but it's a closely guarded secret. Oh, and call me Tom, please."

"And this is Jasmine and I'm Ruby," she reminded him.

"Yes," he said quietly. "I know."

Both Ruby and Tom felt their faces growing red with embarrassment. And maybe excitement . . . Ruby went across and stood beside Jasmine, concentrating on the dancing flames in the stove. Right then, she'd have given any money to have a handy car parked close by. Then they wouldn't have to sit in the Land Rover with Tom later on. She wondered if he would think her rude if she insisted on calling for another taxi. For a few moments there was no sound except for the hammering of the rain on the roof of the shed.

"Now would anybody like a sip of tea?" Tom said stiffly. "I have a packet of paper cups around here somewhere. And a fresh flask of tea."

"Oh thanks, that'd be lovely," Jasmine said, shivering a little bit less. "Do you often invite strange women into your shed for light refreshments? Won't your wife be suspicious?"

"Jasmine, for God's sake, would you stop it," Ruby whispered.

"I'm a widower," Tom said at once. "My wife Kate died just under five years ago. And I never invite anybody back here for light refreshments, as it happens. But this is an emergency, isn't it?"

There was a slight look of hurt in his eyes. Ruby could see that. He wasn't amused that Jasmine had more or less accused him of being a flirt. And really it would be hard to imagine any man being less of a flirt than Tom Lavery. Clearly he was a gentleman of the highest order and Ruby felt herself warming to him enormously. She began to wonder what he looked like out of those shabby clothes, in fact!

"I'd love a sip of hot tea," she said graciously as two flashes of blue lightning lit up the shed and glinted off the bright metal shovels and spades in one corner.

Wordlessly he found the paper cups and poured tea into three of them. Jasmine relaxed into the armchair, leaving Ruby and Tom to stand awkwardly together by the window looking out at the rain battering down the winter plants and shrubs. Ruby didn't dare catch Jasmine's eye as the three of them waited for the worst of the storm to blow over. She knew that if she did, Jasmine would give her a knowing great wink. And if she saw that now, on top of her relief at being rescued from the maze, and her escalating attraction towards Tom Lavery, she might just break down and laugh or cry uncontrollably.

# 20

## The Anniversary

Tom sat down heavily on the beach at Murlough Strand and stared blankly out to sea. The air was bitingly cold and his ears were numb but he barely noticed any minor physical discomfort these days. He was bone tired and quite hungry and he hadn't slept properly in three days. Tom sighed, inhaled deeply and then exhaled all the way down to his worn leather boots.

"Five years, Noah. Five years today! Do you even remember Kate, huh? You were only a puppy when she died."

Noah looked up eagerly at Tom's face and then out to sea and then back at Tom. The dog wanted to go for a breathless run along the beach but he'd been at Murlough enough times already to know that he had to wait a while first. Until his master had been quiet and sad and silent for a few minutes. And then they'd walk and run for miles along the beach and he'd fetch sticks from the water, and then they'd go home for something nice to eat.

"You know, sometimes, I wonder what's the point of anything," Tom said to Noah now, rubbing the top of the dog's head affectionately. "I mean, the house and the grounds look far better nowadays than anyone living at Camberwell in the early days could have imagined. But when you think about it, it's still just a shrine to the dead. With lots of day-trippers eating Irish stew and buying souvenir mugs. We must be mad, the few of us that are left, to keep on working so hard for the pittance they pay us. Who really cares about Camberwell, huh? About the old retainers? Who really cares about any of it? Not the current owners, that's for sure."

And then he thought of Ruby and he wondered if he'd mistaken her expression that day in the storm for something approaching affection for him. Had she looked at him shyly over the rim of her paper cup because she fancied him a little bit? Or was he finally losing the plot with sheer loneliness? He twisted his gold wedding ring round and round on his finger. The cold had made his skin contract and the ring felt slightly loose on his wedding finger.

"What's the point?" he said again. "I can't get over Kate and I can't ask Ruby out!"

And then without realising he was going to do it, he slid the ring off his finger and threw it into the sea with as much force as he could muster. He almost dislocated his shoulder he put that much effort into it. The ring sparkled in the sunlight for a split-second and then vanished beneath the waves with the tiniest of small, sad splashes.

"There you are! Have that as well," he shouted at the crashing breakers. "That's where Kate's ashes are," he told his startled dog. "That's where my heart is, where my life is, at the bottom of the ocean. The sea might as well have the ring too and be done with it."

Noah went racing towards the waves to retrieve whatever it was that Tom had thrown. But Tom caught up with the animal and guided him along the beach instead.

"No, you don't," he said gently. "It's far too cold for you to go swimming today. Come on, boy."

Soon the two of them were running fast along the hard sand at the water's edge, breathing hard. Running towards what, Tom wondered. He wanted to cry but he had no tears left. He felt empty and lost inside. Empty and for the first time ever, he also felt frightened that he wouldn't be able to cope for much longer with so much emptiness in his heart.

However, at that exact moment, just as Tom and Noah were beginning to warm up from their jog along the beach, the postman was delivering a thank-you card to Tom's little cottage. The card was from Ruby and Jasmine to say thanks again for rescuing them from the maze. Jasmine had sent it, of course. Ruby knew nothing about it. And Jasmine had also added a short note at the bottom asking Tom to drop by the shop sometime soon and advise them on what flowers they might plant in the window-boxes for the summer. Ruby would have been furious if she'd known. But Jasmine had decided that Ruby O'Neill was simply too slow in seizing the initiative. So she'd taken it upon herself to make the first move. For as Jasmine always said, where there's life there's hope.

# 21

## The Fifth Secret

It was May and the cold fingers of winter were finally loosening their grip on the small city of Belfast. Pure white snowdrops and cheery yellow daffodils had brightened up the municipal green spaces and everyone seemed happy to be casting off their hats and gloves for the first time in six months. Business at Ruby's shop had settled down into a manageable and satisfactory routine. Her closest neighbours would often wave in at her as they went by and Ruby would wave back, smile and be glad she had bought the shop before the notion went by her. She was almost feeling normal again, she thought to herself. Perhaps not content exactly, but at least she wasn't on the floor with despair any more.

But one day Ruby was incredibly startled when she heard the doorbell chime and looked up from the counter to see Tom Lavery standing outside with his arms full of flowers. Three slate-grey window boxes that were already planted up with pretty pink and white summer flowers and lots of pale-green trailing ivy! She noticed that he'd combed his hair and put on a new-ish jacket though his old weather-beaten boots were still present and correct.

She also noticed that Tom was doing his best to smile though his face seemed to be twitching with the effort of it.

Ruby darted a glance at Jasmine and was horrified to see the mischievous look on her friend's face. "Jasmine, what the heck have you done now?" she hissed as she turned away from the window so that Tom would not see her panicking.

"Just a wee thank-you note for the lift home that Tom gave us that day," Jasmine said quickly. "You remember, when we got caught in the storm at Camberwell? I forgot to tell you I sent a thank-you note, sorry."

"Jasmine, I am going to *kill* you when he leaves," Ruby squeaked as she pressed the buzzer and let Tom in.

"Um, hi," Tom began. "I was just in the area today so I thought I'd drop these flowers off to you . . ."

"Do you mean these *lovely* flowers are for us? How very kind of you," Ruby said, helping Tom to set them down on the floor. "How much do I owe you, Tom?"

"Oh, nothing at all," Tom said breezily, waving away any notion of payment with a wide sweep of his large, square hands.

"But this is just too much, it's far too generous of you. Really, I insist on paying you for your trouble," Ruby protested, feeling as if she were some rich old relic from the eighteenth century, dangling a silk purse full of gold sovereigns before the hired help. Why on earth was she cursed with such blessed politeness!

"No, it's okay. It's just some plants and ivy I had sitting about in the greenhouse," Tom said, smiling. "They were only going to waste, honestly."

"But the window boxes? They're so gorgeous," Ruby said, taking in the raised patterns on the pewter containers. "You can't just give these away!"

"Yes, it's okay," Tom said, shrugging his shoulders.

His very broad and manly shoulders, Ruby couldn't help noticing.

"Anyway, um, that's that done so I'll be seeing you," Tom said, sensing Ruby's unease.

"Wait a minute! Don't rush off, Tom," Jasmine said loudly. "You can't just rush off after bringing those lovely flowers to us. Stay and have a cup of tea, yeah?"

Then she vanished into the kitchenette leaving Ruby and Tom standing together in the middle of the shop.

"Look, I won't stop for the tea," he said, blushing all the way down to his worn leather boots.

"Yes indeed, you will bother," Jasmine said, coming out of the kitchenette again and ushering Tom towards the fancy armchair. "The kettle's boiling now. It'd be rude to refuse."

"I couldn't sit there. I might get dust on that lovely chair," Tom began, looking worried. "These are my old digging trousers. Sure, you might have customers coming in the door any minute as well." He gazed longingly at the pavement outside. This meeting was a lot harder than he'd thought it would be.

"I know! Why don't you bring Tom upstairs for a proper chat?" Jasmine said, winking slyly at Ruby.

"Oh, there's no need for that," Tom began.

"Jasmine, I'm sure Tom has better things to do than sip tea with me," Ruby added.

"Not at all! Away with you now and let me mind the shop in peace," Jasmine said loudly, literally shoving Ruby out the door and onto the pavement and then Tom after her, and then handing out Ruby's handbag from behind the counter. "That's it," she smiled, shutting the shop door firmly so Ruby couldn't get back in without making a scene. Turning away from Ruby's livid face Jasmine scurried into the kitchenette and prayed that Ruby would be too embarrassed to start rattling the door handle. And so she was.

Turning almost cerise with mortification, Ruby found her keys in her bag, unlocked the door to her flat and pointed her visitor towards the stairs. And Tom, also weak with embarrassment, went bounding swiftly up them and into the small entrance hall.

"What a lovely place," he said gently, when confronted with Ruby's tastefully decorated flat. All cream rugs and white furniture and textured cushions and pretty table lamps with ribbon-shades. "And what's that cooking? Smells delicious," he added.

"Oh, that's just a plain old casserole I put in the slow cooker this morning," Ruby said, delighted at least that she had something to do now. She could offer Tom some lunch in return for the expensive-looking window boxes he'd brought. Anything would be better than standing here looking at one another shyly after the complete fool she had made of herself downstairs. "Would you like a small bite of lunch?" she added hopefully.

"Well, I would, yes, if it's no trouble," Tom said, smiling again and the ice was broken at last.

"No trouble whatsoever," Ruby said breathlessly, dropping her bag onto the hall table and going to wash her hands at the kitchen sink. "I often use the slow cooker nowadays as it's such a bore cooking for one. Somehow it's easier to prepare food in the morning than at supper time."

"Yes, I know what you mean. If it wasn't for the hot meals I get at work I'd probably be living on tea and sandwiches myself."

"I went through a little phase of that when I lost my husband," Ruby said carefully. She didn't often talk about Jonathan any more in case she broke down and wept in front of anyone. "Maybe you read about it in the paper?"

"Yes, I did. I'm very sorry."

"Thanks . . . I existed on takeaway food and toast for about six months afterwards. Which is silly, of course, because then you get run down, and you end up feeling more depressed than ever. But Jasmine bullied me into shopping for groceries again and looking after myself. She can be a little minx sometimes but she's also been a great friend. A terrific friend actually."

"Yes, she seems great," Tom said, wondering whether he should be grateful for Jasmine and her meddling, or not.

"Did you have much family support when your wife . . . Kate . . . passed away?" Ruby asked tentatively.

Tom blanched visibly but Ruby knew that to say nothing at all about Kate would be much worse than bringing her up now.

"Um, not really, I suppose. It was breast cancer she had."

"Was it? Oh dear. I'm so sorry, Tom."

"Thanks. Yes, Kate's own family was too grief-stricken to comfort me all that much at the time, or after. We sort of retreated from each other a bit. It was just too difficult, to be fair to them. I reminded them of Kate, and they reminded me of her . . . It's easier all round if we keep things at a distance. Of course, I ring her parents at Christmas-time but that's about it. Kate had four brothers but they all live in Canada now. We don't keep in touch."

"Yes, that can happen sometimes." Ruby served the casserole, thinking of her own parents. "A death in the family affects people in different ways."

"Yeah . . . I've no siblings myself. My parents live in India. They work for a charity there."

"Really? How amazing."

"Um, yeah," Tom sighed.

Ruby thought he must miss them a lot.

Tom rinsed his hands under the kitchen tap and sat down carefully at the small bistro table. Ruby noticed that his long legs could barely fit underneath it and that his arms were huge and rippling with muscles. She tried very hard not to fancy him as she poured boiling water into the teapot and added bread, butter, cutlery and cups to the plates of casserole on the table.

"Salt and pepper?" she asked. "Sugar for your tea?"

"I'm okay, thanks," he said, blushing again. She suddenly felt an urge to kiss him very hard on the lips. But of course, she didn't.

Ruby wondered if she ought to switch the radio on to fill up any awkward silences. But then again she didn't want to spoil the atmosphere with some gruffly spoken Belfast DJ complaining about the traffic congestion or the outrage of having only a fortnightly bin collection. She decided to leave the radio off and risk their lunch descending into silence. Tom lifted his fork and began to eat. Ruby looked away, not wanting him to feel nervous, but soon they were almost feeling relaxed, just sipping tea and enjoying each other's company. A robin redbreast landed on the windowsill and peered in at them with its head to one side.

"Oh look, a robin," Ruby said. "I think that one's following me. I keep seeing a robin and I think it's the same one. He always has his head to one side like that, as if he's thinking about me. Or maybe I'm just going a bit daft in my old age."

"Lovely little birds," Tom agreed. "We have one at Camberwell too. Fat wee thing with long legs. Always perched on the handle of my spade, waiting for crumbs."

"Yes?"

"I know it's silly but I'd miss him if he wasn't there at least once a day. But you look forward to the smallest things when you've lost someone special."

"I know."

"It's just so hard to talk to other people about ordinary things. Because you know they're trying not to say the wrong thing back to you. And you're trying so hard not to be a drain on their kindness. It's tiring for me, to be honest. I'd rather dig over an entire field than try to socialise normally any more."

"Oh, I know what you mean," Ruby said, nodding. "I don't go out much myself but I have to keep telling Jasmine that it's okay for her to go out. And then tell me about her dating exploits and so on. That I won't break down with jealousy if she meets a nice guy some day."

"Yes, I understand."

"I don't want the whole world to tip-toe around me forever," Ruby sighed.

"Yes. Me neither."

"But I'm not quite ready to put on my dancing shoes . . ."

"Me neither . . ." said Tom.

"No."

"Though if you were ever at a loose end any time . . . it'd be nice to go for a walk maybe . . . and have a chat or whatever? Just if you found yourself with time on your hands and all your other friends were busy?"

"Well, of course, yes. Thank you, Tom. I did have lots of friends, casual friends as well as very dear friends, but they've kind of dropped away these last two and a half years," Ruby said slowly, to avoid having to give Tom a direct answer to his invitation. "I think they're afraid to come near me in case the Grim Reaper lets go of my hand and follows them home instead."

"Tell me about it," Tom said and he laughed out loud with empathy. "You can almost see them thinking about death whenever you enter the room. Like it's catching! It's not like I enjoy being bereaved or that I'm proud of it in some way. It's not my fault that Kate died. She had no real symptoms until it had spread and then it was too late. It just happened, you know? Cancer happens to lots of people and there's no point in denying it exists." But Ruby could tell he was still putting a brave face on his grief.

"Believe me, I understand," she said gently. "I used to think it was my fault that Jonathan died because I wanted him to hurry home so we could decorate the Christmas tree together. And he would've known that, do you see? He would've known I was watching the clock that night. And maybe he was driving too fast on my account?"

Tom nodded to show he understood.

"But in my heart I know there's no one to blame when these things happen," she went on. "It wasn't his fault either . . . he was hit by another vehicle. So I can't blame Jonathan and I can't blame myself. Of course, I can blame the other driver but where would that get me? It wouldn't bring Jonathan back. It's just life. And life isn't always fair."

"Yes. I mean no, it isn't fair," Tom agreed sadly.

"So anyway, is your meal okay?"

"It's lovely, thanks."

"And yes, it'd be nice to go for a walk sometime," Ruby said after a minute.

"Really?" Tom asked, slightly shaken with relief.

"Yes, surely. I'll give you my business card and we'll keep in touch. Okay?" Ruby said, slipping him one from her handbag.

"Okay. I'll give you Camberwell's card too. You can leave me a message at the main house if you like."

"You don't have a phone where you live?" Ruby asked, puzzled.

"No. I never bothered getting one installed when I moved into the cottage. I don't have a mobile phone either. I had one years ago but then I dropped it and it broke and I didn't bother getting a new one. Though I must get one soon. It's silly of me to have left it for so long. I hate mobiles anyway, they're so fiddly to use when you've got big hands."

"Yes, they must be," Ruby smiled.

"Nobody phones me anyway except Mrs Kenny to ask me for a lift to work sometimes. If the weather's really rotten."

"I see."

They finished their meal and then Ruby walked her guest back down the stairs again and onto the street.

"Thank you very much," he said simply. "I enjoyed that."

"So did I," Ruby said.

He gave her one of Camberwell's business cards from his jacket pocket. It was a little bit creased round the edges.

Ruby laughed suddenly. "You need a fancy wallet to keep those in," she said.

"Do I?" Tom looked confused.

"No. I'm only joking," she assured him.

"Oh. Okay then, bye," Tom said, turning to go.

"Bye," Ruby said gently.

They gazed at each other for a moment and then Tom set off down the street, taking long strides with his long legs. Ruby watched him go for a few minutes and then she turned her head towards the shop window.

Jasmine was practically kneeling in the bay window, spying on them with her eyes like saucers. Ruby pursed her lips together and narrowed her eyes in mock rage and poor Jasmine sprang from the window and fled into the kitchenette to hide.

"It's okay, Jasmine. I'm not going to kill you," Ruby said when she returned to the shop twenty minutes later. "Not today anyway."

"Thank God for that. I nearly died myself when he turned up with those window boxes. So what was he like then? Was he sexy? Did you fancy him? Did he fancy you? Well, obviously he did! Did you kiss him? Probably not, knowing you! Are you seeing him again? When? Where?" Jasmine was delighted her plan was going so well.

"We swapped numbers," Ruby admitted. "But I don't know if he'll ever call me."

"He'll call," Jasmine said knowingly.

"We'll see."

"C'mere," Jasmine said then. "If we just set these fancy boxes on the windowsills they'll be nicked for sure. I'll phone my dad. He'll come right over and do something useful with his screwdriver."

And then for some reason Ruby and Jasmine collapsed into helpless giggles.

"Are you happy, Ruby?" Jasmine asked, a short while later.

"Yes, I suppose I am," Ruby replied. "Or at least I'm getting there."

"Well then, that's the fifth secret of happiness," Jasmine declared triumphantly.

"What is?" Ruby asked.

"Good deeds. You must do as many good deeds as you can," Jasmine answered. "I've been plotting to set the two of you up on a date for ages. And then I thought about the good deed that Tom did when he drove us home that day in the storm. And so I thought I'd send him a thank-you card just to see what his reaction would be. And I mentioned the flowers, just to give him an excuse to get in touch. I was hoping he'd come by for a visit. And he did."

"Yes, he did," Ruby agreed. "But the next time you feel like doing me a good deed promise me you'll have the decency to let me know well in advance. Oh and by the way, I want you to have the pink handbag as a reward for being such an unholy meddler in my personal affairs. Okay?"

Jasmine just nodded her thanks as Ruby handed her the pink velvet evening bag from her collection. For once in her life Jasmine wasn't able to have the last word.

# 22

## The Date

As it happened, Ruby didn't have long to wait for Tom's phone call. For later that evening she was just about to step into an almond-scented bubble bath when the phone began to ring.

"Now who's that?" she said yawning widely, never imagining it would be Tom Lavery himself.

"Hello? Is that Ruby?" he said in an anxious voice. "It's Tom here. Tom Lavery."

"Oh. Hi, Tom," she replied. An adrenaline surge started up somewhere near her stomach.

"I know this is probably too soon but would you like to go out for dinner next week? With me?"

"Um, next week?" Ruby said, playing for time.

"Yes. Or anytime you like? Whatever suits. Or just a walk round the Botanic Gardens or something?"

What to do? Ruby bit her lip with indecision. But then she remembered the fun she and Jasmine had, betting each other that Tom would or wouldn't phone back. She hadn't laughed so much in ages. And so she forced herself to accept Tom's invitation.

"Yes, thanks," she said as casually as she could. "That would be lovely."

So now here they were, facing each other over a very small table, in a near-empty restaurant, near the Botanic Gardens in the heart of Belfast. Tom had suggested this restaurant because he knew he could see the trees from the main window and in some strange way he felt this would make him less nervous. In a way Ruby was glad the place was almost deserted. She felt as if she were somehow cheating on Jonathan and the last thing she wanted to do was to bump into someone they both knew. Even though she knew in her heart that this was a silly thought.

"You look lovely," Tom said over his menu as they both pretended to give the dishes on offer some serious thought.

"Thank you very much," Ruby said quietly. "You don't look too bad yourself."

Tom had had a haircut and had bought himself a new jacket and shoes. He hoped Ruby wouldn't think he was trying too hard. But Ruby had also spent days deciding what to wear. And in the end she'd chosen a 1950s-style red frock and shoes complete with red lipstick and a cute pillbox handbag.

"Thanks. But really you do look lovely."

"I've probably gone way overboard," she laughed then. "But I always overdo it when I'm nervous."

"I didn't mean to make you nervous," he said at once.

"No, no, not in that sense. It's not you personally that's making me nervous," she added hastily. "It's just that I haven't been out for dinner like this with anyone else but Jonathan."

"Oh, okay."

"We met as students, do you see? So before that I only ever went to the cinema or the pub with my dates." Ruby then blushed slightly and decided she'd have the soup and then the chicken. And a bottle of house white! Probably the quickest items on the menu, she reckoned. If this meal turned out to be excruciatingly embarrassing at least it'd all be over in an hour or so.

"I'll have the same," Tom said to the waitress a minute later and Ruby was glad he wasn't a fussy eater.

"Anyway this is nice," Ruby told him cheerfully. "I haven't been out anywhere new in ages. Not at all! Not since, well, since . . . You know what I mean. It feels funny. Funny and strange."

"Yes, it does. This is my first meal out in five years."

"No? Really?"

"Yes. The time has just flown. I never intended letting five years pass me by. But somehow it has. I guess I just never felt ready to return to normality."

"I feel like that sometimes," she said, smiling sadly. "Will we ever be normal again?"

"Ruby, listen, I really like you."

"That's okay, Tom, I like you too. Let's just talk about other things for a while and see how it goes?"

"Okay."

And so they chatted amicably through the two courses and then ordered coffee. Ruby learnt that Tom had once played rugby for his county and also that he knew how to sail. He wasn't from a wealthy family himself but he'd gone to a good grammar school and had made some well-off friends there. They'd taught him how to sail and also encouraged his interest in professional gardening. Kate on the other hand had been from a very rich family. Her family owned a string of department stores in England. She'd left Tom a lot of money in her will but he'd given it all to a cancer-research charity within a month of her funeral.

"You must think I'm quite shallow by comparison," Ruby said shyly. "I spent all my money on a silly dress shop, after all."

"Not at all, Ruby. I think you've been very brave and sensible. Sometimes I think I should've kept a bit of that money and taken early retirement. I work far too hard for what they pay me at Camberwell."

"Maybe that was exactly why you did give it away, Tom? So you'd be forced to go on working and doing something useful? Keeping yourself busy, you know?"

"Yes, probably," Tom nodded.

Ruby gazed into his dark brown eyes and felt something turn over in her heart. Tom Lavery was very handsome in his own way. If you liked your men weather-beaten and muscular and chronically depressed, that is. She wondered briefly if he'd ever be fun again and if he'd ever laugh out loud again. Really laugh? And if she would?

"Let's go for a walk?" she suggested and Tom swiftly paid the bill and helped her on with her jacket.

Outside the air was full of the clean scents of freshly cut grass and spring flowers coming into bloom. They went in through the massive green wrought-iron gates of the park. Rhododendron bushes lined the paths and Ruby could smell hothouse hyacinths. It was almost dark but Ruby felt safe walking along beside Tom. Surely those massive shoulders of his would scare off the most determined mugger?

"Thanks for dinner, Tom," she said softly and he almost jumped, the way she said his name. Almost tenderly, as if they were lovers already or something. Ruby felt a tiny bit embarrassed but she let it go. Tom was his name, after all. They were walking together, weren't they? They were both consenting adults. They were two lonely people struggling to find the right things to say to one another. They were alive and well, even though most of the time it felt as if they were only watching the world on a television screen.

"Tom, listen, would it be okay if we held hands?" she said suddenly, her heart pounding with nerves. It must have been the wine making her so bold, she thought to herself. But surely he wouldn't be too surprised? He *had* said he liked her . . .

"Sure we can."

Tom looked down at Ruby's hands and she looked at his.

"I'd love to hold hands with a man again – it's been such a long time. Two and a half years . . . And I always loved holding hands with Jonathan. It's silly but it's one of the things I missed most about him. I hope you don't think I'm quite mad?"

Tom stopped walking, took both of Ruby's hands reverently in his and then, ever so slowly, he bent forward and kissed her softly on the cheek. The softest kiss imaginable, like a butterfly's wing brushing against her skin. Immediately Ruby felt a bolt of electricity shoot through her entire body, and she had to try really hard not to let him see how attracted to him she was. She felt a bit reckless, if she was honest with herself. She felt like making love to Tom right then and there. Jonathan had never made her feel quite this reckless. He'd been a much better-looking man than Tom and he'd been much more charming and confident in himself, but Ruby hadn't ever felt like tearing his clothes off in a public place and committing an act of gross indecency. She had a fleeting image of Tom and herself together, tumbling about in the shrubbery, covered with rhododendron petals.

"Was that all right?" Tom asked, bringing her out of her reverie.

"Yes, thanks. It was very nice," she told him, perspiring with equal amounts of emotion and desire.

"Can I kiss you properly?" Tom asked. "Sometime?"

"Yes, sometime," Ruby agreed, walking onwards then and feeling a new and wonderful sensation in her heart. Something new and fresh like a bird singing. Tom kept hold of one hand. They blushed a little as they walked.

No, she told herself. I will not think about tomorrow or the next day or the day after that. I've been doing that all my life and where has it got me? Just live in the moment, Ruby. For once in your life, just live in the moment.

They did three further laps of the park, pointing out flowers and plants they recognised. Stopping here and there to admire an early rose or some unusual exotic bloom. At no point did they stop holding hands. Then they left the park and Tom drove her home and said he would call her the following day.

"Yes, that would be nice," she smiled.

"You're sure?" he said.

"Yes," she nodded firmly.

"Okay then. I'll call you tomorrow evening. Bye, Ruby."

"Bye Tom," she said.

He drove off, waving through the rear window.

It was a chilly now. Ruby inhaled deeply, savouring the familiar smells of old Belfast. Ancient brick dust, the nose-tingling scent of hyacinths, the omnipresent traffic fumes and the aroma of freshly poured lager and stout. She was almost afraid to step out of her bereavement bubble and go forward into the unknown. But she knew she had no other alternative. Tom had promised to call her the next day. And this time, Ruby had no doubt that he'd keep his promise. Smiling and hugging this new feeling of optimism to herself, Ruby unlocked the door to her little flat and traipsed happily up the stairs.

# 23

# The Sixth Secret

That evening, Ruby took a long hot shower, got her photograph albums out and went to bed early. She looked at dozens of pictures of her late husband, marvelling again at how handsome he was. Those cheekbones, those lovely soft eyelashes of his . . . Was she being terribly disloyal to Jonathan's memory now, she wondered? Would he have started seeing someone else within two years and six months of her death, if he'd been in her shoes? Indeed, was it fair to give Tom Lavery false hope? Or was she already developing real feelings for him? Beyond fancying him like mad, that is? And did she fancy him not only because he was tall and rugged and deliciously shy, but also because he was heartbroken himself? Because it would be easier for her to love someone who was as damaged as she was? Because it'd be easier to love Tom than to keep up with some other happier, non-bereaved person?

She lay back on the pillows then and pulled the covers right up to her chin, just resting and thinking. She thought of her parents and their bizarre trial separation. Her father sitting fishing off a small wooden pier at the Lough's edge. Almost hidden behind the reeds. Seeing hardly anyone all day long. Her mother counting out the change in dollars and cents to strangers with American accents. Actually the customers probably had vastly differing accents from all over the world, Ruby mused. Was her mother completely daft or was she only now discovering that she was an adventurous soul at heart, Ruby wondered? Would the pair of them ever be able to fall in love again? Would her mother meet another man in America?

"Oh my God, I never thought of that," Ruby said out loud. "Not really. What if she has a ridiculous fling with another man while she's out there? Poor Daddy!"

But there was no answer to that question so Ruby forced herself to calm down and focus on herself and Tom again. The thought of Tom Lavery kissing her was much less frightening than, say, her mother kissing another man over the baguette tray.

Was she afraid of falling in love again herself, Ruby wondered? She didn't want to grow old alone in this apartment, however pretty and cosy it was. She knew that much. And Tom was a gentleman and he understood her grief and he was pretty sexy in his own way. She smiled and then reached for another photo album.

This one contained pictures of Ruby when she was a very young child. There were pictures of her showing off a new Barbie doll, wearing various garish party frocks, sitting proudly on a new bicycle, icing a lopsided birthday cake for her father. There were pictures of her going in through the school gates for the first time, waving goodbye to her parents and giving the camera a nervous thumbs-up. And there were some pictures of Ruby and her dad at a Halloween bonfire in the town, pointing up at a shower of orange sparks.

And suddenly Ruby had an epiphany: her parents had done their best to bring her up well. They may not have been the best parents in the world lately, but they had definitely done their best during her formative years. Ruby felt a single tear well up in her eye, and then it went rolling down her cheek.

I've been so blinkered, she thought. I've expected them to be there for me always. When I know now that they've had major issues of their own. They've lost their way, the two of them. They've simply drifted off course and they don't know how to get back. Well, I've got to think of some plan to get them back on track. And maybe even friends with one another again.

Ruby sighed and packed away her albums, and switched off the lights. She lay very still in the darkness, thinking of the past and how her childhood hadn't been nearly as bad as she remembered it. The glossy Barbie doll in its brightly coloured box, the old school gates, the shower of Halloween sparks floating up into the night sky. Only little things, yes, but they'd been beautiful in their own way. Yes, the house had been a bit stuffy and less-than-welcoming. And perhaps her parents hadn't been so great with the hugs and kisses and the words of encouragement over the years. But they'd always tried to buy her the most fashionable toys when she was little, and they'd also remembered to bring her to the big fireworks display in Enniskillen town every October. She decided she would call her father in the morning and tell him how much she loved him. And her mother too. She would try to find a list of the bakeries in Manhattan and she would ring them all until she found the one her mother was working in. Then she'd post her out a velvet evening bag. Just as a goodwill gesture. The red one! She'd send her mother the red bag. Red was her mother's favourite colour. And maybe she'd put a small photo of herself and her dad inside it? And a tiny box of hand-made truffles into the parcel too, or something.

The doll, the school gates, the Halloween sparks . . .

"See the beauty in small things," she told herself. "That's the sixth secret of happiness. I must try harder to see the beauty in small things."

# 24

## The Secret of the Maze

"Now, if you tell anyone else the secret of the maze, even Jasmine, especially Jasmine, I could get into major trouble," Tom said, laughing. "And I do mean major trouble. I could maybe do time for this."

They were standing at the arch-shaped entrance to the maze. The early morning sun was shining brightly and there was nobody else about. The day-trippers would not be arriving for another hour or two at least.

"I swear on my own life I won't tell another soul," Ruby began. And then she felt a bit silly and over-dramatic. Plus, swearing on lives was a bit insensitive given both of their personal circumstances.

"Okay then, maybe not *major* trouble," Tom conceded. "But if word gets out I might have to re-lay some of the paths in the maze."

Ruby looked down at her feet, at the pebbly path laid out before her in sweeping swirls and long graceful curving patterns. Egg-shaped white stones interspersed here and there with smaller, rounder blue and grey ones.

"Ah, so there's a secret pattern in the pathway?" she said. "A secret code?"

"You've got it," he smiled. "It's as easy as pie when you know what to look for."

"Don't tell me, I'll work it out," Ruby said happily.

"You won't be able to work it out," Tom told her. "Unless you spend days and days getting to know the maze itself. And most people only venture into it once or twice. It's easy to lose your bearings when you get further in. Plus, sometimes the sun casts long shadows and then it's harder to see the pebbles."

"Okay then, tell me," she begged, eager to be allowed into Tom's exclusive club of dark-green right angles and neatly-clipped archways. "Was the pebble path your idea?"

"No, would you believe it was designed over two centuries ago? The maze was planted but for some reason the path was never laid. And then, over the years, the hedges got overgrown and it all sort of died off. You have to keep the maze in top repair or the light can't get in. I replanted it years ago and laid the paths bit by bit when I had some free time."

"How fascinating," Ruby breathed.

"More of a folly, some people might say," Tom said, smiling sheepishly.

"Yes, but it's so lovely."

"Yes," Tom said quietly. "Anyway, let's get started, shall we?"

"Okay," Ruby said.

They walked slowly into the maze, the light dimming noticeably as they passed beneath the first archway. The walls of the maze were too thick and tightly packed for any rays of sunshine to penetrate at such an early hour.

"How do the shady sides of the hedges get enough sunshine?" Ruby asked suddenly. But Tom only laughed and told her she was a very philosophical kind of girl.

"I'm serious," she said.

"Well, as I said, we just do our best to keep the whole thing well trimmed and fed," Tom said calmly. "The sun moves around during the day, the maze seems to be managing well enough on the bit of sun it does get."

And then they came to the first fork in the path. Ruby looked downwards to see if she could notice any difference in the pebble pattern between the two options. One path had a small but perfect star in the centre and the other one had a small but equally perfect crescent moon.

"The moon or the star?" Ruby asked excitedly.

"The star," Tom smiled. "But it's not the star that's significant. See the blue pebble in the centre there? Well, the correct path to the centre is marked with blue stones. The wrong turnings always have a grey pebble. It's not an obvious colour difference, especially when it's been raining. But if you look really closely you can see what I mean."

"Wow, so I just follow the blue stones all the way to the bench in the centre?" Ruby said, hurrying towards the next junction.

"Yes."

In no time at all they were standing by the willow bench.

"It's just amazing," Ruby said happily. "The day Jasmine and I got lost in here it never crossed our minds to think of a secret code. Yet when you know the secret it seems so totally obvious."

"Yes, it's a lovely bit of topiary, really. Did much better than we'd expected. I enjoyed bringing it back from the brink," Tom admitted.

"Thanks, Tom."

"For what?"

"For sharing this with me," she said, smiling up at him.

"That's okay," he said simply.

"It doesn't seem quite so claustrophobic any more either. Now that I know how to find my way out again."

"Yes, that's true enough."

"Shall we have that fry-up now?" Ruby asked. "I'm starving. You did promise me a full Irish breakfast."

"Why not?" Tom laughed. "But I must warn you that Mrs Kenny is dying to meet you, Ruby. She'll be hovering close by, I'm sure."

"Oh Lord, I forgot about Mrs Kenny. What have you told her about me?" Ruby said giddily.

"Just that you're a very good friend," Tom admitted.

"Okay then, I'll do my best to behave as a very good friend should," Ruby said.

And they set off back towards the café, finding their way out of the maze in less than two minutes flat.

# 25

# The Talkers

"It's very, um, cosy in here," Ruby said cheerfully.

Noah stood right beside her, wagging his tail excitedly. He wasn't used to seeing visitors at the cottage.

"It's a bit of a dump compared to your place," Tom grimaced. "Noah, sit!"

The dog immediately sat down and bowed his head sadly. Tom laughed and patted him on the back.

"Look at him, playing for sympathy," he said. "Clever dog!"

"No, it's lovely and full of character," Ruby smiled, indicating the room once more.

They both surveyed the worn armchairs, the frayed rugs and the sagging bookcases lined with well-read books in the sitting room. The yellowing skirting boards could have done with a lick of fresh paint. There was a big plastic bag of coal sitting crookedly beside the fireplace. One touch and it might have spilled its sooty contents all over the floor.

"You're so polite sometimes, Ruby," Tom laughed. "It's so nice of you to even try to compliment this bedraggled heap of junk."

"Oh Tom, it's fine really," she protested. "Rustic, um, simplicity is all the rage these days. And it's really very . . . charming."

"Well, thanks. It's impossible to keep any place perfect when there's a dog in the house. Especially when it's an old house like this one, with carpets on the floor instead of tiles. You know, when there's a dog and nobody at home during the day to tidy up? A woman's touch is what this house needs. I mean, not that it has to be a woman's touch. Anybody at all could do it. Though women are usually so much better at having ideas for nicer homes, aren't they? God, that sounds so sexist. But I always seem to be too tired to sort it all out." Tom scratched his head and began to sweep out the ashes from the grate. "Okay, that's enough of my rambling, I can't defend this lot, Ruby. Not even to myself. It's a dump."

"Tom, it's *fine*," Ruby said again. "It's getting dark outside anyway. No room looks at its best at dusk. I always think rooms can look quite melancholy at this time of day. The light in them is all blue and cold. Must be the Irish climate?"

"But I've seen your home, remember? Both of them," Tom said quietly. "Like something from a magazine, both the house on the Ravenhill, and now the flat."

"Yes, well, it's my chief hobby reading decorating magazines and then pottering about the shops looking for nice things. I enjoy clearing everything out and starting again from scratch. Lots of lamps and candles to add warmth and atmosphere. A psychologist would probably say I have unresolved issues or something."

"Haven't we all? Um, listen, it's getting cold. I'll light the fire," he said then.

Ruby sat down on the edge of the sofa and folded her hands in her lap, waiting for him to set the fire and get it going. After a few minutes, the small pile of sticks and coal began to spark and crackle into life. Tom stood up and dusted himself down.

"I'll make us some tea and toast," he said next.

"Can I help?" Ruby offered, not quite wanting to be left alone with Noah. She was nervous of dogs, especially large ones with very bright eyes.

"I'll put Noah in his room," Tom said, picking up on her worries. "He wouldn't harm a fly but then again you never know. He's had me all to himself for five years. He's not used to visitors coming to the cottage."

"Thanks, Tom," Ruby said, standing up again.

Tom shooed Noah down the corridor. The dog stepped neatly into his basket and Tom patted him on the head. Then he closed the door and came back to the sitting room, looking slightly unsure of himself.

"Thanks for a lovely day showing me round the gardens," Ruby said then. "I really have enjoyed myself."

"Have you, honestly?"

"Of course I have. I had a lovely time. Just because I own a dinky shop in the city doesn't mean I'm too good for a stroll round the daffodils, you know? I've missed having a garden since I sold the house, to tell you the truth. Even though our little patch on the Ravenhill was about as small a garden as you could get. But it was big enough for a table and two chairs and a pot of flowers in the summertime. We used to sit there for hours, getting quietly pickled."

"I know you still miss him," Tom said as Ruby wiped a tear from her eye and turned to look out of the window at the stars twinkling high above them.

"God, yes, it still hurts so much," she admitted, her voice catching with emotion. "I never thought much about bereavement before it happened to me, Tom. I used to see old widows at church thumbing through their prayer books and I never actually thought of them as human beings. As women who were young girls once, full of dreams and hopes and silly notions. I never thought about growing old myself. I never really thought about anything that might upset me. Now I seem to be fighting off profound thoughts morning, noon and night."

"Yes, I understand," he nodded. "Me too."

"And widowers too, of course. God love them, they must find it so hard being on their own, especially coping with the housekeeping . . . Not that I was referring to you, Tom. Though there's usually far fewer widowers than widows. Or maybe they just blend into the crowd better . . ." She shrugged her shoulders hopelessly.

"About that tea?" Tom smiled.

"Yes, the tea!"

Together they went through to the kitchen. Ruby was pleased to see that this room was large and bright and very clean. It was painted a soft white, with a tiled floor and a smart Roman blind at the window. There were big willow baskets for storing the firewood and old newspapers and even one for carrier bags. She felt a little more relaxed now. Ruby was a bit doubtful of people who let a house go completely to rack and ruin. Surely any reasonable person could pick up a sponge and a bottle of cleaning spray, she sometimes thought to herself, when they showed those awful neglected houses on the TV.

"This room is lovely," she announced, taking in the neatly stacked crockery on the sideboard.

"Mrs Kenny comes in once a month to give it all a decent going over. And she got me organised with the storage baskets and such. But I do my best in the meantime, you know? I can wash up and do my own laundry," he added proudly. "I used to pull my own weight even when Kate was alive. She worked long hours, you see? She was a vet. Mind you, we lived in a very nice house in Hillsborough and we had a full-time housekeeper to take care of all the domestic stuff. I didn't want to live there by myself when Kate died so I sold it. The new owners kept the housekeeper on which was very good of them."

"Yes, that was very kind."

"She was a good housekeeper, though."

214

"Yes, I'm sure she was."

A small but friendly silence descended.

"I love the flowers," Ruby said suddenly, pointing to a row of fragrant blue hyacinths coming into bloom on the windowsill.

"More leftovers from the greenhouse," Tom said proudly, putting several strips of bacon under the grill. "Seemed a shame to waste them. Bacon doorsteps okay for you?"

"Lovely. I'm starving again. All this country air is giving me a huge appetite."

"Yes, it can do that if you're not used to it. Tomato sauce okay for you? White bread?"

"Yes, that's fine. I'll butter the bread."

For a few minutes they worked wordlessly together. Tom fetched plates and cups and filled the teapot while Ruby assembled the sandwiches and cut them into neat triangles. Then they sat down beside the Rayburn range to have their late supper.

"I suppose I'll have to say this formally and get it over with," Tom began, blushing ever so slightly. "I like you, Ruby. I like you a lot."

"Thank you, Tom. And I like you."

"No, I mean I like you in a *romantic* way," he stammered.

"Yes, I had a suspicion you did," she laughed.

"Well, anyway, just so you know," he added, shrugging his shoulders hopelessly.

"Tom, I think you're a very attractive man. I do," she told him then.

"But it's too soon for anything to happen between us?" he asked.

"Yes, oh yes. Far too soon, I suppose. But then again I don't think I'll ever be at the stage where I can say that I'm finally over Jonathan and ready to start dating again. A clean slate will never happen for me, Tom. True love never dies, does it? It only sits down in the corner of your mind and stops talking quite so loudly."

"Yes, I know what you mean. It's like that for me too. It's like I've become two different people. I miss Kate all the time. I've loved her since we were at school together. But I'm lonely for a friend now. More than a friend really. And the loneliness is becoming harder to deal with than my memories of Kate. So what will we do?"

Ruby held Tom's hand across the small pine table and smiled at him.

"We'll talk," she said. "Let's just sit here and talk and see what happens. Like we did at the restaurant that evening."

"Okay."

Tom poured more tea and added a few wooden blocks to the range.

"My grandparents had one of these ranges," Ruby said wistfully. "It was a cream colour too, or maybe they were all cream?"

"Possibly. Great job," Tom nodded. "Just as good as an Aga."

"Yes, I always loved the smell of the turf burning, first thing in the morning. And the way you could make toast on the top of the range in that wire tennis-racket thing. And boil a kettle on the top, too. And have a chicken in the hot oven and an apple pie in the cool oven. *And* tea towels drying on the rail. All that heat and hot water as well."

"Oh yes, they're terrific things."

"I used to stay with my grandparents quite a lot when I was a child. A nice change of scene for me during the school holidays, Mum said. They had a traditional Irish stone cottage near Dungannon. Thatched roof and all on it! And the window frames were painted dark green – it was gorgeous. Anyway one night a huge bomb went off about five miles down the road and the power lines were out of action for three whole days. But because we had the range we barely noticed. Granddad lit his old oil lamp when it happened and we said a prayer for anyone who'd been hurt in the bomb. Then one of the neighbours called in and told us the details."

"Was that the bomb that killed all those soldiers?" Tom asked, mentally checking dates.

"Yes, it was. I was tucked up in bed when I heard it going off. A kind of low roar, it sounded like. It seemed to go on for about five minutes. A soft crumpling sound. Not a loud bang at all . . . Not the way it is in films . . . I couldn't breathe because I was listening so hard."

"God love them," Tom sighed.

"Yes. Thank God we couldn't see the television coverage afterwards. I nearly had a heart attack that night. I had palpitations until the sun came up. Not knowing what had happened or what else was going to happen. Terrible night. That was enough to put me off action movies for life, I'm afraid. I still can't watch James Bond films without remembering the awful sound that bomb made."

"Yeah, explosions aren't quite as much fun in real life."

"No," she shook her head sadly. "They still hang poppy wreaths on the fence at the side of the road where it happened."

"Were you ever political?" Tom asked carefully. Better to get the awkward questions over with, early on. Just in case Ruby turned out to have very strong views in either direction.

"No, definitely not. I was more into *Top of the Pops* than politics when I was young," Ruby said firmly, looking straight into his dark brown eyes and understanding what he meant. It was vital they were honest with each other from the very beginning. There was too much at stake for either of them to start spinning out a false identity.

"Ha, a good answer," he nodded, smiling.

"A safe answer," Ruby said, smiling too. "No, I was never political. We lived in a kind of ivory tower, my parents and me. Just the three of us in our big house in the country and the long drive down to the main road . . . and all the copper beech trees around us. We didn't get very involved in community life. Mind you, in Fermanagh it was always fairly easy-going, politically. Usually there was no pressure to take one side or the other."

"Sounds idyllic."

"It was in a way. We had plenty of money, I suppose. So that insulated us from a lot of things. My mother never sat down long enough to read the local papers or listen to the radio. And Dad was too busy walking by the loughs to get mixed up in any bother or even in silly bits of village gossip. I'm glad they never got sucked into making 'donations to the cause' or anything. I'd have hated to have our lives blighted with all of that business. Police kicking the door down at three o'clock in the morning. It was all pointless in the end, wasn't it?"

"Yeah. Pointless is the right word. I always stayed out of it, even from the harmless talk in the pub. You can't beat the quiet life."

"No, indeed," Ruby said reflectively. "Though when I was a child I found the days very long. Especially the summer holidays. I wanted to grow up as quick as I could and go to London and see a bit of life. I thought it would be all trendy people and brilliant shops and TV presenters on every corner. I thought I'd see famous pop stars buying their groceries in M&S."

"And did you ever go to London?"

"Yes, lots of times. I went shopping on Oxford Street and to pop concerts and stuff. With my best pal from school: her name was Mary Campbell. She met a guy there one summer and stayed in London and eventually she married him. But I didn't like it as much as I'd hoped. I kept getting lost on the Tube. It was too big for me so I went to college in Belfast instead."

She collected up her plate and set it in the sink.

"More tea?" Tom asked, getting to his feet also.

"In a while. I thought we could just enjoy the range for a while?" she said quietly. "At my grandparents' house we used to leave the door of the fire open a little bit. And we'd turn off the lights and just watch the sparks floating up towards the chimney. Does that sound mad?"

"Not at all. I'll just check on Noah," Tom said, opening the door to the range, protecting his hand from the hot handle with an old towel. He flicked off the overhead lights as he left the room and Ruby pulled their chairs closer to the fire and just sat there reminiscing. She understood now why she'd been dropped off at the cottage near Dungannon so often during her childhood. Not only to keep her mother's parents company but to give her mother a rest from her childish enthusiasms and endless questions. Still, there were worse ways to spend a summer than playing with a Rayburn, and eating her gran's tasty cakes and pies.

"He's fine," Tom said, coming back into the kitchen. "Fast asleep. Ha, I sound like a proud parent, God help me . . . Glass of wine?"

"Oh yes, that'd be lovely," Ruby agreed.

"Red or white?"

"Red, please."

"I've a nice Merlot here," Tom said, plucking a bottle from the wine rack.

"Great."

"And if I'm not mistaken I've also got some Kettle Chips. Here they are," he said, finding them at the back of a tall cupboard.

"Aren't you the secret sophisticate?" Ruby teased. "Red Onion Kettle Chips? Oh now, how very posh!"

"Not a bit of me. Mrs Kenny brought them the last day she was here. She said they weren't a big seller at Camberwell. The flavour's good, she said, but the bloody things are as hard as flint."

"Oh yes, I've noticed that too," Ruby agreed at once. "I usually buy tortilla chips because they're a bit softer than crisps. Sometimes I can polish off a whole bag and then I feel terribly guilty, but then I do the exact same thing a few days later," she laughed. "Is that mad?"

"No. Of course not! That's the second time you've asked me if I think you're mad," he added. "Or is it the third time?"

"Sorry," Ruby blushed.

"Don't be," he said tenderly. "I don't think you're mad; not at all. I think you're gorgeous."

He poured the wine into two large glasses and handed one to Ruby.

"Cheers," he said, smiling at her.

"Cheers," she said, clinking glasses and smiling too.

Tom sat down again and they resumed talking. They talked about hyacinths and Noah and Kettle Chips and wine and Rayburn ranges and cottages in the country and things long past. They talked until late into the night and the basket of wood blocks was empty and the room was so warm Tom had to raise the Roman blind and open the window. The wine bottle was long empty and so was a second one. Tom and Ruby were both stifling huge yawns and Noah hadn't moved a muscle for hours. Then Ruby agreed to go home in a taxi and come back later that day for her car.

"I'll pick you up. No need to call another taxi later on," Tom said as they waited by the front door for the taxi to arrive. "I'll wait until the wine has worn off and then pick you up in the Rover, probably sometime in the evening."

"Okay," Ruby said gently.

As she was leaving, Tom kissed her lightly on the cheek. And then very fleetingly on the lips . . .

Ruby thought about the kiss all the way back to the Ravenhill Road in the taxi. Had she felt anything? Yes, she had felt something: a poignant mix of guilt and desire and curiosity. Something definite had happened between them during the night: something very small and tentative but also very real and definite. Not true love: not just yet. But there had certainly been something significant. And Tom's kiss had been lovely too. It had been tender and sexy and light and yet full of longing. Ruby decided she was definitely going to have to kiss him back, one of these days. Kiss him back, and maybe even go to bed with him . . .

# 26

## The Morning After

When Ruby opened her eyes the next day she felt curiously excited but for a moment she couldn't think why. Then she remembered Tom's face glowing with pleasure as they'd gone wandering idly round the maze at Camberwell House. And Mrs Kenny, who was all smiles as they sat down afterwards to a delicious plate of fried bread, bacon and tomatoes in the café. Poor Mrs Kenny had the two of them married off already and halfway to Paris on their honeymoon, she was that happy for them. Tom explained that Mrs Kenny was like a surrogate mother to all the staff at Camberwell and that she simply couldn't help clucking over them all. And Ruby marvelled at this lovely woman who had so many maternal feelings she had some to spare for her co-workers.

Tom was going to call for her later that day and give her a lift to Camberwell to fetch her car. The shop was closed today so she had all day to relax and paint her nails and decide what to wear. She might even go out for lunch by herself, something she hadn't done in years. She might catch the bus into town and have coffee in her favourite bookstore. It was heavenly to feel so normal again. Almost back to her old self!

Ruby got up and wrapped herself in her warmest robe before hurrying to the kitchen for a refreshing cup of Earl Grey. She almost felt like singing, she was feeling so light and breezy. She almost felt like switching on the radio and twirling round the kitchen, singing aloud to herself. She was a real woman again, meeting people again – not lying awake at night wondering if she was going mad. She put a slice of crusty bread in the toaster and filled the kettle.

"Music," she said to herself. "I need music to keep me company."

But when she switched on the radio her heart seemed to fall off the edge of a cliff. The news programme was detailing another car accident that had taken place during the night and this time three people had been killed. Some relative was crying as they told the story of what had happened. And Ruby was immediately plunged straight back into the acute grief she had felt the night she'd lost Jonathan. The shock and the disbelief of it all, and the anger and the rage, and the overwhelming sense that she was now only half the person she used to be. Unexpectedly, she burst into a fit of hysterical sobbing and dark despair. And her new-found happiness seemed to blow away like a straw hut in a hurricane.

I've made a fool of myself, she thought as the slice of golden-brown bread popped up and turned cold in the toaster. I've made an absolute fool of myself running around in the gardens of a big posh house and getting all giddy over blue pebbles, and Mrs Kenny winking at me. What in God's name would Jonathan think of me, if he could see me now? Carrying on like a giddy schoolgirl.

Ruby felt her hands shaking suddenly and she experienced a hot flush all over her body. She sat down on a kitchen chair and continued to sob gently. It would always be like this, she told herself hopelessly. It would always be just like this. Just when she thought she had made a little progress, the rug would be pulled out from underneath her again. Just when she thought she was fitting back into the human race, some news bulletin would shut the door in her face, and remind her that she was a widow. That she was different from most other people now. That she ought to be ashamed of herself for daring to do nice things when she was not entitled to do them any more.

The phone began to ring, making her jump with nerves. She looked at the caller display. It was Tom. He was phoning already? Before she'd even eaten breakfast? He was that keen on her?

"I can't answer it," Ruby gasped.

Most likely he was phoning to arrange a time to collect her later that evening so she could pick up her car. Obviously that was all he wanted. He didn't want to come over and see her right away. But Ruby's breath still began to contract with indecision. She couldn't possibly speak to Tom right now, not when her heart was banging with embarrassment and her eyes were full of tears. She decided to ignore the phone and pretend she'd not heard it. She could always say she was in the shower. But then he might ask why she hadn't called him back when she was out of the shower. The ringing seemed to go on forever.

"Stop it," Ruby wept, covering her ears with her hands. "Stop it, stop it. Leave me alone."

Eventually the ringing stopped. Ruby didn't have an answering machine in the flat yet. And she was grateful for that much at least. For now she could buy some precious time, deciding what to do.

Tom replaced the receiver and sat down on the sofa beside a sulky Noah. His heart was also racing but in his case it had been racing with anticipation. For when he reunited Ruby with her car, he'd been planning to ask her out again. Just for dinner or a drink or even a walk somewhere scenic. But now he was convinced she was avoiding him and he felt that old familiar pang of loneliness tugging at his heart. He'd said too much or moved too fast the day before. He'd ruined their fledgling friendship with his neediness, and by telling Ruby that he really liked her. And also by saying that he wanted to be more than just friends someday. Women hated a man being needy, didn't they?

"I've blown it, Noah," he said quietly. "I met a lovely woman and I really liked her, and she actually seemed to like me back, and yet I blew it."

Noah sat up and barked softly as if to say, I told you so.

"Ah, Christ," Tom sighed sadly. "I thought it was all going so well. I thought it was better to be honest than to try and play the smooth guy or pretend I didn't really care one way or the other. I thought it was better to be straightforward from the beginning. I don't understand how I could've got it so wrong."

Noah looked bored and trotted off towards the hall to look for a toy to play with.

Wait a minute, Tom chided himself then. What am I saying? Ruby could have been asleep? Or maybe she was in the shower? Or out at the shops? I'll ring her again later. I'm just out of practice; that's all it is. It's just been so long since I was dating. God, I'm such an eejit! I'll call Ruby later and do my best to sound easy-going, yeah?

He took Noah out for a good run across the fields, then fed him and then tried calling Ruby again. But there was no answer this time either, even though Tom let the phone ring for a full two minutes.

I can't call her flat for a third time, he fretted. Not in one day. It'll seem as if I'm stalking the poor woman. Maybe I should wait until she rings me? But what if she's lost my number? She could always look up Camberwell in the Yellow Pages though, couldn't she? Maybe she's changed her mind about me being, what did she say, attractive? I bet I'm not a patch on her husband. He was like Brad Pitt in that photograph I saw in the newspaper. Oh my God, that's it! She's come to her senses and realised she must have been mad to even consider going out with me. And I must have been mad too to think that she'd be mine someday.

Tom flopped down in a chair beside the range and folded his arms. There was no sound in the kitchen except for the ticking of an old clock on the dresser.

Back at her flat Ruby was in bed and hiding under the blankets. She heard the phone ringing for the second time and she just put a pillow over her ears and tried her best to ignore it.

I can't go out with him again, she thought. I just can't do it. He'll think we're a proper couple if this keeps up. That we are officially together! He might try to kiss me properly or even sleep with me, God help us both. He might get all serious and intense and then I'd have to break his heart with my babbling and my silly chatter about it being too soon for me. What am I? A born-again virgin! For God's sake . . . Or else I'd get all serious and clingy and then he'd go off me. I mean Kate was a vet with her own practice and what do I do for a living? I sell handbags and bangles! Oh God, I need time to think. We need more time to think. Both of us! We definitely need more time . . .

And then she remembered her car parked neatly at the back door of Tom's cottage. And Tom couldn't even drop it off at her flat because she had the keys safely in her handbag.

Oh fuck this, she thought. My car is still at his house. I forgot all about the stupid bloody car. Oh well, this is just great. This is just sweet altogether. My car is out there in the middle of nowhere. There's no way I can get it back without him seeing me. Noah would bark his head off for a start. And I can't send someone else out to fetch it without insulting the man completely. What the hell am I going to do now?

Ruby stayed in bed all afternoon and didn't even bother to eat lunch.

At eight o'clock that evening the phone rang for a third time.

Tom, three glasses of wine in him, had become desperate. He might as well get the full brush-off and do it properly he told himself as he let the phone ring for a full five minutes. But Ruby didn't hear the phone ringing because at that moment she was in the Errigle Inn with Jasmine, having a third glass of wine herself.

"Ruby, stop being a total wimp and give the guy a call," Jasmine scolded her.

"No, I can't. My confidence has deserted me entirely," Ruby sighed.

"You don't have to sleep with the poor man, Ruby. Just get your car back and then make a date to have another drink with him," Jasmine advised gently.

"I'm afraid to face him again," Ruby admitted.

"Why? Do you still fancy him?" Jasmine asked immediately.

"Sort of. Yes, I do fancy him."

"I knew you did," Jasmine nodded wisely.

"Well, obviously I *fancy* him," Ruby said crossly. "But nothing can happen."

"Not right away," Jasmine agreed. "Not until you feel good and ready."

"Not ever," Ruby said.

"Oh Ruby, you're being silly now," Jasmine scolded.

"But I feel awful, Jasmine. I feel like I'm committing adultery," Ruby whispered.

"I'm going to the bar for a refill," Jasmine groaned. "I'll get you one too, shall I?"

"No, just a lemonade for me, honestly. I'm plastered already on three glasses of wine."

"Ruby, they're only pub measures, for God's sake. Added together they wouldn't even fill a decent-sized wineglass. I'm getting you one more drink and then maybe you'll be able to pick up the phone and ring Tom."

"I won't."

"Well then, I'll ring him for you," Jasmine said, patting Ruby's hand.

"I'll fire you if you do," Ruby said crossly.

"Ruby, you've got to stop threatening to fire me," Jasmine smiled. "We both know you'll never do that. I'm the best sales assistant in Belfast and you know it."

"Okay, I won't fire you," Ruby admitted.

"Look, have a sleep on it and you might feel better tomorrow, yeah?"

"Okay," Ruby nodded with more enthusiasm than she felt.

# 27

## The Mystery Man

As expected, Ruby's nerves were in tatters by the following morning. She had a throbbing hangover and she felt even sicker with shame for avoiding Tom's calls. She knew there were three missed calls altogether on her phone but she simply couldn't bring herself to pick up the receiver and call Tom back. Even though she knew he was a lovely man who'd surely understand that her romantic feelings were in turmoil these days. And to put the final touch to her misery, it was her birthday! She'd almost forgotten about it, given all the emotional upheaval.

"I'll call him for you," Jasmine said firmly as they opened up the shop at nine thirty.

"No, thank you very much, but that'd be a bit childish," Ruby said quickly.

"So tell me, is lying in bed with a pillow over your ears the height of maturity nowadays?" Jasmine said quietly.

"Yes, well, I couldn't help it. I was very upset by that news story on the radio. It brought everything rushing back to me. I thought I was going to be sick. My stomach just flipped over."

"So tell Tom that," Jasmine advised. "He'll understand."

"No. He'd only think I was being hysterical," Ruby sighed.

"Ruby, will you get over yourself? You are not being hysterical at all. You are a very sensitive woman. It's not a *crime* to be sensitive." Jasmine gave Ruby a hug.

"I know it isn't but it's just very bloody awkward sometimes," Ruby said. "I wish I was more of a risk-taker."

"Hasn't it taken Tom five years to begin dating again?"

"I suppose so," Ruby admitted.

"Well then, he must be even more sensitive than you are?"

"That's a good point," Ruby nodded.

"So call him?"

"Um, no."

"Give me his number," Jasmine said.

"No, please don't bother."

"He might think you've been taken ill, Ruby. Have you thought of that?" Jasmine pointed out.

"Oh God no, I haven't," Ruby fretted.

"You've got to put the poor guy out of his misery. Wait a minute, there's a van pulling up outside the shop. A florist's van, a dead posh one! You're getting a bouquet, Ruby. Oh, it's so beautiful. Pink tulips and pink roses, if I'm not mistaken," Jasmine smiled. "There you are, you silly moo, Tom's not cross with you at all."

"Poor Tom. He's been so kind. Jesus, I feel like such an idiot now," Ruby said, blushing, as Jasmine graciously received the flowers and thanked the delivery guy. "Read me the note quickly," Ruby said.

"Give me two seconds to open the envelope, would you? Oh. Hang on a second. These flowers are for me," Jasmine said slowly. "Oh dear, Ruby, I'm so sorry about this! There's no name on the card, which is weird. It just says, *For Jasmine*. Oh God, I hope you're not too disappointed! What do you think, huh? I've got myself a secret admirer or something?"

"You must have," Ruby said primly. It was obvious she was slightly annoyed that the gorgeous flowers were not for her after all.

"*Are* you very disappointed?" Jasmine said gently.

"No, don't be daft. Well, maybe I'm a tiny bit disappointed," Ruby admitted.

"You must be. But I'm sure that if you call Tom back today, you can sort it all out very easily."

"Indeed."

Jasmine was examining the florist's card again. "You know, I bet the florist just forgot to put the sender's name on. Hang on a sec. I'll phone and ask."

But a minute later Jasmine was more puzzled than ever. The sender hadn't given his name. He had come to the shop and paid in cash but the florist wasn't able to describe him – or so she said.

"At least you know it was a man," said Ruby.

"Well, I'll have to wait until he turns up or phones me," said Jasmine with a dismissive shrug. She picked up her flowers. "Look, I'll put these in some water. And then I'll call Tom for you."

"No, no! I won't give you his number anyway."

"Ha, sorry but you can't stop me that easily. Think again. I'll just look up Camberwell in the phone book," Jasmine said lightly. "It's not MI5 he works at. It's only up the road, you numbskull. Honestly I'm going to have to kidnap the pair of you and tie you onto a couple of chairs, and force you to sort out this relationship once and for all."

"Oh right, to heck with it, you win, this is crazy. I'll call him right now," Ruby said bravely, jabbing the numbers into the shop phone. "I'll phone him and tell him something came up last night. Though what could have caused me to be out-of-contact for an entire day, I don't know. Don't listen to me, please. You go into the kitchenette and shut the door. Hurry, it's ringing."

Jasmine went scurrying across the shop with her huge bouquet of tulips and roses. She set the flowers carefully into the sink and filled it half-full with cold water. Then she stood against the door, holding her breath, listening hard.

"Hello? Hello, is that Mrs Kenny? Hi, Mrs Kenny. How are you? Yes, it's only me, Ruby. Listen, can I please speak to Tom for a minute? Is he terribly busy?" Jasmine heard Ruby say nervously. Then there was a pause as Ruby waited for Tom to be found. "Tom? Is that you? It's me, Ruby. You called me last night? Yes, I know, the car . . . Oh, hi Tom, yes, I'm so sorry, yes, I had to go out all day yesterday. Something came up . . . Yes, today after work would be fine. Okay, I'll see you then, thanks, Tom."

Ruby put the phone down and closed her eyes. "He's coming to pick me up after work."

"Well, thanks be to God! That wasn't so hard, was it?" Jasmine said cheerfully, coming out of the kitchenette.

"You rascal, you were listening!" Ruby said.

"Yes, of course, I was listening to every word. Now, did he sound pissed off or anything?"

"No, he sounded fine. A bit nervous but fine," Ruby admitted. "I think he's willing to give me another chance."

"There you are then. You got clean away with your attack of hysterics," Jasmine laughed. "Lucky girl!"

"Oh Jasmine, am I doing the right thing here? I haven't even scattered Jonathan's ashes yet. The urn is still in my sitting room upstairs."

"We'll do it together? Any time you like?" Jasmine offered. "We could go somewhere nice this weekend?"

"What about your secret admirer?" Ruby asked. "What if he turns up with another bouquet for you? An even bigger bouquet, if indeed that's possible?"

"He can wait," Jasmine said at once. "This is far more important."

232

"I don't know what I'd do without you, Jasmine Mulholland, I really don't. Come here and give me a hug."

"It's okay, Ruby, everything will be okay," Jasmine said, squeezing her friend tightly and then backing off again in case anyone saw them through the window and started up a rumour.

"I hope so," Ruby sighed.

"Yes, sure haven't we made it this far in one piece?"

"I suppose," Ruby agreed.

"There's only one thing," Jasmine said then as she flicked her long hair over her shoulders.

"What's that?"

"It's your birthday today."

"Well, yes it is," Ruby said, sighing slightly. "But after what happened with Tom, I didn't exactly feel like celebrating."

"Silly moo! Just as well I got you this," Jasmine said brightly, handing over a small parcel wrapped in pink foil that she'd been hiding behind the counter. "Happy Birthday, Ruby. You bloody idiot."

Ruby carefully opened the dainty present. It contained the most exquisite silver brooch in the shape of a bird. There were red stones for the eyes.

"It's really lovely, Jasmine," Ruby said, welling up with the surprise of it.

"I thought it looked like a phoenix," Jasmine said. "You know, the phoenix rising from the ashes and all that caper?"

"Thank you, you're an angel," Ruby said.

"Ah, I'm not."

"You are," Ruby said.

"Okay then, I am."

# 28

# The Absent Mother

Dorothy Lipman wasn't always happy that she had persuaded Emily Nightingale to join her at the painting group in the Bronx. Yes, it was nice to introduce a friend to a new hobby. The classes didn't cost much and it was a great way to get out of the house and meet people. And Dorothy had been a member of the painting group for so long, she almost felt like one of the teachers herself. But Emily was proving to be a very stubborn beginner. Stubbornness must be an Irish trait, Dorothy eventually decided.

"You see, if you were to put some more Prussian blue on *that* side of the canvas then the sunflowers would look far more intense," Dorothy suggested carefully. "Just a suggestion, of course," she added. Emily could be incredibly touchy about her painting skills. Dorothy had observed this curious phenomenon many times before, usually in the most hopeless of the amateurs labouring away under the illusion that they had talent to equal Vincent Van Gogh.

"Yes, but I like the *green* background," Emily said firmly. "It's nice and summery."

"Well, yes it is. But you've got plenty of green in the leaves of the flowers already."

"All the same, I think some more green would be best," was the curt reply.

"Have it your own way," Dorothy smiled.

"I will," Emily muttered, vigorously mixing yellow paint with a small hint of orange for the outer petals.

"Any sign of your daughter coming over to visit you?" Dorothy asked then, taking a discreet sip of cola from a bottle in her shopping basket.

"Um? What did you say?" Emily was miles away from Ruby just then, in just about every respect.

"Didn't you say once that you had a grown-up daughter back in Ireland?" Dorothy said brightly.

"I did, yes. But I never said she was coming over here on a visit," Emily sniffed, glancing round the warehouse-studio in case anybody else could overhear. But the other painters seemed engrossed enough in their tasks.

"Why is she not coming to see you? Is she very busy?"

Emily sighed gently. Would she ever be able to get away from her responsibilities, she wondered?

"She runs her own business, you see. A dress shop. She's very busy all the time, yes indeed."

"You know, Emily, it's none of my concern but I reckon you should make it up with your daughter. It's a shame when families don't speak. And then one day one of you gets a phone call and it's too late to speak to them any more." Dorothy sounded like the sort of woman who'd known her fair share of suffering down the years.

"Dorothy dear, I am on perfectly fine terms with my family. I'm just having a little break from them, that's all. I'm just having a break from all of it. You don't know what it's like in Ireland. Everybody there is *obsessed* with everybody else's business.

Obsessed beyond reason, I'm telling you. That's why Ireland never had an empire . . . because they were all too busy spying on one another. Mocking each other's regional accents. Trying to find out how many cabbages or carrots everyone had growing secretly among the potato drills."

"I have absolutely no idea what you're talking about, Emily. Secret cabbages! But anyway, do go on. So what happened with your family? Tell me the big story," Dorothy said, washing out her brushes in a big jar of clean water. "Don't you just love acrylics? Oils are so damn messy. And they stink the house out."

"There is no big story," Emily said casually, waving her own paintbrush in the air.

"In New York, *everybody* has a story," Dorothy said then. "But here we don't spy on one another or go around counting cabbages. We just ask the questions straight out. Yes sir, we got enough scripts here for eight million movies . . ."

"Well, there isn't any brilliant movie script with me and mine, honestly. I simply got bored sitting on my arse, sorry, my backside . . . sitting on my backside at home, it's as plain as that. My husband isn't a great one for travel or trying new things. My daughter is too busy with her little shop in Belfast to hang around the bright lights of Fermanagh with me. So I applied to come here for a while. Just for a change of scene."

"Why New York?"

"I had a relative here. The flight was handy enough to arrange. And New York was too far away from Ireland to be bothered getting homesick."

"Okay. Is your daughter married?" Dorothy asked next. "Have you any grandchildren?"

"No . . . she's not married. No children."

"Is she engaged? Seeing anyone?"

"She *was* married. He died if you must know," Emily said briskly.

"Oh my word. When did he die? What happened?"

"A car accident. It was two years ago. Two and a half years ago." Emily stood back and studied her canvas thoughtfully. Maybe there *was* too much green in the composition but she'd never be able to admit that to Dorothy now.

"Emily, forgive me for asking, but why on earth did you come to New York and leave your poor daughter behind like that? She must need you, lady. Hey, there is something big going on here. Why did you come to New York to work in a crumby old bakery when your only child needs you to love her?"

"I'm telling you, Dorothy! Ruby doesn't need me. She never has. She couldn't wait to leave home the minute she turned eighteen. Never wanted anything to do with us, from the moment she went to college in Belfast."

"Honey, I'm sure that's not true. She was only eager to grow up and be an adult, I'm sure. You should be proud of her, Emily. Not like my lazy son, still sitting in my house drinking beer and he's twenty-nine."

"I don't really know any more," Emily sighed, "Children can be so difficult . . ." She dabbed a pale yellow highlight on her central sunflower. "I think you might have been right about the blue background," she murmured, anxious to change the subject. God, but these New Yorkers were a very forthright bunch. Back home in Ireland your husband could be lying stocious in the gutter with a black eye and nobody would dare to open their mouth about it. For a fleeting moment Emily was almost longing for Ireland and its buttoned-up ways.

But Dorothy wasn't quite ready to let the matter rest. She looked Emily right in the eye and took a deep breath. "Honey, I'm right about a lot of things. You just wait and see. Whatever you're doin' over here, it ain't worth it. This ain't no holiday, Emily, let me tell you. You're just running away from something, same as a scared teenager."

"Well, you seem to know an awful lot about human nature," Emily said crossly. "I don't know why you bother with running a dog-grooming parlour, I really don't. You ought to set yourself up in business as a shrink immediately. You'd make an absolute fortune."

"I've been told that before, now you mention it. But I think I'll stick with my dogs," Dorothy said, smiling brightly. "Dogs are a lot easier to deal with than humans. Oftentimes they're smarter. And they're usually a lot more grateful for my kindness as well."

But Emily only pursed her lips together like a clam and began to lather Prussian blue paint onto her canvas like a woman possessed. Well now, here was a fine thing: Dorothy Lipman telling her that she was no better than a scared teenager! What would Dorothy Lipman know anyway! Dorothy was eleven years divorced from an abusive husband, with two high-flying lawyer sons that she rarely saw any more. And a third layabout son that she said was just waiting on her to die and leave him the house. Some day soon she'd have to tell her stay-at-home son that she'd sold half the equity of her three-storey Brownstone house in Brooklyn years ago to an investment company so she could jump the queue for a much-needed hip operation. In fact, Dorothy was only going to give him one more year to get his act together and then she was moving to a smaller apartment in the suburbs to retire. She wanted a little place with better heating, lower ceilings and no stairs. Her son would probably never speak to her again when she discovered that he'd have to fend for himself in the Big Bad World. Poor Dorothy didn't have to look far to see her own problems. Emily felt a bit sorry for her New Best Friend then.

"Okay, I'll think about what you said," Emily said graciously and Dorothy just smiled and nodded wisely.

# 29

## The Letter

**M**rs Emily Nightingale sat up all night in her tiny little apartment just thinking about what Dorothy had said to her in the art class. It was a very hard thing to have to admit but yes, it probably wasn't very nice of her to allow her husband and daughter to go on living in limbo like this. Actually it was rather scandalous. She'd been having such fun being an independent lady in New York that she hadn't really noticed the time passing at all. And possibly she'd been in denial as the months flew by? Yes, there was definitely a fair bit of denial going on. But there was never a minute to spare, she rationalised then. No real time for soul-searching. Between dashing to work and serving hundreds of customers every day, and then dashing home again to shower and change her clothes, and then going out to eat supper or see a show or a film with Dorothy and the gang from the art club. It was non-stop really. It wasn't a deliberate act of neglect on her part.

"It was simply a case of there being too few hours in the day," she muttered to herself. But Emily knew in her heart that she was only being selfish to let things continue the way they were.

The ancient heating pipes in the kitchen began to throb and rumble ominously, and Emily got up off her tiny 1930s-style sofa and went into the other room to make some tea and heat a croissant for breakfast. She lifted her pretty pink cup and plate from the dish-rack and fetched butter and milk from the fridge.

"But I don't want to go home," she said suddenly to her ancient chrome kettle. "I can't go home yet, I'm not ready to give up my adventure. Oh my God, that's why I haven't been honest with anyone. Least of all myself! Because I don't *want* to live in that big house ever again! I don't want to go back to being a robot! Just cleaning and cleaning for six days a week and then going to Mass on Sundays! And if I do go back now, I know I'll go mad with boredom. Really and truly *mad*! Not just jittery-mad! Properly insane!"

And so the decision was made for her. Yes, she was broke and exhausted here in this vast city of eight million people. She barely made enough money working six days a week in the bakery to pay the rent on a run-down studio flat on the outskirts of Manhattan. She knew that people in her neighbourhood had been murdered for their shoes. She knew that it was only a matter of time before she was deported for overstaying her holiday visa, or even developed a health problem of some sort. And she had no health insurance and hardly any savings either. Her husband had always taken care of the money. She had just a few hundred pounds saved in the bank. But still, she felt so young and alive sitting on the bus each morning, wearing her yellow dress for the bakery, smiling at people from every walk of life. Not knowing who any of them were and none of them knowing who she was either. It was a lovely little fantasy that could well come crashing down around her ears at any moment. But while it lasted, she was determined to savour every minute.

I'll write to David today, she said to herself. "I'll write to him today and ask him for a divorce. It's the only decent thing to do. He'll never leave Fermanagh and I don't want to live there any more. So we'll divorce. Then he can decide what to do with the rest of his life. And maybe he can set me up with an allowance of some kind? So I can extend my visa or get health insurance or even move to another city somewhere. One where they don't bother to check up on the immigrants quite so often.

Emily Nightingale knew that she had no concrete plans and very few life skills. But she knew one thing: her life had only begun to take shape at the tender age of sixty-five. Which sounded ancient but it wasn't really. Not since she'd had a relatively easy life and was therefore well preserved looks-wise and in good health generally, even now she was nearing sixty-seven.

"No, that's it. I'm never going back to that big dark house ever again," she told herself sternly. "Just to end up dusting and cleaning for David and myself. And he doesn't notice the cleaning anyway and I don't care about it any more."

It was a revelation to Emily but she knew then, in that exact moment, that she'd be happy to be poor for the rest of her life, as long as she had something useful to do each day. A useful job to go to, or a great hobby to devote hours of time to. Friends to visit and places to see. She wanted to eat out every day even if it was only a coffee and a cheeseburger in one of the cheap places. It had been a long time coming, Emily Nightingale's coming of age. But now she could see it all so clearly in her mind. She wasn't going back to routine and solitude, and peeling spuds over the kitchen sink, and eventually joining the rest of the Nightingales in their private plot in the village cemetery.

"Oh my God," she sighed with relief. "It's over."

She had another two hours to fill before she had to be at work.

"I'll write the letter now," she said.

She took her tea and croissant and sat down by the window. She yawned widely and began the letter to her husband, writing slowly and carefully on a notepad she'd bought for fifty cents in a discount store.

*Dear David, I've thought a lot about this and I want a divorce.*

No, that was too abrupt. She tore out the page and rolled it up into a ball.

*Dear David, how are you? This is going to come as a bit of a shock to you but I want a divorce.*

God no, that was still too brutal. Another page was ripped out.

*Dear David, how are you?*

*Thank you for being so patient and understanding. I have always loved you very much. And I know you have always loved me. And that it hasn't always been easy to live with me. But I've changed a lot in recent months and I don't want to live in Fermanagh any more. It's not Fermanagh that's the problem or even yourself. It's just that I need my own space. I love New York and I want to live on my own from now on and I'm sorry but I want a divorce. There is nobody else involved, I promise you. It's just something I need to do for my own happiness. I hope you can find happiness too someday soon.*

*Yours sincerely,*

*Emily*

Yes, that would do for starters, she decided. She'd post the letter on her way to work, and hope that she didn't fall asleep today, standing behind the counter. She hadn't sat up all night worrying for years. It was quite exciting really to have something to sit up all night for, to be honest. She'd have to put her address on the letter now too, for David would have to go to a solicitor and there'd be forms to sign. They'd been living apart for eighteen months already. Surely it wouldn't take too long to get the formalities over and done with? Lots of mature ladies were leaving their husbands these days, in America as well as in Ireland and Britain. She'd read about it in the *New York Times*. It was a golden time for older ladies, she told herself bravely. Not just resigned to the housework any more. Not just picking up after their husbands any more. Until their backs gave out or their fingers got arthritis and then they had to get the home help in.

"I've got ten good years left in me yet," Emily said, sipping her cup of weak tea. The only thing that bothered her about America was the weak tea, she thought suddenly. They had coffee you could stand a spoon up in, yes. But their tea was like warm water no matter how many teabags you put in the pot. No wonder so many Americans said they never drank tea. Still, bad tea aside, she wasn't going to spend the rest of her days asking her husband what he fancied for his lunch.

She would call Ruby as well, she decided. She'd call that very day and tell her daughter not to worry about her any more, and that she wasn't coming home for a good while yet. She was happy here in New York and she was enjoying her job at the bakery and she wasn't ready to come home to Ireland and take her seat in God's Waiting Room. And maybe Ruby could send her out a few packets of good strong tea from M&S if she had a minute to spare anytime? The Fair Trade stuff had the best flavour, she reckoned.

No, then again, maybe not.

Tea was probably not the most suitable thing to be asking for at this particular stage, she decided. But anyhow she'd talk to Ruby this morning also. It was high time they cleared the air. Poor Ruby, Emily thought to herself. Ruby was headed down the same path that she herself had been on for so many years. A dull daily routine in that little dress shop of hers: like a hamster on a wheel, every day exactly the same.

At least when I get sick of the sight of iced doughnuts, I can move on, Emily told herself smugly.

She folded the pages of the letter to her husband and slipped them into a cheap envelope. Stamps she could buy on the way to work. Emily yawned again and went to lie down for an hour. But she remembered to set her alarm clock so that she didn't sleep in.

"Don't want to get fired," she told herself. Oh, it was so

fabulous to think that she was now in a position to even get fired. God bless America.

Back home in Belfast, Ruby was lifting the red velvet evening bag out of the display case. The red bag she would parcel up and send to her mother just as soon as she had an address to send it to.

# 30

# The Lonely Father

Ruby parked her car at the front door and this time her father came out to greet her. He practically flew across the gravel he was going that fast. He looked a lot better than he had in recent months, though. He'd put on some weight and his clothes were neatly pressed.

"Steady on, Dad," Ruby said, getting out of the car and reaching out her arms towards him.

They hugged each other fiercely for about half a minute.

"Thanks for coming, love. I don't know why I'm being so stupid about it," he said, sniffling. It was clear he'd been crying for hours. "She's been gone long enough. I should have known she was never coming back to me."

"Oh Dad, are you all right?" Ruby said, giving him another big hug and pushing the car door shut with her foot.

"Not too bad, considering," he said in a low, tired voice. "There's never a dull moment with your mother."

"Divorce, huh? Did she really ask you for a divorce?" Ruby asked.

"Yes, I have the letter here in my pocket," he said. "Come inside and I'll show you."

Together, arms linked, they went into the house. Ruby was surprised to see it was looking splendid. The entire place was immaculate, in fact. The straggly weeds were gone from the drive and there were fresh flowers in a tall vase on the hall table.

"I see the housekeeper and the gardener have worked out well?" Ruby said, very impressed with such a high standard of tidiness.

"Yes, they're lovely people," Ruby's father said at once. "The parish priest put me on to them. He's a great man and he's been very supportive in all of this. I had a wee chat with him a few days ago. Anyway, yes, the housekeeper and the gardener, they were glad to get the bit of work, God bless them indeed. But what do you think is going on over there in New York? Has your mother met someone, do you think? She *said* there was nobody else but I don't know what to believe. She's a very good-looking woman still. I mean, why has she waited all this time to ask me for a divorce?"

"Dad, I honestly don't know what to think. She's told me next to nothing on the phone, all the time she's been away . . . just little bits of trivia. Jasmine says that she thinks Mum is having the mother of all crises."

"You mean, it's just a phase? A hormonal thing."

"More or less. Yes."

"And she doesn't really mean it?"

"Well, that's just it. I don't *know* if she means it, Dad. I guess the two of you will have to start communicating *properly* soon. For a start, you need to decide what you want. I feel weird even asking you this . . . but do you even want Mum back? You seem to be managing quite well on your own these days."

"I suppose I am. But how will we sort things out? What will I do to get in touch? She doesn't have a phone in this place where she's staying, her mobile is never on, and we still don't know where she works exactly. Will I go over there and wait on the doorstep, do you think? There's an address on the envelope."

"Oh Dad, I'm not sure. Would it be too much for you if she refused to talk to you? It would, wouldn't it? You'd be very upset. And you'd still have to travel home again. It's an eight or nine-hour flight, don't forget. And that's each way, obviously. That's a lot of travelling to do when you're not in good form."

"Would you come with me, Ruby?"

"Dad, to be honest, I'd rather not," Ruby said.

"Why not?"

"Because it's not really my business, that's why," Ruby sighed. "I'm not getting involved in a big thing like this. This is between you and Mum."

"But she's your mother."

"I know she is, Dad, but she's your wife. I'm in my thirties now, you know! Some children are only babies when their parents get divorced."

"Still and all?" he pleaded. "We could make a holiday out of it?"

"No, honestly, it'd be too much emotional upheaval for me, I think. I'm still getting over the funeral. I mean, it's only recently I could face going into a restaurant without Jonathan by my side, for heaven's sake. And it's so crowded in New York. So much to think about."

"Of course, I'm so sorry. Listen, I'll get you some lunch," Ruby's father said, nodding his head with resignation. "I had a notion you wouldn't want to get involved. And of course, you're quite right not to. It's high time your mother and I got our lives organised. Come through to the kitchen."

While Ruby sat down, her father donned a pair of oven gloves, lifted a big Shepherd's Pie out of the oven and set it gently on the kitchen table.

"Wow, this smells lovely, Dad," Ruby said, pleased that he'd gone to so much effort for her.

"I made it myself," he announced proudly.

"Really? Did you? I thought the housekeeper made it?"

"No, I went on a little cookery course they were running at the Buttermarket Centre," he admitted shyly. "Just a wee social sort of thing, nothing too fancy."

"Dad, I'm delighted for you," Ruby said, fetching two plates from the cupboard and helping them each to a huge slice. "This is a great sign altogether."

"I don't know about a great sign, Ruby, but at least I won't starve. Do you think I should call her bluff? Agree to the divorce and see if that shocks her back to reality?"

"No, I think you should decide what *you* want to do, and then proceed with dignity and caution."

"Um, very sensible advice! You know what, I was speaking to the gardener about it this morning. Niall is his name. He's divorced. He's only twenty-seven years of age and he's divorced. What is the world coming to?"

"Twenty-seven, huh? What happened to his marriage? Did he say?"

"His wife had an affair with an older fella, it seems. A rich businessman in his forties that she met when he came into her salon to have his hair cut. They got chatting and one thing led to another, so Niall said. She left him a note beside the telephone. To say they'd gone to England to start a new life together."

"Oh my God."

"Aye! Niall said it wasn't too bad in the end really. They had no children and hardly any equity in the house. So he bought her out, divorced her and just carried on as normal with his job in the call-centre. Mind you, that's why he's doing the bit of gardening on the side now. Because he needs the extra money to pay the mortgage on his own." He shook his head sadly. "It seems no big deal to get divorced these days. Niall says all of his pals are either single or divorced or just living together. But none of them are actually married."

"I know. Sure I'm widowed and Jasmine is single. And Teresa Morris is a widow too. You know that poor woman, her husband was killed in a farming accident?"

"Oh sorry, I clean forgot to tell you," Ruby's father said, making a guilty face.

"It's all right, Dad. You've clearly had a lot on your mind these last few years."

After dinner they went for a long walk around the village and then along the lough path.

"These reeds aren't as high as I remember them," Ruby said sadly.

"They're still as sharp, pet, so mind yourself," her father replied. "Fierce cut you can get from a reed. Right to the bone."

"Are there still dragonflies?"

"Of course there are."

"Dad?"

"Yes?"

"Do you love Mum?"

"Of course I love her."

"Why do you love her?" Ruby asked.

"That's a silly question," he said crossly.

"No, it isn't. Tell me."

"Well, she was beautiful. Still is. And she was a lot of fun in the early days, always laughing and carrying on, telling the funniest jokes you can imagine. Doing all the silly voices. She made me laugh a lot."

"And when did that stop?"

"It didn't stop exactly."

"What then?"

"There were quiet days. And then quiet weeks. And then she would go off for a day on her own somewhere."

"And that became the pattern, did it?" Ruby asked gently.

"Yes."

"But you still loved each other?"

"Yes."

"And Mum said in her letter that she still loved you?"

"Yes . . . She did . . . Where is this all going, Ruby?"

"Well, I'm no expert but from what I can see it's a basic personality clash, that sort of thing. Mum loves you but she needs excitement as well. She needs change. For you it's enough to go walking around the loughs. Or maybe listening to the radio. Or just pottering in the shed and making things."

"Yes?"

"So, if you're to get back with Mum, one of you is going to have to compromise. And obviously it's not going to be her. So it'll have to be you, Dad."

"How do you mean?" he asked. He sounded mystified.

"I mean, you might have to start doing what she wants for a change."

"Like what?"

"Like selling the house and moving to Enniskillen or even to Belfast. Or maybe even abroad somewhere, though you'll have to be careful where you buy nowadays, some resorts are going downhill. And you'd have to start taking Mum out more. And going on holiday more. Anything she wants, really. So she'll start to laugh again."

"But I'm a home bird, Ruby. She knew that when she married me," he said in a worried voice. "I don't want to be a jet-setter out partying every night of the week at some trendy Spanish resort. And some ridiculous holiday clothes on me! We're retired now. We're past all that."

"Dad love, I don't think *Mum's* past all that. Do you see? I think it's now or never, for this marriage. Mum has thrown down the gauntlet here. She's going to divorce you unless you make major changes. And it's up to you now whether you join her in her little world or stay here in yours. And to be brutally honest, maybe there's nothing you can do to make her change her mind. Maybe it's too late already?"

"What do you think I should do, Ruby?"

"That's entirely up to you, Daddy."

"I knew you'd say that."

"I'm sorry. I only wish I had some better advice to give you."

"Ah, it's okay. I'll think of something," he smiled.

"I've met someone. I suppose I should tell you," she said then.

"Really? A man?" he asked.

"Yes, a man. I'm not bisexual, Dad."

"Shush, for God's sake!" Ruby's father said, looking over his shoulder. "Someone might hear you. Bisexual indeed!"

"He's a gardener too," Ruby laughed. "A proper gardener and not just a weekend handyman. Tom Lavery is his name. Seriously though, he's a lovely man. He's a widower. His wife died of cancer five years ago."

"Is that right? God bless the two of them. Isn't that desperate altogether? But I suppose that's something major you have in common now. Where did you meet this Tom Lavery?"

"It's a long story," Ruby said. "He delivered my Christmas tree ages back."

"I see. And are you very fond of him?"

"Yes, I am. I mean, we haven't had a big talk about the future or anything, it's early days for us, but I like him a lot. We've been out together a few times and we just get on well, you know? It's easy to talk to him. He's very easy-going when you get to know him. But he's quiet at first."

"Fair enough. I never could stand these life-and-soul types. The majority of them seem to hang their fiddles on the back of the door. They use up all their energy and *craic* on their friends and hangers-on and then the poor wife gets nothing but a grumpy mood and a scowl."

"He's not like that, believe me," Ruby smiled.

"And there's been no, what did you call it, no personality clash?"

"Not yet, no. And then Jasmine and I sprinkled Jonathan's ashes a few days ago in the Mourne Mountains."

"Ah, love . . ."

"It was early in the morning, a glorious sunny morning . . . there was nobody else there . . . I think I'm ready to move on, Dad. Or at least begin to move on. I trust Tom. There's a kind of peace about him and that's what I need right now. We had a little misunderstanding a while back. Well, I got cold feet, to tell you the truth. I didn't think I was ready to start seeing anyone else. But he was really nice and understanding about it. And so we decided to carry on. There's sadness too. I mean, he loved his wife very much. And he always will. But I understand that. I loved Jonathan with all my heart too."

"I hope it works out for you both then. I really do," Ruby's father said, patting her affectionately on the arm. "You deserve it."

"Thanks. And what will you do? About Mum?"

"I'm going to have a good, long think," he said, nodding his head, and smiling. "You know me, Ruby! It takes me a while to get my act together! But don't you be worrying about me, love, I'll get myself sorted out . . . eventually . . ."

# 31

# The Return of the Snow

The months flew by and soon it was Christmas time again. Ruby's father had written to his wife twice, offering to make some significant changes to their lifestyle, and even to go for a few sessions of relationship counselling, but so far she'd not replied.

Emily called Ruby every week now to keep in touch, however, which was something of a development. And she'd also called to thank her for the beautiful red handbag and all the goodies (a packet of strong tea included) that she'd sent over from Belfast.

And then one day Emily had asked Ruby to please tell her husband that she was very sorry, but that she still wanted to divorce him. There was no point in answering her husband's very nice letters, she said to Ruby, because he'd only expect her to stop her silliness in New York and come home again, and behave herself. And she wasn't going to do that, not ever. And offering to go to the cinema more, and for weekend breaks to Dublin, just wasn't going to be enough to save their marriage, unfortunately. "Too little, too late", had been the exact phrase she'd used. So he'd better just start getting used to it.

SHARON OWENS

Ruby duly passed on the message and her father seemed to take it well enough. He had signed up for another cookery course, he told Ruby, and he'd made some new friends there and also in the church choir. So he was getting out and about at least once a week and it was doing him "the power of good".

Ruby and Tom saw each other every week too. They'd go for long, meandering walks along the beach or around the gardens at Camberwell. Occasionally they held hands if nobody else was around to see them. They had dinner sometimes in the quiet restaurant near the park that they both liked. Or they had lunch at Ruby's flat or at the café at Camberwell. Mrs Kenny was always happy to see Ruby and she always gave her a small basket of scones to take back to her flat.

So far though, Ruby and Tom hadn't spent the night together. They both wanted to, though. That much was patently obvious by now, so it wasn't down to a lack of sexual chemistry or anything. No, they were both dying to take that next step. It was all they could do sometimes not to just run to the nearest private space and tear each other's clothes off . . . They'd just had some very tender and delicious kisses, mostly in the maze when it was closed to the public. But spending the night together might mean they were officially a couple, perhaps even ready to live together, and they both wanted to be one hundred per cent sure before they took things to that final stage.

Early on Christmas Eve it began to snow again. They'd been predicting it for a while on the weather forecast but nobody in Belfast really worried about the snow unless it persisted for more than three or four days. That was usually when the patience of the locals began to run out. However, Ruby felt very emotional when she opened her bedroom curtains at seven o'clock in the morning and saw the soft white flurries brushing past her frozen window. It was the third anniversary of Jonathan's death.

254

Ruby stood there, statue-still for a minute, just gazing out at the blizzard. The streets were still clear but by the looks of it they'd be under a few inches of snow by lunchtime. Ruby blew a tender kiss skywards, to Jonathan, and then she went into the kitchen to make breakfast.

She was going to keep the shop open all day today. And Jasmine and herself were planning to give a small packet of chocolates away free to every customer. They were going to play Christmas songs on the stereo and had even put up a small Christmas tree in one corner. One of Tom's trees, as it happened . . .

"Can you believe it's snowing?" Jasmine gasped when she arrived for work at nine o'clock. There were even snowflakes stuck to her eyelashes.

"No, I can't," Ruby replied, shaking her head.

"What's going on with the bloody weather?"

"Search me."

"I mean that's three years in a row now we've had heavy snow."

"I know. I don't remember getting weather like this every year in the past," Ruby said thoughtfully. "Must be a cold snap?"

"I thought it was supposed to be getting warmer?" Jasmine muttered, brushing snow out of her hair. "Global warming, my foot."

"Um, I'm not sure but I think if Ireland loses the Gulf Stream effect and also gets more rain, well, we could end up with a climate like Iceland's – under snow and ice for months at a time."

"Christ, I hope not. Typical bloody Ireland! This place has little enough going for it already," Jasmine groaned. "Without us all having to wear fur coats to the Spar shop for a loaf of bread! Talk about Narnia!"

"You said last week that it wasn't all that bad here," Ruby reminded her. "You know, like, compared to Africa or the Middle East?"

"Yes, well, I'm just a bit fed up today. I still have no idea who the hell's been sending me these blasted flowers!" Jasmine said, hanging up her coat and changing into a dry pair of shoes. "A great big bunch of pink tulips or roses or lilies every month and no message on it?" The florist still wouldn't tell her who they were from. Said it was confidential. "I'm definitely thinking of refusing to accept the next one. Or maybe even going to the police, like my parents suggested."

"I told you it'd be a stalker," Ruby said in a sympathetic voice.

"Yes, I know you did. Thank you for the vote of confidence! I might have known if something nice like this happened to me, there'd be a stalker on the other end of it. God's sake!"

"I mean, it's a lovely gesture and everything," Ruby soothed. "But one bouquet a month, for the last six months! That's just too long to wait for any mystery man to come forward."

"Yes, I was hoping it'd be some lovely shy guy. Like your Tom. And that he'd have come in here, in person, by now. I'm getting very bored with all the suspense, Ruby."

"So am I," Ruby agreed meaningfully. Sometimes Jasmine could speak of little else!

"Right, so what are our plans for today?" Jasmine wanted to know.

"Nothing more to do really. You've gift-wrapped lots of nice things, the shop is spotless, we've all our chocolates ready to give out. I think we've only to open up and hope the shoppers can still be bothered to venture forth in this awful weather."

"Okay. Is Tom coming round to see you later?"

"Maybe. I said I'd phone him and let him know how I'm feeling. I thought I might prefer to spend the third anniversary of Jonathan's death by myself. But now that it's snowing and everything, well, it might be nice to have some company."

"You're very brave, Ruby."

"Not at all. The bravest thing I've ever done is put a burgundy rinse in my hair without doing the allergy test first," Ruby smiled.

"No really, you are the bravest person I know," Jasmine said gently, thinking back to the night when Jonathan had been so tragically killed. She wanted to ask Ruby if she was falling in love with Tom but she didn't dare. Not yet anyway. Whatever Tom and Ruby had together was obviously still very vulnerable and fragile and might be spoiled by too much outside attention. Or joking around . . .

"What are you doing tonight? Still going to that swanky party?" Ruby asked.

"At Café Vaudeville? Yes. Might as well go, seeing as my mystery man is still a complete bloody mystery. Can I have a staff discount on one of these short black cardigans with the big buttons, please, Ruby? It'd just go perfectly with my lovely new dress from Dotty P."

"Of course," Ruby said, smiling. "Be my guest. Have a corsage as well, on the house."

"Oh you sweetheart!"

Then the first customer of the day arrived. A well-dressed man came bustling in the door, red in the face with rushing, and a list of twenty-one names in his hand.

"I'm so sorry," he said apologetically, "But I've left it all to the last minute as usual. Could you ever help me out? I need gifts for my four teenage nieces, two sisters-in-law, the ten ladies who work for me in the office, my mother, my grandmother, two aunts and my cleaning lady. I'm just giving all the males on my list either a bottle of wine or a voucher for HMV depending on whether they're over thirty or under it. But I daresay the ladies will be very upset if I don't get them something a bit more thoughtful. Especially my cleaning lady – she's very sensitive about getting a Christmas present."

Ruby and Jasmine exchanged smug glances: this was going to be a breeze now with Jasmine's super-speedy, pre-wrapped gift service. In less than five minutes Jasmine had all twenty-one gifts safely packed in two large carrier bags. With the initials of each recipient written in pencil on the back of the gift tag, the receipt printed out and the free box of chocolates handed over with a smile.

"Thank you so much," the man said, beaming from ear to ear. "What a terrific little shop this is! I thought I'd be stuck here all morning. At this rate I might even be early for my first meeting. I must tell all my friends about you. Happy Christmas!"

"Happy Christmas," Ruby and Jasmine replied, delighted with such a good start to Christmas Eve.

The shop was busy all day, and Ruby and Jasmine even had to stagger their lunch breaks to cope with the influx. They'd never had so many customers in one day, in fact. The cabinets were almost empty and every one of Jasmine's special gifts had been sold. By closing time the shop was stripped bare and Ruby and Jasmine were utterly exhausted.

"So much for my wee hobby-shop," Ruby yawned. "That was unbelievable. Every bone in my body is aching."

"Me too," Jasmine agreed. "My feet are in shreds. I could lie down there on the armchair and sleep, right now."

"Will you be fit to go to your party?" Ruby asked.

"I don't know if I'll have the energy, Ruby. I might faint if I drink too much, feeling this tired. I'll go home now and sleep for a bit, and maybe I'll find my second wind. What time is it?"

"Six fifteen."

"Well, if I sleep until nine I might be able to make it," Jasmine said, peering out at the snow. "Mind you, the weather is so awful. It's just like the North Pole out there. I'm tempted to stay in bed and watch TV instead."

"So am I," Ruby agreed. The idea of her cosy bed was sheer heaven to her just then but Tom was coming around later.

"Did you get a chance to ring Tom at lunchtime?" Jasmine asked just then.

"Yes, I did, just for a minute. He has a mobile now."

"Wow. Progress!"

"I know. It's great not to have to ring the café all the time. I love Mrs Kenny but it makes me feel like a teenager – asking my boyfriend's mummy if I can please speak to him for two seconds."

"Are Tom's parents coming home for Christmas, by the way?"

"No, they're staying in India. They're having a party in the orphanage they run there. He showed me some photographs of them both last week. They seem a lovely couple."

"Right." Jasmine wasn't overly interested in Indian orphanages; she had a very useful knack of blocking out the various miseries of the human condition. "So is Tom coming over to see you tonight?"

"Yes, the Land Rover is fine in the snow, he said. God, I hope so. I get so nervous of anyone travelling to see me in bad weather," Ruby confessed.

"I know you do," Jasmine nodded. "That's perfectly understandable."

"So anyway, I'll see you out. And will you please call me if you can't get a taxi home or anything?" Ruby said then.

"Yes, Mummy," Jasmine teased.

"Jasmine, honestly, I don't want you walking home alone, anything could happen," Ruby said sternly. "Promise me you'll call if you're stranded? I don't care what time it is. Tom and I will come and fetch you home in the Land Rover."

"Okay, I promise. And thanks."

"Oh, and here's your present," Ruby said, going to the kitchenette and handing over a medium-sized box. "You can't open it till tomorrow," she beamed, hoping Jasmine would love the quirky, bone China, rose-patterned teacups and saucers in a leather box within.

"Thanks, Ruby," Jasmine said delightedly. "And here's yours." She gave Ruby a smaller box containing a pair of red glass earrings to match the silver brooch she'd given her for her birthday.

The two women hugged each other tightly and then Jasmine put on her coat, boots, scarf and gloves and set off into the snowy gloom. Her flat was quite close by, otherwise Ruby would have insisted on her waiting on a lift from Tom.

When she was alone in the shop Ruby glanced round at the little Christmas tree and the depleted cabinets and wardrobes. They had taken an absolute fortune in money; she would have to get it into the bank as soon as possible. Switching off the lights now she carefully glanced out the window to make sure no robbers were waiting in the shadows. Then she locked the shop door behind her, and opened the door to her flat and hurried up the stairs. Tom was due to arrive at seven, and she knew that he'd not be one minute late. He knew the story of what Ruby had been through one Christmas Eve three years ago.

Ruby glanced at herself in the hall mirror. She looked tired. She looked worn out, really.

"I'd sooner go to bed now myself," she told her reflection. "I'm that wrecked."

But still, it was nice to have someone special coming to visit. More than nice, to be honest. It was lovely. And with the snow lying, they might as well spend the evening in. Ruby had made one of her famous slow-cooker casseroles and judging by the aroma in from the kitchen, it was almost ready. She had two bottles of red wine in the rack and a small Christmas cake in the cupboard. There were some Christmas DVDs they could watch and there was bound to be something on the telly, a nice romantic movie maybe? And if the weather got even worse Tom could always sleep over . . .

"Oh, help!" Ruby laughed out loud. But she knew the time was coming when they'd have run out of excuses not to sleep together, and also the will power to say no . . .

She'd have a warm shower now to soothe her aching feet. Maybe rub on some of that lovely peppermint foot balm. And even though she was utterly exhausted she'd make an effort to dress up for him. She'd wear her red silk skirt from Monsoon with black opaque tights, red pumps and a black fitted sweater.

Her father was going to a dinner-dance in a hotel in Enniskillen tonight with some of his friends from the cookery course, so that was all right. She wouldn't have to worry about him being too lonely. Her mother was going to a party in her friend Dorothy's house. Apparently Dorothy's lazy son had finally found himself a job and had moved in with his pregnant girlfriend after being given an ultimatum by both women. So Dorothy was throwing a massive party for everyone at the art club and then after Christmas she was going to downsize to something more manageable. All in all things were looking up.

At seven o'clock on the dot Ruby heard Tom knocking gently on the front door, down below in the snow-filled street. She hoped he'd like the scarf and gloves she'd bought for him. She didn't want to overdo the gift, not for their first Christmas together. And Tom spent so much time out of doors he was bound to need all the gloves and scarves he could get. Smiling to herself she quickly applied some pale bronze lipstick to her lips and a spray of light perfume to both wrists and then she went hurrying down the stairs to greet him.

But when Ruby saw Tom standing there in a new coat with the collars turned up, sturdy black boots on his feet and fresh snowflakes in his hair, she almost forgot how tired she was.

"You look absolutely *gorgeous*," she told him warmly.

And Tom simply laughed out loud.

# 32

## Some Things are Best Kept Secret

It was midway between Christmas Day and New Year's Eve, and Ruby and Jasmine were having lunch in Ruby's flat. They weren't going to open the shop today, Ruby decided. They had hardly any stock left, for one thing. And for another, the snow was frozen into great muddy ridges on most of the roads in Belfast. And nobody was venturing out of their home unless it was really necessary. Jasmine hadn't bothered going to her party in the end, she said. She'd slept right through the alarm and only woke up when her mother phoned her on Christmas morning to ask what time she'd be round for dinner.

Ruby and Tom, on the other hand, had spent a wonderful evening together on Christmas Eve. Magical, really . . .

Ruby wondered if she ought to tell Jasmine about it now? The poor girl was worn out with curiosity. Though she could tell that Jasmine was doing her best not to ask a thousand questions, all of them deeply personal!

Should she tell Jasmine, for instance, that when she'd seen Tom standing in the snow on Christmas Eve, she'd been overcome with affection for him, and lust! His dark eyes looked so pleased when she complimented his new coat. Should she reveal that she'd practically pulled him in over the doorstep and kissed him passionately until the snow in his hair melted and trickled down both their faces? Would Jasmine like to know that they'd staggered up the steps together, still kissing, and went straight into Ruby's pretty white bedroom? Where they proceeded to undress in less than thirty seconds flat! And that Tom had looked incredible, naked. A gorgeous hairy chest on him, and the most amazing, muscular legs. And that he'd kissed Ruby *all over* before making love to her for more than two hours! And that when they'd finally reached *that moment*, it was the most incredible sense of release and well-being Ruby had ever known? And that immediately afterward, Tom had told her he loved her, and that she'd said she was falling in love with him too. And now they were both counting the minutes until they could be together again.

No, better not tell Jasmine any of that, Ruby decided.

Some things were best kept a secret.

"More wine, Jasmine?" she said instead.

Meanwhile Tom was sitting in his shed; wondering if Ruby had liked the Christmas gift he'd given her. A small wooden box containing some rare lily bulbs. Yes, it was a bit obvious he'd give her something horticultural but then again he didn't want to give her jewellery or anything too personal like that, not just yet. Not until she felt ready to accept such intimate presents from him. And then she'd amazed him by kissing him hungrily and taking him to bed . . .

The snow was still lying today and Tom wondered if they should make plans to cope with this sort of weather on a regular basis at Camberwell? The main lawns might even start to die back in the shadier areas if their summers didn't improve very soon.

He started to idly play with some loose strands of florist's wire that were lying on the table and without really thinking about it he formed them into a large circle and twisted the ends together. He could make a wreath for Ruby, he decided suddenly. He could hang it on her door as a surprise, or would that be totally silly of him? Only since the manager at Camberwell had decided to hang wreaths on all the doors for Christmas, Tom had become rather adept at putting them together quickly. Well, it would pass a bit of time for him anyway. It was too cold and snowy to do anything else. He collected some stray evergreen branches and bits of holly and set to work, adding some small white roses as a finishing touch. Then he wrapped up in his warmest coat, put on the scarf and gloves Ruby had given him and drove in to the Ravenhill Road to hang the wreath on Ruby's front door. There was no answer when he knocked so he assumed she was still asleep. The shops were all closed today and there was hardly any traffic.

But as he was walking away he heard a tapping sound above him and he was delighted to see Ruby waving to him from her sitting-room window. Moments later she came outside, pulling on her winter coat and some bright blue and purple gloves.

"I was just about to go for a walk," she said. "I was getting a touch of cabin fever in there. Just up the road a few minutes or until my feet go numb. Would you like to come with me?"

"Surely," Tom replied.

"Sorry I almost didn't hear you knocking before," Ruby told him as they held hands and set off down the street, their feet crunching through almost six inches of fresh snow. "I was on the phone to my father."

"Oh, that's okay. I thought you'd be sleeping anyway. We were awake all night, you know, the night we . . ."

"I know and it was wonderful, Tom. I only wish you hadn't offered to help out at Camberwell over Christmas. I'd have stayed in bed all week with you, if you'd been free."

"Oh, Ruby, thank you so much for saying that! How's your dad?"

"Surprisingly enough he's not too bad. He's having some people from his cookery course over for dinner today and would you believe it, he's cooking a fourteen-pound turkey with all the trimmings? And they're all bringing side dishes and desserts."

"Sounds great," Tom said. "Sounds like he's having a great time on that course."

"Yes, I know, isn't it? I nearly fainted when he told me he was having a dinner party. He's such a recluse normally."

"Good for him, then. And good for your mother too, I suppose."

"Oh yes, surely, of course. I only wish that he and my mother could have been this enterprising and resourceful years and years ago. It's like they had to split up to get going again, you know? All the years they were together they did nothing but sit in that big fancy house imagining everyone in the village was jealous of their money."

"Maybe they were?"

"Maybe, but I doubt it. It's an easy-going sort of village."

"Ruby, there's no such thing as an easy-going sort of village."

"I suppose not."

"Are you not going to see your dad today? I could drive you?" Tom offered.

"No, thanks a million but no. They're all keen cooks so it'll be all cookery-chat and I think half of them are lonely hearts. Dad keeps mentioning this one woman. I don't expect there's anything to it but you never know. He did ask me for some advice on what to wear tonight . . . God help him! They'll have much more fun if I'm not there to spy on them." Ruby smiled. "And anyway it'd be no fun driving in this weather."

"And how's your mother getting on?"

"She's amazing, she really is. She rang me this morning. She said her New Best Friend Dorothy got her out of her old frumpy skirts and blouses and now she's wearing combats and Converse.

And she's had her hair cut really short like Mia Farrow in the 1960s. So handy in the mornings, she told me. No more bother with getting her hair curled and set any more. And today they're having dinner in a retro-style diner in Dorothy's neighbourhood in Brooklyn."

"Well, as long as she's happy," Tom said, holding Ruby's hand a little tighter.

"Yes. I never realised how just dull their lives had become. I suppose I'm glad for them both really. I just miss them so much, you know, as a couple? Christ, I hope my mother gets tired of this New York thing before she gets mugged or stabbed or worse."

"I know. It's kinda weird but as you said, it's hopefully just a phase. She'll be home soon. And you know that any of us could get mugged right here in dear old Belfast. Every weekend almost, there's a pensioner burgled."

"True. Anyway, what are you doing for dinner today?"

"Nothing special. I might pop round to Mrs Kenny's later for a bite of supper. She always cooks far too much for her own family," Tom said fondly. "They've got Noah today, by the way. Her grandchildren love playing with him when they come to visit."

Ruby stopped walking then and turned to face Tom. She noticed he was wearing the scarf and gloves she'd bought him and she was very touched. Tom's eyes were sparkling with interest in her and in her crazy parents and suddenly Ruby felt like kissing him again. Kissing him passionately right there on the street. They were standing beside the railings to the park and there were no other people about yet. She turned her face up towards his and looked at his lips with a twinkle in her eye. Tom's expression was only quizzical for a moment before he held Ruby closer to him and kissed her tenderly. A long, lingering kiss that sent both their pulses racing. Ruby felt a familiar tingly feeling shooting up and down her body. Tom was such an expert kisser. They barely noticed a sprinkling of fresh snowflakes swirling around their shoulders.

"You're having dinner with me today, Tom Lavery," Ruby said, laughing, when they eventually came up for air. "Or maybe it'll be supper by the time we get around to it."

"I thought you'd never ask," he replied in a low voice.

As they were making their way back to the flat a little robin redbreast watched them from the shelter of an ancient oak tree in the park. The robin had his head to one side almost as if he was approving of their heady romance. Then as Ruby and Tom reached the flat and went inside, the robin puffed up his feathers and flew away.

# 33

## Camberwell Revisited

By New Year's Eve the snow had melted away, and the citizens of Belfast staggered up off their sofas and ventured out of doors again. Filled to the brim with turkey sandwiches and microwave plum pudding, rich chocolates and fine wines, they were eager to breathe some fresh air into their lungs and stretch their legs. And Ruby and Tom were no exception. Now officially relaxed in each other's company, they were filled with a new energy and vitality, and a renewed sense of hope for the new year ahead. The season that had once smothered both of them with sheer dread had become a happy time once more.

But as Ruby arrived at Camberwell to go for a long walk with Tom she was dismayed to find him sitting on the doorstep of his cottage with tears in his eyes.

"What's happened?" she said, hurrying from her car to hug him.

"It's Noah."

"Is he ill?"

Tom shook his head. "Worse than that."

"Oh Tom, don't tell me he's died?"

"Yes, I found him this morning in his basket. The vet said he must have been ill for a while but not in any pain."

"I'm so sorry, Tom."

"Well, I just wish he'd have gone on for another while yet."

"I know."

Ruby urged Tom into the kitchen where she made tea for him. He wouldn't eat toast or anything.

"I'm going to bury him," Tom said then.

"Okay. Do you want to be alone?" Ruby asked.

"No, I'd like you to come with me if that's okay?"

"Of course I will."

"He's in his basket," Tom said, sighing heavily. "You won't have to look at him."

"That's all right, Tom," Ruby assured him. "I'm fine."

"Okay. Thanks, Ruby."

"I'm going to bury him beside that statue in the Christmas tree plantation. I've already dug the . . ."

"It's okay. We'll just go and do it whenever you're ready. Don't worry about me," Ruby said, starting to wash the dishes that had been left to soak in the sink.

"There's just you and me now," Tom said, half-laughing with abject misery. He leaned forward on his chair, holding his head in his hands.

Ruby thought he was crying but she didn't know whether to go to him or not. Jonathan had always liked a cuddle when he was unhappy but maybe Tom was the strong, silent type.

"Will you be all right?" Ruby asked him after a few minutes.

"Yes, I'll be all right," Tom sighed. He sat up straight and dried his eyes. "Sorry for the dramatics, Ruby. I always knew I'd lose him one day. That's the thing about pets, we know we'll probably outlive them. Maybe that's why we love them so much?"

"Maybe," Ruby agreed.

"And Noah was the last link I had to Kate, you see. You know what I mean?"

"Yes, I understand."

"I mean there's always her family . . . but Noah was her dog. She chose him."

"Shush, it's okay, Tom, really, I do understand."

"Come on then," Tom said gently.

"It's all right if you need more time to say goodbye to him?"

"No, I'll do it now and then we'll go for that walk. Is Murlough beach okay with you? I scattered Kate's ashes there. I want to throw a flower into the sea for her and one for Noah too."

"That's a lovely idea," Ruby said, nodding her head. Obviously Tom would want to mark the occasion in some way and she wasn't surprised that it involved both flowers and walking. Two things she'd come to associate closely with Tom Lavery.

After the burial, Tom laid a wreath of greenery and white roses on Noah's grave and Ruby offered him her hand to hold as they walked back to his cottage. They had a light lunch before climbing sombrely into the Land Rover and heading for the beach.

Tom was exceptionally quiet so Ruby filled the silence by telling him about her six secrets of happiness. And the little story that had led to each one.

"I daresay you think it's silly," she said, blushing slightly. "Or just common sense. But somehow it all seemed like a great revelation to me."

"I think that's a lovely idea and very true," Tom said at last as they parked by the sand dunes and set off towards the beach. "Some people live their whole lives and never find happiness. Maybe they just don't know what to look for?"

"Maybe."

As they walked, Ruby invited Tom to come back to her flat and spend the night there.

"Just in case it's too lonesome for you at the cottage without Noah?" she said gently. "We don't have to do anything, you know? Just be together; just be company for each other . . . I don't think we should spend New Year's Eve being lonely."

"Thanks, Ruby," he said, putting his arm around her shoulders. "I'd like that very much."

# 34

# The Mystery Man Revealed

"I'm really sorry, Jasmine. I thought I was being terribly romantic," Mark Crawford said shyly. He was blushing all the way from his trendy trainers up to his natural blond hairline.

"Well, you might have thought you were being terribly romantic, Mark. But I thought I was about to be murdered by a stalker!"

"Look, I'm really sorry," he said, scratching his head. "I'm really sorry if I've upset you."

"The florist wouldn't give me your name and address," she said accusingly.

"I told her not to."

"Idiot!"

"What can I say? I *am* an idiot! But I've fancied you ever since we were in secondary school together. And I once heard you tell your pal Megan that you'd love it if a mystery admirer sent you bouquets of pink flowers."

Jasmine rolled her eyes. "I was about thirteen for Christ's sake!"

"Well, I remembered. And I just wanted to do something stylish to impress you. You know, the sort of things guys do in romantic films . . ."

"Okay, whatever. But why didn't you come in here yourself and ask me out sooner, though?" Jasmine wanted to know. "I've been going crazy trying to work out who was sending me those damn flowers. Ruby was convinced I was being followed home from work some nights."

"Oh, I'm such a dick head! It didn't occur to me that you would think that. I couldn't have come any sooner, Jasmine. I was too bloody shy – afraid to take the plunge," he said sheepishly. "In case you said no. But all those long nights in the hospital, all I could think of was you."

"Oh my God, were you very ill? Nothing too serious, I hope?" Jasmine asked. Suddenly she was very worried. She didn't want to go falling for a man with a terminal illness, even if he was totally sexy and charming and extremely kissable. She didn't want to end up like Ruby, left reeling in her early thirties with a broken heart.

But Mark began to laugh. He sensed Jasmine was warming to him. "I wasn't a patient, Jasmine. I'm a doctor working here in Belfast. Just finished my studies in Birmingham last year and now I'm working here. I was very lucky to get a place in Belfast, what with the cutbacks and everything."

"Oh wow! Well, that's amazing. A doctor, huh! I thought you always said you were going to be a rally car driver?" Jasmine was completely embarrassed now. And more than a little stunned. A man with good prospects was sending her pink flowers every month. A doctor, no less! A gorgeous looking doctor, with blond hair and cool clothes . . . Oh wow.

"Aye, well, the rally driving didn't pan out. Nice of you to remember that much about me! I'm only just starting out in my medical career, mind," Mark said then as if reading her thoughts. "I'm not exactly minted up yet."

"Well! That's fine by me," Jasmine said, fluttering her eyelashes uncontrollably at him. "I'm not the shallow sort of girl to go all giddy and silly over a medical man, you understand?"

"No, of course not! Does that mean you're not going to let me down then?" Mark asked hopefully, clasping his hands together in mock-prayer.

"Um . . . Are you sure you still like me now though, Mark Crawford? Or is this some trip down Memory Lane for you?"

"Just me being nostalgic, do you mean? No, I've always liked you, Jasmine Mulholland. I had a crush on you all through school but you fancied Jimmy White."

"I did not indeed. He used to spike his hair up with sugar. Anyway, he's a criminal now."

"I know! Did you see the papers! But you did fancy him. You told Megan that you did. You said he had lovely hair. I heard you!"

"You must have spent a lot of time spying on Megan and myself!" Jasmine said, laughing her head off.

"I did, I'm ashamed to say. And I've never forgotten you. But I didn't know where you lived. Or worked. Or even if you were still living in Belfast. I didn't even know where your family was living, only that it was somewhere in Sandy Row. And you don't want to go nosing about in Sandy Row, really. And you're not on one of those networking sites. I checked. Then a few months ago one of my brothers came in here to buy a present for his girlfriend and he recognised you. I came along a few times and looked in and saw you but stalled at the door. Then I got the idea of doing my 'mystery man' act with the pink flowers . . . to intrigue you and I guess to prove how well I remembered you and knew you . . . or so I thought. Seems stupid now in retrospect . . . but it seemed a good idea at the time!"

"Show me your ID," Jasmine said suddenly, almost unable to accept his story.

He showed it. It seemed to check out.

"Swear to me this is all true?" Jasmine said sternly.

"I swear."

"And you're not a married man?"

"No, I'm definitely single."

"Because if I find out you're married or even seeing anyone else, I promise you I'll go straight round to their house or their work or whatever and tell them the truth, point blank. I'm serious."

"That's fine by me."

"Right then."

"Right then."

"Well, in that case I'll be happy to go for that drink with you at the weekend," Jasmine said graciously.

"Great. That's really great – thanks, Jasmine."

At that exact moment Ruby came back from running an errand. Or rather she came back from pretending to be running an errand. Just to give Jasmine and her secret admirer a chance to get to know one another again. And Mark Crawford did look very pleased indeed with himself. He began backing towards the shop door as if he were going to say cheerio. Jasmine was absolutely puffed up with pride, flicking her long hair over her shoulders and fluttering her fingers behind the counter with excitement.

"Jasmine, why don't you get your coat now?" Ruby said, trying not to laugh.

"What for?" Jasmine asked.

"You can leave early today," Ruby said at once. "It's dead quiet. Always is in early January. I can lock up on my own."

"Great idea," Mark said. "Why wait until the weekend to go for that drink?"

Jasmine didn't need asking twice. She grabbed her coat and bag and left the shop arm-in-arm with Mark.

"Shall we have a bite to eat before we go to the pub?" Mark said happily.

"Okay," Jasmine agreed. "We'll just nip back to my apartment first though. I need to freshen up my make-up."

"Okay but you look fine to me. I'll have a good snoop round while you get ready. I've often wondered if you were tidy or messy around the house," Mark laughed. "I'm very tidy, me. Medical training, you know?"

"I'll have you know I'm an excellent housekeeper," Jasmine said mock-huffily.

Five minutes later, Jasmine and Mark were standing in the bedroom of her immaculate apartment in the Bell Towers. They'd got to the end of the tour of Jasmine's home . . . and were now kissing passionately. Jasmine thought she was going to die with happiness. Her feelings for Mark had been so sudden and overwhelming. Thank God she'd made the bed before going to work that morning, she thought as she tore off Mark's clothes to reveal a perfect body underneath. Perfect in every way, in fact. Jasmine began to giggle uncontrollably.

"What's wrong?" Mark said anxiously, glancing downwards.

"Nothing's wrong. Do you know, Doctor Crawford, I think I might have something urgent that you can help me with . . . Oh wow!" Jasmine said for the third time that day as Mark chased her round the bedroom, scooped her up into his tanned, bare arms and then leapt onto the bed with her. In no time at all her clothes had joined his on the floor and somehow both of them knew that the dinner-and-drinks plan would have to be put on hold. In the flat below, the ceiling pendant began to swing back and forth ever so slightly.

# 35

## The Beach

"I've never seen her like this before about a boyfriend. She's as giddy as a Lotto winner. She's *higher* than that old school pal of hers who won the Lotto last year. In fact, she's probably happier than most of them ever are. It's all *Mark says this* and *Mark says that*. She's just head over heels about him," Ruby told Tom as she poured the tea from a shiny new flask and handed him a cup.

It was Valentine's Day but they'd both decided not to put too much focus on the occasion, out of respect for past loves. Instead they were having a picnic at the beach. Or rather they were having a picnic in Ruby's car, as it was too cold to sit outside.

"And he's a doctor, you say?"

"Yes, just newly qualified, would you believe it? He's tall and handsome and his ID checks out. And she's met his family too so that's a good sign. I always think it's a red flag when there are no relatives clamouring to meet you."

"I didn't have anyone clamouring to meet you," Tom pointed out.

Oops, Ruby thought to herself. Tom Lavery was no dozer, was he? "Yes, but your parents live abroad, and anyway you had all the staff at Camberwell," she said lightly. "Mrs Kenny and all the waitresses. Proper little fan club you've got there. You're not the sad loner you think you are, you know! They all adore you!"

"Stop teasing me!" he laughed.

"It's true – they all adore you at Camberwell."

"And I haven't met your parents either."

"Ah well, Tom, it's different for us. We both have, shall we say, eccentric families?"

"Yes indeed. A bit eccentric! I thought when my parents said they were going to India to open a school for equal numbers of boys and girls that they'd be home again in six weeks. They always were a couple of old lefties, I thought to myself, but this is ridiculous. But fair play to them, they did it. And now they say they can't imagine sitting in traffic for an hour on the M2 in the pouring rain, or waiting in a queue for twenty minutes to buy one cushion in IKEA. One *imported* cushion!"

"Oh God, yeah, I daresay they're Fair Trade nuts too! To be honest, I agree with them, we should all support our local factories a lot more than we do . . . So anyway Jasmine is completely in love with this Mark lad. He's practically living with her already from what she tells me. I'm just worried she's moving too fast. I hope he doesn't break her heart."

"Why would he do that?" Tom said, puzzled.

"Oh you know, the usual story? He might just be dallying with a humble shop girl before marrying someone more *suitable*, as our old boss Theodora would have put it."

"Come on, Ruby, that's a bit old-fashioned, isn't it?" Tom asked, shaking his head in disagreement.

"Yes, old-fashioned and snobbish!" Ruby agreed.

"But surely if he's going to be well paid some day he won't care what Jasmine does for a living? I don't think all that many men are bothered what job their girlfriend or wife has, to be fair."

"We'll see."

"No, really. She's a lovely girl. I'm sure this guy knows when he's well off," Tom said firmly. "So don't be worrying. Now what have you got in that basket? I'm starving."

"I've got salmon and cucumber sandwiches on brown bread, Cheddar and lettuce sandwiches on white bread, a small jam and cream sponge and a bit of cooked chicken," she told him, opening the dainty picnic basket and wedging it in between them on the back seat. They were sitting on a neatly folded car rug that was helping to take the chill off the leather seats. Ruby only wished she had a second blanket to go over her knees. Or to cuddle up with Tom under . . .

"Yes to everything," Tom said, holding out his plate.

"I suppose we were mad to come here today? It's so bloody cold. When is this damn winter going to end? My hands keep getting stiff in the shop. I'll have to wear gloves soon just to be able to operate the cash register."

"Yeah, I know. You should try digging over a frozen flowerbed," Tom agreed.

"Rather you than me," Ruby said, slightly embarrassed now that she was complaining about chilly fingers when Tom was out of doors all day. She reached out to the dashboard and turned the heating up full-blast. They ate their picnic quickly, keeping their hands wrapped round cups of hot tea. The cold weather kept making them hungry, Ruby noted. Tom was a big man and her small, neat sandwiches looked almost comical in his large hands. He kept dropping them when there was only a bite left. Next time she would use a larger-size loaf of bread.

"How's the business doing?" Tom asked suddenly. "I don't mean the money end of things. I mean, are you still enjoying it?"

"Yes, it's fine, I haven't got bored yet anyway. Or gone bankrupt. I think the trick is to keep most of the stock very affordable and only sell a small amount of really expensive stuff. I was worried the downturn would be disastrous for the shop but it seems we girls still want our shiny trinkets and glittery what-nots."

"Fair enough," Tom said, nodding. He had no idea what a glittery what-not was but he didn't feel inclined to ask.

"I don't mean to harp on but it's a bit funny to see Jasmine falling in love overnight like this," Ruby mused then as they sat gazing out of the car windows.

"How come?"

"She's so unafraid of being hurt, you know? She just accepts that this guy has always liked her and now they've got together at last and it's all going to be fine."

"And it will be, hopefully."

"Ah. You said the word, *hopefully*."

"Yes, of course. None of us can see into the future."

"No." Ruby knew he was thinking of Kate.

"Well, if this incredible romance keeps up I'm sure we'll be hearing wedding bells soon," Ruby said then.

"What? You mean you and me?" Tom said, obviously joking. But not really joking.

"No. Jasmine and Mark, you eejit! I mean, the pair of them will be getting married in no time. Both so young and full of energy. I'm sure they'll be getting engaged any day now. I'm telling you, it's the love story of the century!"

"Hey! We're not too old ourselves to be getting engaged," Tom said, winking at Ruby over his chicken leg.

"What? Oh, don't be outrageous."

"We aren't past it, Ruby. Jesus, we're in the prime of our lives! Hell, I never thought I'd say that again! But meeting you has changed my life, changed everything . . . What if I was to propose to you right now? Right here in this car! What if I got down on one knee and asked you to marry me? What would you say?"

Ruby's heart turned over in her chest with sheer excitement. Marriage! It seemed like only yesterday she was wishing her own life away. And now she had met this lovely man and he was asking her to marry him! And even though she knew it was sheer bloody madness to even think of marrying again, some vain and feminine part of her was utterly delighted at Tom's proposal. Best not to give in right away, though, Ruby thought to herself. If she said yes now, she'd look a right flake. She decided to make a joke out of the whole thing.

"I'd say you'd have trouble getting down on one knee in the back of this car," Ruby said and then laughed her head off. "Your legs are far too long. Come on, let's go for a ten-minute walk and then go straight back to mine to thaw out? I am so, so over winter now. I used to adore winter but I can't stand it any more. All that snow . . . and even when the snow clears away it's still freezing. I'm numb from head to toe."

They wiped their hands on paper napkins and ventured out of the car and towards the beach. But before they'd even made it past the sand dunes, the driving wind blew an ice-cold blast into their faces, making it impossible for them to talk to one another. Or even see one another easily as their eyes were watering that much. Ruby's face was pure white with the cold and even Tom's scarf wrapped round her neck was no help.

"This is just stupid," Tom shouted eventually. "We'll go back now and I'll make you a hot chocolate while you warm up in the bath. I'm worried you might get pneumonia."

Ruby just nodded and together they raced back to the car

park. Luckily there was hardly any traffic on the road home and soon Ruby was running a hot bath while Tom tried not to make too much of a mess in Ruby's petite yet perfect kitchen. Then they went to bed and made love until the sun came up.

# 36

# The Cottage

Now it was March and the shops were full of Easter eggs in pale green packaging and pink and yellow ribbons. Jasmine and Mark were so in love with each other it was heartening for everyone to see. The two of them kept finishing each other's sentences, and calling and sending texts to one another at lunchtimes. Mark was even talking of selling his tiny terrace near the hospital and buying something bigger in the suburbs. Something near the good schools, he said once or twice. Jasmine wasn't quite ready to say goodbye to the ivory tower that was the Bell Towers but sometimes she would find herself pausing by the estate agent's window.

"Just having a look," she said. "Just keeping an eye on the market to see if there are any bargains to be had."

Ruby wasn't a bit jealous of her best friend's new-found bliss. She'd had that sort of all-encompassing love with Jonathan. Entire days spent in bed, either making love or sharing secrets of the heart. And now she was having it all again with Tom. Or at least the days spent in bed. She wasn't at the stage yet where she wanted to make actual plans. All she wanted to do was run her business and spend a good percentage of her spare time with Tom and enjoy his company and feel safe and cherished with him. She didn't want a big grand house any more or even children, she decided. She wanted a quiet life now, just some peace and quiet.

Tonight Ruby was going to cook a meal for Tom at his cottage. And they might even spend the night together there. Actually they would almost definitely be spending the night together. Ruby hadn't spent a night in Tom's house yet and so she was giddy with anticipation. She could tell he wanted her desperately, all the time, and it was getting to the stage where she was finding it hard to resist him long enough to even have a chat first when they met. If things kept going the way they were, Ruby could see the two of them having frantic sex before they'd even said hello to one another. But what could she do about it? He was so warm and comforting to hold. So tender and loving afterwards . . .

The only downside was, she was spending increasing amounts of time in the bathroom getting ready to meet Tom. As they invariably ended up in bed together, she couldn't afford to let her personal grooming slip even a little bit.

She wanted tonight to be special as she was staying over at Tom's house for the first time. And so, aware that she wouldn't be able to nip into her own bathroom for any last-minute tweaks, Ruby went through her checklist for the tenth time that day. She'd shaved her legs and underarms with scented shaving foam and a brand-new razor. She'd bought new underwear in M&S: a beautiful, turquoise, polka-dot padded bra and lace-trimmed shorts. She was wearing a black dress and black stockings that were easy to take off in a hurry but which weren't too provocative in themselves. And only a small heel on her shoes in case they decided to go for yet another long stroll around Camberwell afterwards. She had brushed and flossed her teeth, rinsed twice with mouthwash, plucked her eyebrows, applied scented moisturiser to her knees and elbows, and checked her back and cleavage for pimples. She'd not worn ankle socks for two days because they always left an imprint on her skin. She'd painted her toenails and fingernails pale pink so it wouldn't be too noticeable if they got chipped. She'd even remembered not to use hairspray in case it landed on her face and neck and ended up on Tom's lips again when he kissed her. She had a spare set of underwear and a toothbrush in her bag. She hadn't eaten or drunk anything that might give her indigestion or hiccups. She'd put perfume everywhere, even on the soles of her feet.

"Right, that must be everything now," she said, switching off the lights in the flat and going outside to her car.

Two minutes later, however, Ruby had to nip back up the stairs to pick up the tuna steaks, the bag of other ingredients and the bottle of wine from the fridge. She'd almost forgotten she was supposed to be cooking Tom his supper.

In the large and roomy kitchen of Tom's cottage, Ruby was suddenly all thumbs.

"I'm so sorry," she said as the grill pan clattered loudly onto the terracotta tiles. "Did I crack the floor just then? I'm used to cooking in a confined space, do you see? This kitchen is so huge compared to my little one."

"It's fine," Tom said gently. "This is a humble country cottage, Ruby. Not the Fat Duck restaurant."

"Oh yes, I know, I know. Well, lucky for you it isn't the Fat Duck. I can't promise snail ice-cream or dry ice billowing over the mashed potatoes," Ruby laughed.

"I'll open the wine," Tom offered.

"Yes, yes, the wine," Ruby said.

Tom opened the wine and poured Ruby a glass. "Here," he said. "Get this into you and relax. You don't have to cook if you're too tired or stressed out."

"I know that – and I'm looking forward to cooking for you – it's just that I want this to be special."

"It already is. I don't care what I eat as long as I'm close to you."

He caught her in his arms then, held her close to him and kissed her hard. As usual, Ruby's knees turned instantly to jelly. She hoped the scent of her perfume would smell stronger than the small pool of perspiration that was forming in her cleavage. Tom was caressing her breasts now; his hand having miraculously found the side-zip in her dress and gently pulled it down. Ruby melted into his embrace and her appetite for the meal faded away and was replaced with another kind of appetite. Tom's other hand was reaching for the hem of her dress now. Ruby closed her eyes again. They couldn't possibly do it standing up, could they? She'd never done it that way before. What then? The table? She'd never made love on a kitchen table before either.

She felt her temperature go up and up. Suddenly she'd had a delicious ripple of pleasure that went zig-zagging up and down her entire body, and Tom had barely touched her. A moment later, she began to unbuckle his belt. Exactly what she was going to do when she'd removed Tom's jeans, she hadn't quite decided . . . would she lead him into the bedroom or just playfully push him down to the floor? Anything was possible, she thought, she was feeling so turned on tonight . . .

Suddenly Ruby realised that the tuna steaks were beginning to char. She reached down to try pulling them out of the oven, and ended up burning the edge of Tom's wrist with the smoking grill pan.

"Oh my God, I'm so sorry," she cried. "What have I done? For heaven's sake! Quick! Get your arm under a cold tap!"

"It's nothing," he told her, still breathless with desire. "You hardly touched me with it. Relax!"

"You'll have a little scar, Tom."

"I'm covered in little scars, Ruby. I work with wire and tools all day long . . . Honestly, you're hilarious!"

"I'm a liability!" she said sadly.

"No, you're not," he laughed. "You're wonderful."

Then Tom set the grill pan on the draining board, scooped Ruby up into his arms and carried her straight to the bedroom.

"We'll just let the tuna rest there for a minute or twenty," he said firmly.

Oh wow, Ruby thought to herself. Sometimes having steamy sex *and* trying to cook interesting meals on a daily basis was just too much of a challenge.

# 37

## The Kiss

"That was a lovely dinner," Tom sighed contentedly, putting down his knife and fork and smiling at Ruby. He'd eaten everything on the table, even the six bread rolls that Ruby had laid out in a wicker serving-dish. "I'll eat anything, you know, so I don't expect this sort of treatment every day or even every week. But really, it was delicious."

"It was only a tuna steak," Ruby said modestly.

"It was a char-grilled tuna steak with stuffed onions, baked mushrooms, red wine gravy, new potatoes, a green salad, garden peas and crusty bread rolls," Tom corrected her. The cooking had taken over two hours. The sex had taken about ten minutes . . .

"Well, yes," Ruby said. "Char-grilled, huh? How's the wrist?"

"It's fine. Do you want to leave the dishes till tomorrow, and we'll go into the sitting room for another drink?"

"No, I like it here," Ruby told him.

"Because of the range?"

"Yes."

"Right. Thanks again for dinner, Ruby. It was delicious, the entire evening has been delicious . . ."

"That's okay, you're worth it! Sometimes I feel like cooking. When I have the time, you know?"

"Yes, sometimes it's nice to stay home," Tom agreed.

"Yes, it is."

They smiled at one another.

"So how's everybody?" Tom asked, clearing away a few plates so he had room to make coffee.

"Oh Lord! Let me see . . . Mum's still working in the bakery in Manhattan. Still loving all the fuss she's creating back here, no doubt. Dad's told her he's considering a divorce now but I think he's only trying to scare her into coming home. But then sometimes I think he actually means it because he sounds happier than I've ever known him. I think he might have met a wee lady on this cookery course."

"Wow. Really?"

"Yeah, there's one lady he keeps mentioning. And Jasmine is so besotted with Mark Crawford she's doodling his name on the margins of my order book. Mark's got a full-time placement in the Royal Victoria Hospital and they're both obsessed with looking at houses."

"Good luck to them on that front."

"Indeed. They want something near to a good school, if you don't mind. Theodora Kelly sent us a postcard to the shop. She's having a great time ballroom dancing in Essex with her sister Amelia. They're out on the tiles three nights a week. And Theodora's getting on great with all Amelia's friends. The two of them are sharing Amelia's house but it's working out well and now they've got so much money to spend that they're going on a three-week cruise."

"Great stuff."

"Yes, they're terrific company for one another, Theodora said. They're getting on just as if they were young girls again. Then Mary Stone wrote to us to tell us that she's all fixed up with a job in Yorkshire looking after horses and ponies in a rescue sanctuary. She was that customer I told you about. Do you remember?"

"Yes, the one who bought the first bag?"

"Yes. And her kids love it there and her husband's agreed to stay away from her in return for a suspended sentence. Their lawyers are still hammering out a financial settlement. He's trying to pretend he has no savings, the swine, but Mary doesn't really care. She's just happy to be rid of him."

"Okay. Hope she gets some money though . . ."

"Yes, poor woman. And speaking of the law, the police came to see me again yesterday but they said the trial is still some way off. And because there was only one witness it might not be possible to get a custodial sentence for the lorry driver. And I said that was okay because I still wasn't ready to talk about what happened. I don't want to think about the lorry driver up in the dock, I suppose. Or myself either. I'm past caring if he goes to prison or not. It won't change what happened . . . And it's ruined his life too. As long as he's banned from driving or something. As long as he's learned his lesson now and doesn't hurt anybody else on the roads. Oh, let's change the subject!"

"Okay," Tom nodded.

"What else? Well, I told you I'd been to another school reunion. Teresa Morris was given a special mention during the speeches. She's so brave to be bringing up those five kids all by herself. They gave her a big bouquet of yellow roses and a giant box of chocolates though she joked that a set of earplugs would have been a lot handier. She's a great girl."

"Yes, she is."

"And then there's Rebecca McCann – she's the one who was Jasmine's arch-nemesis at school? Well, she's currently dating some guy who was in a boy-band in the 1990s. I can't remember his name but he wears a back-to-front baseball cap to this day. And he's just out of rehab for addiction to soft drugs and prescription painkillers and she met him in a spa somewhere in Leeds. They were both having a massage at the same time apparently. It was in the local paper. I reckon he was on the lookout for a rich woman and now he's found one. And so they're living together in a big house in Birmingham with electronic gates, and her mum and dad are also living with them which is a bit weird. But at least it shows she hasn't deserted them, I suppose? But the stress of all the press intrusion has been bad for Rebecca's mother's nerves and she's become agoraphobic almost overnight. Jasmine got all the gossip from her mum, who knows a woman who knows Rebecca's Aunt Mabel."

"Jesus Christ, I don't know how you keep track of it all," Tom laughed.

"Women are very good at multi-tasking. And we're also very good at being very bloody nosy. Will we have another glass of wine?" Ruby asked then, sipping the last of her coffee.

"Sure," Tom said, pouring what was left in the bottle into two fresh glasses. It wasn't really enough to make up a decent glassful. "I have a nice red wine here somewhere but maybe we shouldn't get too smashed?"

"One more *small* glass each would be okay, I think?"

"Whatever you say," Tom nodded, getting up to fetch it. When he was reaching up to a high shelf, Ruby saw his shirt pull out from his jeans to reveal his washboard stomach. Smooth white skin and a neat swirl of soft brown hair spreading up from the top of his jeans. She could still hardly believe they were lovers.

"Lovers," she whispered absentmindedly.

"What did you say?" Tom asked.

"Nothing," she said.

"I thought you said something?"

"No, I didn't."

"Okay."

He poured the wine and sat down again. The room was very warm. Ruby felt as if she might faint with sheer contentment. She couldn't get the picture of Tom's super-taut stomach out of her mind and it was getting dark outside and they couldn't sit in the kitchen all night. She longed to be curled up in bed with him, that beautiful hard stomach of his pressed against her body . . .

"Lovely wine," she said, the glass trembling slightly in her hand.

"Yes, it's not bad."

"Kiss me again," she said.

Leaning across the table, Tom kissed Ruby softly on the cheek and then on the lips. He didn't say anything and neither did she. The kiss seemed to go on for ages. Ruby felt as if she were floating away on a summer cloud. Her racing pulse slowed right down.

"Will we go to bed now, Ruby? I mean, just to sleep? Just let me hold you and we can go to sleep together?" Tom said in a husky voice.

"Yes," she said in a whispery wobble. "Yes, I'd love that."

It wasn't the first time they would be spending the entire night together. But somehow it felt magical, as if they were a confirmed couple now. As if they both knew their relationship was going to last for a very long time. They kissed again and somehow the bottle of red wine got knocked over and spilled all across Tom's best jeans.

# 38

## The Lovers

Ruby walked slowly into Tom's bedroom and sat down gently on the side of the bed. The sheets were still crumpled from earlier. She smelt a faint aroma of lavender fabric conditioner and felt pleased that he'd gone to such an effort to impress her. The pillowcases were freshly ironed and all of Tom's old gardening clothes had been cleared away. She thought she remembered seeing piles of ancient sweaters and worn leather boots sitting around the room the day before, when she'd glanced into it on her way down the corridor to the bathroom. But now all was tidy and clean.

After a short while Tom came out of the shower, fully dressed again but with damp hair. He smelled of after-shave; Ruby guessed it was Chanel. She wondered if he'd bought it specially or if someone had given it to him for Christmas or something. Maybe it was Mrs Kenny?

"Hopefully I don't smell like a winery any more," Tom said.

"Trust me," Ruby replied, "to burn you with the pan and then plaster you in red wine."

"Ah, it was worth it," he smiled.

"I'll have a quick shower myself," she said quietly. "If that's okay? I'd like to freshen up?"

"Sure," he said. "There's towels and so on, on the shelf."

"Thanks, Tom. I won't be long," Ruby said, briefly touching his hand.

"I'll be right here," he replied.

"Okay," Ruby said.

A few minutes later Ruby returned to the bedroom to find Tom sitting casually on the bed. The lights had been turned off and only a sliver of moonlight stole in across the carpet. He turned to look at her as she stood there in her bare feet and wet hair, with no make-up on and wearing only a bath towel. He thought she had never looked more beautiful. He crossed the room in an instant with his long legs and stood beside her.

"Well, here I am," she said playfully, shrugging her shoulders. "It seemed such a bother to get dressed again."

"I'm not complaining. You look gorgeous."

She held his hand.

"Let's go to bed," she said. "I'm exhausted."

He followed her to the bed, peeled off his clothes and they got in and lay close together.

They gazed at one another for a moment. Then Tom swept Ruby into his arms, kissing her gently.

"I don't know what I'd have done if I hadn't met you," he whispered. "I don't know how much longer I'd have been able to wear myself out with work." He fell silent for a moment. "Ruby?"

"Yes?"

"Will we always be able to talk like this, and be friends?"

"I hope so," Ruby said, kissing him tenderly.

"I don't mean to put any pressure on you though."

"I know."

The moon went in behind a cloud and the room was pitch dark.

"Ruby, I just want you to know that if things don't work out between us, I'm still grateful you gave me this chance to feel normal . . . and happy again . . . and –"

But he didn't get to finish his sentence because Ruby was kissing him. Tom had his arms wrapped round her and it was good to feel warm and safe and cherished.

"It'll be okay," she told him. "We'll be okay."

Then they kissed each other goodnight softly and went to sleep.

# 39

## Breakfast at Tom's

Next morning, the sun was shining brightly. Ruby woke up feeling wonderfully calm and refreshed. When she turned her head to look at Tom she saw that he was just waking up too. He looked very handsome, first thing in the morning. The sleepy crinkles round his eyes gave him a softer, more vulnerable edge that was very appealing.

"Good morning," she smiled.

"Good morning," he said, and kissed her softly.

He reached across beneath the sheets and held Ruby's hand.

"Tom?"

"Yes?" he said.

"Thanks."

"What for?"

"For everything. For asking me out in the first place and for being so sensitive about my circumstances and everything."

"I'd have waited for you, you know? If you needed more time to think about going out with me. I'd have waited for you, no matter how long it took."

"Would you, Tom?"

"Of course. Yes, I would. I mean, you can't expect to grow a mature garden overnight."

"You can if you're rich enough," she laughed.

"Not really. I don't think it ever looks quite the same when they just deliver the lot on the back of a lorry," Tom said. "All concrete tubs and designer colour schemes. It never looks right to me. A real garden takes fifty years to get right. And it shouldn't look brand new. It should look timeless."

"I know what you mean," she said, touching his face tenderly.

"And I just wanted you to know that I'm serious about you, Ruby. Really serious, and not just passing the time with you, okay? You mean everything to me."

"Okay."

They looked at each other for a minute and then began to kiss again. Tom moved his hands down under the duvet and Ruby gasped as he began to push her knees apart.

"Oh, already?" she said as he began to make love to her again. "Oh, Tom, you're something else. Shouldn't we have breakfast first? Freshen up a little?"

"I can't wait. Is it okay?" he asked, kissing her passionately.

"Um, yes, oh, well, oh . . . yes! Oh yes!"

# 40

# The Stork

"Oh no . . . Oh God . . ." Jasmine said simply. Then she sat down on the edge of the bath and burst into tears. She was definitely pregnant. There was no doubt about it. And why wouldn't she be? She'd had more sex in the last few weeks than in the last five years put together. Sometimes she and Mark had sex three times a day! Mornings, evenings and in the middle of the night.

She picked up her mobile phone and rang Ruby.

"Guess what?"

"What?" Ruby said.

"I'm pregnant," Jasmine said slowly.

"Really? Oh my God. Are you sure?"

"Yes, I'm sure."

"Have you done a second test to confirm?"

"Yes. I did ten tests today. And ten yesterday! Cost me a bloody fortune from the chemist's." And so it had. She'd be living on sliced bread and tinned soup for the rest of the month.

"Oh, well then," Ruby said. "Twenty pregnancy tests can't be wrong. Congratulations, love!"

"Congratulations? Oh hell. What am I going to do now?" Jasmine sighed heavily.

"Well, let me see. You're having a baby. So that means you might get very sick in the mornings, possibly. Put on a bit of weight round your tummy area. Get varicose veins, piles and stretch marks? I daresay bigger boobs are a definite maybe. And you'll buy a cot and a pram and hundreds of cuddly toys. And a breast pump. And at the end of all that, you'll have a beautiful baby in your arms and life will never be the same again."

"Shut up, Ruby. I'm scared stiff here."

"I'm sorry. I was only trying to make you laugh. Or feel happy."

"It's okay. But I'm not happy, I'm terrified."

"You are keeping the baby, aren't you?" Ruby asked nervously.

"I guess so," Jasmine said, feeling her stomach for any little baby-shaped lumps. "I'm not getting any younger."

"Well that's silly, you're no age. But that's brilliant news," Ruby said, almost weak with relief and happiness. "I know it's utterly selfish of me to say it but if you weren't going to keep the baby I'd rather not have known about the pregnancy at all."

"Ruby O'Neill!" Jasmine scolded. "How could you not support my right to choose?"

"I know, I know. And I do support your right to choose . . . But it's just, you're both so bloody good-looking. You and Mark both, you're like supermodels. This baby will be only *beautiful*."

"You shallow little cow."

"Aye, whatever. It's true. You can't go wrong with your genes and Mark's together."

"A beautiful baby, huh?"

"Yup! Bound to be," Ruby laughed.

"I hope so, too, actually! Is that awful of me? You do see some pig-nosed little creatures around in buggies . . . some wee boys who look like mini-thugs already . . . and then you look at the fathers and they've got the same tough-nut expressions, and you think to yourself, Jesus Christ, how could the mother have got herself up the duff to such an ugly git?"

"Jasmine, you're a snobby bitch!"

"I know I am. But I would never sleep with a man who had a piggy nose, just in case the kids all ended up looking like wee piglets! I'd be mortified at the school gates. God, I really am a right bitch!" Jasmine said happily.

"Ah, you're not the worst of them, don't worry. Yes, any child of yours will be a total beauty. An absolute angel. You're so lucky to be having a wee baby, you know. I'd love to have a baby myself." Ruby sighed.

"Would you really?"

"Of course I would."

"Well then, tell Tom to get on and do the business," Jasmine giggled.

"Just like that?" Ruby laughed.

"Yes, why not? He's very good at planting seeds, isn't he?"

"Ha, ha. Some day, maybe."

"Some day? You're thirty-four, love. I'll have a word with him for you, shall I?"

"No thanks, don't you bother yourself."

"Ruby, will you fire me if I get morning sickness?" Jasmine asked.

"No, of course not. You can throw up in one of our candy-striped carriers."

"Oh yeah," Jasmine said. "They're very well made. Strong enough to withstand projectile vomiting."

"Um, I take that offer back now you've painted such a pretty picture for me. Seriously, Jasmine, it'll be fine. You're not a kid any more."

"I feel like one sometimes. I feel like a total eejit."

"Yes, I know you do, but you're not. We'll sort out suitable hours for you if you want to go on working. And Mark's a lovely man. You'll be fine. Have you told him yet?"

"No, I'll tell him tonight," Jasmine sighed. "He's coming over for dinner."

"Okay. How pregnant are you? Do you know?"

"About four weeks, I think. Or maybe five weeks or maybe six? I lost track of the time. It must have happened very soon after we met up again."

"Do you feel pregnant?"

"Not terribly. A little bit off my food. Can't face eggs or chips."

"Don't you feel any different?"

"My boobs do look bigger but I thought it was my new balcony bra. Or else it was all the extra sex giving my auld hormones a boost?"

"Oh Jasmine!"

"I know. I'm fucking hopeless."

"No you're not. Jasmine listen, can I be the official godmother, please? I know it's not a role that's really talked about much these days but I'd love to be the godmother. I'll baby-sit for you any time you like. And I'll do up the nursery too when you get one. And remind you when it's time to go for vaccinations. And when to apply to a primary school. You've got to put your name down years in advance to get into a top primary school, you know?"

"I know, Mark mentioned that once. God, he's going to get the shock of his life when I tell him. Oh Ruby, thank you for being so great about this. I've been so worried about how I'd cope. I didn't know how I was going to tell everybody. Especially my parents! But now I feel sort of okay about the baby coming. The baby, imagine that! You're the best friend ever."

"I know I am and don't you forget it, Miss," Ruby said happily.

# 41

# The Engagement

Jasmine put down her knife and fork and began toying with the red tulips Mark had just brought her.

"Listen, Mark, I've something really important to tell you," Jasmine began nervously. Wondering how she could break the news to him without making him have a heart attack. Or think she'd done it on purpose. She knew they'd been taking a few risks with birth control but then again the pill had always made her feel queasy and they hadn't always bothered with a condom if Jasmine thought it wasn't her most fertile time of the month. She'd never been caught out before. Somehow she'd assumed her body would only make a baby whenever she wanted it to.

"Are we pregnant?" Mark asked gently, hopefully.

"What did you say? What are you talking about?"

"I said, are we pregnant?"

It was so scary hearing him say it out loud like that.

"Where's this come from?" she said, playing for time.

"Well, you've not touched your wine all evening. Not a single sip and it was a really good bottle too. The lamb chops were very well done, almost charred. Usually we have them just medium. You keep touching your stomach and your boobs look a tiny, tiny bit bigger. Am I right or am I right?"

"You don't miss much, I'll give you that. I'm not in the mood for wine, that's all. And I lost track of the time when I was cooking and I'm wearing a new bra," Jasmine said defensively, shrugging her shoulders.

"Oh, that's fine then. It's just I thought you hugged me a bit differently too when I got here this evening? Not as tightly as you normally hug me?"

"You sound almost disappointed, Mark. Do you want a baby?"

"Sure I do."

"Really?"

"Yeah, really."

"I thought most men would run for the hills if their new girlfriend was suddenly preggers?"

"Not me. I'd be delighted. I'd love to have a family of my own, one day. Of *our* own."

"Interesting, very interesting," Jasmine said thoughtfully, a slight twinkle in her eyes.

"Obviously it'd be nice to have a couple of years to ourselves before the sprogs come along," Mark said matter-of-factly.

"Yes, obviously," she agreed, feeling strangely elated. To listen to Mark, it was almost as if they were married already.

"But still, a baby would be lovely," he said, his eyes beseeching hers.

"Maybe."

"Jasmine, love, I can't play this game any more. I know you're pregnant," Mark said, holding her hand tenderly across the table.

"You do? How come?"

"Because when I was in the bathroom earlier I went to throw the empty loo roll tube in the bin. I'm a bit funny like that. I just go and tidy up without thinking. It goes with the job."

"And you saw the test sticks?"

"Yes. A big load of them. All with blue lines."

"Oh no, I should've hidden them better," Jasmine said crossly. "I'm such a twit."

"Well, are you going to put me out of my misery or aren't you? Are we having a baby? Or were those tests for somebody else? A friend of yours?"

"They're mine," she admitted, sighing so much her chin practically hit the glass table.

"Oh Jasmine, that's brilliant news! I knew it. Marry me? Please marry me?"

"What?"

He got down on one knee and kissed her hand.

"I'll be a good husband," he promised. "We'll buy the ring tomorrow morning."

"Marriage?" Jasmine gasped.

"Yes, why not?" he said.

"It's too weird," she said. "Only old people get married."

"Nonsense, we're the perfect age to get married."

"Oh my God!"

"What's wrong?" he said.

"Nothing. I can't imagine myself as Mrs Crawford."

"What's wrong with it?"

"Nothing. It's just too *weird*. I'm too young to get married."

"Some people get married when they're only twenty or twenty-one."

"Yeah, name me somebody you know who got married at that age! Nobody normal gets married in their early twenties."

"Oh Jesus, Jasmine Mulholland! Your head is a mystery to me," Mark laughed.

"It's a mystery to me and all," Jasmine laughed. "I was only just getting used to the idea of having a baby. Getting married as well is a bit overwhelming for me."

"Please, just think about it?" he said.

"You'd better be a bloody good husband, Mark Crawford. Because I'm a bona fide tough nut from Sandy Row and I've got a load of hard brothers to back me up," she laughed.

"I'll be good to you," he said. "And the baby. Don't you worry about that."

"You don't have to marry me just for the baby," she said then, beginning to cry with relief.

"I want to marry you, you daft thing."

"Do you?"

"Of course I do. How could I not?"

"Are you sure?"

"Yes, I'm sure. I love you."

"I love you too," she said quietly.

"Well then?"

"I don't want a pity-proposal. And I don't want you to marry me just so you'll have father's rights."

"Jasmine, how could you even think that about me?" he said, genuinely mystified.

"We've not been together very long, Mark. I'm sorry but I can't help being a little paranoid. And you're such a high achiever. Are you sure you're not asking me to marry you because it's the old-fashioned thing to do?"

"Okay, I understand you're worried about the practicalities and that's okay. But that's not why I want us to get married. I've always loved you, Jasmine. Always."

"Have you?"

"Yes. And now I've fallen for you, head over heels. So it doesn't feel too soon to me."

"Um . . ."

"And I want to be a proper father to our baby."

"Yeah, I know. Oh, maybe I don't know, Mark."

"Don't hold my wanting us to get married against me, please,

Jasmine? Yes, I want us all to have the same name and to be a proper family. Please don't say you want to go all modern on me now, and just live in two houses, and never get married and all that malarkey? Please, Jasmine?"

"Oh all right then, I'll marry you," she said, as if it was no big deal to her. Even though it was. "But if you turn out to be some psycho control-freak I'll get my brothers to beat you up. And they will too, they'd be happy to oblige me."

Jasmine's brothers weren't actually thugs at all but she'd been pretending they were, to her various boyfriends, all her life.

"Fair enough," Mark said.

"Right," she nodded. "And I can't be bothered to cook every night either. So it'll be microwave rice, and cheese sandwiches, most of the time, right?"

"Right. Jasmine, I can throw an egg on the pan myself if I'm hungry enough. Or eat a bowl of cornflakes. Hooray, we're getting married! Let's drink a toast to celebrate? Is that wine still chilled? Oh, I mean, let's have a cup of tea to celebrate?"

"Celebrate what? The baby or our engagement?"

"Both. You twit. In whatever order you wish."

"Okay then. Let's get married and have the baby, in that order," she said, kissing him happily. "Might as well! God, this is so normal it's embarrassing. No paternity suit on *Jeremy Kyle* or anything."

"Hooray," Mark mumbled, through their longest kiss ever. "We're actually getting married?"

"It'll keep my mother happy, I suppose. Mark?"

"Yeah?"

"There's just one more thing?"

"It's twins?" he laughed.

"Will you stop kidding around, you eejit? I don't know anything about the baby, or babies, yet. No, it's not that," she sighed.

"What is it?"

"I really, really don't want a big white wedding."

"I don't believe you. Why not?"

"Because my parents couldn't afford it and neither can I. And I don't want you to pay for it, or your parents either. And I hate stuffy things anyway. They make me so nervous and flustered. And when I'm nervous I feel sick. And I might feel a bit sick in the mornings as it is, and I can't drink champagne or even cocktails for ages. And I'm not getting roped into a big, grand wedding if I can't even have a glass of champagne."

"Okay then. Agreed. But I don't want to wait for ages and ages either."

"We can get married as soon as possible, Mark. Just not a big fancy wedding! Please?"

"Leave it with me," he said, scratching his head. "I'll think of something nice but not too expensive. In the meantime let's get you a proper check-up and then we can start looking at houses."

"Houses?"

"Yes, houses. We're going to need a bigger place for the baby, aren't we?"

"Oh my God, yes, we are. But my lovely built-in wardrobes? My recessed spotlights? My dinky balcony with the metal chair?"

"Don't worry, we'll get loads of wardrobes and spotlights put into our new place. Can't promise you a balcony but I'll go halves on a top-of-the-range tumble dryer?"

"I've never had one of those."

"They're great gizmos, my love. You don't need to iron a thing if you hang the clothes up while they're still warm. Old student tricks!"

"You're so romantic," she laughed.

"We've got to be practical. I don't want my beautiful wife to spend all day in the kitchen," he said, hugging her as tightly as he dared.

"Can I have that in writing, please? I love you, Mark."

"I love you too."

"If all this gets too much for me, though, can we hire a cleaning lady? Even once a week to do the bathrooms? I can't be doing with living in a messy house, you know? And there's no way on this earth I am picking up after you, mate, so we'd better start as we mean to go on."

"Yes, all right. We'll have it written into our wedding vows."

"Really?"

"No, I'm joking about the vows but yes, we can hire a cleaner. I'll work out a complete budget tonight. I'll have to deduct a cleaner's wages from our new mortgage estimate. Though I can always downsize on my car and start saving for a private room at the maternity hospital . . ."

"All right," she sighed happily. "Let's talk about all of that tomorrow. The practicalities and so on. Tonight I just want to be happy about the baby."

"And the wedding?"

"And the wedding, of course."

"And I can go ahead and plan anything I like?"

"Yes, you can. But remember what I said about nothing too fancy."

"Right."

And so it was agreed.

# 42

# The Wedding

It was August. Every last citizen in Sandy Row and the surrounding streets had been told by Jasmine's mother to pray for unbroken sunshine on Mark and Jasmine's wedding day. Not just asked to pray either. But actually told to pray for a clear blue sky and not so much as a speck of grimy drizzle or a gust of cold air.

"Vicky love, you've got to stop telling complete strangers to pray for good weather," her husband told her over and over. "Somebody might report you to the men in white coats."

"I know, Sam. I know. But sure what harm can it do?" she replied breathlessly, lighting yet another row of strawberry candles and holding one up towards the window.

"And please will you stop all this business with the candles, love? You're scaring the life out of me. I keep thinking you're going to convert to Catholicism. Either that or burn the bloody house down."

"Shush, Sam, they're not holy candles. They're only scented tea-lights from M&S. But I won't light another candle for the wedding, I promise you. If it bothers you that much."

But he knew in his heart that she would.

On the day itself, Vicky slept in. She'd been awake half the night fretting that the rain would come on and spoil their open-air ceremony. That's all Mark would tell them. That the ceremony was to be held in the open air . . . He'd send black cabs to collect them at eleven o'clock, he said.

And so Vicky had been in a deep sleep when the alarm finally went off at eight o'clock. Her husband quickly shut off the beeps, slipped out of bed and went to put the kettle on.

"Another hour or two of sleep will do her no harm," he told Jasmine, who was just coming out of the shower.

And also they all needed some peace and quiet before the hoopla kicked off. But he'd barely had a lovely sip of nuclear-hot tea down his throat before the first callers began to arrive at the house.

"Come in, come in, it's good to see you," he said warmly, throwing open the door in his old blue dressing gown. "But try not to make any noise. We've just got Vicky off to sleep."

Vicky was afraid to open her eyes when she eventually woke up at ten o'clock. But as she lay rigid as a statue on the pillow she could feel the warmth of the sun stealing across her face and she began to relax and breathe normally.

"Thank God," she sighed. It felt so nice and warm in the room. Then she thought: was it really a fine day outside? Or had Sam just turned the heating on full-blast for Jasmine's big day?

"Wakey, wakey!" Sam called then, coming into the room with a cup of freshly brewed coffee and two warm croissants for his wife. "It's like Piccadilly Circus downstairs. Bridesmaids, beauticians, hairdressers, nosy neighbours! You name it, they're drinking tea out of our best cups and eating all our chocolate biscuits."

They both knew he was enjoying every minute of it.

"Tell me it's a beautiful day," his wife asked, her eyes still closed.

"Yes, well, it is a scorcher. But probably the fact it's the height of summer had something to do with it."

A scorcher? Vicky finally opened her eyes.

"Thank God," she said happily. "I hoped it would be a beautiful day. It was the candles that clinched it."

"Here, woman, get this breakfast down your neck and then will you please give our Jasmine a hand getting ready? She's been up for ages. Fussing like I don't know what about her make-up. You women and your flippin' make-up. It always looks the same to us blokes." He set down the tray and opened the bedroom curtains. "Oh heck, the flowers have arrived. I'll get the door."

He hurried down the stairs.

"Jasmine, pet?" her mother called.

"What?"

"Is the shower free?"

"Yes. But don't be long in the bathroom. I need the loo, like, every five minutes," Jasmine called back. She was rummaging in her old bedroom for a safety pin. One of the bridesmaids had lost a button off her dress. "I hope the flowers are nice."

"They'll be lovely," Vicky said happily, stuffing half a croissant in her mouth. "Never mind lovely, they'll be bloody brilliant. Have the bridesmaids been here long?"

"Yes. Ages."

"Are they all in their dresses?"

"Yes. Of course."

"Is their hair done?"

"Yes, Mum. I'm getting mine done next."

"Right. Have the rest of those wedding presents been taken over to your flat?"

"Yes. The boys took them over half an hour ago."

"Good. They'll be safer at the flat. Everybody round here knows we'll be out all day. Has the minister been in touch?"

312

"Yes! Mum, will you please stop asking me questions and get out of bed and help me? I'm having an anxiety attack," Jasmine gasped. "I'm completely mad. This is sheer utter madness. I barely know Mark and now I'm having his baby and we're getting married. And I keep forgetting his surname. I'm going to miss my flat so much. I'm going to miss working with Ruby every day. The cars are coming in fifty minutes. And Mark's family are all dead posh types from Hillsborough. Oh God . . . Oh God . . . Oh God . . ."

Vicky flung off the bedcovers and went dashing across the small, creaking landing to Jasmine's old room. Jasmine was sitting on the bed, wearing a pink dressing gown and slippers and hyperventilating into a small paper bag from Eason's that had recently contained three boxes of biodegradable confetti.

"Sweetheart, love, you'll be fine," Jasmine's mother soothed, sitting down and sweeping her only daughter into her arms.

"Mummy, help me," Jasmine said between sobs.

"You'll be fine, love, I promise you. Today will be fine. I know it."

"I'm scared to death, Mum."

"What of, pet?"

"Of growing up."

"I know, it's not easy," her mother sighed.

"I feel as sick as a parrot," Jasmine said, wheezing.

"Nerves or morning sickness?"

"Both? I don't know, maybe it's too late in the pregnancy for morning sickness? Oh, I don't know any more . . ."

"Right, wait here. I'll get you a barley sugar sweet and some herbal sedatives."

"And a double vodka and Coke?" Jasmine joked.

"No, not a double vodka on your wedding day," her mother said firmly, not realising it was a joke. "We're not savages. And you're pregnant besides! I'll get you a tiny, tiny glass of pink fizz."

"Okay. Thanks, Mum." Jasmine laid her paper bag on the bed and took a deep breath.

"Will I send the stylist up in a minute?" Vicky asked gently.

"Yes, okay. I love you, Mum."

"I love you too."

"Mum?"

"Yes, love?"

"Will you do lots of baby-sitting for us, Mum?" Jasmine asked tearfully.

"You try and stop me," her mother smiled. "I'll be round at your house every day for breakfast. You'll be sick of the sight of me, I promise you."

"Thanks, Mum. Thanks a million."

"Now listen, I have to get ready myself. Are you definitely okay here? I'm only in the bathroom, remember? Has your breathing returned to normal yet?"

"Yeah, I guess so. Just send up the fizz along with the stylist, will you?" She gazed at her black and white designer wedding dress (a gift from Ruby) as it hung on the front of the wardrobe door. "I can always divorce Mark if it doesn't work out," she added doubtfully.

"Divorce, huh? That's the spirit," Vicky said, giving her beautiful daughter a double thumbs-up.

"Let's get this show on the road then," Jasmine said, plugging in her hairdryer.

"Right," Vicky said. She was halfway down the stairs already.

"So much for modern marriage," Jasmine sighed as she ran her fingers through her hair. Not that she truly believed she would ever want to divorce Mark, no way. But still, it was a comfort to know that there was a get-out available if Mark turned out to be weird in some way. And then she thought of how he'd looked so earnest and even a tiny bit goofy when he'd smiled at her after they'd made love two days earlier, and she knew in her heart, she was doing the right thing.

The happy convoy of black cabs parked in a neat line and the guests gathered in the grounds of the Transport Museum at Cultra. The sun was splitting the stones and the entire place was immaculately tidy.

"And we've just to wait here?" Sam said to the driver.

"Yes, mate."

"Yes, Dad," Jasmine said.

"That's what Mark said? Definitely now?"

"Yes, Dad."

"We've not to go in to the Reception desk or anything?"

"No, Dad."

"Flippin' mystery man! I hope your Mark hasn't come up with anything too mental," Sam muttered, fixing his oversized tie for the tenth time.

"Leave that tie alone, Sam, would you?" scolded his wife. "There's nothing wrong with it. It's meant to look that big."

"Leave it alone, Dad," Jasmine said.

"It feels too loose. It's gonna' fall open any minute," he muttered.

"No, it isn't. Leave it *alone*," Vicky said sharply.

She slapped his hand away and almost dislodged her own hat in the process. A huge great woven thing with coffee-coloured feathers that made her resemble a bird of prey.

"Stop fussing, the pair of you. You're making me nervous again," Jasmine complained, rubbing her stomach gently.

Immediately they were both contrite. "Sorry, love."

The line of cabs set off again, leaving the guests from both sides of the family to mingle as best they could on the lawn.

"We all look *gorgeous*, Dad. Even your hat looks nice, Mum. Now that I've got used to it a bit more. The thing is, I *did* say I wanted this wedding to be a surprise," Jasmine said in a watery voice. "I just hope that the surprise part isn't Mark doing a fucking runner on me."

"Don't say *fuck* on your wedding day, Jasmine," her mother sighed.

"Sorry, Mum. Oh, I wish Ruby was here! Why isn't she here yet anyway?"

Jasmine looked like an illustration from *Vogue* magazine in her very stylish, three-quarter-length white tulle dress with black embroidery on the bodice. She had a small spherical bouquet of black roses studded with green stones and green silk banana leaves. Her long hair was simply braided into a loose plait. And she wore a pair of beautiful green silk shoes with a black rose on each toe.

"Relax, everyone. It's probably an open-air ceremony somewhere in the Museum grounds and then a traditional cream tea in the café or something?" Vicky said cheerfully. "No doubt that's what the fashionable folk of Hillsborough are doing these days."

"Speaking of which, I suppose we ought to go and say hello to the snobs?" Sam said doubtfully.

"Shush, they're not snobs. They're actually quite human," Jasmine said, waving across to Mark's parents. "Where's Ruby? I want Ruby. Was she in one of those cabs, did anybody notice?"

"Here she comes now," Vicky said happily, not at all jealous that her only daughter was looking round for another female for comfort and reassurance.

"Jasmine, hi! Oh, you look fabulous!" Ruby said, hurrying up to her friend. Tom was lagging slightly behind, looking very dapper indeed in his single-breasted black suit and a metallic bronze tie, both chosen by Ruby, naturally.

"My God, he *does* scrub up well," Jasmine said approvingly to Ruby.

"I know, doesn't he?" Ruby whispered back.

At that exact moment a great cheer went up from the small gathering of excited guests as Mark and the minister came sailing up the drive in a vintage bus. Mark was wearing a white suit and a green tie and waving furiously at them all.

"Oh my God," Sam said, shielding his eyes from the sun. "A bus!"

"Oh my God," said his wife, fumbling in her handbag for the camera. "A rickety old bus!"

"Oh my God," Jasmine said and she began to laugh hysterically. "I don't care if he is in a rickety old bus! At least he's here!"

"You're not getting married in that bloody thing," her father said then. "Not if I have anything to do with it."

"Oh now," Vicky said in a worried voice. "Don't make a scene, and Mark's gone to so much trouble as well."

"It's okay," Ruby assured them both, giving Jasmine a big hug. "You won't be getting married in a bus, love."

"You were in on this?" Jasmine asked.

"Yes, sorry for not telling you but Mark wanted something really memorable," Ruby smiled. "This is just his wee joke to get the *craic* going. You're actually getting married on a steam train."

"That's pretty memorable, you've got to admit," Tom added, waving back to Mark.

"And we don't have to get into that auld bus there?" Sam asked, visibly relieved.

"No," Ruby told them.

"And is there going to be food and all, by the steam trains after the wedding?" Sam asked hopefully. "I'd love to have a picnic by the trains even if they aren't moving."

"He loves steam trains," Vicky said affectionately. "He always says they remind him of his childhood, and going to Bangor on day trips."

"Yes indeed, it's your lucky day, Sam. The reception is going to be held *on* the biggest steam train," Ruby laughed. "That one's inside the Museum building. It'll not be moving anywhere but the servers are going to be wearing 1940s' uniforms. I've seen it already this morning and it looks fabulous. We've been here for an hour already. Mark asked myself and Tom to come here early, and give him a call if there were any problems. But it all looks totally amazing so don't worry. They've got bunting up everywhere and the wedding cake's in the ticket booth. Oh dear, I shouldn't have told you that!"

"Ruby, tell me everything," Jasmine gasped. "I don't think my nerves can take any more surprises."

"That's it really, sweetheart. We'll be going for a drive round Belfast after the food and the speeches, in one of the old open-top buses. But it's a big, roomy bus and not a wee bean-tin of a thing. Do you like the sound of that?"

"That sounds like heaven," Sam said, patting his giant tie with sheer relief. "I get to have my lunch on the train and then I get to show off round Belfast on an open-topped bus. Hooray!"

The emotional, open-air wedding ceremony was over within a few short minutes and everyone shouted and cheered and threw confetti over the happy couple. Then they all went inside for the reception. Photographs were taken of everyone posing merrily beside the buses and trains. Speeches were made and toasts were drunk. Then they all piled onto the bus for the Grand Finale, an hour's tour of the city.

"This is the best wedding I've ever been to," Ruby sighed as the ancient bus went serenely up the wide sunny road. "I mean, as a guest."

"Me too," Tom agreed, putting his arm round her tenderly. They were sitting on the lower deck in a quiet corner, carefully nursing two glasses of very expensive champagne: Mark's father's contribution to the festivities. Neither of them mentioned their own wedding days. This was a day to make happy memories.

"It was all so relaxed, wasn't it?" Ruby said contentedly.

"Yes, it was," Tom agreed.

"I like the idea of a buffet, too. It's nice to be able to wander around and not have to sit beside one person for, like, six hours," Ruby said thoughtfully. "Especially if you don't know them very well."

"True. Let's drink a toast to buffets?"

"Cheers!" Ruby said, raising her glass.

"Cheers," Tom said, laughing.

"You look so nice in that suit," Ruby told him then.

"Do I?"

"Of course. You should get dressed up more often."

Tom looked at Ruby's perfect cleavage in her red dress and also at her slim ankles in matching, red shoes.

"Don't get me thinking about clothes," he begged Ruby.

"Why not?" she said.

"Because then I'll only be thinking about taking yours off," he whispered into her ear.

"Stop it," she giggled.

"I can't help it," he said in a low voice. "You're turning me into a sex addict."

"Oh, am I now?" Ruby said quietly.

"Sorry, I shouldn't have said 'sex addict' on a vintage bus," Tom whispered.

"Why not?"

"It just seems inappropriate," he said, rolling his eyes towards Jasmine's parents, who were chatting animatedly with the minister.

"Kiss me," Ruby said then.

"Okay but just a quick one," Tom replied.

When Mark and Jasmine came downstairs from the top deck a few minutes later, Tom and Ruby were lost in a lingering kiss. Jasmine was extremely impressed.

"Tom was once so shy he ran away up the Ravenhill Road rather than say hello to us," she told her new husband quietly.

"Seems to be making up for it now," Mark said gently.

"Do you think we'll ever be as in love as they are?" Jasmine jokingly asked him.

"Jasmine, nobody could ever love anyone as much as I love you," Mark said, giving her yet another hug.

And he meant it.

# 43

# The Baby

The months seemed to fly by. Jasmine continued to work in Ruby's shop even though she was sitting on the luxury armchair for most of the day towards the end of her pregnancy. Ruby was constantly answering the doorbell and unpacking the new stock and ringing up the purchases as Jasmine pottered round the shop with a duster in one hand and a book of baby names in the other.

"I can't say a word to her though," Ruby told Tom on one of their regular walks along the beach, pretending to be cross with Jasmine for being unable to whizz about the way she used to.

"God, no," he agreed, playing along.

"It would be an utter betrayal of the sisterhood," Ruby said firmly.

"Yes. She'd be very upset as well," Tom said, nodding wisely.

"And we mustn't upset a pregnant woman," Ruby said.

"No, we definitely shouldn't do that."

"Seriously, I wonder if Jasmine will go on working after the baby comes?" Ruby wondered. "It might not look so good having a pram parked by the changing-room curtains. Or maybe it would!"

"I'm sure she'll be able to work part-time," Tom said. "Unless she decides to be a full-time mum."

"I don't know. I can't see Jasmine turning into an earth mother."

"She might do," Tom said.

"I suppose anything's possible," Ruby said doubtfully. "I know she'll adore the baby. It's just I can't see her giving up the shop altogether. She loves it."

"She can work part-time, then?"

"Okay, okay, I know I'm fretting. I'll miss her so much if she doesn't come back, that's all."

By the time Ruby came rushing into the maternity unit in early November it was all over. And Jasmine had safely delivered an eight-pound baby girl. She hadn't decided on a name yet. She was quite keen on Harlow, she said, inspired by the name Nicole Richie had given her daughter. Mark thought Amy was a lovely name but he also worried the name was too closely linked with the singer Amy Winehouse. Sam and Vicky thought Kylie was a great and bubbly sort of name. But again, Mark felt that Kylie wasn't quite unique enough. And of course, Mark's conservative parents favoured the classic names like Alice, Beatrice, Charlotte and Victoria. Everyone knew that Jasmine would be the one to choose the new baby's name in the end. After all, she'd been the one in labour for fourteen hours.

"She's absolutely gorgeous," Ruby sighed, touching the baby's tiny pink hand with the tip of her finger.

"Isn't she?" Jasmine said proudly.

"Just perfect. Where's Mark?"

"Working again this afternoon. But he'll take a couple of days off when I go home from hospital. When *we* go home. Me and the baby . . . my daughter!"

"Any idea when you'll be going home?" Ruby said, sitting down on a comfy chair beside Jasmine's bed. And whispering so she didn't wake the baby.

"I have no idea," Jasmine replied. "We're going to stay on at Mark's house until we buy a new place."

"I think that's wise. I mean, I know your apartment is nicer but it is on the fifth floor."

"Yes, it's only a little house but we'll look for something bigger as soon as we can. I mean, I know he's only just starting out in his career but I'm sure we'll get a big enough mortgage. And Mark says he'll take whatever price he can get for his current house, you know, just to get the deposit together? We were talking about it last night. Mark said he'd rather not sell the house to a landlord because the street is mostly retired people and young families. But if nothing else turns up he might have to reconsider."

"Okay." Ruby just nodded. It wouldn't be easy house hunting with a new baby and Mark's very demanding job. "Is there anything I can do to help?" she added.

"Will you come with me? Looking at houses?" Jasmine asked. "I can look at some on my own, Mark says. If he's too busy, I can start the ball rolling. Will you come with me, though? You're the expert on houses."

"Surely I will. I'll start collecting brochures right away. Thank God you can drive, Jasmine. That'll make life so much easier for you."

"Mum said she would mind the baby any time I ask her," Jasmine said, suddenly tearful. "Isn't she a sweetheart?"

"She is indeed. She's so good to you, Jasmine," Ruby said wistfully.

"Is your mum ever coming home again?" Jasmine asked gently. She usually kept off this thorny subject and Ruby hadn't volunteered an update for ages.

"Who knows?"

"Are you still raging at her?"

"Not any more, no."

"That's good," Jasmine said quietly, suddenly all aware and terribly defensive of the mother – daughter relationship.

"She loves me in her own way," Ruby nodded sadly. "It's just that she has to do something independently now. Something for herself, you know? And I sort of understand that need. Sort of . . . So anyway we'll keep in touch and she'll come home again when she's good and ready. Hopefully . . . And if she just goes on travelling forever, well, I guess I'll just have to respect her wishes."

"You're very wise, Ruby."

"I don't know about that."

"You're only four years older than me but sometimes you feel like a second mother to me."

"Thanks, Jasmine. I *think* that's a compliment!" Ruby laughed.

"Oh, it is, definitely," Jasmine said quickly. "No use in the two of us being total eejits. One eejit is more than enough in any friendship."

"Okay then."

"How's your dad these days?" Jasmine asked suddenly.

"It's funny but I think Dad is getting used to the peace. That's my only worry now. He doesn't talk about Mum any more when we chat on the phone."

"You mean he might not want your mother to come back?"

"I'm not sure, no. He seems very happy on his own. Content, you know?"

"Oh dear. Out of sight, out of mind, huh?"

"I know," Ruby sighed.

"Isn't it funny, Ruby? The current generation of over-60s, I mean? All out ballroom dancing like Theodora Kelly. And gallivanting like your mother. SKI-ers, they're called. Spending Kids' Inheritance, you know?."

"Yes, I know," Ruby nodded.

"What'll be left for you if your parents split up?"

"I don't know or care really. I just want them to be happy."

"Huh, you're far too nice. I'll be getting one sixth of a terrace in Sandy Row when my parents kick the bucket. Or maybe even less than that if they count in all the grandchildren."

"Never mind that now. You did bag a doctor, didn't you? You jammy cow!"

"Yes, I did, didn't I?" Jasmine giggled. "But I do love him madly," she added. "When he came into the shop that day, I had no idea that he'd done so well for himself. I just thought how good-looking and sexy and nice he'd become. I do love him for himself, you know."

"I know you do," Ruby said, smiling brightly at Jasmine and then marvelling at Jasmine's gorgeous baby daughter once again.

A nursing assistant brought them tea and biscuits then and for a while the two friends just sat gazing at Baby Crawford's exquisite rosebud lips, long fluttering eyelashes and perfect round cheeks.

"She's so beautiful," Ruby sighed. "I thought babies were supposed to be all red and wrinkly and screaming the house down when they were born?"

"Not all of them," Jasmine said smugly.

"Was it sheer agony?" Ruby ventured.

"Not really," Jasmine said sheepishly.

"Seriously, Jasmine, was it?"

"No."

"Liar."

"It wasn't easy," Jasmine admitted.

"How sore was it exactly?"

"I'm not telling you," Jasmine said, sipping her tea demurely.

"It's a conspiracy," Ruby said, leaning back in her chair.

"No, it isn't."

"Yes, it is. All new mothers clam up about the birth. Just so you don't deter the rest of us poor suckers. Are you being kind, I wonder? Or do you just want us all to suffer as much as you did?"

"You forget the pain, Ruby. Immediately afterwards, you forget all the bad stuff," Jasmine admitted shyly.

"Oh my God, so it *was* agony?"

"Ruby, look, don't torture yourself. I'm not going to dwell on the details of it. She's here now and all I want to do is get a house bought so you and me can decorate the nursery together. And go for lovely long walks in Ormeau Park, and take hundreds of photos, and all of that caper."

"Yes, indeed," Ruby said brightly. She didn't like to point out to Jasmine that she still had a shop to run. Single-handedly now, possibly. She daren't mention hiring a new assistant in case Jasmine was offended.

"It'll be so weird, won't it? Me, a mummy?" Jasmine sighed.

"Not at all. You'll be the gold standard that all yummy mummies will aspire to," Ruby said, patting her friend's hand enviously. "You might have to swap those five-inch heels of yours for beaded flip-flops, mind. But you'll still look totally amazing."

"Ruby?"

"Yes?"

"Can I still work in the shop on Fridays and Saturdays?"

"Of course you can."

"Mum said she would look after the baby so I could still get out of the house sometimes. Mum says it's important to keep one foot in the door of the workplace, or else you become a baby bore and a social outcast."

"Okay then. We can't have you becoming a social outcast. It wouldn't suit you! I'll struggle on as best I can between Mondays and Wednesdays, shall I? Maybe I'll close the shop on Thursdays actually? Have a day off myself."

"Yes! We could make Thursday our 'Ladies who Lunch' day? And Mark says that if I'm going stir-crazy at home I can always put the baby into a good nursery and go back to work full-time. Even though it would end up costing us more than I earn. But obviously I'm going to try to look after her myself first."

"Okay."

"And my dad says babies do best when they stay with their mothers."

"Okay."

"But Mark's parents are all for working mothers. They think I should do some childcare courses and open up my own nursery. They say there's a shortage of good nurseries in Belfast and everywhere."

"Okay," Ruby said again. She thought the idea of Jasmine running her own nursery was *slightly* ambitious to say the least but she decided to say nothing for now. Wait and see how Jasmine got on with *one* child initially, she told herself. She must remember not to interfere too much. Anyway, your own life was so much simpler when you didn't interfere in other people's . . .

"What do you think I should do, Ruby?" Jasmine asked suddenly.

Ruby bit her lip. She mustn't say the wrong thing.

"Oh God, don't ask me for advice," she muttered, blushing slightly. "What would I know about babies?"

"But you're so clever and everything."

"Not where babies are concerned. I haven't a clue about babies."

"Fair enough. It's just so hard to decide."

"Give it a few weeks, yes? See how you feel?"

"Yes, okay. I'll see how motherhood agrees with me."

"Good girl."

"It's funny how being a mother reduces you though," Jasmine said quietly.

"How do you mean?"

"Well, you become so dependent on other people. Before this

one here came into the world, I needed nobody to help me. I had my job and my lovely flat. I could come and go whenever I wanted. I could sleep with any man I wanted. Or just stay in bed reading magazines on my days off. Now I need Mark to support me financially. And he'll get a major say in where we live. And I need Mum and Dad to baby-sit. And I need you to give me some hours in the shop that suit me and the baby . . . I feel like a great big fat burden."

"Don't swear near the baby, Jasmine love. You don't want her first word to be a naughty one, do you?"

"You see? I can't even swear now. My life's not my own any more," Jasmine complained. "I have to be a proper Goody Two Shoes from now on, don't I?"

"Relax, pet. Your life is your own. That's just the hormones talking."

"Ah, fuck it. Sorry, I didn't mean to say that! Oh well, I'll just have to do my best, I suppose."

"Yes," Ruby agreed.

"I'll tell you what else I've changed my mind about," Jasmine said quietly.

"What?"

"Casual sex. I've gone right off it."

"Well, you are a married woman now, Jasmine. You can't be having one-night stands any more, can you?"

"No, not for me, silly, I love Mark now! I meant, casual sex in general."

"Oh?"

"Yes. After what I went through in there last night," she nodded towards the delivery room, "I'll never be able to read about casual sex or see it on the telly or in a film ever again without wincing. I reckon ninety-nine per cent of men just aren't worth it, basically. It's just five minutes in bed for them but it's life and death for the woman."

"I knew it was agony," Ruby smiled.

"Yes, well."

"But Mark and the baby are worth it, aren't they?" Ruby asked hopefully.

"Yes. Just about."

"Oh come on, let's pick a name," Ruby said brightly. "What about Harlow? That was your favourite, wasn't it?"

"Yes, but everyone'll be choosing that name now. Five years from now there'll be five girls called Harlow in every Primary One class in the western world."

"I suppose."

"And Kylie's a no-no for the same reason."

"Yes, I agree. Kylie Crawford doesn't sound right anyway."

"I'll have to have a good long think about it," Jasmine sighed.

"Yes, you will."

"But Harlow is a gorgeous name, isn't it?" Jasmine yawned.

"Yes, it is."

"Really nice . . ."

Then Ruby slipped Jasmine's teacup gently out of her hand as Jasmine yawned again prettily and drifted off to sleep.

# 44

# The Odd Couple

When she looked up from the cash register and saw her abandoned husband standing silently at the bakery counter, Emily Nightingale almost fainted with shock.

"Christ preserve us!" she said loudly.

"No need to faint, it's only me. That yellow dress really suits you," he said, smiling gently.

"Oh my God."

"Hello, Emily."

"What are you doing here?" she gasped, nervously glancing over her shoulder in case the supervisor was watching from the office window. They weren't supposed to receive social visits at work. "Don't you dare make a scene in here," she hissed nervously.

"Don't worry," he said calmly. "I won't make a scene. I wouldn't dream of it. I'm not a scene-maker by nature."

"Then what are you doing here?" she repeated, cold sweat beginning to pool on her neck and collarbones with the worry and anticipation of what lay ahead.

"I came to New York to say goodbye to you," he said simply.

"Goodbye?"

"Yes, goodbye. We were married for forty years, Emily. I think that warrants a face-to-face goodbye, don't you? And this is it. You didn't think our marriage would just fade away, did you?"

"Well, yes, I did."

"No, there was a formal wedding ceremony and there has to be a formal ending. So it's *goodbye* then. I'm sorry you weren't happy being my wife. I did my best to be a good husband and a faithful companion to you. But clearly I got it wrong. Spectacularly wrong."

"Is there a problem here?" asked the bakery supervisor, who'd just come out of his office and noticed the lengthy queue forming behind Emily's current customer.

"Hello, I'm Emily's husband, David Nightingale. I just came to tell my wife I'm going to grant her the divorce she asked for," he said, offering his hand with a little flourish.

The supervisor shrugged his shoulders and shook David's hand warmly. He was divorced himself.

"Not an easy thing to go through," he said kindly. "It was less traumatic having my kidney tumour removed last year than it was getting divorced. And she got the house. And the dog."

"Oh my God," Emily said again, closing her eyes with sheer embarrassment.

"Well, you wanted a divorce, Emily. So I'm giving you one now. What's the matter? Don't you want it all out in the open? I thought you were tired and bored of hiding away in our big house behind the trees?"

"David, would you shush!" she hissed.

"We are getting divorced," her husband told the other customers who were standing close by.

"Good luck to you, buddy," said one man. "But is there any chance I could get some bread around here?"

The other customers just rolled their eyes and looked at their watches. Divorce was not big news here in the Big Apple.

"Take five, Emily," said the supervisor. "Actually, take the rest of the day off," he added, reaching for an apron from the rack on the wall. "But be here tomorrow morning, nine o'clock sharp, yeah? Or you're fired."

"Okay, thanks," Emily said, fetching her purse and coat and hurrying her soon-to-be ex-husband out of the Sunnyside Bakery.

"I can't believe you just did that," she said, almost in tears. "A simple letter would have sufficed."

"No, it wouldn't. I'm here now so let's talk."

They walked down the street together and went into a small diner that Emily liked. It was all chrome stools and pink curtains. The tables were very clean and the water was nicely chilled.

"Two coffees, please?" she called to the waiter.

The waiter immediately brought them over.

"Have a nice day," he said, smiling, as David paid him and left a large tip on the saucer. "Thank *you*, Sir."

Emily and David nodded but did not smile back.

"This is a silly bloody stunt you've pulled," Emily said at last.

"No, it isn't."

"You have no intention of divorcing me. I've been waiting for ages to hear from your solicitor."

"I have. It will happen. I've already started the proceedings. We've not lived together for some time, Emily. As you might have noticed? It will only be a formality at this stage of the game, or so I'm told."

"Oh, right."

"Needless to say, I'm keeping the house in Blackskull."

"Now wait a minute. I'm totally broke here."

"Not for much longer. I'm keeping the house because I love where it's situated. And there's no way I'd get permission to build something that big ever again. You couldn't get permission for a small shed round there nowadays. The planners have gone all hard-line. So I'm keeping the house but I'm giving you the lion's share of our savings."

"Oh, right," she said again.

"I have the cheque here in my jacket pocket. All you have to do is sign some papers and we won't have to see each other ever again. Okay? Not as a married couple, I mean. You're always welcome to visit me as a friend. And Ruby says to say hello, and you're welcome to visit her any time also."

"You mean, Ruby's not over here with you? You came here on your own? How did you manage it all?"

"I'm not completely dense, Emily," he sighed.

"Well, this is something I definitely wasn't expecting. Where are these divorce papers? Let me see them."

"Not here. We have to go to this address," he said, showing her a page in his address book. "It's a lawyer's office. They set it all up for me at the solicitor's, back home."

"Is this some sort of a trap, David? If I go to this place will I be arrested?" she said, eyeing him suspiciously.

"No, I promise you. It's all very straightforward. We'll be divorced within six months. And you can have the money today."

"How much?"

He told her.

"That's very generous of you, David."

"I know it is."

"But why are you giving in so easily?" she asked, mystified.

"Because I'm tired of failing you," he replied sadly.

"What do you mean?"

"I'm so tired, Emily. I just want a rest," he said simply.

"Oh, I see."

"I don't want to spend the time I've got left in this world fighting and arguing with you or anyone," he said simply. "I've got better things to do."

"There's no need to be hurtful, David," she began.

"I'm not trying to be hurtful. You started this. Is that really all we had, Emily? Hurt and boredom? A forty-year sentence of hurt and boredom? Not a real marriage at all. Just a low-level conflict punctuated with the odd bust-up? Not to mention your various disappearances."

"David, please don't do this . . ."

"Ah, fine . . . You were right to leave me, Emily. Really you were. Otherwise we would have gone on the same way until either I keeled over with a heart attack or old age. Or you did. That's not a life."

"It wasn't that bad."

"It was. It was only our marriage vows that were keeping us together. Not love."

"Do you think so?"

"We never laughed together enough – I mean, we never really laughed enough at all. Until our sides ached."

"We had a few laughs," she said hopelessly.

He looked at her levelly. "I'm sorry, Emily. I give in. It's over."

"You're calling my bluff," she said.

"No, I'm not."

"Yes, you are. You're trying to frighten me into coming home with you."

"No, honestly I'm not. I don't want you to come home with me. I'm having the house re-decorated anyway. It's all ladders and dustsheets at the moment."

"What?"

"The wallpaper was steamed off last week. All the walls are being re-plastered and painted white. Oak floors will then be laid and stained dark brown. And I've bought a rocking chair to go by the fireplace in the kitchen. You know how you always hated rocking chairs? You said they reminded you of the Famine? Well, now I've got one."

"My chintz curtains, though? My lovely floral sofas?"

"Don't worry. They've gone too . . . but only into storage. I've put them, and all of your other stuff, into a storage place for you in Belfast. It'll be safe there for one year and then they can either sell it on or dump it; that's up to you. I'll give you their business card later at the lawyer's office."

Then he went up to the counter of the diner and asked for a double cheeseburger with extra onions and extra pickles. And a large helping of fries.

"Have you gone mad?" Emily asked when he came back and sat down to await his meal.

"No, hopefully not. But I've quit smoking and I'm eating healthier foods these days. Mainly healthier foods anyway. This is my one treat of the week. I'm allowing myself one treat every week and this is it. Well, I am in New York. So I've got to have a burger, haven't I?"

"Where are you staying?" she asked.

He told her.

"How long for?"

"Just for tonight. I'm going home tomorrow morning."

"Why not stay a while longer? See the sights?"

"I don't want to see the sights, Emily. I don't like crowds, queues, trains, noise or museums. You know that."

"Fair enough."

They sat in silence then for a few minutes, each lost in thought.

"Here comes my burger. That was pretty quick! Are you having any lunch yourself?" he asked. "My shout."

"I'm not hungry," she said, beginning to cry.

"It'll be okay, Emily," he told her then. "Please don't cry. You know this is for the best. We should have talked things over ages ago, maybe even away at the very beginning. We should have split up decades ago, I daresay. I blame the church, not you or myself. It made our generation frightened of thinking for ourselves. We knew we weren't compatible but we were afraid to admit it to everyone. Even to ourselves, Emily."

"Yes. It's true. I just feel so scared now it's finally happening," she confessed.

"You'll be fine. You can come back to Ireland if you like? Open your own business if you want to? Live near Ruby in Belfast or wherever you fancy."

"But not live with you?"

"No. I don't think so."

"Why not, David? Would you not give me another chance?"

"No, Emily, I can't do that."

"Why not?"

"Because I can never forget what you said to me the day you left. About me being boring. I can never forget that. I *am* boring, Emily. But that's just the way I am. I don't want to change and I don't think I *can* change. I like living by myself now – it's very peaceful. I've taken up fishing and joined a cookery club." He decided not to tell Emily he was very fond of one particular lady on his cookery course. Nothing had happened yet so there was no point in throwing another name into the mix.

"But that all sounds great," Emily said.

"It's okay," he admitted. "We only meet every other Saturday now but it's enough for me."

"Why didn't we do this years ago?" she wondered. "Join clubs? Travel a bit?"

"We were too shy," he said flatly.

"Yes. I suppose we were."

"Yes."

"Have you told Ruby you're divorcing me?"

"Yes, I've told her that *we* are getting divorced. A mutual decision. You know it's what you wanted. It's not just me. You started it, remember? But it's for the best, Emily."

"Yes, I suppose. What did Ruby say?"

"She said it was okay with her." He sprinkled more salt on his burger. "Jesus but this is a big burger. Talk about value for money, hey. I'll not eat for a solid week when I get home. It's lovely though, I can't fault the taste of it. Lovely bit of beef."

"I don't believe you, David – what you said about Ruby. She just said it was *okay* if we split up? Just *okay*?"

"Yes, she was very calm about it, Emily, if you must know. She said if she could survive losing Jonathan she could survive anything. I mean, we'll still be her parents, won't we? I mean, we're not divorcing Ruby. She's seeing someone now, you know. A lovely chap called Tom Lavery. She probably told you about him already? We had dinner together last week in the hotel. They drove down to visit me. He's very protective of her. Not quite the looker that Jonathan was, of course. But she's very settled and content with him all the same. I hope they get married some day. Marriage seems to suit Ruby. Even if it never suited you and me, huh?"

"Oh my God," Emily sighed. "The two of you have clearly been doing just fine without me. You're cooking in a club. And fishing. And doing up the house. And Ruby's seeing another man. And it sounds pretty serious."

"Isn't that what you wanted? For both of us to get on with our lives and give you a rest?"

"No. I mean, yes. I mean, no."

"We're not cutting you off, Emily. You're free to come home and see Ruby and myself any time you like. I'm only here to tell you, in person, that our marriage is officially over."

Emily ordered more coffees and they sat again in silence for a while as David finished his meal, just listening to Tom Petty on the radio and watching the shoppers going by their window. Rich old ladies with fur coats and too much make-up on them. Blonde young things with tiny dogs in cute baskets, and gay couples casually holding hands in a way they never could back home in Ireland. Homeless men shuffling in tattered shoes, muttering to themselves. Businessmen talking loudly on tiny mobile phones. Tourists who were blocking the pavements, as they took photographs of the tallest buildings.

"David?" she asked suddenly.

"Yes?" he said.

"Did you ever love me?"

"Yes, of course I did. That's a silly question."

"But not any more?" she asked.

"Not in the same way, no. I'm sorry."

"Why not? Do you mind if I ask you why not?"

"I've already told you why not. I can't love a woman who finds me boring." He smiled sadly at her. "I can't love a woman that left me on my own for all this time with barely a few phone calls. I can't love a woman who didn't answer even one of my letters. That would be pathetic of me, Emily. And I'm not pathetic. I might be boring but I'm not *pathetic*."

"I see. Have we really been apart for so long?"

"Yes. Years! Doesn't that show you how weak our marriage was? You didn't miss me at all, obviously. You'd rather stand on your feet all day long in a busy bakery, and live in some tip, than live with me, Emily. Jesus Christ, now that I've finally opened my eyes and given you a bloody divorce, don't tell me you've changed your mind?"

She was on fire with embarrassment now. This was too real, too raw.

"I'm sorry," she said simply.

"It's okay, it's not your fault, it just didn't work out. I'll miss the good times though," he said, sensing her shame. "We had some good times, didn't we? With Ruby, when she was little?"

"Yes we did. Ruby was a lovely little girl, wasn't she? I'll miss the good times too. David?"

"Yes?"

"Thank you for coming to New York to say goodbye to me. I took you for granted all these years and I'm sorry about that. Shall we go and sign those papers now?"

"Okay," he agreed, dabbing some ketchup off his chin with a pink paper napkin. "I'm stuffed."

"And then maybe afterwards we could just go for one last walk together?"

"Okay. If you like."

"Yes. We'll go shopping and buy a nice gift for Ruby. You can take it home with you tomorrow. What about a nice leather handbag from Bloomingdales? She sent me a lovely bag and I'd like to send her one."

"Okay. And I'll give you the cheque after we've signed the papers. I've been told that's the right way to do things. It must be properly witnessed, do you see? They won't ask about your status here. But the divorce and the settlement will be final now? You understand that? The house and what's left in my personal account are mine for keeps. This is the end of it?"

"Okay," she nodded sadly. "I won't trouble you any further after today. I didn't mean to hurt you, David. Do you know that? I never meant to make you feel pathetic. I'm very sorry if that's the way I made you feel."

"That's fine, Emily. I know you didn't do it on purpose. We were never suited, that's all. We were never suited to one another. I never meant to make you feel bored. I'm very sorry about that too. I was only trying to keep you safe."

"I understand that now."

"And the very best of luck to you in the future, Emily. And all of that auld shenanigans! You know the score? Whatever you decide to do and wherever you decide to live. Good luck to you. And I mean that most sincerely, Emily."

"Thank you, David. And good luck to you too. And I mean that."

We'll go to your bank before we go shopping, by the way. I don't want that cheque to get lost," he said, and they both laughed.

339

"Sensible to the last, that's you," she said affectionately.

"Yes, that's me," he agreed, nodding back and smiling.

They shook hands tenderly across the spotless pink Formica table in Harry's Original New York Diner.

And so forty years of marriage came to an end.

# 45

# The Seventh Secret

Ruby made up her bed with pretty new sheets and opened the bedroom window to let in some fresh air. She dusted the dressing table and emptied the wastepaper basket into a bin bag. She vacuumed the cream carpet and tidied away two shopping bags from the local Faith shoe store. She loved this bedroom, she thought to herself. She loved the emptiness of the room, the feeling of space. The spotless carpets and the tiny scented heart-shaped cushion hanging on the door handle. She loved her cute kitchen and her handy slow cooker, and her elegant bistro table and chairs and her pink ceramic biscuit jar. Would she be able to give up her cosy little sanctuary and share her life with a man again, she wondered now.

A man with a broken heart like Tom Lavery. A man who might rescue another dog from the dogs' home some day soon? A man who wore muddy boots and muddy jeans and muddy jackets to work? A man who would never forget his first wife.

But then she thought of his tenderness towards her when they were cuddled up in bed together. The way he was always so gentle and yet so intense and the way he always held her close to him after they made love. Caressing her shoulders and kissing her face softly. Perhaps they *could* make it work, she decided. Perhaps they really could give each other some comfort and friendship and even fun and good times? But love? Could she ever say the words "I love you" to him? She did love him. But was it the same sort of love that she'd had for Jonathan? Could she really and truly find enough space in her heart for another man? She'd be seeing him again at the weekend and she sensed he'd probably want to ask if they had a future together . . .

"Well, that shop won't open by itself," she said briskly, checking her watch.

Some days Ruby wondered what she'd have done without her beloved little shop to keep her busy.

However, Ruby was amazed when she went downstairs to open up her shop and found Mrs Kenny standing there on the doorstep.

"Mrs Kenny, is anything wrong?" Ruby asked worriedly.

"Not at all. I just wanted a wee word with you," Tom's co-worker and dear friend said sheepishly.

"Well, surely, come in," Ruby said, unlocking the door and switching on the lights.

"What a gorgeous place," the older woman said.

"Thanks, it's not bad," Ruby smiled. She was glad the heating was on the timer and the shop was cosy and warm already. "You take a seat there on the armchair and I'll make us a cup of tea."

"Okay."

Mrs Kenny perched politely on the edge of the sumptuous chair, nervously clutching her handbag to her chest as if it contained her life savings.

"Right, what can I help you with?" Ruby said when she came out of the kitchenette a minute later with two mugs of tea.

"Are you on your own today, Ruby?"

"Yes, Jasmine works part-time at the moment."

"Oh right, that's great, because I wanted to talk in private – about Tom."

"Tom?"

"Yes, I think he's going to ask you to marry him, Ruby dear."

"Well now, I can't say I'm terribly surprised," Ruby said lightly, even though her heart was soaring.

"Ruby, I just wanted to ask you to give him a chance. He's a good man, better than most."

"I know that," Ruby smiled.

"And he would never, ever, in a million years, treat you badly."

"I know that too," Ruby nodded.

"Yes, of course you know that. The two of you were made for each other. So you'll say yes?"

"I don't know, Mrs Kenny. I'll have to listen to my heart, if and when he asks me," Ruby said carefully.

"No, that won't do at all, Ruby," Mrs Kenny said.

"What?"

"You'll have to make up your mind in advance. Don't you see? That's why I came here this morning: to give you more time."

"Oh?"

"Yes. Because if you hesitate at all when he asks you, he'll think you don't want to marry him. He may not ask again, do you see? He's a very proud man, Ruby."

"But, Mrs Kenny, I'm still in mourning for my husband, Jonathan. Well, I know I'm seeing Tom. And I do love Tom. But in my heart, I still love Jonathan too."

"Listen to me now, love, because I'm an old woman and I've collected up a bit of wisdom over the years. You've got to *let go of the past*, Ruby. You don't have to forget the past, or pretend it never happened. You just have to keep moving onwards and keep looking to the future."

"Well, thanks very much for the advice, and for the advance notice of Tom's proposal. How do you know he's thinking of proposing, by the way?" Ruby said.

"It's the cottage. He said he might not be living there much longer."

"I see."

Both women sipped their tea thoughtfully. Then Mrs Kenny got up and began walking round the shop, glancing into the various cabinets and wardrobes, and admiring the clothes and scarves. When she got to the glass case beside the window, she was very taken with the last handbag in Ruby's collection, the purple one.

"This is very pretty," she said.

"I made it," Ruby told her absentmindedly.

"Did you? Well, do you know, I think I'll just buy this wee bag. There's a wedding I'm going to in the near future, and this bag would really go with my good purple coat."

"Put your money away, Mrs Kenny. I'll give it to you."

"You will not indeed. I'll pay for it," Mrs Kenny said firmly.

"Please let me give it to you? Or even for half-price?"

"No way!" Mrs Kenny laughed. "I'm not taking it unless I pay you the full price. I'm a very proud and independent woman!"

"Okay, point taken."

She counted out the banknotes carefully.

Ruby wrapped up the bag swiftly and handed the carrier to Mrs Kenny.

"Where's the wedding?" she asked casually.

"Oh, it's likely to be in Belfast," Mrs Kenny said meaningfully.

"What? Oh! You're incorrigible!" Ruby laughed.

"I am. Now listen – you won't tell Tom I was here, sure you won't?"

"I won't."

"Promise me?"

"Yes, I promise."

"I just wanted to give you a bit of time to think things over, do you see? So you could then say yes right away, and make Tom very happy. Or you could let him down gently. God knows, I don't want to meddle, Ruby."

"I know you don't."

"It's just, I'm very fond of you. And you've been the salvation of Tom. And I love Tom as a son."

"That's okay, and thanks so much for taking the trouble to come all this way today."

"You're welcome."

"There's just one thing," Ruby said.

"What?"

"That carrier bag! If you don't want Tom to know you were here, you'd better hide it when you go back to Camberwell."

"You're right! I'll wrap it up in my coat so Tom doesn't see it."

"Okay. And thanks again."

"Aye! I'll be off now then, I've a taxi booked to take me back up the road in half an hour. So I'll go for a coffee to pass the time."

"I can make you some more tea?" Ruby offered.

"No, you're all right. I kind of like sitting in a café when I don't have to work in it," Mrs Kenny explained.

"Fair enough."

"So I'll say cheerio for now."

"Right," Ruby nodded.

"And remember what I said, Ruby dear? You've got to let go of the past."

"I'll remember."

When Mrs Kenny had left the shop, Ruby looked at the empty shelf in her glass case, where the seven handbags had once sat. All gone now, all seven of them.

"That's the seventh secret of happiness," Ruby sighed to herself, as she stood there, all alone in her little shop. "Let go of the past. I've got to let go of my past, haven't I? Jonathan, if you can hear me, sweetheart, I still love you and I always will. And I'll never forget you. Not ever, I promise. But maybe it is time to move on, or to keep moving onwards, as Mrs Kenny said. Meddler that she is, I think the lady is very wise."

Ruby and Tom were sitting on the willow bench in the centre of the maze. It was a sunny but cold Sunday morning in December and there was nobody else about yet. Tom turned to Ruby and took her hand.

"Have you thought any more about us living together?" he asked gently.

"I have, yes," she smiled.

"And what do you think?" Tom said, not wanting to presume anything.

"I think we should give it a go," Ruby said, holding his hand tightly.

"Really? That's great. I'm so glad you said that," Tom said, exhaling with relief.

"Mind you, I'm a little disappointed."

"How come?"

"I thought you were going to ask me to marry you," she laughed.

"Would you say yes if I did ask you?" he said, his eyes glittering with hope.

"I might say yes . . ." she teased him.

"Well then, marry me," he said at once, getting down on one

knee. "I didn't ask because I thought it might be too soon for you to think about getting married, that's all. That's the only reason I didn't ask sooner. I've loved you from the first moment I saw you."

"Oh Tom! Well, my answer is . . . yes."

"Ruby, do you really mean it?"

"I do."

"Oh God, this is amazing. Whatever happened to make you so . . . reckless?" Tom asked.

"Nothing. I've just decided to add one more secret to my collection, that's all," she told him. "Remember my little secrets of happiness? There was emotional independence, good health, getting rid of envy, holding on to your friends, doing good deeds and seeing the beauty in small things. Well, that's the last secret, Tom. Letting go of the past. So that's what I'm going to do now. I'm going to let go of the past."

"Okay, and I will too," he said gently.

"We'll see about that," she said, smiling at him. "It won't be easy for either of us."

"I'll try my best," he promised.

"So will I. Really hard," Ruby said.

"So what happens now?" he asked.

"We set a date, look at houses . . . I'm going to keep my flat," Ruby said then.

"Okay."

"I mean, I'm not going to rent it out or anything. I'm just going to keep it as it is, so we can stay there sometimes, maybe? I don't want anyone else to live in it. Not yet. It's not that I don't have faith in us. I just need to know it's there."

"That's okay. I understand."

"Do you, Tom?"

"Of course. I'll have to let the cottage go though. It's not really worth hanging onto. The rent isn't that high but I want a fresh start."

"Okay. What will you do if we don't make it?"

"I'll find another old cottage, don't you worry. But I'm one hundred per cent sure it'll never come to that. God, I'm so happy, Ruby! You've made me so happy!"

"I do want us to make it, Tom," she said, her eyes welling up with tears of joy.

"So do I. I love you, Ruby."

He kissed her tenderly on the lips.

"I love you too," she said.

It was the first time she had said it so directly to him. So seriously, without any hint of a joke or a smile attached to the words. She did love him, and he loved her. It was a miracle after all the pain and sadness they had both endured.

They hugged each other tightly. The words had not been all that hard to say really, she thought to herself. Now that she had said them at last, it hadn't really been hard at all. She would always keep the replacement engagement ring Jonathan had bought for her. As well as her old ring. She would always keep the expensive shoes she had bought for him. But these things she would wrap in tissue paper and store away for the time being. She would never forget Jonathan, not ever. But Tom was right for her now and she knew she was right for him also.

A robin redbreast landed on the ground beside them and looked at them both before flying away again.

"Was that your robin or mine?" Ruby said.

"Who knows?" he replied.

"I do love you, Tom. I mean that."

"And I love you too."


Ruby and Tom were amazed at the changes to the house in Blackskull when they went to visit for the grand re-opening. Or rather, for the very low-key re-opening. Ruby's father had asked the cookery club round for a few sandwiches and canapés in the kitchen. A glass of fizz and a cup of tea.

"What do you think?" he said to Ruby and Tom as they came in the front door.

"Wow! The light! It's so airy and light, Dad," Ruby sighed.

"It's fantastic, Mr Nightingale," Tom agreed.

"How did you manage all of this?" Ruby asked.

"It was nothing to do with me," her father said modestly. "It was the decorators. They did it all. I just told them I wanted it fully modernised."

"It's certainly modern now," Ruby nodded.

"The walls are immaculate, aren't they?" he said proudly.

"Yes, they are," Ruby nodded again.

"Inside and out?"

"Yes, indeed."

The pristine walls were glowing with reflected light and the windows looked much bigger without their floral pelmets and pleats blocking out the sunshine. The dark brown floors were gleaming brightly and smelling deliciously of beeswax polish. There was hardly any furniture in the house. Just a few Shaker-style antiques. It seemed even bigger than before. There was a fishing rod in one corner, and a wicker picnic basket.

"You look so well, Dad," Ruby whispered, hugging him tightly. "Have you got something else to tell me? Have you?"

"You mean, is there a new lady in my life?" he laughed.

"Yes? Is there someone special in the cookery club?"

"No, not at all," he smiled. "We're all just very good friends. Well, there is someone . . . but it's early days – very early days . . ."

"Okay, I believe you. Though thousands wouldn't."

"Listen, if you promise to be very discreet, I'll introduce you to her a bit later on. She's very shy so don't be making any big loud jokes about us getting married, right?"

"Right, Dad, I promise."

Ruby and Tom went into the kitchen and said hello to everybody, shaking hands and sampling the food and saying how gorgeous the house looked. Even the kitchen had been given a makeover with the cabinets all painted white and the brown plastic counter replaced with black granite slabs.

"I think you have to open the windows every day for five minutes to let out the radiation?" Ruby said helpfully. "From the granite?"

"Yes, that's true," Ruby's father nodded happily. Though Tom and Ruby could tell he wasn't all that bothered about radiation.

"It's gorgeous, Dad," Ruby hugged him again.

Everybody clapped and agreed the house was truly fabulous.

Later when the cookery club had gone home, Tom and Ruby sat down to supper with David Nightingale. Some fish he'd caught and then fried himself.

"Have you heard from Mum recently?" Ruby asked.

"Yes, she sent me a postcard from Florida," David said. "She's left the bakery in New York, as you know. And she's having a holiday in Florida with her friend Dorothy and then she's coming home to see you and Tom in Belfast, she said."

"And is that going to be a problem for you?" Ruby asked. "Will you miss her all over again if she comes to Belfast on a visit?"

"Nope. Not a bit of it. We've said our goodbyes."

"Honestly, Dad?"

"No, truly. I'm fine," he said, patting her hand. "I can handle it. I'll maybe see her the next time she's home. Just as an old friend."

"Oh, Dad. You're so good."

"Never you mind about me. I can take care of myself. Now, what I want to know is, how are the two of you getting on, huh? Am I going to be a Father of the Bride any time soon?"

"Daddy, stop it," Ruby scolded him.

"Maybe," Tom said, blushing furiously. "Maybe you are."

"What! Have you set the date?" Ruby's father asked happily.

"Yes," Ruby said gently. "Yes, we have."

Ruby and Tom found a lovely new house to rent in Saintfield village, halfway between Camberwell House and Ruby's shop on the Ravenhill Road. It was in a secluded cul-de-sac near the shops and was large enough to give them both plenty of personal space. There was a small conservatory for Tom to potter in if he was ever feeling low. And a little spare bedroom for Ruby's sewing machine, just in case she felt like running up some more velvet handbags in the middle of the night.

"I'll leave the decorating up to you, if you don't mind?" Tom said, looking at the stark white walls and the empty rooms. "It's kind of nice the way it is. It reminds me of your father's house. But anyway it's up to you."

"Thanks a million, Tom. I have it all planned out in my head already," Ruby told him happily. "Nothing too floaty and fussy, don't worry."

"I wouldn't know floaty and fussy if it punched me in the face," Tom laughed, opening the lids of their delivery pizza, garlic bread and potato wedges. "Do you want the barbeque sauce or the chilli sauce?"

"Just a pinch of salt for me," Ruby said, fetching two large glasses and a bottle of red wine from a cardboard box on the kitchen counter. "I never have the dipping sauces. I'm a potato wedge purist."

"We still have so much to learn about one another," Tom said, looking slightly downcast.

"That's okay, isn't it?" Ruby smiled. "We have all the time in the world."

Neither of them knew for sure how much time they had, of course. Fate could intervene at any time. Another car accident, or an illness . . . But it was better to be optimistic, Ruby decided.

"I suppose. I just want to know everything about you," he said.

"Ask me then," she said brightly.

"Ask you what?"

"Ask me anything."

"Anything?"

"Yes. Five questions every day. Would that do you?"

"Okay," he said as they sat down at the table. He thought about it for a while and then he began.

"What's your favourite flower?"

"Any kind of white rose, small or large. I don't know the names of them. Just white roses in general. Next question?"

"Favourite perfume?"

"Chanel. Any one in the range."

"Because of the scent or the brand name?"

"Both, but mostly because I like the shape of the square glass bottles. I love glass bottles that are heavy and thick. That counts as your third question, by the way."

"Okay. Do you like surprises?"

"No, I don't think I'd be able to cope with a really big surprise any more. So no holiday tickets under my pillow, okay? Small surprises are fine though."

"What would constitute a small yet good surprise?"

"A triple-layer chocolate cake from M&S, breakfast in bed occasionally, a bunch of white roses on a miserable wet day. That's your five questions."

"Okay. I like this game. Do you want to ask me anything?"

"Not yet," she laughed, pouring the wine. "For the time being I quite enjoy you being so mysterious."

"I'm not mysterious at all, Ruby," he said in a low voice. "I was in the wilderness since losing Kate. I had nothing worth living for except Noah. And now I've found something to live for again. I love you, Ruby. And thanks for giving my life back to me."

She kissed him softly on the lips.

"It was my pleasure, and I love you too," she said tenderly. "Now eat your pizza."

THE END

If you enjoyed *The Seven Secrets of Happiness* by
Sharon Owens, why not try

# It Must be Love

also published by Poolbeg?

Here's a sneak preview of Chapter One.

# 1

## Big Mouth Strikes Again

It was eight thirty on a frosty Friday night in December. The air outside the tube station was bitterly cold and the end of Sarah's nose was soon bright red and nearly numb. The sudden drop in temperature always caught her by surprise at this time of year. She hurried down the street and into the smartly decorated foyer of her building. A quick dash up four flights of stairs (her only exercise, usually) and she was almost there. Now, where had she put her green-apple key-chain?

"Honey, I'm home!" Sarah said brightly, even though she knew most nights there was no one there to answer her.

Her fiancé, Mackenzie, lived near a tiny village called Glenallon (on the east coast of Scotland, about forty minutes' drive from Edinburgh) all year round, taking care of his country estate. It'd been romantically titled Thistledown in 1776 though in reality it was an austere and draughty place. A four-storey Gothic mansion complete with three turrets, four gargoyles and an ancient, nail-studded, black-painted front door. Perched right on the edge of the cliffs, it was a bit foreboding for Sarah. But Mackenzie was very proud of the manor house and he enjoyed country life. And Sarah loved him with all her heart, and after the wedding she knew she would grow as fond of Thistledown as he was.

In the meantime, this prestigious address in London was a much nicer spot in which to live and the furniture was a lot more comfortable, too. There was a small M&S at the end of the street and two gorgeous boutiques just round the corner. The apartment had formed part of Mackenzie's inheritance after his father died. And Sarah had been living here for the last three years – ever since getting engaged to him, in fact. (They'd been together for five years.) He came down to London to see her as often as he could and she went up to Thistledown most Fridays after work. Still, it was lonely sometimes, this long-distance love. It was nice to pretend, therefore, when she was coming home from work, that Mackenzie was pottering in the kitchen or singing in the shower or sitting in his favourite wingback chair reading the evening paper.

Sarah set her large black-patent handbag down on the hall table and switched on one or two of the electric radiators. The only downside to having such high ceilings, she admitted glumly, was having to shiver in the winter, in permanently freezing rooms.

She was exhausted after a long day spent taking photographs of a duck-egg-blue soup tureen full of lamb casserole and floury dumplings. And then a fantastically tall sponge cake, studded with silver balls and topped with sugar rose-petals. Sarah was a professional photographer by trade, currently working for a glossy cookery magazine. "Gastro-porn" her best friend Abigail called it. Dishes that most people weren't able to make, displayed in houses most people weren't able to afford or weren't talented enough to decorate for themselves, even if they could be bothered to gather up the typically long list of ingredients.

"An entire bottle of expensive sherry?" Abigail had once remarked. "Just to add one teaspoon of it to the recipe? Madness. Who drinks sherry anyway? And who's got a long-handled serving spoon going spare? I mean, a silver spoon, for heaven's sake?"

"Don't blame me," Sarah had replied indignantly. "I only take the pictures for them. I only follow orders."

"That's what Colonel Paul Tibbets used to say."

"Who?"

"The pilot of *Enola Gay*, the man who dropped the atomic bomb on Hiroshima."

"Swot!"

Abigail had always been the clever one. She worked as a clinical psychologist in a top London clinic, counselling the depressed, the bewildered and the broken-hearted. Sarah knew Abigail didn't have to justify her work to anybody. Nobody went around making fun of clinical psychologists.

Well, she wouldn't be working in the gastro-porn industry for much longer, Sarah thought happily. Because on Christmas Eve, Sarah Quinn, thirty years old, professional photographer and dedicated fashionista, would be giving up her glamorous career in publishing, moving to Scotland and marrying Mackenzie Campbell, gentleman farmer and gorgeous older man. She was going to wear her Grandmother Ruby's cream satin wedding dress with the long line of covered buttons up the back and carry a huge bouquet of cream roses and trailing ivy. And for once in her life, she'd willingly be swapping her comfy ankle boots for a pair of cream satin shoes. She was counting down the days, the very hours, until the ceremony.

Ever since she'd first met Mackenzie on a location-shoot at Thistledown Manor (featuring Thistledown Fine Foods, his small cheese- and jam-making business), she'd been hopelessly in love with him. He was tall and broad shouldered, gorgeous looking with tousled grey-blond hair and bright blue eyes. He'd been married before, to the beautiful Jane, but she'd died in a car accident years earlier. Jane had been expecting their first child at the time. So that was all incredibly poignant and tragic, of course, but he didn't talk about it much. And Sarah respected his privacy and never asked him anything about Jane. But she wanted to look after Mackenzie when they were married, the way he'd always looked after her. And have at least one child with him. Hopefully two or maybe even three. Then Mackenzie wouldn't be the last of the Campbells of Glenallon to live at Thistledown. (Seven hundred years, they'd been there.) She'd have the nursery walls painted with a delicate pastel mural of interlocking trees; she'd have a huge crib with warm curtains around it to keep out the draughts. She would be the best mother of all time.

Speaking of which, Mackenzie's mother, Millicent, was a bit of a dragon, it had to be said. And she lived with him at Thistledown Manor. Relentless in her daily routine, she was always doing something. Never sitting down, never relaxing. And Sarah was a London girl who didn't really know how to sew or cook or handle dogs, and Mackenzie had six prize-winning German Pointers. In truth, she still knew next to nothing about running a country estate with a big house and a dairy herd and a small business attached. But these were minor things. She would learn the ropes soon enough.

"Soon enough," she said to herself now, slipping off her boots. "Okay, first a drink and then I'll order pizza."

The flat was dark and humming with silence as she sloped through to the grand sitting room, took off her trench coat and polka-dot scarf and selected a large glass and a screw-top bottle of Merlot from the walnut cabinet. She'd forgotten to open the blinds before going to work that morning and now the room was cold and had a forlorn feeling, the way rooms do when they haven't been aired all day. The walls of the sitting room were painted a dark grey-blue and a huge resin-cast mirror from Italy hung above the mantelpiece. Far below on the street outside she could hear the evening traffic trundling past, some impatient tooting of horns and the occasional angry shout at those drivers still determined to double-park outside their favourite shops despite the stricter parking laws that had recently been introduced. Sarah blew a kiss to the back of Mackenzie's wingback chair and sank onto the sofa. She opened the wine and poured some very carefully into her glass. She didn't want to spill any on the red brocade cushions.

"I'm getting married," she said as she raised a glass to her reflection in the beautiful, silvery mirror. "I'm actually getting married. Little old me. Who'd have thought it?"

It was so exciting. She had to talk to someone, she had to go over all the girly details one more time. She decided to give Abigail a call. Fridays were Abigail's "admin" days at work and hopefully she wouldn't be too tired for a good, long chat about personalised books of matches and tiny pink boxes of sugared almonds. But there was no answer at Abigail's house – a sleek and modernised two-bed maisonette in Chelsea. She could have moved further out and got something bigger, she said. But she valued her privacy more than anything and her neighbourhood was quietly exclusive with its established trees and close-knit community of long-term residents. Sarah hung up and dialled her friend's mobile number.

"Hello? Sarah? Sorry, I must have nodded off," Abigail mumbled, yawning. "God, this thing has a loud ring on it. I must work out how to turn it down one of these days."

"Hi there," Sarah replied, immediately feeling guilty for waking her friend. "Didn't mean to wake you up."

"It's fine, I'll go to bed soon. How are you?"

"Oh, I'm good. Just fancied an old chinwag. I'm home alone tonight. Are you busy?"

"Not at the moment, obviously! I was lying on the sofa with my feet up, waiting for something decent to come on the telly. Are you not on your way to Mackenzie's by now? Don't tell me you've mislaid your tiara again?" That was Abigail, always teasing Sarah about her posh boyfriend and his landed-gentry lifestyle.

"Ha, ha. No, I was too tired to go this weekend – we were way behind on the latest shoot. It was nothing in particular I wanted, only a chat with you about the wedding. I know I'm completely obsessed with it all but indulge me, please. Did you ever get around to buying that nice diamanté clasp for your hair? You know, the one you saw in the antique shop in Notting Hill?"

"Not yet, no. But I will. I'll go tomorrow morning, first thing."

"Yes, well, the wedding's only three weeks away and you *are* my chief bridesmaid. And you haven't bought any shoes yet either. I'll have to get Big Millie onto your case."

"Very funny."

"Yes, Big Millie will sort you out. I'll get her to slither under your bedroom door at midnight and scare the living daylights out of you."

And they both dissolved into fits of girlish laughter. For Millicent Campbell stood six foot two in her sock soles and was very, very skinny. Sarah and Abigail secretly called her Big Millie when they were feeling mischievous. In fact, Sarah used to joke privately to Abigail that if they ever lost the knives at Thistledown Fine Foods, they could use Big Millie as a cheese wire.

"She's not fattened up then on the Christmas fare?" laughed Abigail.

"No, tweeds and all, she'd still be thin enough to slice through that Cheddar like a dream," Sarah spluttered.

"Can't wait to see her in the flesh, so to speak!"

(Abigail hadn't met Millie yet but she'd seen the photographs.)

"I'm only sorry it's too late to get her a walk-on part in *Harry Potter*," said Sarah, giggling. "With that long white hair of hers and those long coats, she'd be a natural. Not to mention she knows her way around old castles. Up and down the stairs she goes like a panther, completely silent. You never know where she is, you just turn a corner and there's Big Millie, dusting away at the antlers like nobody's business. So watch what you say when you come to Thistledown, won't you?"

"I will. I'll be on my best behaviour, I promise."

"Honestly, Abigail, when you meet Big Millie, you'll be terrified. She's even scarier in real life than she is in pictures. And when she looks at you, it's as if she can read your mind."

"Oh, you're mean!"

"Yes, I know. I'm a bit giddy tonight but I'm just so excited. I wish the wedding was tomorrow morning. I wish I was in the church right this minute. I wish Big Millie was flying off into the sunset on her broomstick so Mackenzie and I had the house to ourselves for a while."

"Wow, go easy on the poor guy, won't you? He's pushing fifty, remember. We don't want him croaking it before you've got the heir and the spare safely in their cradles."

"Now who's being mean? Mackenzie is in great shape. Oh, wait till you hear what happened today at work. I forgot to tell you, but at the end of the shoot when I was out of the room switching things off, Eliza dropped a chocolate penis into the casserole. And then she took a picture of my face when I came back and clocked it sticking up between the dumplings. She said she was going to post it on MySpace tonight. I'm going to look beyond ridiculous – my eyes were out on stalks."

"Oh wow, I've got to see that."

"It was disgustingly vulgar really, but we were falling about the place. Eliza is priceless, isn't she? I know she only joined the magazine last year but I'm glad I asked her to be my second bridesmaid. We'll have great craic in Thistledown on the hen night."

"Would you listen to Miss London Irish 2007! We'll have great *craic*, indeed. Our parents might be Irish but you and I were born and bred here in London town, m'lady!"

"I *know* that. For your information, I am getting into the Celtic spirit. In preparation for my imminent move to Scotland."

"Fair enough. But in Scotland they don't say *craic*, they say something else – oh, what was it again?"

All in all, a very enjoyable chat. Just two best friends having a laugh on a quiet Friday night in.

It was only a pity that Mackenzie himself was merely a few feet away from Sarah and heard almost every word. Well, it wasn't his fault he'd fallen asleep in the wingback chair, was it? And then woken up just in time to hear his mother being ridiculed. He'd come to London on a whim to take Sarah out to dinner. But he'd been awake since dawn working on the farm, and then she'd been late home from work. And then he'd had a few drinks while he was waiting and dozed off in the chair. Now he was going to have to let her know he was in the flat. She'd probably have a heart attack. Coughing gently, he leaned round the edge of the chair and waved at Sarah with an apologetic hand.

Predictably, she nearly collapsed with fright. Her wineglass leapt from her hand and splattered dark red Merlot all across the carpet. She quickly hung up the phone without even saying cheerio to Abigail.

"What's going on?" she gasped, both hands over her mouth in shock and acute embarrassment.

"Hello, Sarah."

"Mackenzie, oh my God, what are you doing here?"

"I came to see you – why else would I be in town? With the wedding so close, I didn't want us to spend a weekend apart, that's all. And I didn't mean to overhear your conversation. It was just, well, I couldn't help it. It was so interesting."

"Look, I'm sorry," said Sarah. "I'm sorry for what I said about Big Millie. I mean, Millicent. I was joking, Mackenzie. I didn't mean any of it. You didn't think I was serious, did you? We were only having a bit of a laugh."

"It doesn't matter," he said, smiling fondly at her.

But it did.

• ◆ •

If you enjoyed this chapter from

*It Must Be Love*
why not order the full book online
@ www.poolbeg.com

See page 375 for details.

• ◆ •

# Author interview with Sharon Owens

**1. Your first love was art. How does this influence your writing?**

ANS: I like to describe everything, I suppose. I love detail. Tiny details are so personal. Like whether a character has a button missing on their coat. I always think a person's appearance says so much about them. About their personality, I mean. We all know someone who claims to be a big Socialist, and then you notice that every stitch they have on their body is by some designer or other. Or they're driving a huge car. And you think to yourself, maybe you are a Socialist, my dear, but I would say you're a bit of a Champagne Socialist, and good luck to you!

My house is full of paintings, both mine and also my husband's. We both love looking at art and going to exhibitions; usually on a quiet day when the gallery is empty, and you actually have peace to see the work.

## 2. Would you have preferred to become a hugely successful artist rather than a hugely successful writer?

**ANS:** I'm not sure. If I could finish a painting in a week and sell it for £25,000 then obviously it would be better for my bank balance to be a hugely successful painter. But there's something wonderful about knowing my books are stocked in little shops all around the world. And books are so much more affordable than paintings so I can reach a wider audience with them. And even though I do love art, I don't really like talking about art, or hobnobbing with buyers and collectors, as it can be quite a snobbish field. Whereas all the authors, editors, publishers, agents and booksellers I have met so far have been lovely, warm-hearted people. And very kind and down-to-earth and human! So, overall I would say I'm glad I got my little break in publishing and not art. I can still enjoy painting even if I don't have the time to exhibit and network in this area any more.

## 3. Do you have a secret ambition?

**ANS:** Well, I do have a secret fantasy... I'd love to have been the drummer in a punk band. I just adore loud drumming. The louder and more aggressive, the better. Some of my favourite artists nowadays, such as Morrissey and also new band Florence & the Machine are using concert drums, and the sound they make in a rock band setting is just nectar for my soul.

I went to see Morrissey, in Belfast, in May of this year, and the drumming was so good the fans were visibly moved. I confess I did shed a few tears myself in the darkness, I enjoyed the concert that much.

If I could be a rock star for just three minutes I'd play the drums for Florence & the Machine, on their song "Cosmic Love". Or maybe it'd be on "Something is Squeezing my Skull" for Morrissey. Or maybe it'd be "Brassneck" for the Wedding Present. Or "Sonne" for German rockers Rammstein. I could give you a list of about 500 of my favourite songs but I won't! I read somewhere that music does have a calming effect on the brain and it can produce very powerful endorphins.

I don't expect I'd have enjoyed all the travelling involved in being a rock star, and I'd not have bothered with the heavy drinking and the drugs either. But I probably would have had the tattoos and possibly got an eyebrow pierced. I've always fancied having a small set of very ornate, wrought-iron gates tattooed on the back of my neck. Thank God I never actually got around to having it done, though! I'd be totally mortified now, at my age.

I still wear DM boots. That's my only rock-n-roll affectation. I'm never going to be shuffling about the place in flimsy little ballerina pumps. I love a good old solid shoe.

I'd also like to write a play about mental illness, and pass the driving test: possibly a play featuring both of these painful themes. They are very closely linked…

4. **Many of your characters achieve happiness by throwing off convention. Do you consider yourself a rebel?**

ANS: Not really a rebel, as such. I'm just stubborn. Incredibly stubborn! A true northerner! I think about things very deeply, and I make up my mind, and that's it. I don't try to push my views onto other people, absolutely not. But I won't be swayed by public opinion either. I can't stand Reality TV, or the current obsession with fame for fame's sake, or any hint of sectarianism. I can't stand bullies or bossy people, or lazy people who let other mothers clean their houses for them. But I never interfere! I say nothing and I make my excuses and I leave. Life is far, far too short to get embroiled in a silly row with a casual acquaintance over their political views or who does their housework. I sometimes enjoy seeing the frustration on the face of another person when they can see I don't agree with them, but they know I won't have an argument with them about it. Everyone is entitled to their own opinion, after all. They are not entitled to break the law but they are entitled to be lazy, bigoted, fame-obsessed, a pompous man or a selfish little madam.

My only area of true rebellion really is my DM footwear fetish. I simply will not wear shoes that are not comfortable. I won't do it. I can't do it. How can any woman say she is truly a feminist, or even very sane, and then she goes hobbling round the place in seven-inch heels, with big shiny bunions on her toes and huge water blisters on her soles and possibly even a pair of dislocated kneecaps? Come on, ladies: stop the madness! Get some biker boots or even trainers on your feet. Stop worrying about silly shoes and start living your life in comfort.

## 5. Where do you get your quirky sense of humour from?

**ANS:** Suppressed rage, probably! It's a lot easier to laugh about the various injustices in this world than to get angry. Anger is very wearying on the soul. Plus, pompous bullies hate to be laughed at. They'd rather see everyone going red in the face with rage. So I won't give it to them! I love comedy shows like *Seinfeld, Curb Your Enthusiasm, Frasier, The King of Queens* and *Everybody Loves Raymond*. I love to laugh! My favourite comedy characters are George Costanza from *Seinfeld*, and Arthur Spooner from *The King of Queens*. I love it when they roar with frustration! I wish I could do that but I'm far too polite. Last week in my local DIY store they wouldn't let me buy a watering can because the price code wouldn't scan. I had to say thank you and leave it behind on the counter. When I really wanted to announce I was taking the watering can, and there was the money, and they could like it or lump it.

## 6. Your books are full of wonderful eccentrics. Is this acceptance of human foibles your philosophy in life?

**ANS:** Yes, absolutely. Throughout my forty-one years on this earth I've known a lot of people who were classed as eccentric and I was always taught to respect their mannerisms and to "pass no remarks". With the benefit of hindsight I now believe these so-called eccentrics were possibly suffering from depression, anxiety, post-traumatic stress, alcoholism, extreme grief, OCD or maybe even schizophrenia. But they were accommodated within the community, and people were gentle with them, and spoke to them as if nothing was the matter.

Sometimes, of course, it's better to get the individual into therapy, and perhaps onto medication. But sometimes it's better to let them potter along in their own little world, if that is what makes them happy. I do often wonder where all the eccentrics of my youth are now, and if anyone is being kind to them, and inviting them round for Christmas dinner.

The only "foible" I cannot tolerate in other people is aggressive depression, because it unsettles me too much. I am fine with clinical or manic depression. But that compulsive habit some people have of trying to project their personal unhappiness onto other people is just too much for me to cope with. So I avoid people like that, I'm ashamed to say.

I've got a few foibles myself, mind you. I'm quite claustrophobic so I don't like planes, trains, traffic jams or stuffy meetings. I don't know where it comes from but I've always felt panicky in claustrophobic situations. Maybe it was triggered by a bomb scare in my childhood. I do remember wondering, when I was only about seven or eight, how my family would cope if a civil war broke out in the north. My great plan was to make a big packet of sandwiches and then walk across the fields, under cover of darkness, to the safety of Donegal, and then hire a caravan and live in it until the war was over. A caravan, with seven people in it!

I couldn't bear to live in a caravan, actually: I think I'd rather stick out the riots in my Belfast semi... I can laugh about my childhood fears now but at the time civil war was a genuine possibility.

I have no interest in extreme politics these days. And I think that anyone who has is a bit mad.

### 7. What character & scene was most difficult to write?

ANS: It was all pretty okay! I never find writing too hard, thank heaven. It just seems to flow for me. I have a cosy little desk in the corner of our bedroom, with all my pens and notebooks and CDs round me. And I just go in there with a big mug of tea, and off I go, typing away. My husband Dermot and daughter Alice are very supportive of my work and they understand I sometimes have to work in the evenings or at weekends. I don't notice the time passing when I write.

It's only the publicity I find daunting. I suppose I don't feel worthy of all the nice attention I get when a book comes out. I was brought up in a different era, really, before the obsession with fame really kicked off. I remember when I was a teenager, if I ever asked anybody if I looked nice, the usual retort would be, "Who the hell's looking at you anyway?" And I suppose that phrase is still in the back of my mind today, when I'm getting preened up to go on the telly. I'm only an auld eejit from Belfast and who do I think I am, going on the telly and talking about books?

## 8. What is happiness for you?

ANS: Peace and quiet. I love peace and quiet. So no theme parks for me. Just a nice sunny day pottering round the garden centre, then having lunch in a favourite cafe, then home to watch a few films on DVD. As long as my family is safe and well, then I'm happy. If I won a fortune on the Lotto tomorrow I'd give most of it away. I honestly wouldn't want to end up going mad behind a set of ten-foot high security gates, worrying about kidnap threats and everyone being jealous of me. That sounds like a living nightmare to me. It's lovely to have enough money to live well, don't get me wrong. I just don't hanker after a second home or a chauffeur-driven car.

9. **Handbags play a huge part in the magical storyline of the book - why are handbags so important/special for women, do you think?!**

ANS: This is a lovely question, thank you. I believe that handbags have attained such cult-like status because they are one of the few places in this male-dominated world that are exclusively feminine and private. Women traditionally owned so little, and had so little power and influence, that perhaps their little handbag became a kind of secret world to them? Containing only their own personal possessions, and nothing to do with housework or children or husbands or work!

I have 10 handbags; mostly they are big and black and very clean and tidy! My favourite one is a Lulu Guinness bag I got as a gift some years ago. It's black with a green clasp and the lining has navy and cream stripes. In there, I've got my phone, purse, wallet, sunglasses, make-up bag, notebook and pen, blank postcards, my iPod, a sun hat, a bottle of Vera Wang's Rock Princess perfume and some tissues. It's a very heavy bag!

10. **Love and friendship are central themes in the book, but so is loss . . .**

ANS: Yes, loss is never far away in this life, is it? There's no getting away from that so it's better to be prepared, I think. I imagine I could cope with losing just about anything in my life: my career, my health or my home... Just as long as I have my family around me, and my friends, hopefully I'll be okay.

# POOLBEG WISHES TO

# THANK YOU

for buying a Poolbeg book.
As a loyal customer we will give you
**10% OFF (and free postage\*)**
on any book bought on our website
**www.poolbeg.com**

Select the book(s) you wish to buy
and click to checkout.

Then click on the 'Add a Coupon' button
(located under 'Checkout') and enter
this coupon code

 **USMWR15173**

POOLBEG (Not valid with any other offer!) POOLBEG

WHY NOT JOIN OUR MAILING LIST
@ www.poolbeg.com and get some
fantastic offers on Poolbeg books

\*See website for details

All orders despatched within 24 hours!

# The Trouble with Weddings

## SHARON OWENS

978-1-84223-298-9

Glamorous Julie Sultana runs Dream Weddings from a converted lighthouse outside Belfast. Julie doesn't actually believe in marriage or love everlasting but this is exactly what makes her a superb wedding planner – calm, cool and unflappable in a crisis.

That is, until she meets gorgeous young barman, Jay O'Hanlon, on a spa-trip to County Galway and suddenly the unflappable Julie is swept off her feet.

Mags, Julie's PA, is left to run the business single-handedly while Julie and Jay continue their sizzling affair. It doesn't help when Mags' family life is plunged into chaos. Death, birth and disaster – Mags has to handle it all, while dealing with Julie's jilted boyfriend and an hysterical bride as well!

And all that's before a middle-aged rock star and his supermodel girlfriend turn up asking for a Gothic-themed wedding . . . complete with bats and 666 guests . . .